Windy McPherson's Son

Windy
McPherson's Son
Sherwood Anderson

MINT EDITIONS

Windy McPherson's Son was first published in 1916.

This edition published by Mint Editions 2021.

ISBN 9781513283494 | E-ISBN 9781513288512

Published by Mint Editions®

 MINT
EDITIONS

minteditionbooks.com

Publishing Director: Jennifer Newens
Design & Production: Rachel Lopez Metzger
Project Manager: Micaela Clark
Typesetting: Westchester Publishing Services

Contents

BOOK I

I

At the beginning of the long twilight of a summer evening, Sam McPherson, a tall big-boned boy of thirteen, with brown hair, black eyes, and an amusing little habit of tilting his chin in the air as he walked, came upon the station platform of the little corn-shipping town of Caxton in Iowa. It was a board platform, and the boy walked cautiously, lifting his bare feet and putting them down with extreme deliberateness on the hot, dry, cracked planks. Under one arm he carried a bundle of newspapers. A long black cigar was in his hand.

In front of the station he stopped; and Jerry Donlin, the baggage-man, seeing the cigar in his hand, laughed, and slowly drew the side of his face up into a laboured wink.

"What is the game tonight, Sam?" he asked.

Sam stepped to the baggage-room door, handed him the cigar, and began giving directions, pointing into the baggage-room, intent and business-like in the face of the Irishman's laughter. Then, turning, he walked across the station platform to the main street of the town, his eyes bent on the ends of his fingers on which he was making computations with his thumb. Jerry looked after him, grinning so that his red gums made a splash of colour on his bearded face. A gleam of paternal pride lit his eyes and he shook his head and muttered admiringly. Then, lighting the cigar, he went down the platform to where a wrapped bundle of newspapers lay against the building, under the window of the telegraph office, and taking it in his arm disappeared, still grinning, into the baggage-room.

Sam McPherson walked down Main Street, past the shoe store, the bakery, and the candy store kept by Penny Hughes, toward a group lounging at the front of Geiger's drug store. Before the door of the shoe store he paused a moment, and taking a small note-book from his pocket ran his finger down the pages, then shaking his head continued on his way, again absorbed in doing sums on his fingers.

Suddenly, from among the men by the drug store, a roaring song broke the evening quiet of the street, and a voice, huge and guttural, brought a smile to the boy's lips:

> *"He washed the windows and he swept the floor,*
> *And he polished up the handle of the big front door.*
> *He polished that handle so carefullee,*
> *That now he's the ruler of the queen's navee."*

The singer, a short man with grotesquely wide shoulders, wore a long flowing moustache, and a black coat, covered with dust, that reached to his knees. He held a smoking briar pipe in his hand, and with it beat time for a row of men sitting on a long stone under the store window and pounding on the sidewalk with their heels to make a chorus for the song. Sam's smile broadened into a grin as he looked at the singer, Freedom Smith, a buyer of butter and eggs, and past him at John Telfer, the orator, the dandy, the only man in town, except Mike McCarthy, who kept his trousers creased. Among all the men of Caxton, Sam most admired John Telfer and in his admiration had struck upon the town's high light. Telfer loved good clothes and wore them with an air, and never allowed Caxton to see him shabbily or indifferently dressed, laughingly declaring that it was his mission in life to give tone to the town.

John Telfer had a small income left him by his father, once a banker in the town, and in his youth he had gone to New York to study art, and later to Paris; but lacking ability or industry to get on had come back to Caxton where he had married Eleanor Millis, a prosperous milliner. They were the most successful married pair in Caxton, and after years of life together they were still in love; were never indifferent to each other, and never quarrelled; Telfer treated his wife with as much consideration and respect as though she were a sweetheart, or a guest in his house, and she, unlike most of the wives in Caxton, never ventured to question his goings and comings, but left him free to live his own life in his own way while she attended to the millinery business.

At the age of forty-five John Telfer was a tall, slender, fine looking man, with black hair and a little black pointed beard, and with something lazy and care-free in his every movement and impulse. Dressed in white flannels, with white shoes, a jaunty cap upon his head, eyeglasses hanging from a gold chain, and a cane lightly swinging from his hand, he made a figure that might have passed unnoticed on the promenade before some fashionable summer hotel, but that seemed a breach of the laws of nature when seen on the streets of a corn-shipping town in Iowa. And Telfer was aware of the extraordinary figure he cut; it was a part of his programme of life. Now as Sam approached he laid a hand on Freedom Smith's shoulder to check the song, and, with his eyes twinkling with good-humour, began thrusting with his cane at the boy's feet.

"He will never be ruler of the queen's navee," he declared, laughing and following the dancing boy about in a wide circle. "He is a little mole that works underground intent upon worms. The trick he has of tilting up his nose is only his way of smelling out stray pennies. I have it from Banker Walker that he brings a basket of them into the bank every day. One of these days he will buy the town and put it into his vest pocket."

Circling about on the stone sidewalk and dancing to escape the flying cane, Sam dodged under the arm of Valmore, a huge old blacksmith with shaggy clumps of hair on the back of his hands, and sought refuge between him and Freedom Smith. The blacksmith's hand stole out and lay upon the boy's shoulder. Telfer, his legs spread apart and the cane hooked upon his arm, began rolling a cigarette; Geiger, a yellow skinned man with fat cheeks and with hands clasped over his round paunch, smoked a black cigar, and as he sent each puff into the air, grunted forth his satisfaction with life. He was wishing that Telfer, Freedom Smith, and Valmore, instead of moving on to their nightly nest at the back of Wildman's grocery, would come into his place for the evening. He thought he would like to have the three of them there night after night discussing the doings of the world.

Quiet once more settled down upon the sleepy street. Over Sam's shoulder, Valmore and Freedom Smith talked of the coming corn crop and the growth and prosperity of the country.

"Times are getting better about here, but the wild things are almost gone," said Freedom, who in the winter bought hides and pelts.

The men sitting on the stone beneath the window watched with idle interest Telfer's labours with paper and tobacco. "Young Henry Kerns has got married," observed one of them, striving to make talk. "He has married a girl from over Parkertown way. She gives lessons in painting—china painting—kind of an artist, you know."

An exclamation of disgust broke from Telfer: his fingers trembled and the tobacco that was to have been the foundation of his evening smoke rained on the sidewalk.

"An artist!" he exclaimed, his voice tense with excitement. "Who said artist? Who called her that?" He glared fiercely about. "Let us have an end to this blatant misuse of fine old words. To say of one that he is an artist is to touch the peak of praise."

Throwing his cigarette paper after the scattered tobacco he thrust one hand into his trouser pocket. With the other he held the cane, emphasising his points by ringing taps upon the pavement. Geiger, taking the cigar between his fingers, listened with open mouth to the outburst that followed. Valmore and Freedom Smith dropped their conversation and with broad smiles upon their faces gave attention, and Sam McPherson, his eyes round with wonder and admiration, felt again the thrill that always ran through him under the drum beats of Telfer's eloquence.

"An artist is one who hungers and thirsts after perfection, not one who dabs flowers upon plates to choke the gullets of diners," declared Telfer, setting himself for one of the long speeches with which he loved to astonish the men of Caxton, and glaring down at those seated upon the stone. "It is the artist who, among all men, has the divine audacity. Does he not hurl himself into a battle in which is engaged against him all of the accumulative genius of the world?"

Pausing, he looked about for an opponent upon whom he might pour the flood of his eloquence, but on all sides smiles greeted him. Undaunted, he rushed again to the charge.

"A business man—what is he?" he demanded. "He succeeds by outwitting the little minds with which he comes in contact. A scientist is of more account—he pits his brains against the dull unresponsiveness of inanimate matter and a hundredweight of black iron he makes do the work of a hundred housewives. But an artist tests his brains against the greatest brains of all times; he stands upon the peak of life and hurls himself against the world. A girl from Parkertown who paints flowers upon dishes to be called an artist—ugh! Let me spew forth the thought! Let me cleanse my mouth! A man should have a prayer upon his lips who utters the word artist!"

"Well, we can't all be artists and the woman can paint flowers upon dishes for all I care," spoke up Valmore, laughing good naturedly. "We can't all paint pictures and write books."

"We do not want to be artists—we do not dare to be," shouted Telfer, whirling and shaking his cane at Valmore. "You have a misunderstanding of the word."

He straightened his shoulders and threw out his chest and the boy standing beside the blacksmith threw up his chin, unconsciously imitating the swagger of the man.

"I do not paint pictures; I do not write books; yet am I an artist," declared Telfer, proudly. "I am an artist practising the most difficult of all arts—the art of living. Here in this western village I stand and fling my challenge to the world. 'On the lip of not the greatest of you,' I cry, 'has life been more sweet.'"

He turned from Valmore to the men upon the stone.

"Make a study of my life," he commanded. "It will be a revelation to you. With a smile I greet the morning; I swagger in the noontime; and in the evening, like Socrates of old, I gather a little group of you benighted villagers about me and toss wisdom into your teeth, striving to teach you judgment in the use of great words."

"You talk an almighty lot about yourself, John," grumbled Freedom Smith, taking his pipe from his mouth.

"The subject is complex, it is varied, it is full of charm," Telfer answered, laughing.

Taking a fresh supply of tobacco and paper from his pocket, he rolled and lighted a cigarette. His fingers no longer trembled. Flourishing his cane he threw back his head and blew smoke into the air. He thought that in spite of the roar of laughter that had greeted Freedom Smith's comment, he had vindicated the honour of art and the thought made him happy.

To the newsboy, who had been leaning against the storefront lost in admiration, it seemed that he had caught in Telfer's talk an echo of the kind of talk that must go on among men in the big outside world. Had not this Telfer travelled far? Had he not lived in New York and Paris? Without understanding the sense of what had been said, Sam felt that it must be something big and conclusive. When from the distance there came the shriek of a locomotive, he stood unmoved, trying to comprehend the meaning of Telfer's outburst over the lounger's simple statement.

"There's the seven forty-five," cried Telfer, sharply. "Is the war between you and Fatty at an end? Are we going to lose our evening's diversion? Has Fatty bluffed you out or are you growing rich and lazy like Papa Geiger here?"

Springing from his place beside the blacksmith and grasping the bundle of newspapers, Sam ran down the street, Telfer, Valmore, Freedom Smith and the loungers following more slowly.

When the evening train from Des Moines stopped at Caxton, a blue-coated train news merchant leaped hurriedly to the platform and began looking anxiously about.

"Hurry, Fatty," rang out Freedom Smith's huge voice, "Sam's already half through one car."

The young man called "Fatty" ran up and down the station platform. "Where is that bundle of Omaha papers, you Irish loafer?" he shouted, shaking his fist at Jerry Donlin who stood upon a truck at the front of the train, up-ending trunks into the baggage car.

Jerry paused with a trunk dangling in mid-air. "In the baggage-room, of course. Hurry, man. Do you want the kid to work the whole train?"

An air of something impending hung over the idlers upon the platform, the train crew, and even the travelling men who began climbing off the train. The engineer thrust his head out of the cab; the conductor, a dignified looking man with a grey moustache, threw back his head and shook with mirth; a young man with a suit-case in his hand and a long pipe in his mouth ran to the door of the baggage-room, calling, "Hurry! Hurry, Fatty! The kid is working the entire train. You won't be able to sell a paper."

The fat young man ran from the baggage-room to the platform and shouted again to Jerry Donlin, who was now slowly pushing the empty truck along the platform. From the train came a clear voice calling, "Latest Omaha papers! Have your change ready! Fatty, the train newsboy, has fallen down a well! Have your change ready, gentlemen!"

Jerry Donlin, followed by Fatty, again disappeared from sight. The conductor, waving his hand, jumped upon the steps of the train. The engineer pulled in his head and the train began to move.

The fat young man emerged from the baggage-room, swearing revenge upon the head of Jerry Donlin. "There was no need to put it under a mail sack!" he shouted, shaking his fist. "I'll be even with you for this."

Followed by the shouts of the travelling men and the laughter of the idlers upon the platform he climbed upon the moving train and began running from car to car. Off the last car dropped Sam McPherson, a smile upon his lips, the bundle of newspapers gone, his pocket jingling with coins. The evening's entertainment for the town of Caxton was at an end.

John Telfer, standing by the side of Valmore, waved his cane in the air and began talking.

"Beat him again, by Gad!" he exclaimed. "Bully for Sam! Who says the spirit of the old buccaneers is dead? That boy didn't understand what I said about art, but he is an artist just the same!"

II

Windy McPherson, the father of the Caxton newsboy, Sam McPherson, had been war touched. The civilian clothes that he wore caused an itching of the skin. He could not forget that he had once been a sergeant in a regiment of infantry and had commanded a company through a battle fought in ditches along a Virginia country road. He chafed under the fact of his present obscure position in life. Had he been able to replace his regimentals with the robes of a judge, the felt hat of a statesman, or even with the night stick of a village marshal life might have retained something of its sweetness, but to have ended by becoming an obscure housepainter in a village that lived by raising corn and by feeding that corn to red steers—ugh!—the thought made him shudder. He looked with envy at the blue coat and the brass buttons of the railroad agent; he tried vainly to get into the Caxton Cornet Band; he got drunk to forget his humiliation and in the end he fell to loud boasting and to the nursing of a belief within himself that in truth not Lincoln nor Grant but he himself had thrown the winning die in the great struggle. In his cups he said as much and the Caxton corn grower, punching his neighbour in the ribs, shook with delight over the statement.

When Sam was a twelve year old, barefooted boy upon the streets a kind of backwash of the wave of glory that had swept over Windy McPherson in the days of '61 lapped upon the shores of the Iowa village. That strange manifestation called the A. P. A. movement brought the old soldier to a position of prominence in the community. He founded a local branch of the organisation; he marched at the head of a procession through the streets; he stood on a corner and pointing a trembling forefinger to where the flag on the schoolhouse waved beside the cross of Rome, shouted hoarsely, "See, the cross rears itself above the flag! We shall end by being murdered in our beds!"

But although some of the hard-headed, money-making men of Caxton joined the movement started by the boasting old soldier and although for the moment they vied with him in stealthy creepings through the streets to secret meetings and in mysterious mutterings behind hands the movement subsided as suddenly as it had begun and only left its leader more desolate.

In the little house at the end of the street by the shores of Squirrel Creek, Sam and his sister Kate regarded their father's warlike pretensions with scorn. "The butter is low, father's army leg will ache tonight," they whispered to each other across the kitchen table.

Following her mother's example, Kate, a tall slender girl of sixteen and already a bread winner with a clerkship in Winney's drygoods store, remained silent under Windy's boasting, but Sam, striving to emulate them, did not always succeed. There was now and then a rebellious muttering that should have warned Windy. It had once burst into an open quarrel in which the victor of a hundred battles withdrew defeated from the field. Windy, half-drunk, had taken an old account book from a shelf in the kitchen, a relic of his days as a prosperous merchant when he had first come to Caxton, and had begun reading to the little family a list of names of men who, he claimed, had been the cause of his ruin.

"There is Tom Newman, now," he exclaimed excitedly. "Owns a hundred acres of good corn-growing land and won't pay for the harness on the backs of his horses or for the ploughs in his barn. The receipt he has from me is forged. I could put him in prison if I chose. To beat an old soldier!—to beat one of the boys of '61!—it is shameful!"

"I have heard of what you owed and what men owed you; you had none the worst of it," Sam protested coldly, while Kate held her breath and Jane McPherson, at work over the ironing board in the corner, half turned and looked silently at the man and the boy, the slightly increased pallor of her long face the only sign that she had heard.

Windy had not pressed the quarrel. Standing for a moment in the middle of the kitchen, holding the book in his hand, he looked from the pale silent mother by the ironing board to the son now standing and staring at him, and, throwing the book upon the table with a bang, fled the house. "You don't understand," he had cried, "you don't understand the heart of a soldier."

In a way the man was right. The two children did not understand the blustering, pretending, inefficient old man. Having moved shoulder to shoulder with grim, silent men to the consummation of great deeds Windy could not get the flavour of those days out of his outlook upon life. Walking half drunk in the darkness along the sidewalks of Caxton on the evening of the quarrel the man became inspired. He threw back his shoulders and walked with martial tread; he drew an imaginary sword from its scabbard and waved it aloft; stopping, he aimed carefully at a body of imaginary men who advanced yelling toward him across a wheatfield; he felt that life in making him a housepainter in a farming village in Iowa and in giving him an unappreciative son had been cruelly unfair; he wept at the injustice of it.

The American Civil War was a thing so passionate, so inflaming, so vast, so absorbing, it so touched to the quick the men and women of those pregnant days that but a faint echo of it has been able to penetrate down to our days and to our minds; no real sense of it has as yet crept into the pages of a printed book; it yet wants its Thomas Carlyle; and in the end we are put to the need of listening to old fellows boasting on our village streets to get upon our cheeks the living breath of it. For four years the men of American cities, villages and farms walked across the smoking embers of a burning land, advancing and receding as the flame of that universal, passionate, death-spitting thing swept down upon them or receded toward the smoking sky-line. Is it so strange that they could not come home and begin again peacefully painting houses or mending broken shoes? A something in them cried out. It sent them to bluster and boast upon the street corners. When people passing continued to think only of their brick laying and of their shovelling of corn into cars, when the sons of these war gods walking home at evening and hearing the vain boastings of the fathers began to doubt even the facts of the great struggle, a something snapped in their brains and they fell to chattering and shouting their vain boastings to all as they looked hungrily about for believing eyes.

When our own Thomas Carlyle comes to write of our Civil War he will make much of our Windy McPhersons. He will see something big and pathetic in their hungry search for auditors and in their endless war talk. He will go filled with eager curiosity into little G. A. R. halls in the villages and think of the men who coming there night after night, year after year, told and re-told endlessly, monotonously, their story of battle.

Let us hope that in his fervour for the old fellows he will not fail to treat tenderly the families of those veteran talkers; the families that with their breakfasts and their dinners, by the fire at evening, through fast day and feast day, at weddings and at funerals got again and again endlessly, everlastingly this flow of war words. Let him reflect that peaceful men in corn-growing counties do not by choice sleep among the dogs of war nor wash their linen in the blood of their country's foe. Let him, in his sympathy with the talkers, remember with kindness the heroism of the listeners.

On a summer day Sam McPherson sat on a box before Wildman's grocery lost in thought. In his hand he held the little yellow account book and in this he buried himself, striving to wipe from his consciousness a scene being enacted before his eyes upon the street.

The realisation of the fact that his father was a confirmed liar and braggart had for years cast a shadow over his days and the shadow had been made blacker by the fact that in a land where the least fortunate can laugh in the face of want he had more than once stood face to face with poverty. He believed that the logical answer to the situation was money in the bank and with all the ardour of his boy's heart he strove to realise that answer. He wanted to be a money-maker and the totals at the foot of the pages in the soiled yellow bankbook were the milestones that marked the progress he had already made. They told him that the daily struggles with Fatty, the long tramps through Caxton's streets on bleak winter evenings, and the never-ending Saturday nights when crowds filled the stores, the sidewalks, and the drinking places, and he worked among them tirelessly and persistently were not without fruit.

Suddenly, above the murmur of men's voices on the street, his father's voice rose loud and insistent. A block further down the street, leaning against the door of Hunter's jewelry store, Windy talked at the top of his lungs, pumping his arms up and down with the air of a man making a stump speech.

"He is making a fool of himself," thought Sam, and returned to his bankbook, striving in the contemplation of the totals at the foot of the pages to shake off the dull anger that had begun to burn in his brain. Glancing up again, he saw that Joe Wildman, son of the grocer and a boy of his own age, had joined the group of men laughing and jeering at Windy. The shadow on Sam's face grew heavier.

Sam had been at Joe Wildman's house; he knew the air of plenty and of comfort that hung over it; the table piled high with meat and potatoes; the group of children laughing and eating to the edge of gluttony; the quiet, gentle father who amid the clamour and the noise did not raise his voice, and the well-dressed, bustling, rosy-cheeked mother. As a contrast to this scene he began to call up in his mind a picture of life in his own home, getting a kind of perverted pleasure out of his dissatisfaction with it. He saw the boasting, incompetent father telling his endless tales of the Civil War and complaining of his wounds; the tall, stoop-shouldered, silent mother with the deep lines in her long face, everlastingly at work over her washtub among the soiled clothes; the silent, hurriedly-eaten meals snatched from the kitchen table; and the long winter days when ice formed upon his mother's skirts and Windy idled about town while the little family subsisted upon bowls of cornmeal mush everlastingly repeated.

Now, even from where he sat, he could see that his father was half gone in drink, and knew that he was boasting of his part in the Civil War. "He is either doing that or telling of his aristocratic family or lying about his birthplace," he thought resentfully, and unable any longer to endure the sight of what seemed to him his own degradation, he got up and went into the grocery where a group of Caxton citizens stood talking to Wildman of a meeting to be held that morning at the town hall.

Caxton was to have a Fourth of July celebration. The idea, born in the heads of the few, had been taken up by the many. Rumours of it had run through the streets late in May. It had been talked of in Geiger's drug store, at the back of Wildman's grocery, and in the street before the New Leland House. John Telfer, the town's one man of leisure, had for weeks been going from place to place discussing the details with prominent men. Now a mass meeting was to be held in the hall over Geiger's drug store and to a man the citizens of Caxton had turned out for the meeting. The housepainter had come down off his ladder, the clerks were locking the doors of the stores, men went along the streets in groups bound for the hall. As they went they shouted to each other. "The old town has woke up," they called.

On a corner by Hunter's jewelry store Windy McPherson leaned against a building and harangued the passing crowd.

"Let the old flag wave," he shouted excitedly, "let the men of Caxton show the true blue and rally to the old standards."

"That's right, Windy, expostulate with them," shouted a wit, and a roar of laughter drowned Windy's reply.

Sam McPherson also went to the meeting in the hall. He came out of the grocery store with Wildman and went along the street looking at the sidewalk and trying not to see the drunken man talking in front of the jewelry store. At the hall other boys stood in the stairway or ran up and down the sidewalk talking excitedly, but Sam was a figure in the town's life and his right to push in among the men was not questioned. He squirmed through the mass of legs and secured a seat in a window ledge where he could watch the men come in and find seats.

As Caxton's one newsboy Sam had got from his newspaper selling both a living and a kind of standing in the town's life. To be a newsboy or a bootblack in a small novel-reading American town is to make a figure in the world. Do not all of the poor newsboys in the books become great men and is not this boy who goes among us so industriously day after day likely to become such a figure? Is it not a duty we of the town owe to future greatness that we push him forward? So reasoned the men of Caxton and paid a kind of court to the boy who sat on the window ledge of the hall while the other boys of the town waited on the sidewalk below.

John Telfer was chairman of the mass meeting. He was always chairman of public meetings in Caxton. The industrious silent men of position in the town envied his easy, bantering style of public address, while pretending to treat it with scorn. "He talks too much," they said, making a virtue of their own inability with apt and clever words.

Telfer did not wait to be appointed chairman of the meeting, but went forward, climbed the little raised platform at the end of the hall, and usurped the chairmanship. He walked up and down on the platform bantering with the crowd, answering gibes, calling to well-known men, getting and giving keen satisfaction with his talent. When the hall was filled with men he called the meeting to order, appointed committees and launched into a harangue. He told of plans made to advertise the big day in other towns and to get low railroad rates arranged for excursion parties. The programme, he said, included a musical carnival with brass bands from other towns, a sham battle by the military company at the fairgrounds, horse races, speeches from the steps of the town hall, and fireworks in the evening. "We'll show them a live town here," he declared, walking up and down the platform and swinging his cane, while the crowd applauded and shouted its approval.

When a call came for voluntary subscriptions to pay for the fun, the audience quieted down. One or two men got up and started to go out, grumbling that it was a waste of money. The fate of the celebration was on the knees of the gods.

Telfer arose to the occasion. He called out the names of the departing, and made jests at their expense so that they dropped back into their chairs unable to face the roaring laughter of the crowd, and shouted to a man at the back of the hall to close and bolt the door. Men began getting up in various parts of the hall and calling out sums, Telfer repeating the name and the amount in a loud voice to young Tom

Jedrow, clerk in the bank, who wrote them down in a book. When the amount subscribed did not meet with his approval, he protested and the crowd backing him up forced the increase he demanded. When a man did not rise, he shouted at him and the man answered back an amount.

Suddenly in the hall a diversion arose. Windy McPherson emerged from the crowd at the back of the hall and walked down the centre aisle to the platform. He walked unsteadily straightening his shoulders and thrusting out his chin. When he got to the front of the hall he took a roll of bills from his pocket and threw it on the platform at the chairman's feet. "From one of the boys of '61," he announced in a loud voice.

The crowd shouted and clapped its hands with delight as Telfer picked up the bills and ran his finger over them. "Seventeen dollars from our hero, the mighty McPherson," he shouted while the bank clerk wrote the name and the amount in the book and the crowd continued to make merry over the title given the drunken soldier by the chairman.

The boy on the window ledge slipped to the floor and stood with burning cheeks behind the mass of men. He knew that at home his mother was doing a family washing for Lesley, the shoe merchant, who had given five dollars to the Fourth-of-July fund, and the resentment he had felt on seeing his father talking to the crowd before the jewelry store blazed up anew.

After the taking of subscriptions, men in various parts of the hall began making suggestions for added features for the great day. To some of the speakers the crowd listened respectfully, at others they hooted. An old man with a grey beard told a long rambling story of a Fourth-of-July celebration of his boyhood. When voices interrupted he protested and shook his fist in the air, pale with indignation.

"Oh, sit down, old daddy," shouted Freedom Smith and a murmur of applause greeted this sensible suggestion.

Another man got up and began to talk. He had an idea. "We will have," he said, "a bugler mounted on a white horse who will ride through the town at dawn blowing the reveille. At midnight he will stand on the steps of the town hall and blow taps to end the day."

The crowd applauded. The idea had caught their fancy and had instantly taken a place in their minds as one of the real events of the day.

Again Windy McPherson emerged from the crowd at the back of the hall. Raising his hand for silence he told the crowd that he was a bugler, that he had been a regimental bugler for two years during the Civil War. He said that he would gladly volunteer for the place.

The crowd shouted and John Telfer waved his hand. "The white horse for you, McPherson," he said.

Sam McPherson wriggled along the wall and out at the now unbolted door. He was filled with astonishment at his father's folly, and was still more astonished at the folly of these other men in accepting his statement and handing over the important place for the big day. He knew that his father must have had some part in the war as he was a member of the G. A. R., but he had no faith at all in the stories he had heard him relate of his experiences in the war. Sometimes he caught himself wondering if there ever had been such a war and thought that it must be a lie like everything else in the life of Windy McPherson. For years he had wondered why some sensible solid person like Valmore or Wildman did not rise, and in a matter-of-fact way tell the world that no such thing as the Civil War had ever been fought, that it was merely a figment in the minds of pompous old men demanding unearned glory of their fellows. Now hurrying along the street with burning cheeks, he decided that after all there must have been such a war. He had had the same feeling about birthplaces and there could be no doubt that people were born. He had heard his father claim as his birthplace Kentucky, Texas, North Carolina, Louisiana and Scotland. The thing had left a kind of defect in his mind. To the end of his life when he heard a man tell the place of his birth he looked up suspiciously, and a shadow of doubt crossed his mind.

From the mass meeting Sam went home to his mother and presented the case bluntly. "The thing will have to be stopped," he declared, standing with blazing eyes before her washtub. "It is too public. He can't blow a bugle; I know he can't. The whole town will have another laugh at our expense."

Jane McPherson listened in silence to the boy's outburst, then, turning, went back to rubbing clothes, avoiding his eyes.

With his hands thrust into his trousers pocket Sam stared sullenly at the ground. A sense of justice told him not to press the matter, but as he walked away from the washtub and out at the kitchen door, he hoped there would be plain talk of the matter at supper time. "The old fool!" he protested, addressing the empty street. "He is going to make a show of himself again."

When Windy McPherson came home that evening, something in

SHERWOOD ANDERSON

the eyes of the silent wife, and the sullen face of the boy, startled him. He passed over lightly his wife's silence but looked closely at his son. He felt that he faced a crisis. In the emergency he was magnificent. With a flourish, he told of the mass meeting, and declared that the citizens of Caxton had arisen as one man to demand that he take the responsible place as official bugler. Then, turning, he glared across the table at his son.

Sam, openly defiant, announced that he did not believe his father capable of blowing a bugle.

Windy roared with amazement. He rose from the table declaring in a loud voice that the boy had wronged him; he swore that he had been for two years bugler on the staff of a colonel, and launched into a long story of a surprise by the enemy while his regiment lay asleep in their tents, and of his standing in the face of a storm of bullets and blowing his comrades to action. Putting one hand on his forehead he rocked back and forth as though about to fall, declaring that he was striving to keep back the tears wrenched from him by the injustice of his son's insinuation and, shouting so that his voice carried far down the street, he declared with an oath that the town of Caxton should ring and echo with his bugling as the sleeping camp had echoed with it that night in the Virginia wood. Then dropping again into his chair, and resting his head upon his hand, he assumed a look of patient resignation.

Windy McPherson was victorious. In the little house a great stir and bustle of preparation arose. Putting on his white overalls and forgetting for the time his honourable wounds the father went day after day to his work as a housepainter. He dreamed of a new blue uniform for the great day and in the end achieved the realisation of his dreams, not however without material assistance from what was known in the house as "Mother's Wash Money." And the boy, convinced by the story of the midnight attack in the woods of Virginia, began against his judgment to build once more an old dream of his father's reformation. Boylike, the scepticism was thrown to the winds and he entered with zeal into the plans for the great day. As he went through the quiet residence streets delivering the late evening papers, he threw back his head and revelled in the thought of a tall blue-clad figure on a great white horse passing like a knight before the gaping people. In a fervent moment he even drew money from his carefully built-up bank account and sent it to a firm in Chicago to pay for a shining new bugle that would complete the picture he had in his mind. And when the evening papers were distributed he hurried home to sit on the porch before the house discussing with his sister Kate the honours that had alighted upon their family.

WITH THE COMING OF DAWN on the great day the three McPhersons hurried hand in hand toward Main Street. In the street, on all sides of them, they saw people coming out of houses rubbing their eyes and buttoning their coats as they went along the sidewalk. All of Caxton seemed abroad.

In Main Street the people were packed on the sidewalk, and massed on the curb and in the doorways of the stores. Heads appeared at windows, flags waved from roofs or hung from ropes stretched across the street, and a great murmur of voices broke the silence of the dawn.

Sam's heart beat so that he was hard put to it to keep back the tears from his eyes. He thought with a gasp of the days of anxiety that had passed when the new bugle had not come from the Chicago company, and in retrospect he suffered again the horror of the days of waiting. It had been all important. He could not blame his father for raving and shouting about the house, he himself had felt like raving, and had put another dollar of his savings into telegrams before the treasure was finally in his hands. Now, the thought that it might not have come sickened him, and a little prayer of thankfulness rose from his lips. To be sure one might have been secured from a nearby town, but not a new shining one to go with his father's new blue uniform.

A cheer broke from the crowd massed along the street. Into the street rode a tall figure seated upon a white horse. The horse was from Culvert's livery and the boys there had woven ribbons into its mane and tail. Windy McPherson, sitting very straight in the saddle and looking wonderfully striking in the new blue uniform and the broad-brimmed campaign hat, had the air of a conqueror come to receive the homage of the town. He wore a gold band across his chest and against his hip rested the shining bugle. With stern eyes he looked down upon the people.

The lump in the throat of the boy hurt more and more. A great wave of pride ran over him, submerging him. In a moment he forgot all the past humiliations the father had brought upon his family, and understood why his mother remained silent when he, in his blindness, had wanted to protest against her seeming indifference. Glancing furtively up he saw a tear lying upon her cheek and felt that he too would like to sob aloud his pride and happiness.

SHERWOOD ANDERSON

Slowly and with stately stride the horse walked up the street between the rows of silent waiting people. In front of the town hall the tall military figure, rising in the saddle, took one haughty look at the multitude, and then, putting the bugle to his lips, blew.

Out of the bugle came only a thin piercing shriek followed by a squawk. Again Windy put the bugle to his lips and again the same dismal squawk was his only reward. On his face was a look of helpless boyish astonishment.

And in a moment the people knew. It was only another of Windy McPherson's pretensions. He couldn't blow a bugle at all.

A great shout of laughter rolled down the street. Men and women sat on the curbstones and laughed until they were tired. Then, looking at the figure upon the motionless horse, they laughed again.

Windy looked about him with troubled eyes. It is doubtful if he had ever had a bugle to his lips until that moment, but he was filled with wonder and astonishment that the reveille did not roll forth. He had heard the thing a thousand times and had it clearly in his mind; with all his heart he wanted it to roll forth, and could picture the street ringing with it and the applause of the people; the thing, he felt, was in him, and it was only a fatal blunder in nature that it did not come out at the flaring end of the bugle. He was amazed at this dismal end of his great moment—he was always amazed and helpless before facts.

The crowd began gathering about the motionless, astonished figure, laughter continuing to send them off into something near convulsions. Grasping the bridle of the horse, John Telfer began leading it off up the street. Boys whooped and shouted at the rider, "Blow! Blow!"

The three McPhersons stood in a doorway leading into a shoe store. The boy and the mother, white and speechless with humiliation, dared not look at each other. In the flood of shame sweeping over them they stared straight before them with hard, stony eyes.

The procession led by John Telfer at the bridle of the white horse marched down the street. Looking up, the eyes of the laughing, shouting man met those of the boy and a look of pain shot across his face. Dropping the bridle he hurried away through the crowd. The procession moved on, and watching their chance the mother and the two children crept home along side streets, Kate weeping bitterly. Leaving them at the door Sam went straight on down a sandy road toward a small wood. "I've got my lesson. I've got my lesson," he muttered over and over as he went.

At the edge of the wood he stopped and leaning on a rail fence watched until he saw his mother come out to the pump in the back yard. She had begun to draw water for the day's washing. For her also the holiday was at an end. A flood of tears ran down the boy's cheeks, and he shook his fist in the direction of the town. "You may laugh at that fool Windy, but you shall never laugh at Sam McPherson," he cried, his voice shaking with excitement.

III

O ne evening, when he had grown so that he outtopped Windy, Sam McPherson returned from his paper route to find his mother arrayed in her black, church-going dress. An evangelist was at work in Caxton and she had decided to hear him. Sam shuddered. In the house it was an understood thing that when Jane McPherson went to church her son went with her. There was nothing said. Jane McPherson did all things without words, always there was nothing said. Now she stood waiting in her black dress when her son came in at the door and he hurriedly put on his best clothes and went with her to the brick church.

Valmore, John Telfer, and Freedom Smith, who had taken upon themselves a kind of common guardianship of the boy and with whom he spent evening after evening at the back of Wildman's grocery, did not go to church. They talked of religion and seemed singularly curious and interested in what other men thought on the subject but they did not allow themselves to be coaxed into a house of worship. To the boy, who had become a fourth member of the evening gatherings at the back of the grocery store, they would not talk of God, answering the direct questions he sometimes asked by changing the subject. Once Telfer, the reader of poetry, answered the boy. "Sell papers and fill your pockets with money but let your soul sleep," he said sharply.

In the absence of the others Wildman talked more freely. He was a spiritualist and tried to make Sam see the beauties of that faith. On long summer afternoons the grocer and the boy spent hours driving through the streets in a rattling old delivery wagon, the man striving earnestly to make clear to the boy the shadowy ideas of God that were in his mind.

Although Windy McPherson had been the leader of a Bible class in his youth, and had been a moving spirit at revival meetings during his early days in Caxton, he no longer went to church and his wife did not ask him to go. On Sunday mornings he lay abed. If there was work to be done about the house or yard he complained of his wounds. He complained of his wounds when the rent fell due, and when there was a shortage of food in the house. Later in his life and after the death of Jane McPherson the old soldier married the widow of a farmer by whom he had four children and with whom he went to church twice on

Sunday. Kate wrote Sam one of her infrequent letters about it. "He has met his match," she said, and was tremendously pleased.

In church on Sunday mornings Sam went regularly to sleep, putting his head on his mother's arm and sleeping throughout the service. Jane McPherson loved to have the boy there beside her. It was the one thing in life they did together and she did not mind his sleeping the time away. Knowing how late he had been upon the streets at the paper selling on Saturday evenings, she looked at him with eyes filled with tenderness and sympathy. Once the minister, a man with brown beard and hard, tightly-closed mouth, spoke to her. "Can't you keep him awake?" he asked impatiently. "He needs the sleep," she said and hurried past the minister and out of the church, looking ahead of her and frowning.

The evening of the evangelist meeting was a summer evening fallen on a winter month. All day the warm winds had come up from the southwest. Mud lay soft and deep in the streets and among the little pools of water on the sidewalks were dry spots from which steam arose. Nature had forgotten herself. A day that should have sent old fellows to their nests behind stoves in stores sent them forth to loaf in the sun. The night fell warm and cloudy. A thunder storm threatened in the month of February.

Sam walked along the sidewalk with his mother bound for the brick church, wearing a new grey overcoat. The night did not demand the overcoat but Sam wore it out of an excess of pride in its possession. The overcoat had an air. It had been made by Gunther the tailor after a design sketched on the back of a piece of wrapping paper by John Telfer and had been paid for out of the newsboy's savings. The little German tailor, after a talk with Valmore and Telfer, had made it at a marvellously low price. Sam swaggered as he walked.

He did not sleep in church that evening; indeed he found the quiet church filled with a medley of strange noises. Folding carefully the new coat and laying it beside him on the seat he looked with interest at the people, feeling within him something of the nervous excitement with which the air was charged. The evangelist, a short, athletic-looking man in a grey business suit, seemed to the boy out of place in the church. He had the assured business-like air of the travelling men who come to the New Leland House, and Sam thought he looked like a man who had goods to be sold. He did not stand quietly back of the pulpit giving out the text as did the brown-bearded minister, nor did he sit with closed eyes and clasped hands waiting for the choir to finish singing. While the choir sang he ran up and down the platform waving his arms and shouting excitedly to the people on the church benches, "Sing! Sing! Sing! For the glory of God, sing!"

When the song was finished, he began talking, quietly at first, of life in the town. As he talked he grew more and more excited. "The town is a cesspool of vice!" he shouted. "It reeks with evil! The devil counts it a suburb of hell!"

His voice rose, and sweat ran off his face. A sort of frenzy seized him. He pulled off his coat and throwing it over a chair ran up and down the platform and into the aisles among the people, shouting, threatening, pleading. People began to stir uneasily in their seats. Jane McPherson stared stonily at the back of the woman in front of her. Sam was horribly frightened.

The newsboy of Caxton was not without a hunger for religion. Like all boys he thought much and often of death. In the night he sometimes awakened cold with fear, thinking that death must be just without the door of his room waiting for him. When in the winter he had a cold and coughed, he trembled at the thought of tuberculosis. Once, when he was taken with a fever, he fell asleep and dreamed that he had died and was walking on the trunk of a fallen tree over a ravine filled with lost souls that shrieked with terror. When he awoke he prayed. Had some one come into his room and heard his prayer he would have been ashamed.

On winter evenings as he walked through the dark streets with the papers under his arm he thought of his soul. As he thought a tenderness came over him; a lump came into his throat and he pitied himself; he felt that there was something missing in his life, something he wanted very badly.

Under John Telfer's influence, the boy, who had quit school to devote himself to money making, read Walt Whitman and had a season of admiring his own body with its straight white legs, and the head that was poised so jauntily on the body. Sometimes he would awaken on summer nights and be so filled with strange longing that he would creep out of bed and, pushing open the window, sit upon the floor, his bare legs sticking out beyond his white nightgown, and, thus sitting, yearn eagerly toward some fine impulse, some call, some sense of bigness and of leadership that was absent from the necessities of the life he led. He looked at the stars and listened to the night noises, so filled with longing that the tears sprang to his eyes.

Once, after the affair of the bugle, Jane McPherson had been ill—and the first touch of the finger of death reaching out to her—had sat with her son in the warm darkness in the little grass plot at the front of the house. It was a clear, warm, starlit evening without a moon, and as the two sat closely together a sense of the coming of death crept over the mother.

At the evening meal Windy McPherson had talked voluminously, ranting and shouting about the house. He said that a housepainter who had a real sense of colour had no business trying to work in a hole like Caxton. He had been in trouble with a housewife about a colour he had mixed for painting a porch floor and at his own table he raved about the woman and what he declared her lack of even a primitive sense of colour. "I am sick of it all," he shouted, going out of the house and up the street with uncertain steps. His wife had been unmoved by his outburst, but in the presence of the quiet boy whose chair touched her own she trembled with a strange new fear and began to talk of the life after death, making effort after effort to get at what she wanted to say, and only succeeding in finding expression for her thoughts in little sentences broken by long painful pauses. She told the boy she had no doubt at all that there was some kind of future life and that she believed she should see and live with him again after they had finished with this world.

One day the minister who had been annoyed because he had slept in his church, stopped Sam on the street to talk to him of his soul. He said that the boy should be thinking of making himself one of the brothers in Christ by joining the church. Sam listened silently to the talk of the man, whom he instinctively disliked, but in his silence felt there was something insincere. With all his heart he wanted to repeat a sentence he had heard from the lips of grey-haired, big-fisted Valmore—"How can they believe and not lead a life of simple, fervent devotion to their belief?" He thought himself superior to the thin-lipped man who talked with him and had he been able to express what was in his heart he might have said, "Look here, man! I am made of different stuff from all the people there at the church. I am new clay to be moulded into a new man. Not even my mother is like me. I do not accept your ideas of life just because you say they are good any more than I accept Windy McPherson just because he happens to be my father."

During one winter Sam spent evening after evening reading the Bible in his room. It was after Kate's marriage—she had got into an affair with a young farmer that had kept her name upon the tongues of whisperers for months but was now a housewife on a farm at the edge of a village some miles from Caxton, and the mother was again at her endless task among the soiled clothes in the kitchen and Windy McPherson off drinking and boasting about town. Sam read the book in secret. He had a lamp on a little stand beside his bed and a novel, lent him by John Telfer, beside it. When his mother came up the stairway he slipped the Bible under the cover of the bed and became absorbed in the novel. He thought it something not quite in keeping with his aims as a business man and a money getter to be concerned about his soul. He wanted to conceal his concern but with all his heart wanted to get hold of the message of the strange book, about which men wrangled hour after hour on winter evenings in the store.

He did not get it; and after a time he stopped reading the book. Left to himself he might have sensed its meaning, but on all sides of him were the voices of the men—the men at Wildman's who owned to no faith and yet were filled with dogmatisms as they talked behind the stove in the grocery; the brown-bearded, thin-lipped minister in the brick church; the shouting, pleading evangelists who came to visit the town in the winter; the gentle old grocer who talked vaguely of the spirit world,—all these voices were at the mind of the boy pleading, insisting, demanding, not that Christ's simple message that men love one another to the end, that they work together for the common good, be accepted, but that their own complex interpretation of his word be taken to the end that souls be saved.

In the end the boy of Caxton got to the place where he had a dread of the word soul. It seemed to him that the mention of the word in conversation was something shameful and to think of the word or the shadowy something for which the word stood an act of cowardice. In his mind the soul became a thing to be hidden away, covered up, not thought of. One might be allowed to speak of the matter at the moment of death, but for the healthy man or boy to have the thought of his soul in his mind or word of it on his lips—one might better become blatantly profane and go to the devil with a swagger. With delight he imagined himself as dying and with his last breath tossing a round oath into the air of his death chamber.

In the meantime Sam continued to have inexplicable longings and hopes. He kept surprising himself by the changing aspect of his own viewpoint of life. He found himself indulging in the most petty meannesses, and following these with flashes of a kind of loftiness of mind. Looking at a girl passing in the street, he had unbelievably mean thoughts; and the next day, passing the same girl, a line caught from the babbling of John Telfer came to his lips and he went his way muttering, "June's twice June since she breathed it with me."

And then into the complex nature of this boy came the sex motive. Already he dreamed of having women in his arms. He looked shyly at the ankles of women crossing the street, and listened eagerly when the crowd about the stove in Wildman's fell to telling smutty stories. He sank to unbelievable depths of triviality in sordidness, looking shyly into dictionaries for words that appealed to the animal lust in his queerly perverted mind and, when he came across it, lost entirely the beauty of the old Bible tale of Ruth in the suggestion of intimacy between man and woman that it brought to him. And yet Sam McPherson was no evil-minded boy. He had, as a matter of fact, a quality of intellectual honesty that appealed strongly to the clean-minded, simple-hearted old blacksmith Valmore; he had awakened something like love in the hearts of the women school teachers in the Caxton schools, at least one of whom continued to interest herself in him, taking him with her on walks along country roads, and talking to him constantly of the development of his mind; and he was the friend and boon companion of Telfer, the dandy, the reader of poems, the keen lover of life. The boy was struggling to find himself. One night when the sex call kept him awake he got up and dressed, and went and stood in the rain by the creek in Miller's pasture. The wind swept the rain across the face of the water and a sentence flashed through his mind: "The little feet of the rain run on the water." There was a quality of almost lyrical beauty in the Iowa boy.

And this boy, who couldn't get hold of his impulse toward God, whose sex impulses made him at times mean, at times full of beauty, and who had decided that the impulse toward bargaining and money getting was the impulse in him most worth cherishing, now sat beside his mother in church and watched with wide-open eyes the man who took off his coat, who sweated profusely, and who called the town in which he lived a cesspool of vice and its citizens wards of the devil.

The evangelist from talking of the town began talking instead of heaven and hell and his earnestness caught the attention of the listening boy who began seeing pictures.

Into his mind there came a picture of a burning pit of fire in which great flames leaped about the heads of the people who writhed in the pit. "Art Sherman would be there," thought Sam, materialising the picture he saw; "nothing can save him; he keeps a saloon."

Filled with pity for the man he saw in the picture of the burning pit, his mind centered on the person of Art Sherman. He liked Art Sherman. More than once he had felt the touch of human kindness in the man. The roaring, blustering saloonkeeper had helped the boy sell and collect for newspapers. "Pay the kid or get out of the place," the red-faced man roared at drunken men leaning on the bar.

And then, looking into the burning pit, Sam thought of Mike McCarthy, for whom he had at that moment a kind of passion akin to a young girl's blind devotion to her lover. With a shudder he realised that Mike also would go into the pit, for he had heard Mike laughing at churches and declaring there was no God.

The evangelist ran upon the platform and called to the people demanding that they stand upon their feet. "Stand up for Jesus," he shouted; "stand up and be counted among the host of the Lord God."

In the church people began getting to their feet. Jane McPherson stood with the others. Sam did not stand. He crept behind his mother's dress, hoping to pass through the storm unnoticed. The call to the faithful to stand was a thing to be complied with or resisted as the people might wish; it was something entirely outside of himself. It did not occur to him to count himself among either the lost or the saved.

Again the choir began singing and a businesslike movement began among the people. Men and women went up and down the aisles clasping the hands of people in the pews, talking and praying aloud. "Welcome among us," they said to certain ones who stood upon their feet. "It gladdens our hearts to see you among us. We are happy at seeing you in the fold among the saved. It is good to confess Jesus."

Suddenly a voice from the bench back of him struck terror to Sam's heart. Jim Williams, who worked in Sawyer's barber shop, was upon his knees and in a loud voice was praying for the soul of Sam McPherson. "Lord, help this erring boy who goes up and down in the company of sinners and publicans," he shouted.

In a moment the terror of death and the fiery pit that had possessed him passed, and Sam was filled instead with blind, dumb rage. He remembered that this same Jim Williams had treated lightly the honour of his sister at the time of her disappearance, and he wanted to get upon his feet and pour out his wrath on the head of the man, who, he felt, had betrayed him. "They would not have seen me," he thought; "this is a fine trick Jim Williams has played me. I shall be even with him for this."

He got to his feet and stood beside his mother. He had no qualms about passing himself off as one of the lambs safely within the fold. His mind was bent upon quieting Jim Williams' prayers and avoiding the attention of the people.

The minister began calling on the standing people to testify of their salvation. From various parts of the church the people spoke out, some loudly and boldly and with a ring of confidence in their voices, some tremblingly and hesitatingly. One woman wept loudly shouting between the paroxysms of sobbing that seized her, "The weight of my sins is heavy on my soul." Girls and young men when called on by the minister responded with shamed, hesitating voices asking that a verse of some hymn be sung, or quoting a line of scripture.

At the back of the church the evangelist with one of the deacons and two or three women had gathered about a small, black-haired woman, the wife of a baker to whom Sam delivered papers. They were urging her to rise and get within the fold, and Sam turned and watched her curiously, his sympathy going out to her. With all his heart he hoped that she would continue doggedly shaking her head.

Suddenly the irrepressible Jim Williams broke forth again. A quiver ran over Sam's body and the blood rose to his cheeks. "Here is another sinner saved," shouted Jim, pointing to the standing boy. "Count this boy, Sam McPherson, in the fold among the lambs."

On the platform the brown-bearded minister stood upon a chair and looked over the heads of the people. An ingratiating smile played about his lips. "Let us hear from the young man, Sam McPherson," he said, raising his hand for silence, and, then, encouragingly, "Sam, what have you to say for the Lord?"

Become the centre for the attention of the people in the church Sam was terror-stricken. The rage against Jim Williams was forgotten in the spasm of fear that seized him. He looked over his shoulder to the door at the back of the church and thought longingly of the quiet street outside. He hesitated, stammered, grew more red and uncertain, and finally burst out: "The Lord," he said, and then looked about hopelessly, "the Lord maketh me to lie out in green pastures."

In the seats behind him a titter arose. A young woman sitting among the singers in the choir put her handkerchief to her face and throwing back her head rocked back and forth. A man near the door guffawed loudly and went hurriedly out. All over the church people began laughing.

Sam turned his eyes upon his mother. She was staring straight ahead of her, and her face was red. "I'm going out of this place and I'm never coming back again," he whispered, and, stepping into the aisle, walked boldly toward the door. He had made up his mind that if the evangelist tried to stop him he would fight. At his back he felt the rows of people looking at him and smiling. The laughter continued.

In the street he hurried along consumed with indignation. "I'll never go into any church again," he swore, shaking his fist in the air. The public avowals he had heard in the church seemed to him cheap and unworthy. He wondered why his mother stayed in there. With a sweep of his arm he dismissed all the people in the church. "It is a place to make public asses of the people," he thought.

Sam McPherson wandered through Main Street, dreading to meet Valmore and John Telfer. Finding the chairs back of the stove in Wildman's grocery deserted, he hurried past the grocer and hid in a corner. Tears of wrath stood in his eyes. He had been made a fool of. He imagined the scene that would go on when he came upon the street with the papers the next morning. Freedom Smith would be there sitting in the old worn buggy and roaring so that all the street would listen and laugh. "Going to lie out in any green pastures tonight, Sam?" he would shout. "Ain't you afraid you'll take cold?" By Geiger's drug store would stand Valmore and Telfer, eager to join in the fun at his expense. Telfer would pound on the side of the building with his cane and roar with laughter. Valmore would make a trumpet of his hands and shout after the fleeing boy. "Do you sleep out alone in them green pastures?" Freedom Smith would roar again.

Sam got up and went out of the grocery. As he hurried along, blind with wrath, he felt he would like a stand-up fight with some one. And, then, hurrying and avoiding the people, he merged with the crowd on the street and became a witness to the strange thing that happened that night in Caxton.

IN MAIN STREET HUSHED PEOPLE stood about in groups talking. The air was heavy with excitement. Solitary figures went from group to group whispering hoarsely. Mike McCarthy, the man who had denied God and who had won a place for himself in the affection of the newsboy, had assaulted a man with a pocket knife and had left him bleeding and wounded beside a country road. Something big and sensational had happened in the life of the town.

Mike McCarthy and Sam were friends. For years the man had idled upon the streets of the town, loitering about, boasting and talking. He had sat for hours in a chair under a tree before the New Leland House, reading books, doing tricks with cards, engaging in long discussions with John Telfer or any who would stand up to him.

Mike McCarthy got into trouble in a fight over a woman. A young farmer living at the edge of Caxton had come home from the fields to find his wife in the bold Irishman's arms and the two men had gone out of the house together to fight in the road. The woman, weeping in the house, followed to ask forgiveness of her husband. Running in the gathering darkness along the road she had found him cut and bleeding terribly, lying in a ditch under a hedge. On down the road she ran and appeared at the door of a neighbour, screaming and calling for help.

The story of the fight in the road got to Caxton just as Sam came out of the corner, back of the stove in Wildman's and appeared on the street. Men ran from store to store and from group to group along the street saying that the young farmer had died and that murder had been done. On a street corner Windy McPherson harangued the crowd declaring that the men of Caxton should arise in the defence of their homes and string the murderer to a lamp post. Hop Higgins, driving a horse from Culvert's livery, appeared on Main Street. "He will be at the McCarthy farm," he shouted. When several men, coming out of Geiger's drug store, stopped the marshal's horse, saying, "You will have trouble out there; you had better take help," the little red-faced marshal with the crippled leg laughed. "What trouble?" he asked—"To get Mike McCarthy? I shall ask him to come and he will come. The rest of that lot won't cut any figure. Mike can wrap the entire McCarthy family around his finger."

There were six of the McCarthy men, all, except Mike, silent, sullen men who only talked when they were in liquor. Mike furnished the town's social touch with the family. It was a strange family to live there in that fat, corn-growing country, a family with something savage and primitive about it, one that belonged among western mining camps or among the half savage dwellers in deep alleys in cities, and the fact that it lived on a corn farm in Iowa was, in the words of John Telfer, "something monstrous in Nature."

The McCarthy farm, lying some four miles east of Caxton, had once

SHERWOOD ANDERSON

contained a thousand acres of good corn-growing land. Lem McCarthy, the father of the family, had inherited it from a brother, a gold miner, a forty-niner, a sport owning fast horses, who planned to breed race horses on the Iowa land. Lem had come out of the back streets of an eastern city, bringing his brood of tall, silent, savage boys to live upon the land and, like the forty-niner, to be a sport. Thinking the wealth that had come to him vast beyond spending, he had plunged into horse racing and gambling. When, within two years, five hundred acres of the farm had to be sold to pay gambling debts, and the wide acres lay covered with weeds, Lem became alarmed, and settled down to hard work, the boys working all day in the field and at long intervals coming into town at night to get into trouble. Having no mother or sister, and knowing that no Caxton woman could be hired to go upon the place, they did their own housework; and on rainy days sat about the old farmhouse playing cards and fighting. On other days they would stand around the bar in Art Sherman's saloon in Piety Hollow drinking until they had lost their savage silence and had become loud and quarrelsome, going from there upon the streets to seek trouble. Once, going into Hayner's restaurant, they took stacks of plates from shelves back of the counter and, standing in the doorway, threw them at people passing in the street, the crash of the breaking crockery accompanying their roaring laughter. When they had driven the people to cover they got upon their horses and with wild shouts raced up and down Main Street between the rows of tied horses until Hop Higgins, the town marshal, appeared, when they rode off into the country awakening the farmers along the darkened road as they fled, shouting and singing, toward home.

When the McCarthy boys got into trouble in Caxton, old Lem McCarthy drove into town and got them out of it, paying for the damage done and going about declaring the boys meant no harm. When told to keep them out of town he shook his head and said he would try.

Mike McCarthy did not ride swearing and singing with the five brothers along the dark road. He did not work all day in the hot corn fields. He was the family gentleman, and, wearing good clothes, strolled instead upon the street or loitered in the shade before the New Leland House. Mike had been educated. For some years he had attended a college in Indiana from which he was expelled for an affair with a woman. After his return from college he stayed in Caxton, living at the hotel and making a pretence of studying law in the office of old Judge Reynolds.

He paid slight attention to the study of law, but with infinite patience had so trained his hands that he became wonderfully dexterous with coins and cards, plucking them out of the air and making them appear in the shoes, the hats, and even in the mouths, of bystanders. During the day he walked the streets looking at the girl clerks in the stores, or stood upon the station platform waving his hand to women passengers on passing trains. He told John Telfer that the flattery of women was a lost art that he intended to restore. Mike McCarthy carried in his pockets books which he read sitting in a chair before the hotel or on the stones before store windows. When on Saturdays the streets were filled with people, he stood on the corners giving gratuitous performances of his magical art with cards and coins, and eyeing country girls in the crowd. Once, a woman, the town stationer's wife, shouted at him, calling him a lazy lout, whereupon he threw a coin in the air, and when it did not come down rushed toward her shouting, "She has it in her stocking." When the stationer's wife ran into her shop and banged the door the crowd laughed and shouted with delight.

Telfer had a liking for the tall, grey-eyed, loitering McCarthy and sometimes sat with him discussing a novel or a poem; Sam in the background listened eagerly. Valmore did not care for the man, shaking his head and declaring that such a fellow could come to no good end.

The rest of the town agreed with Valmore, and McCarthy, knowing this, sunned himself in the town's displeasure. For the sake of the public furor it brought down upon his head he proclaimed himself a socialist, an anarchist, an atheist, a pagan. Among all the McCarthy boys he alone cared greatly about women, and he made public and open declarations of his passion for them. Before the men gathered about the stove in Wildman's grocery store he would stand whipping them into a frenzy by declaring for free love, and vowing that he would have the best of any woman who gave him the chance.

For this man the frugal, hard working newsboy had conceived a regard amounting to a passion. As he listened to McCarthy he got continuous delightful little thrills. "There is nothing he would not dare," thought the boy. "He is the freest, the boldest, the bravest man in town." When the young Irishman, seeing the admiration in his eyes, flung him a silver dollar saying, "That is for your fine brown eyes, my boy; it I had them I would have half the women in town after me," Sam kept the dollar in his pocket and counted it a kind of treasure like the rose given a lover by his sweetheart.

It was past eleven o'clock when Hop Higgins returned to town with McCarthy, driving quietly along the street and through an alley at the back of the town hall. The crowd upon the street had broken up. Sam had gone from one to another of the muttering groups, his heart quaking with fear. Now he stood at the back of the mass of men gathered at the jail door. An oil lamp, burning at the top of the post above the door, threw dancing, flickering lights on the faces of the men before him. The thunder storm that had threatened had not come, but the unnatural warm wind continued and the sky overhead was inky black.

Through the alley, to the jail door, drove the town marshal, the young McCarthy sitting in the buggy beside him. A man rushed forward to hold the horse. McCarthy's face was chalky white. He laughed and shouted, raising his hand toward the sky.

"I am Michael, son of God. I have cut a man with a knife so that his red blood ran upon the ground. I am the son of God and this filthy jail shall be my sanctuary. In there I shall talk aloud with my Father," he roared hoarsely, shaking his fist at the crowd. "Sons of this cesspool of respectability, stay and hear! Send for your females and let them stand in the presence of a man!"

Taking the white, wild-eyed man by the arm Marshal Higgins led him into the jail, the clank of locks, the low murmur of the voice of Higgins and the wild laughter of McCarthy floating out to the group of silent men standing in the mud of the alley.

Sam McPherson ran past the group of men to the side of the jail and finding John Telfer and Valmore leaning silently against the wall of Tom Folger's wagon shop slipped between them. Telfer put out his arm and laid it upon the boy's shoulder. Hop Higgins, coming out of the jail, addressed the crowd. "Don't answer if he talks," he said; "he is as crazy as a loon."

Sam moved closer to Telfer. The voice of the imprisoned man, loud, and filled with a startling boldness, rolled out of the jail. He began praying.

"Hear me, Father Almighty, who has permitted this town of Caxton to exist and has let me, Thy son, grow to manhood. I am Michael, Thy son. They have put me in this jail where rats run across the floor and they stand in the mud outside as I talk with Thee. Are you there, old Truepenny?"

A breath of cold air blew up the alley followed by a flaw of rain. The group under the flickering lamp by the jail entrance drew back against the walls of the building. Sam could see them dimly, pressing closely against the wall. The man in the jail laughed loudly.

"I have had a philosophy of life, O Father," he shouted. "I have seen men and women here living year after year without children. I have seen them hoarding pennies and denying Thee new life on which to work Thy will. To these women I have gone secretly talking of carnal love. With them I have been gentle and kind; them I have flattered."

A roaring laugh broke from the lips of the imprisoned man. "Are you there, oh dwellers in the cesspool of respectability?" he shouted. "Do you stand in the mud with cold feet listening? I have been with your wives. Eleven Caxton wives without babes have I been with and it has been fruitless. The twelfth woman I have just left, leaving her man in the road a bleeding sacrifice to thee. I shall call out the names of the eleven. I shall have revenge also upon the husbands of the women, some of whom wait with the others in the mud outside."

He began calling off the names of Caxton wives. A shudder ran through the body of the boy, sensitised by the new chill in the air and by the excitement of the night. Among the men standing along the wall of the jail a murmur arose. Again they grouped themselves under the flickering light by the jail door, disregarding the rain. Valmore, stumbling out of the darkness beside Sam, stood before Telfer. "The boy should be going home," he said; "this isn't fit for him to hear."

Telfer laughed and drew Sam closer to him. "He has heard enough lies in this town," he said. "Truth won't hurt him. I would not go myself, nor would you, and the boy shall not go. This McCarthy has a brain. Although he is half insane now he is trying to work something out. The boy and I will stay to hear."

The voice from the jail continued calling out the names of Caxton wives. Voices in the group before the jail door began shouting: "This should be stopped. Let us tear down the jail."

McCarthy laughed aloud. "They squirm, oh Father, they squirm; I have them in the pit and I torture them," he cried.

An ugly feeling of satisfaction came over Sam. He had a sense of the fact that the names shouted from the jail would be repeated over and over through the town. One of the women whose names had been called out had stood with the evangelist at the back of the church trying to induce the wife of the baker to rise and be counted in the fold with the lambs.

The rain, falling on the shoulders of the men by the jail door, changed to hail, the air grew colder and the hailstones rattled on the roofs of buildings. Some of the men joined Telfer and Valmore, talking in low, excited voices. "And Mary McKane, too, the hypocrite," Sam heard one of them say.

The voice inside the jail changed. Still praying, Mike McCarthy seemed also to be talking to the group in the darkness outside.

"I am sick of my life. I have sought leadership and have not found it. Oh Father! Send down to men a new Christ, one to get hold of us, a modern Christ with a pipe in his mouth who will swear and knock us about so that we vermin who pretend to be made in Thy image will understand. Let him go into churches and into courthouses, into cities, and into towns like this, shouting, 'Be ashamed! Be ashamed of your cowardly concern over your snivelling souls!' Let him tell us that never will our lives, so miserably lived, be repeated after our bodies lie rotting in the grave."

A sob broke from his lips and a lump came into Sam's throat.

"Oh Father! help us men of Caxton to understand that we have only this, our lives, this life so warm and hopeful and laughing in the sun, this life with its awkward boys full of strange possibilities, and its girls with their long legs and freckles on their noses, that are meant to carry life within themselves, new life, kicking and stirring, and waking them at night."

The voice of the prayer broke. Wild sobs took the place of speech. "Father!" shouted the broken voice, "I have taken a life, a man that moved and talked and whistled in the sunshine on winter mornings; I have killed."

THE VOICE INSIDE THE JAIL became inaudible. Silence, broken by low sobs from the jail, fell on the little dark alley and the listening men began going silently away. The lump in Sam's throat grew larger. Tears stood in his eyes. He went with Telfer and Valmore out of the alley and into the street, the two men walking in silence. The rain had ceased and a cold wind blew.

The boy felt that he had been shriven. His mind, his heart, even his tired body seemed strangely cleansed. He felt a new affection for Telfer and Valmore. When Telfer began talking he listened eagerly, thinking that at last he understood him and knew why men like Valmore, Wildman, Freedom Smith, and Telfer loved each other and went on being friends year after year in the face of difficulties and misunderstandings. He thought that he had got hold of the idea of brotherhood that John Telfer talked of so often and so eloquently. "Mike McCarthy is only a brother who has gone the dark road," he thought and felt a glow of pride in the thought and in the apt expression of it in his mind.

John Telfer, forgetting the boy, talked soberly to Valmore, the two men stumbling along in the darkness intent upon their own thoughts.

"It is an odd thought," said Telfer and his voice seemed far away and unnatural like the voice from the jail; "it is an odd thought that but for a quirk in the brain this Mike McCarthy might himself have been a kind of Christ with a pipe in his mouth."

Valmore stumbled and half fell in the darkness at a street crossing. Telfer went on talking.

"The world will some day grope its way into some kind of an understanding of its extraordinary men. Now they suffer terribly. In success or in such failures as has come to this imaginative, strangely perverted Irishman their lot is pitiful. It is only the common, the plain, unthinking man who slides peacefully through this troubled world."

At the house Jane McPherson sat waiting for her boy. She was thinking of the scene in the church and a hard light was in her eyes. Sam went past the sleeping room of his parents, where Windy McPherson snored peacefully, and up the stairway to his own room. He undressed and, putting out the light, knelt upon the floor. From the wild ravings of the man in the jail he had got hold of something. In the midst of the blasphemy of Mike McCarthy he had sensed a deep and abiding love of life. Where the church had failed the bold sensualist succeeded. Sam felt that he could have prayed in the presence of the entire town.

"Oh, Father!" he cried, sending up his voice in the silence of the little room, "make me stick to the thought that the right living of this, my life, is my duty to you."

By the door below, while Valmore waited on the sidewalk, Telfer talked to Jane McPherson.

"I wanted Sam to hear," he explained. "He needs a religion. All young men need a religion. I wanted him to hear how even a man like Mike McCarthy keeps instinctively trying to justify himself before God."

SHERWOOD ANDERSON

IV

John Telfer's friendship was a formative influence upon Sam McPherson. His father's worthlessness and the growing realisation of the hardship of his mother's position had given life a bitter taste in his mouth, and Telfer sweetened it. He entered with zeal into Sam's thoughts and dreams, and tried valiantly to arouse in the quiet, industrious, money-making boy some of his own love of life and beauty. At night, as the two walked down country roads, the man would stop and, waving his arms about, quote Poe or Browning or, in another mood, would compel Sam's attention to the rare smell of a hayfield or to a moonlit stretch of meadow.

Before people gathered on the streets he teased the boy, calling him a little money grubber and saying, "He is like a little mole that works underground. As the mole goes for a worm so this boy goes for a five-cent piece. I have watched him. A travelling man goes out of town leaving a stray dime or nickel here and within an hour it is in this boy's pocket. I have talked to banker Walker of him. He trembles lest his vaults become too small to hold the wealth of this young Croesus. The day will come when he will buy the town and put it into his vest pocket."

For all his public teasing of the boy Telfer had the genius to adopt a different attitude when they were alone together. Then he talked to him openly and freely as he talked to Valmore and Freedom Smith and to other cronies of his on the streets of Caxton. Walking along the road he would point with his cane to the town and say, "You and that mother of yours have more of the real stuff in you than the rest of the boys and mothers of the town put together."

In all Caxton Telfer was the only man who knew books and who took them seriously. Sam sometimes found his attitude toward them puzzling and would stand with open mouth listening as Telfer swore or laughed at a book as he did at Valmore or Freedom Smith. He had a fine portrait of Browning which he kept hung in the stable and before this he would stand, his legs spread apart, and his head tilted to one side, talking.

"A rich old sport you are, eh?" he would say, grinning. "Getting yourself discussed by women and college professors in clubs, eh? You old fraud!"

Toward Mary Underwood, the school teacher who had become Sam's friend and with whom the boy sometimes walked and talked, Telfer had no charity. Mary Underwood was a sort of cinder in the eyes of Caxton. She was the only child of Silas Underwood, the town harness maker, who once had worked in a shop belonging to Windy McPherson. After the business failure of Windy he had started independently and for a time did well, sending his daughter to a school in Massachusetts. Mary did not understand the people of Caxton and the people misunderstood and distrusted her. Taking no part in the life of the town and keeping to herself and to her books she awoke a kind of fear in others. Because she did not join them at church suppers, or go from porch to porch gossiping with other women through the long summer evenings, they thought her something abnormal. On Sundays she sat alone in her pew at church and on Saturday afternoons, come storm, come sunshine, she walked on country roads and through the woods accompanied by a collie dog. She was a small woman with a straight, slender figure and had fine blue eyes filled with changing lights, hidden by the eye-glasses she almost constantly wore. Her lips were very full and red, and she sat with them parted so that the edges of her fine teeth showed. Her nose was large, and a fine reddish-brown colour glowed in her cheeks. Though different, she had, like Jane McPherson, a habit of silence; and under her silence, she, like Sam's mother, possessed an unusually strong and vigorous mind.

As a child she was a sort of half invalid and had not been on friendly footing with other children. It was then that her habit of silence and reticence had been established. The years in the school in Massachusetts restored her health but did not break this habit. She came home and took the place in the schools to earn money with which to take her back East, dreaming of a position as instructor in an eastern college. She was that rare thing, a woman scholar, loving scholarship for its own sake.

Mary Underwood's position in the town and in the schools was insecure. Out of her silent, independent way of life had sprung a misunderstanding that, at least once, had taken definite form and had come near driving her from the town and schools. That she did not succumb to the storm of criticism that for some weeks beat about her head was due to her habit of silence and to a determination to get her own way in the face of everything.

It was a suggestion of scandal that had put the grey hairs upon her head. The scandal had blown over before the time of her friendship for Sam, but he had known of it. In those days he knew of everything that went on in the town—his quick ears and eyes missed nothing. More

　　　　　　　　　　　　　　　　　　　　　　SHERWOOD ANDERSON

than once he had heard the men waiting to be shaved in Sawyer's barber shop speak of her.

The tale ran that she had been involved in an affair with a real estate agent who had afterward left town. It was said that the man, a tall, fine-looking fellow, had been in love with Mary and had wanted to desert his wife and go away with her. One night he had driven to Mary's house in a closed buggy and the two had driven into the country. They had sat for hours in the covered buggy at the side of the road and talked, and people driving past had seen them there talking together.

And then she had got out of the buggy and walked home alone through snow drifts. The next day she was at school as usual. When told of it the school superintendent, a puttering old fellow with vacant eyes, had shaken his head in alarm and declared that it must be looked into. He called Mary into his little narrow office in the school building, but lost courage when she sat before him, and said nothing. The man in the barber shop, who repeated the tale, said that the real estate man drove on to a distant station and took a train to the city, and that some days later he came back to Caxton and moved his family out of town.

Sam dismissed the story from his mind. Having begun a friendship for Mary he put the man in the barber shop into a class with Windy McPherson and thought of him as a pretender and liar who talked for the sake of talk. He remembered with a shock the crude levity with which the loafers in the shop had greeted the repetition of the tale. Their comments had come back to his mind as he walked through the streets with his newspapers and had given him a kind of jolt. He went along under the trees thinking of the sunlight falling upon the grey hair as they walked together on summer afternoons, and bit his lip and opened and closed his fist convulsively.

During Mary's second year in the Caxton schools her mother died, and at the end of another year, her father, failing in the harness business, Mary became a fixture in the schools. The house at the edge of the town, the property of her mother, had come down to her and she lived there with an old aunt. After the passing of the wind of scandal concerning the real estate man the town lost interest in her. She was thirty-six at the time of her first friendship with Sam and lived alone among her books.

Sam had been deeply moved by her friendship. It had seemed to him something significant that grown people with affairs of their own should be so in earnest about his future as she and Telfer were. Boylike, he counted it a tribute to himself rather than to the winsome youth in him, and was made proud by it. Having no real feeling for books, and only pretending to have out of a desire to please, he sometimes went from one to the other of his two friends, passing off their opinions as his own.

At this trick Telfer invariably caught him. "That is not your notion," he would shout, "you have it from that school teacher. It is the opinion of a woman. Their opinions, like the books they sometimes write, are founded on nothing. They are not the real things. Women know nothing. Men only care for them because they have not had what they want from them. No woman is really big—except maybe my woman, Eleanor."

When Sam continued to be much in the company of Mary, Telfer grew more bitter.

"I would have you observe women's minds and avoid letting them influence your own," he told the boy. "They live in a world of unrealities. They like even vulgar people in books, but shrink from the simple, earthy folk about them. That school teacher is so. Is she like me? Does she, while loving books, love also the very smell of human life?"

In a way Telfer's attitude toward the kindly little school teacher became Sam's attitude. Although they walked and talked together the course of study she had planned for him he never took up and as he grew to know her better, the books she read and the ideas she advanced appealed to him less and less. He thought that she, as Telfer held, lived in a world of illusion and unreality and said so. When she lent him books, he put them in his pocket and did not read them. When he did read, he thought the books reminded him of something that hurt him. They were in some way false and pretentious. He thought they were like his father. One day he tried reading aloud to Telfer from a book Mary Underwood had lent him.

The story was one of a poetic man with long, unclean fingernails who went among people preaching the doctrine of beauty. It began with a scene on a hillside in a rainstorm where the poetic man sat under a tent writing a letter to his sweetheart.

Telfer was beside himself. Jumping from his seat under a tree by the roadside he waved his arms and shouted:

"Stop! Stop it! Do not go on with it. The story lies. A man could not write love letters under the circumstances and he was a fool to pitch his tent on a hillside. A man in a tent on a hillside in a storm would be cold and wet and getting the rheumatism. To be writing letters he would need to be an unspeakable ass. He had better be out digging a trench to keep the water from running through his tent."

Waving his arms, Telfer went off up the road and Sam followed thinking him altogether right, and, if later in life he learned that there are men who could write love letters on a piece of housetop in a flood, he did not know it then and the least suggestion of windiness or pretence lay heavy in his stomach.

Telfer had a vast enthusiasm for Bellamy's "Looking Backward," and read it aloud to his wife on Sunday afternoons, sitting under the apple trees in the garden. They had a fund of little personal jokes and sayings that they were forever laughing over, and she had infinite delight in his comments on the life and people of Caxton, but did not share his love of books. When she sometimes went to sleep in her chair during the Sunday afternoon readings he poked her with his cane and laughingly told her to wake up and listen to the dream of a great dreamer. Among Browning's verses his favourites were "A Light Woman" and "Fra Lippo Lippi," and he would recite these aloud with great gusto. He declared Mark Twain the greatest man in the world and in certain moods he would walk the road beside Sam reciting over and over one or two lines of verse, often this from Poe:

> *Helen, thy beauty is to me*
> *Like some Nicean bark of yore.*

Then, stopping and turning upon the boy, he would demand whether or not the writing of such lines wasn't worth living a life for.

Telfer had a pack of dogs that always went with them on their walks at night and he had for them long Latin names that Sam could never remember. One summer be bought a trotting mare from Lem McCarthy and gave great attention to the colt, which he named Bellamy Boy, trotting him up and down a little driveway by the side of his house for hours at a time and declaring he would be a great trotting horse. He could recite the colt's pedigree with great gusto and when he had been talking to Sam of some book he would repay the boy's attention by saying, "You, my boy, are as far superior to the run of boys about town as the colt, Bellamy Boy, is superior to the farm horses that are hitched along Main Street on Saturday afternoons." And then, with a wave of his hand and a look of much seriousness on his face, he would add, "And for the same reason. You have been, like him, under a master trainer of youth."

ONE EVENING SAM, NOW GROWN to man's stature and full of the awkwardness and self-consciousness of his new growth, was sitting on a cracker barrel at the back of Wildman's grocery. It was a summer evening and a breeze blew through the open doors swaying the hanging oil lamps that burned and sputtered overhead. As usual he was listening in silence to the talk that went on among the men.

Standing with legs wide apart and from time to time jabbing with his cane at Sam's legs, John Telfer held forth on the subject of love.

"It is a theme that poets do well to write of," he declared. "In writing of it they avoid the necessity of embracing it. In trying for a well-turned line they forget to look at well-turned ankles. He who sings most passionately of love has been in love the least; he woos the goddess of poesy and only gets into trouble when he, like John Keats, turns to the daughter of a villager and tries to live the lines he has written."

"Stuff and nonsense," roared Freedom Smith, who had been sitting tilted far back in a chair with his feet against the cold stove, smoking a short, black pipe, and who now brought his feet down upon the floor with a bang. Admiring Telfer's flow of words he pretended to be filled with scorn. "The night is too hot for eloquence," he bellowed. "If you must be eloquent talk of ice cream or mint juleps or recite a verse about the old swimming pool."

Telfer, wetting his finger, thrust it into the air.

"The wind is in the north-west; the beasts roar; we will have a storm," he said, winking at Valmore.

Banker Walker came into the store, followed by his daughter. She was a small, dark-skinned girl with black, quick eyes. Seeing Sam sitting with swinging legs upon the cracker barrel she spoke to her father and went out of the store. At the sidewalk she stopped and, turning, made a quick motion with her hand.

Sam jumped off the cracker barrel and strolled toward the street door. A flush was on his cheeks. His mouth felt hot and dry. He went with extreme deliberateness, stopping to bow to the banker, and for a moment lingering to read a newspaper that lay upon the cigar case, to avoid the comments he feared his going might excite among the men by the stove. In his heart he trembled lest the girl should have disappeared down the street, and with his eyes, he looked guiltily at the banker, who had joined the group at the back of the store and who now stood listening to the talk, while he read from a list held in his hand and Wildman went here and there doing up packages and repeating aloud the names of articles called off by the banker.

At the end of the lighted business section of Main Street, Sam found the girl waiting for him. She began to tell of the subterfuge by which she had escaped her father.

"I told him I would go home with my sister," she said, tossing her head.

Taking hold of the boy's hand, she led him along the shaded street. For the first time Sam walked in the company of one of the strange beings that had begun to bring him uneasy nights, and overcome with the wonder of it the blood climbed through his body and made his head reel so that he walked in silence unable to understand his own emotions. He felt the soft hand of the girl with delight; his heart pounded against the walls of his chest and a choking sensation gripped at his throat.

Walking along the street, past lighted residences where the low voices of women in talk greeted his ears, Sam was inordinately proud. He thought that he should like to turn and walk with this girl through the lighted Main Street. Had she not chosen him from among all the boys of the town; had she not, with a flutter of her little, white hand, called to him with a call that he wondered the men upon the cracker barrels had not heard? Her boldness and his own took his breath away. He could not talk. His tongue seemed paralysed.

Down the street went the boy and girl, loitering in the shadows, hurrying past the dim oil lamps at street crossings, getting from each other wave after wave of exquisite little thrills. Neither spoke. They were beyond words. Had they not together done this daring thing?

In the shadow of a tree they stopped and stood facing each other; the girl looked at the ground and stood facing the boy. Putting out his hand he laid it upon her shoulder. In the darkness on the other side of the street a man stumbled homeward along a board sidewalk. The lights of Main Street glowed in the distance. Sam drew the girl toward him. She raised her head. Their lips met, and then, throwing her arms about his neck, she kissed him again and again eagerly.

Sam's return to Wildman's was marked by extreme caution. Although he had been absent but fifteen minutes it seemed to him that hours must have passed and he would not have been surprised to see the stores locked and darkness settled down on Main Street. It was inconceivable that the grocer could still be wrapping packages for banker Walker. Worlds had been remade. Manhood had come to him. Why! the man should have wrapped the entire store, package after package, and sent it to the ends of the earth. He lingered in the shadows at the first of the store lights where ages before he had gone, a mere boy, to meet her, a mere girl, and looked with wonder at the lighted way before him.

Sam crossed the street and, from the front of Sawyer's barber shop, looked into Wildman's. He felt like a spy looking into the camp of an enemy. There before him sat the men into whose midst he had it in his power to cast a thunderbolt. He might walk to the door and say, truthfully enough, "Here before you is a boy that by the flutter of a white hand has been made into a man; here is one who has wrung the heart of womankind and eaten his fill at the tree of the knowledge of life."

In the grocery the talk still continued among the men upon the cracker barrels who seemed unconscious of the boy's slinking entrance. Indeed, their talk had sunk. From talking of love and of poets they talked of corn and of steers. Banker Walker, his packages of groceries lying on the counter, smoked a cigar.

"You can fairly hear the corn growing tonight," he said. "It wants but another shower or two and we shall have a record crop. I plan to feed a hundred steers at my farm out Rabbit Road this winter."

The boy climbed again upon a cracker barrel and tried to look unconcerned and interested in the talk. Still his heart thumped; still a throbbing went on in his wrists. He turned and looked at the floor hoping his agitation would pass unnoticed.

The banker, taking up the packages, walked out at the door. Valmore and Freedom Smith went over to the livery barn for a game of pinochle. And John Telfer, twirling his cane and calling to a troup of dogs that loitered in an alley back of the store, took Sam for a walk into the country.

"I will continue this talk of love," said Telfer, striking at weeds along the road with his cane and from time to time calling sharply to the dogs that, filled with delight at being abroad, ran growling and tumbling over each other in the dusty road.

"That Freedom Smith is a sample of life in this town. At the word love he drops his feet upon the floor and pretends to be filled with disgust. He will talk of corn or steers or of the stinking hides that he buys, but at the mention of the word love he is like a hen that has seen a hawk in the sky. He runs about in circles making a fuss. 'Here! Here! Here!' he cries, 'you are making public something that should be kept hidden. You are doing in the light of day what should only be done with a shamed face in a darkened room.' Why, boy, if I were a woman in this town I would not stand it—I would go to New York, to France, to Paris—To be wooed for but a passing moment by a shame-faced yokel without art—uh—it is unthinkable."

The man and the boy walked in silence. The dogs, scenting a rabbit, disappeared across a long pasture, their master letting them go. From time to time he threw back his head and took long breaths of the night air.

"I am not like banker Walker," he declared. "He thinks of the growing corn in terms of fat steers feeding on the Rabbit Run farm; I think of it as something majestic. I see the long corn rows with the men and the horses half hidden, hot and breathless, and I think of a vast river of life. I catch a breath of the flame that was in the mind of the man who said, 'The land is flowing with milk and honey.' I am made happy by my thoughts not by the dollars clinking in my pocket.

"And then in the fall when the corn stands shocked I see another picture. Here and there in companies stand the armies of the corn. It puts a ring in my voice to look at them. 'These orderly armies has mankind brought out of chaos,' I say to myself. 'On a smoking black ball flung by the hand of God out of illimitable space has man stood up these armies to defend his home against the grim attacking armies of want.'"

Telfer stopped and stood in the road with his legs spread apart. He took off his hat and throwing back his head laughed up at the stars.

"Freedom Smith should hear me now," he cried, rocking back and forth with laughter and switching his cane at the boy's legs so that Sam had to hop merrily about in the road to avoid it. "Flung by the hand of God out of illimitable space—eh! not bad, eh! I should be in Congress. I am wasted here. I am throwing priceless eloquence to dogs who prefer to chase rabbits and to a boy who is the worst little money grubber in the town."

The midsummer madness that had seized Telfer passed and for a time he walked in silence. Suddenly, putting his arm on the boy's shoulder, he stopped and pointed to where a faint light in the sky marked the lighted town.

"They are good people," he said, "but their ways are not my ways or your ways. You will go out of the town. You have genius. You will be a man of finance. I have watched you. You are not niggardly and you do not cheat and lie—result—you will not be a little business man. What have you? You have the gift of seeing dollars where the rest of the boys of the town see nothing and you are tireless after those dollars—you will be a big man of dollars, it is plain." Into his voice came a touch of bitterness. "I also was marked out. Why do I carry a cane? why do I not buy a farm and raise steers? I am the most worthless thing alive. I have the touch of genius without the energy to make it count."

Sam's mind that had been inflamed by the kiss of the girl cooled in the presence of Telfer. In the summer madness of the talking man there was something soothing to the fever in his blood. He followed the words eagerly, seeing pictures, getting thrills, filled with happiness.

At the edge of town a buggy passed the walking pair. In the buggy sat a young farmer, his arm about the waist of a girl, her head upon his shoulder. Far in the distance sounded the faint call of the dogs. Sam and Telfer sat down on a grassy bank under a tree while Telfer rolled and lighted a cigarette.

"As I promised, I will talk to you of love," he said, making a wide sweep with his arm each time as he put his cigarette into his mouth.

The grassy bank on which they lay had the rich, burned smell of the hot days. A wind rustled the standing corn that formed a kind of wall behind them. The moon was in the sky and shone down across bank after bank of serried clouds. The grandiloquence went out of the voice of Telfer and his face became serious.

"My foolishness is more than half earnest," he said. "I think that a man or boy who has set for himself a task had better let women and girls alone. If he be a man of genius, he has a purpose independent of all the world, and should cut and slash and pound his way toward his mark, forgetting every one, particularly the woman that would come to grips with him. She also has a mark toward which she goes. She is at war with him and has a purpose that is not his purpose. She believes that the pursuit of women is an end for a life. For all they now condemn Mike McCarthy who went to the asylum because of them and who, while loving life, came near to taking life, the women of Caxton do not condemn his madness for themselves; they do not blame him for loitering away his good years or for making an abortive mess of his good

SHERWOOD ANDERSON

brain. While he made an art of the pursuit of women they applauded secretly. Did not twelve of them accept the challenge thrown out by his eyes as he loitered in the streets?"

The man, who had begun talking quietly and seriously, raised his voice and waved the lighted cigarette in the air and the boy who had begun to think again of the dark-skinned daughter of banker Walker listened attentively. The barking of the dogs grew nearer.

"If you as a boy can get from me, a grown man, an understanding of the purpose of women you will not have lived in this town for nothing. Set your mark at money making if you will, but drive at that. Let yourself but go and a sweet wistful pair of eyes seen in a street crowd or a pair of little feet running over a dance floor will retard your growth for years. No man or boy can grow toward the purpose of a life while he thinks of women. Let him try it and he will be undone. What is to him a passing humour is to them an end. They are diabolically clever. They will run and stop and run and stop again, keeping just without his reach. He sees them here and there about him. His mind is filled with vague, delicious thoughts that come out of the very air; before he realises what he has done he has spent his years in vain pursuit and turning finds himself old and undone."

Telfer began jabbing at the ground with his stick.

"I had my chance. In New York I had money to live on and time to have made an artist of myself. I won prize after prize. The master, walking up and down back of us, lingered longest over my easel. There was a fellow sat beside me who had nothing. I made sport of him and called him Sleepy Jock after a dog we used to have about our house here in Caxton. Now I am here idly waiting for death and that Jock, where is he? Only last week I saw in a paper that he had won a place among the world's great artists by a picture he has painted. In the school I watched for a look in the eyes of the girl students and went about with them night after night winning, like Mike McCarthy, fruitless victories. Sleepy Jock had the best of it. He did not look about with open eyes but kept peering instead at the face of the master. My days were full of small successes. I could wear clothes. I could make soft-eyed girls turn to look at me in a dance hall. I remember a night. We students gave a dance and Sleepy Jock came. He went about asking for dances and the girls laughed and told him they had none to give, that the dances were taken. I followed him and had my ears filled with flattery and my card with names. In riding the wave of small success I got the habit of small success. When I could not catch the line I wanted to make a drawing live, I dropped my pencil and, taking a girl upon my arm, went for a day in the country. Once, sitting in a restaurant, I overheard two women talking of the beauty of my eyes and was made happy for a week."

Telfer threw up his hands in disgust.

"My flow of words, my ready trick of talking; to what does it bring me? Let me tell you. It has brought me to this—that at fifty I, who might have been an artist fixing the minds of thousands upon some thing of beauty or of truth, have become a village cut-up, a pot-house wit, a flinger of idle words into the air of a village intent upon raising corn.

"If you ask me why, I tell you that my mind was paralysed by small success and if you ask me where I got the taste for that, I tell you that I got it when I saw it lurking in a woman's eyes and heard the pleasant little songs that lull to sleep upon a woman's lips."

The boy, sitting upon the grassy bank beside Telfer, began thinking of life in Caxton. The man smoking the cigarette fell into one of his rare silences. The boy thought of girls that had come into his mind at night, of how he had been thrilled by a glance from the eyes of a little blue-eyed school girl who had once visited at Freedom Smith's home and of how he had gone at night to stand under her window.

In Caxton adolescent love had about it a virility befitting a land that raised so many bushels of yellow corn and drove so many fat steers through the streets to be loaded upon cars. Men and women went their ways believing, with characteristic American what-boots-it attitude toward the needs of childhood, that it was well for growing boys and girls to be much alone together. To leave them alone together was a principle with them. When a young man called upon his sweetheart, her parents sat in the presence of the two with apologetic eyes and presently disappeared leaving them alone together. When boys' and girls' parties were given in Caxton houses, parents went away leaving the children to shift for themselves.

"Now have a good time and don't tear the house down," they said, going off upstairs.

Left to themselves the children played kissing games and young men and tall half-formed girls sat on the front porches in the darkness, thrilled and half frightened, getting through their instincts, crudely and without guidance, their first peep at the mystery of life. They kissed passionately and the young men, walking home, lay upon their beds fevered and unnaturally aroused, thinking thoughts.

Young men went into the company of girls time and again without knowing aught of them except that they caused a stirring of their whole being, a kind of riot of the senses to which they returned on other evenings as a drunkard to his cups. After such an evening they found themselves, on the next morning, confused and filled with vague longings. They had lost their keenness for fun, they heard without hearing the talk of the men about the station and in the stores, they went slinking through the streets in groups and people seeing them nodded their heads and said, "It is the loutish age."

If Sam did not have a loutish age it was due to his tireless struggle to increase the totals at the foot of the pages in the yellow bankbook, to the growing ill health of his mother that had begun to frighten him, and to the society of Valmore, Wildman, Freedom Smith, and the man who now sat musing beside him. He began to think he would have nothing more to do with the Walker girl. He remembered his sister's affair with a young farmer and shuddered at the crude vulgarity of it. He looked over the shoulder of the man sitting beside him absorbed in thought, and saw the rolling fields stretched away in the moonlight and into his mind came Telfer's speech. So vivid, so moving, seemed the picture of the armies of standing corn which men had set up in the fields to protect themselves against the march of pitiless Nature, and Sam, holding the picture in his mind as he followed the sense of Telfer's talk, thought that all society had resolved itself into a few sturdy souls who went on and on regardless, and a hunger to make of himself such another arose engulfing him. The desire within him seemed so compelling that he turned and haltingly tried to express what was in his mind.

"I will try," he stammered, "I will try to be a man. I will try to not have anything to do with them—with women. I will work and make money—and—and—"

Speech left him. He rolled over and lying on his stomach looked at the ground.

"To Hell with women and girls," he burst forth as though throwing something distasteful out of his throat.

In the road a clamour arose. The dogs, giving up the pursuit of rabbits, came barking and growling into sight and scampered up the grassy bank, covering the man and the boy. Shaking off the reaction upon his sensitive nature of the emotions of the boy Telfer arose. His *sang froid* had returned to him. Cutting right and left with his stick at the dogs he cried joyfully, "We have had enough of eloquence from man, boy, and dog. We will be on our way. We will get this boy Sam home and tucked into bed."

V

S am was a half-grown man of fifteen when the call of the city came to him. For six years he had been upon the streets. He had seen the sun come up hot and red over the corn fields, and had stumbled through the streets in the bleak darkness of winter mornings, when the trains from the north came into Caxton covered with ice, and the trainmen stood on the deserted little platform whipping their arms and calling to Jerry Donlin to hurry with his work that they might get back into the warm stale air of the smoking car.

In the six years the boy had grown more and more determined to become a man of money. Fed by banker Walker, the silent mother, and in some subtle way by the very air he breathed, the belief within him that to make money and to have money would in some way make up for the old half-forgotten humiliations in the life of the McPherson family and would set it on a more secure foundation than the wobbly Windy had provided, grew and influenced his thoughts and his acts. Tirelessly he kept at his efforts to get ahead. In his bed at night he dreamed of dollars. Jane McPherson had herself a passion for frugality. In spite of Windy's incompetence and her own growing ill health, she would not permit the family to go into debt, and although, in the long hard winters, Sam sometimes ate cornmeal mush until his mind revolted at the thought of a corn field, yet was the rent of the little house paid on the scratch, and her boy fairly driven to increase the totals in the yellow bankbook. Even Valmore, who since the death of his wife had lived in a loft above his shop and who was a blacksmith of the old days, a workman first and a money maker later, did not despise the thought of gain.

"It is money makes the mare go," he said with a kind of reverence as banker Walker, fat, sleek, and prosperous, walked pompously out of Wildman's grocery.

Of John Telfer's attitude toward money-making, the boy was uncertain. The man followed with joyous abandonment the impulse of the moment.

"That's right," he cried impatiently when Sam, who had begun to express opinions at the gatherings in the grocery, pointed out hesitatingly that the papers took account of men of wealth no matter what their achievements, "Make money! Cheat! Lie! Be one of the men of the big world! Get your name up for a modern, high-class American!"

And in the next breath, turning upon Freedom Smith who had begun to berate the boy for not sticking to the schools and who predicted that the day would come when Sam would regret his lack of book learning, he shouted, "Let the schools go! They are but musty beds in which old clerkliness lies asleep!"

Among the travelling men who came to Caxton to sell goods, the boy, who had continued the paper selling even after attaining the stature of a man, was a favourite. Sitting in chairs before the New Leland House they talked to him of the city and of the money to be made there.

"It is the place for a live young man," they said.

Sam had a talent for drawing people into talk of themselves and of their affairs and began to cultivate travelling men. From them, he got into his nostrils a whiff of the city and, listening to them, he saw the great ways filled with hurrying people, the tall buildings touching the sky, the men running about intent upon money-making, and the clerks going on year after year on small salaries getting nowhere, a part of, and yet not understanding, the impulses and motives of the enterprises that supported them.

In this picture Sam thought he saw a place for himself. He conceived of life in the city as a great game in which he believed he could play a sterling part. Had he not in Caxton brought something out of nothing, had he not systematised and monopolised the selling of papers, had he not introduced the vending of popcorn and peanuts from baskets to the Saturday night crowds? Already boys went out in his employ, already the totals in the bank book had crept to more than seven hundred dollars. He felt within him a glow of pride at the thought of what he had done and would do.

"I will be richer than any man in town here," he declared in his pride. "I will be richer than Ed Walker."

Saturday night was the great night in Caxton life. For it the clerks in the stores prepared, for it Sam sent forth his peanut and popcorn venders, for it Art Sherman rolled up his sleeves and put the glasses close by the beer tap under the bar, and for it the mechanics, the farmers, and the labourers dressed in their Sunday best and came forth to mingle with their fellows. On Main Street crowds packed the stores, the sidewalks, and drinking places, and men stood about in groups talking while young girls with their lovers walked up and down. In the hall over Geiger's drug store a dance went on and the voice of the caller-off rose above the clatter of voices and the stamping of horses in the street. Now and then a fight broke out among the roisterers in Piety Hollow. Once a young farm hand was killed with a knife.

In and out through the crowd Sam went, pressing his wares.

"Remember the long quiet Sunday afternoon," he said, pushing a paper into the hands of a slow-thinking farmer. "Recipes for cooking new dishes," he urged to the farmer's wife. "There is a page of new fashions in dress," he told the young girl.

Not until the last light was out in the last saloon in Piety Hollow, and the last roisterer had driven off into the darkness carrying a Saturday paper in his pocket, did Sam close the day's business.

And it was on a Saturday night that he decided to drop paper selling.

"I will take you into business with me," announced Freedom Smith, stopping him as he hurried by. "You are getting too old to sell papers and you know too much."

Sam, still intent upon the money to be made on that particular Saturday night, did not stop to discuss the matter with Freedom, but for a year he had been looking quietly about for something to go into and now he nodded his head as he hurried away.

"It is the end of romance," shouted Telfer, who stood beside Freedom Smith before Geiger's drug store and who had heard the offer. "A boy, who has seen the secret workings of my mind, who has heard me spout Poe and Browning, will become a merchant, dealing in stinking hides. I am overcome by the thought."

The next day, sitting in the garden back of his house, Telfer talked to Sam of the matter at length.

"For you, my boy, I put the matter of money in the first place," he declared, leaning back in his chair, smoking a cigarette and from time to time tapping Eleanor on the shoulder with his cane. "For any boy I put money-making in the first place. It is only women and fools who despise money-making. Look at Eleanor here. The time and thought she puts into the selling of hats would be the death of me, but it has been the making of her. See how fine and purposeful she has become. Without the millinery business she would be a purposeless fool intent upon clothes and with it she is all a woman should be. It is like a child to her."

Eleanor, who had turned to laugh at her husband, looked instead at the ground and a shadow crossed her face. Telfer, who had begun talking thoughtlessly, out of his excess of words, glanced from the woman to the boy. He knew that the suggestion regarding a child had touched a secret regret in Eleanor, and began trying to efface the shadow on her face by throwing himself into the subject that chanced to be on his tongue, making the words roll and tumble from his lips.

"No matter what may come in the future, in our day money-making precedes many virtues that are forever on men's lips," he declared fiercely as though trying to down an opponent. "It is one of the virtues that proves man not a savage. It has lifted him up—not money-making, but the power to make money. Money makes life livable. It gives freedom and destroys fear. Having it means sanitary houses and well-made clothes. It brings into men's lives beauty and the love of beauty. It enables a man to go adventuring after the stuff of life as I have done.

"Writers are fond of telling stories of the crude excesses of great wealth," he went on hurriedly, glancing again at Eleanor. "No doubt the things they tell of do happen. Money, and not the ability and the instinct to make money, is at fault. And what of the cruder excesses of poverty, the drunken men who beat and starve their families, the grim silences of the crowded, unsanitary houses of the poor, the inefficient, and the defeated? Go sit around the lounging room of the most vapid rich man's city club as I have done, and then sit among the workers of a factory at the noon hour. Virtue, you will find, is no fonder of poverty than you and I, and the man who has merely learned to be industrious, and who has not acquired that eager hunger and shrewdness that enables him to get on, may build up a strong dexterous body while his mind is diseased and decaying."

Grasping his cane and beginning to be carried away by the wind of his eloquence Telfer forgot Eleanor and talked for his love of talking.

"The mind that has in it the love of the beautiful, that stuff that makes our poets, artists, musicians, and actors, needs this turn for shrewd money getting or it will destroy itself," he declared. "And the really great artists have it. In books and stories the great men starve in garrets. In real life they are more likely to ride in carriages on Fifth Avenue and have country places on the Hudson. Go, see for yourself. Visit the starving genius in his garret. It is a hundred to one that you will find him not only incapable in money getting but also incapable in the very art for which he starves."

After the hurried word from Freedom Smith, Sam began looking for a buyer for the paper business. The place offered appealed to him and he wanted a chance at it. In the buying of potatoes, butter, eggs, apples, and hides he thought he could make money, also, he knew that the dogged persistency with which he had kept at the putting of money in the bank had caught Freedom's imagination, and he wanted to take advantage of the fact.

Within a few days the deal was made. Sam got three hundred and fifty dollars for the list of newspaper customers, the peanut and popcorn business and the transfer of the exclusive agencies he had arranged with the dailies of Des Moines and St. Louis. Two boys bought the business, backed by their fathers. A talk in the back room of the bank, with the cashier telling of Sam's record as a depositor, and the seven hundred dollars surplus clinched the deal. When it came to the deal with Freedom, Sam took him into the back room at the bank and showed his savings as he had shown them to the fathers of the two boys. Freedom was impressed. He thought the boy would make money for him. Twice within a week Sam had seen the silent suggestive power of cash.

The deal Sam made with Freedom included a fair weekly wage, enough to more than take care of all his wants, and in addition he was to have two-thirds of all he saved Freedom in the buying. Freedom on the other hand was to furnish horse, vehicle, and keep for the horse, while Sam was to take care of the horse. The prices to be paid for the things bought were to be fixed each morning by Freedom, and if Sam bought at less than the prices named two-thirds of the savings went to him. The arrangement was suggested by Sam, who thought he would make more from the saving than from the wage.

Freedom Smith discussed even the most trivial matter in a loud voice, roaring and shouting in the store and on the streets. He was a great inventor of descriptive names, having a name of his own for every man, woman and child he knew and liked. "Old Maybe-Not" he called Windy McPherson and would roar at him in the grocery asking him not to shed rebel blood in the sugar barrel. He drove about the country in a low phaeton buggy that rattled and squeaked enormously and had a wide rip in the top. To Sam's knowledge neither the buggy nor Freedom were washed during his stay with the man. He had a method of his own in buying. Stopping in front of a farm house he would sit in his buggy and roar until the farmer came out of the field or the house to talk with him. And then haggling and shouting he would make his deal or drive on his way while the farmer, leaning on the fence, laughed as at a wayward child.

Freedom lived in a large old brick house facing one of Caxton's best streets. His house and yard were an eyesore to his neighbours who liked him personally. He knew this and would stand on his front porch laughing and roaring about it. "Good morning, Mary," he would shout at the neat German woman across the street. "Wait and you'll see me clean up about here. I'm going at it right now. I'm going to brush the flies off the fence first."

Once he ran for a county office and got practically every vote in the county.

Freedom had a passion for buying up old half-worn buggies and agricultural implements, bringing them home to stand in the yard, gathering rust and decay, and swearing they were as good as new. In the lot were a half dozen buggies and a family carriage or two, a traction engine, a mowing machine, several farm wagons and other farm tools gone beyond naming. Every few days he came home bringing a new prize. They overflowed the yard and crept onto the porch. Sam never knew him to sell any of this stuff. He had at one time sixteen sets of harness all broken and unrepaired in the barn and in a shed back of the house. A great flock of chickens and two or three pigs wandered about among this junk and all the children of the neighbourhood joined Freedom's four and ran howling and shouting over and under the mass.

Freedom's wife, a pale, silent woman, rarely came out of the house. She had a liking for the industrious, hard-working Sam and occasionally stood at the back door and talked with him in a low, even voice at evening as he stood unhitching his horse after a day on the road. Both she and Freedom treated him with great respect.

As a buyer Sam was even more successful than at the paper selling. He was a buyer by instinct, working a wide stretch of country very systematically and within a year more than doubling the bulk of Freedom's purchases.

There is a little of Windy McPherson's grotesque pretentiousness in every man and his son soon learned to look for and to take advantage of it. He let men talk until they had exaggerated or overstated the value of their goods, then called them sharply to accounts, and before they had recovered from their confusion drove home the bargain. In Sam's day, farmers did not watch the daily market reports, in fact, the markets were not systematised and regulated as they were later, and the skill of the buyer was of the first importance. Having the skill, Sam used it constantly to put money into his pockets, but in some way kept the confidence and respect of the men with whom he traded.

The noisy, blustering Freedom was as proud as a father of the trading ability that developed in the boy and roared his name up and down the streets and in the stores, declaring him the smartest boy in Iowa.

"Mighty little of old Maybe-Not in that boy," he would shout to the loafers in the store.

Although Sam had an almost painful desire for order and system in his own affairs, he did not try to bring these influences into Freedom's affairs, but kept his own records carefully and bought potatoes and apples, butter and eggs, furs and hides, with untiring zeal, working always to swell his commissions. Freedom took the risks in the business and many times profited little, but the two liked and respected each other and it was through Freedom's efforts that Sam finally got out of Caxton and into larger affairs.

One evening in the late fall Freedom came into the stable where Sam stood taking the harness off his horse.

"Here is a chance for you, my boy," he said, putting his hand affectionately on Sam's shoulder. There was a note of tenderness in his voice. He had written to the Chicago firm to whom he sold most of the things he bought, telling of Sam and his ability, and the firm had replied making an offer that Sam thought far beyond anything he might hope for in Caxton. In his hand he held this offer.

When Sam read the letter his heart jumped. He thought that it opened for him a wide new field of effort and of money making. He thought that at last he had come to the end of his boyhood and was to have his chance in the city. Only that morning old Doctor Harkness had stopped him at the door as he set out for work and, pointing over his shoulder with his thumb to where in the house his mother lay, wasted and asleep, had told him that in another week she would be gone, and Sam, heavy of heart and filled with uneasy longing, had walked through the streets to Freedom's stable wishing that he also might be gone.

Now he walked across the stable floor and hung the harness he had taken from the horse upon a peg in the wall.

"I will be glad to go," he said heavily.

Freedom walked out of the stable door beside the young McPherson who had come to him as a boy and was now a broad-shouldered young man of eighteen. He did not want to lose Sam. He had written the Chicago company because of his affection for the boy and because he believed him capable of something more than Caxton offered. Now he walked in silence holding the lantern aloft and guiding the way among the wreckage in the yard, filled with regrets.

By the back door of the house stood the pale, tired-looking wife who, putting out her hand, took the hand of the boy. There were tears in her eyes. And then saying nothing Sam turned and hurried off up the street, Freedom and his wife walked to the front gate and watched him go. From a street corner, where he stopped in the shadow of a tree, Sam could see them there, the wind swinging the lantern in Freedom's hand and the slender little old wife making a white blotch against the darkness.

VI

S am went along the board sidewalk homeward bound, hurried by the driving March wind that had sent the lantern swinging in Freedom's hand. At the front of a white frame residence a grey-haired old man stood leaning on the gate and looking at the sky.

"We shall have a rain," he said in a quavering voice, as though giving a decision in the matter, and then turned and without waiting for an answer went along a narrow path into the house.

The incident brought a smile to Sam's lips followed by a kind of weariness of mind. Since the beginning of his work with Freedom he had, day after day, come upon Henry Kimball standing by his gate and looking at the sky. The man was one of Sam's old newspaper customers who stood as a kind of figure in the town. It was said of him that in his youth he had been a gambler on the Mississippi River and that he had taken part in more than one wild adventure in the old days. After the Civil War he had come to end his days in Caxton, living alone and occupying himself by keeping year after year a carefully tabulated record of weather variations. Once or twice a month during the warm season he stumbled into Wildman's and, sitting by the stove, talked boastfully of the accuracy of his records and the doings of a mangy dog that trotted at his heels. In his present mood the endless sameness and uneventfulness of the man's life seemed to Sam amusing and in some way sad.

"To depend upon going to the gate and looking at the sky to give point to a day—to look forward to and depend upon that—what deadliness!" he thought, and, thrusting his hand into his pocket, felt with pleasure the letter from the Chicago company that was to open so much of the big outside world to him.

In spite of the shock of unexpected sadness that had come with what he felt was almost a definite parting with Freedom, and the sadness brought on by his mother's approaching death, Sam felt a strong thrill of confidence in his own future that made his homeward walk almost cheerful. The thrill got from reading the letter handed him by Freedom was renewed by the sight of old Henry Kimball at the gate, looking at the sky.

"I shall never be like that, sitting in a corner of the world watching a mangy dog chase a ball and peering day after day at a thermometer," he thought.

The three years in Freedom Smith's service had taught Sam not to doubt his ability to cope with such business problems as might come in his way. He knew that he had become what he wanted to be, a good business man, one of the men who direct and control the affairs in which they are concerned because of a quality in them called Business Sense. He recalled with pleasure the fact that the men of Caxton had stopped calling him a bright boy and now spoke of him as a good business man.

At the gate before his own house he stopped and stood thinking of these things and of the dying woman within. Back into his mind came the old man he had seen at the gate and with him the thought that his mother's life had been as barren as that of the man who depended for companionship upon a dog and a thermometer.

"Indeed," he said to himself, pursuing the thought, "it has been worse. She has not had a fortune on which to live in peace nor has she had the remembrance of youthful days of wild adventure that must comfort the last days of the old man. Instead she has been watching me as the old man watches his thermometer and Father has been the dog in her house chasing playthings." The figure pleased him. He stood at the gate, the wind singing in the trees along the street and driving an occasional drop of rain against his cheek, and thought of it and of his life with his mother. During the last two or three years he had been trying to make things up to her. After the sale of the newspaper business and the beginning of his success with Freedom he had driven her from the washtub and since the beginning of her ill health he had spent evening after evening with her instead of going to Wildman's to sit with the four friends and hear the talk that went on among them. No more did he walk with Telfer or Mary Underwood on country roads but sat, instead, by the bedside of the sick woman or, the night falling fair, helped her to an arm chair upon the grass plot at the front of the house.

The years, Sam felt, had been good years. They had brought him an understanding of his mother and had given a seriousness and purpose to the ambitious plans he continued to make for himself. Alone together, the mother and he had talked little, the habit of a lifetime making much speech impossible to her and the growing understanding of her making it unnecessary to him. Now in the darkness, before the house, he thought of the evenings he had spent with her and of the pitiful waste that had been made of her fine life. Things that had hurt him and against which he had been bitter and unforgiving became of small import, even the doings of the pretentious Windy, who in the face of

Jane's illness continued to go off after pension day for long periods of drunkenness, and who only came home to weep and wail through the house, when the pension money was gone, regretting, Sam tried in fairness to think, the loss of both the washwoman and the wife.

"She has been the most wonderful woman in the world," he told himself and tears of happiness came into his eyes at the thought of his friend, John Telfer, who in bygone days had praised the mother to the newsboy trotting beside him on moonlit roads. Into his mind came a picture of her long gaunt face, ghastly now against the white of the pillows. A picture of George Eliot, tacked to the wall behind a broken harness in the kitchen of Freedom Smith's house, had caught his eye some days before, and in the darkness he took it from his pocket and put it to his lips, realising that in some indescribable way it was like his mother as she had been before her illness. Freedom's wife had given him the picture and he had been carrying it, taking it out of his pocket on lonely stretches of road as he went about his work.

Sam went quietly around the house and stood by an old shed, a relic of an attempt by Windy to embark in raising chickens. He wanted to continue the thoughts of his mother. He began recalling her youth and the details of a long talk they had held together on the lawn before the house. It was extraordinarily vivid in his mind. He thought that even now he could remember every word that had been said. The sick woman had talked of her youth in Ohio, and as she talked pictures had come into the boy's mind. She had told him of her days as a bound girl in the family of a thin-lipped, hard-fisted New Englander, who had come West to take a farm, and of her struggles to obtain an education, of the pennies saved to buy books, of her joy when she had passed examinations and become a school teacher, and of her marriage to Windy—then John McPherson.

Into the Ohio village the young McPherson had come, to cut a figure in the town's life. Sam had smiled at the picture she drew of the young man who walked up and down the village street with girls on his arms, and who taught a Bible class in the Sunday school.

When Windy proposed to the young school teacher she had accepted him eagerly, thinking it unbelievably romantic that so dashing a man should have chosen so obscure a figure among all the women of the town.

"And even now I am not sorry although it has meant nothing but labour and unhappiness for me," the sick woman had told her son.

After marriage to the young dandy, Jane had come with him to Caxton where he bought a store and where, within three years, he had put the store into the sheriff's hands and his wife into the position of town laundress.

In the darkness a grim smile, half scorn, half amusement, had flitted across the face of the dying woman as she told of a winter when Windy and another young fellow went, from schoolhouse to schoolhouse, over the state giving a show. The ex-soldier had become a singer of comic songs and had written letter after letter to the young wife telling of the applause that greeted his efforts. Sam could picture the performances, the little dimly-lighted schoolhouses with the weatherbeaten faces shining in the light of the leaky magic lantern, and the delighted Windy running here and there, talking the jargon of stageland, arraying himself in his motley and strutting upon the little stage.

"And all winter he did not send me a penny," the sick woman had said, interrupting his thoughts.

Aroused at last to expression, and filled with the memory of her youth, the silent woman had talked of her own people. Her father had been killed in the woods by a falling tree. Of her mother she told an anecdote, touching it briefly and with a grim humour that surprised her son.

The young school teacher had gone to call upon her mother once and for an hour had sat in the parlour of an Ohio farmhouse while a fierce old woman looked at her with bold questioning eyes that made the daughter feel she had been a fool to come.

At the railroad station she had heard an anecdote of her mother. The story ran, that once a burly tramp came to the farmhouse, and finding the woman alone tried to bully her, and that the tramp, and the woman, then in her prime, fought for an hour in the back yard of the house. The railroad agent, who told Jane the story, threw back his head and laughed.

"She knocked him out, too," he said, "knocked him cold upon the ground and then filled him up with hard cider so that he came reeling into town declaring her the finest woman in the state."

In the darkness by the broken shed Sam's mind turned from thoughts of his mother to his sister Kate and of her love affair with the young farmer. He thought with sadness of how she too had suffered because of the failings of the father, of how she had been compelled to go out of the house to wander in the dark streets to avoid the endless evenings of war talk always brought on by a guest in the McPherson household, and of the night when, getting a rig from Culvert's livery, she had driven off alone into the country to return in triumph to pack her clothes and show her wedding ring.

Before him there rose a picture of a summer afternoon when he had seen a part of the love making that had preceded this. He had gone into the store to see his sister when the young farmer came in, looked awkwardly about and pushed a new gold watch across the counter to Kate. A sudden wave of respect for his sister had pervaded the boy. "What a sum it must have cost," he thought, and looked with new interest at the back of the lover and at the flushed cheek and shining eyes of his sister. When the lover, turning, had seen young McPherson standing at the counter, he laughed self-consciously and walked out at the door. Kate had been embarrassed and secretly pleased and flattered by the look in her brother's eyes, but had pretended to treat the gift lightly, twirling it carelessly back and forth on the counter and walking up and down swinging her arms.

"Don't go telling," she had said.

"Then don't go pretending," the boy had answered.

Sam thought that his sister's indiscretion, which had brought her a babe and a husband in the same month had, after all, ended better than the indiscretion of his mother in her marriage with Windy.

Rousing himself, he went into the house. A neighbour woman, employed for the purpose, had prepared the evening meal and now began complaining of his lateness, saying that the food had got cold.

Sam ate in silence. While he ate the woman went out of the house and presently returned, bringing a daughter.

There was in Caxton a code that would not allow a woman to be alone in a house with a man. Sam wondered if the bringing of the daughter was an attempt on the part of the woman to abide by the letter of the code, if she thought of the sick woman in the house as one already gone. The thought amused and saddened him.

"You would have thought her safe," he mused. She was fifty, small, nervous and worn and wore a set of ill-fitting false teeth that rattled as she talked. When she did not talk she rattled them with her tongue because of nervousness.

In at the kitchen door came Windy, far gone in drink. He stood by the door holding to the knob with his hand and trying to get control of himself.

"My wife—my wife is dying. She may die any day," he wailed, tears standing in his eyes.

The woman with the daughter went into the little parlour where a bed had been put for the sick woman. Sam sat at the kitchen table dumb with anger and disgust as Windy, lurching forward, fell into a chair and began sobbing loudly. In the road outside a man driving a horse stopped and Sam could hear the scraping of the wheels against the buggy body as the man turned in the narrow street. Above the scraping of the wheels rose a voice, swearing profanely. The wind continued to blow and it had begun to rain.

"He has got into the wrong street," thought the boy stupidly.

Windy, his head upon his hands, wept like a brokenhearted boy, his sobs echoing through the house, his breath heavy with liquor tainting the air of the room. In a corner by the stove the mother's ironing board stood against the wall and the sight of it added fuel to the anger smouldering in Sam's heart. He remembered the day when he had stood in the store doorway with his mother and had seen the dismal and amusing failure of his father with the bugle, and of the months before Kate's wedding, when Windy had gone blustering about town threatening to kill her lover and the mother and boy had stayed with the girl, out of sight in the house, sick with humiliation.

The drunken man, laying his head upon the table, fell asleep, his snores replacing the sobs that had stirred the boy's anger. Sam began thinking again of his mother's life.

The effort he had made to repay her for the hardness of her life now seemed utterly fruitless. "I would like to repay him," he thought, shaken with a sudden spasm of hatred as he looked at the man before him. The cheerless little kitchen, the cold, half-baked potatoes and sausages on the table, and the drunken man asleep, seemed to him a kind of symbol of the life that had been lived in that house, and with a shudder he turned his face and stared at the wall.

He thought of a dinner he had once eaten at Freedom Smith's house. Freedom had brought the invitation into the stables on that night just as tonight he had brought the letter from the Chicago company, and just as Sam was shaking his head in refusal of the invitation in at the stable door had come the children. Led by the eldest, a great tomboy girl of fourteen with the strength of a man and an inclination to burst out of her clothes at unexpected places, they had come charging into the stables to carry Sam off to the dinner, Freedom laughingly urging

SHERWOOD ANDERSON

them on, his voice roaring in the stable so that the horses jumped about in their stalls. Into the house they had dragged him, the baby, a boy of four, sitting astride his back and beating on his head with a woollen cap, and Freedom swinging a lantern and giving an occasional helpful push with his hand.

A picture of the long table covered with the white cloth at the end of the big dining room in Freedom's house came back into the mind of the boy now sitting in the barren little kitchen before the untasted, badly-cooked food. Upon it lay a profusion of bread and meat and great dishes heaped with steaming potatoes. At his own house there had always been just enough food for the single meal. The thing was nicely calculated, when you had finished the table was bare.

How he had enjoyed that dinner after the long day on the road. With a flourish and a roar at the children Freedom heaped high the plates and passed them about, the wife or the tomboy girl bringing unending fresh supplies from the kitchen. The joy of the evening with its talk of the children in school, its sudden revelation of the womanliness of the tomboy girl, and its air of plenty and good living haunted the mind of the boy.

"My mother never knew anything like that," he thought.

The drunken man who had been sleeping aroused himself and began talking loudly—some old forgotten grievance coming back to his mind, he talked of the cost of school books.

"They change the books in the school too often," he declared in a loud voice, turning and facing the kitchen stove, as though addressing an audience. "It is a scheme to graft on old soldiers who have children. I will not stand it."

Sam, enraged beyond speech, tore a leaf from a notebook and scrawled a message upon it.

"Be silent," he wrote. "If you say another word or make another sound to disturb mother I will choke you and throw you like a dead dog into the street."

Reaching across the table and touching his father on the hand with a fork taken from among the dishes, he laid the note upon the table under the lamp before his eyes. He was fighting with himself to control a desire to spring across the room and kill the man who he believed had brought his mother to her death and who now sat bellowing and talking at her very death bed. The desire distorted his mind so that he stared about the kitchen like one seized with an insane nightmare.

Windy, taking the note in his hand, read it slowly and then, not understanding its import and but half getting its sense, put it in his pocket.

"A dog is dead, eh?" he shouted. "Well you're getting too big and smart, lad. What do I care for a dead dog?"

Sam did not answer. Rising cautiously, he crept around the table and put his hand upon the throat of the babbling old man.

"I must not kill," he kept telling himself aloud, as though talking to a stranger. "I must choke until he is silent, but I must not kill."

In the kitchen the two men struggled silently. Windy, unable to rise, struck out wildly and helplessly with his feet. Sam, looking down at him and studying the eyes and the colour in the cheeks, realised with a start that he had not for years seen the face of his father. How vividly it stamped itself upon his mind now, and how coarse and sodden it had become.

"I could repay all of the years mother has spent over the dreary washtub by just one long, hard grip at this lean throat. I could kill him with so little extra pressure," he thought.

The eyes began to stare at him and the tongue to protrude. Across the forehead ran a streak of mud picked up somewhere in the long afternoon of drunken carousing.

"If I were to press hard now and kill him I would see his face as it looks now all the days of my life," thought the boy.

In the silence of the house he heard the voice of the neighbour woman speaking sharply to her daughter. The familiar, dry, tired cough of the sick woman followed. Sam took the unconscious old man in his arms and went carefully and silently out at the kitchen door. The rain beat down upon him and, as he went around the house with his burden, the wind, shaking loose a dead branch from a small apple tree in the yard, blew it against his face, leaving a long smarting scratch. At the fence before the house he stopped and threw his burden down a short grassy bank into the road. Then turning he went, bareheaded, through the gate and up the street.

"I will go for Mary Underwood," he thought, his mind returning to the friend who years before had walked with him on country roads and whose friendship he had dropped because of John Telfer's tirades against all women. He stumbled along the sidewalk, the rain beating down upon his bare head.

"We need a woman in our house," he kept saying over and over to himself. "We need a woman in our house."

SHERWOOD ANDERSON

VII

Leaning against the wall under the veranda of Mary Underwood's house, Sam tried to get in his mind a remembrance of what had brought him there. He had walked bareheaded through Main Street and out along a country road. Twice he had fallen, covering his clothes with mud. He had forgotten the purpose of his walk and had tramped on and on. The unexpected and terrible hatred of his father that had come upon him in the tense silence of the kitchen had so paralysed his brain that he now felt light-headed and wonderfully happy and carefree.

"I have been doing something," he thought; "I wonder what it is."

The house faced a grove of pine trees and was reached by climbing a little rise and following a winding road out beyond the graveyard and the last of the village lights. The wild spring rain pounded and rattled on the tin roof overhead, and Sam, his back closely pressed against the front of the house, fought to regain control of his mind.

For an hour he stood there staring into the darkness and watched with delight the progress of the storm. He had—an inheritance from his mother—a love of thunderstorms. He remembered a night when he was a boy and his mother had got out of bed and gone here and there through the house singing. She had sung softly so that the sleeping father did not hear, and in his bed upstairs Sam had lain awake listening to the noises—the rain on the roof, the occasional crash of thunder, the snoring of Windy, and the unusual and, he thought, beautiful sound of the mother singing in the storm.

Now, lifting up his head, he looked about with delight. Trees in the grove in front of him bent and tossed in the wind. The inky blackness of the night was relieved by the flickering oil lamp in the road beyond the graveyard and, in the distance, by the lights streaming out at the windows of the houses. The light coming out of the house against which he stood made a little cylinder of brightness among the pine trees through which the raindrops fell gleaming and sparkling. An occasional flash of lightning lit up the trees and the winding road, and the cannonry of the skies rolled and echoed overhead. A kind of wild song sang in Sam's heart.

"I wish it would last all night," he thought, his mind fixed on the singing of his mother in the dark house when he was a boy.

The door opened and a woman stepped out upon the veranda and stood before him facing the storm, the wind tossing the soft kimono in which she was clad and the rain wetting her face. Under the tin roof, the air was filled with the rattling reverberation of the rain. The woman lifted her head and, with the rain beating down upon her, began singing, her fine contralto voice rising above the rattle of the rain on the roof and going on uninterrupted by the crash of the thunder. She sang of a lover riding through the storm to his mistress. One refrain persisted in the song—

"He rode and he thought of her red, red lips,"

sang the woman, putting her hand upon the railing of the little porch and leaning forward into the storm.

Sam was amazed. The woman standing before him was Mary Underwood, who had been his friend when he was a boy in school and toward whom his mind had turned after the tragedy in the kitchen. The figure of the woman standing singing before him became a part of his thoughts of his mother singing on the stormy night in the house and his mind wandered on, seeing pictures as he used to see them when a boy walking under the stars and listening to the talk of John Telfer. He saw a broad-shouldered man shouting defiance to the storm as he rode down a mountain path.

"And he laughed at the rain on his wet, wet cloak," went on the voice of the singer.

Mary Underwood's singing there in the rain made her seem near and likeable as she had seemed to him when he was a barefoot boy.

"John Telfer was wrong about her," he thought.

She turned and faced him. Tiny streams of water ran from her hair down across her cheeks. A flash of lightning cut the darkness, illuminating the spot where Sam, now a broad-shouldered man, stood with the mud upon his clothes and the bewildered look upon his face. A sharp exclamation of surprise broke from her lips:

"Hello, Sam! What are you doing here? You had better get in out of the rain."

"I like it here," replied Sam, lifting his head and looking past her at the storm.

Walking to the door and standing with her hand upon the knob, Mary looked into the darkness.

"You have been a long time coming to see me," she said, "come in."

Within the house, with the door closed, the rattle of the rain on the veranda roof sank to a subdued, quiet drumming. Piles of books lay upon a table in the centre of the room and there were other books on the shelves along the walls. On a table burned a student's lamp and in the corners of the room lay heavy shadows.

Sam stood by the wall near the door looking about with half-seeing eyes.

Mary, who had gone to another part of the house and who now returned clad in a long cloak, looked at him with quick curiosity, and began moving about the room picking up odds and ends of woman's clothing scattered on the chairs. Kneeling, she lighted a fire under some sticks piled in an open grate at the side of the room.

"It was the storm made me want to sing," she said self-consciously, and then briskly, "we shall have to be drying you out; you have fallen in the road and got yourself covered with mud."

From being morose and silent Sam became talkative. An idea had come into his mind.

"I have come here courting," he thought; "I have come to ask Mary Underwood to be my wife and live in my house."

The woman, kneeling by the blazing sticks, made a picture that aroused something that had been sleeping in him. The heavy cloak she wore, falling away, showed the round little shoulders imperfectly covered by the kimono, wet and clinging to them. The slender, youthful figure, the soft grey hair and the serious little face, lit by the burning sticks caused a jumping of his heart.

"We are needing a woman in our house," he said heavily, repeating the words that had been on his lips as he stumbled through the storm-swept streets and along the mud-covered roads. "We are needing a woman in our house, and I have come to take you there.

"I intend to marry you," he added, lurching across the room and grasping her roughly by the shoulders. "Why not? I am needing a woman."

Mary Underwood was dismayed and frightened by the face looking down at her, and by the strong hands clenched upon her shoulders. In his youth she had conceived a kind of maternal passion for the newsboy and had planned a future for him. Her plans if followed would have made him a scholar, a man living his life among books and ideas. Instead, he had chosen to live his life among men, to be a money-maker, to drive about the country like Freedom Smith, making deals with farmers. She had seen him driving at evening through the street to Freedom's house, going in and out of Wildman's, and walking through the streets with men. In a dim way she knew that an influence had been at work upon him to win him from the things of which she had dreamed and she had secretly blamed John Telfer, the talking, laughing idler. Now, out of the storm, the boy had come back to her, his hands and his clothes covered with the mud of the road, and talked to her, a woman old enough to be his mother, of marriage and of coming to live with him in his house. She stood, chilled, looking into the eager, strong face and the eyes with the pained, dazed look in them.

Under her gaze, something of the old feeling of the boy came back to Sam, and he began vaguely trying to tell her of it.

"It was not the talk of Telfer drove me from you," he began, "it was because you talked so much of the schools and of books. I was tired of them. I could not go on year after year sitting in a stuffy little schoolroom when there was so much money to be made in the world. I grew tired of the school teachers, drumming with their fingers on the desks and looking out at the windows at men passing in the street. I wanted to get out of there and into the streets myself."

Dropping his hands from her shoulders, he sat down in a chair and stared into the fire, now blazing steadily. Steam began to rise from his trousers legs. His mind, still working beyond his control, began to reconstruct an old boyhood fancy, half his own, half John Telfer's, that had years before come into his mind. It concerned a picture he and Telfer had made of the ideal scholar. The picture had, as its central figure, a stoop-shouldered, feeble old man stumbling along the street, muttering to himself and poking in a gutter with a stick. The picture was a caricature of puttering old Frank Huntley, superintendent of the Caxton schools.

Sitting before the fire in Mary Underwood's house, become, for the moment, a boy, facing a boy's problems, Sam did not want to be such a man. He wanted only that in scholarship which would help him to be the kind of man he was bent on being, a man of the world doing the work of the world and making money by his work. Things he had been unable to get expressed when he was a boy and her friend, coming again into his mind, he felt that he must here and now make it plain to Mary Underwood that the schools were not giving him what he wanted. His brain worked on the problem of how to tell her about it.

Turning, he looked at her and said earnestly: "I am going to quit the schools. It is not your fault, but I am going to quit just the same."

Mary, who had been looking down at the great mud-covered figure in the chair began to understand. A light came into her eyes. Going to the door opening into a stairway leading to sleeping rooms above, she called sharply, "Auntie, come down here at once. There is a sick man here."

A startled, trembling voice answered from above, "Who is it?"

Mary Underwood did not answer. She came back to Sam and, putting her hand gently on his shoulder, said, "It is your mother and you are only a sick, half-crazed boy after all. Is she dead? Tell me about it."

Sam shook his head. "She is still there in the bed, coughing." He roused himself and stood up. "I have just killed my father," he announced. "I choked him and threw him down the bank into the road in front of the house. He made horrible noises in the kitchen and mother was tired and wanted to sleep."

Mary Underwood began running about the room. From a little alcove under a stairway she took clothes, throwing them upon the floor about the room. She pulled on a stocking and, unconscious of Sam's presence, raised her skirts and fastened it. Then, putting one shoe on the stockinged foot and the other on the bare one, she turned to him. "We will go back to your house. I think you are right. You need a woman there."

In the street she walked rapidly along, clinging to the arm of the tall fellow who strode silently beside her. A cheerfulness had come over Sam. He felt he had accomplished something—something he had set out to accomplish. He again thought of his mother and drifting into the notion that he was on his way home from work at Freedom Smith's, began planning the evening he would spend with her.

"I will tell her of the letter from the Chicago company and of what I will do when I go to the city," he thought.

At the gate before the McPherson house Mary looked into the road below the grassy bank that ran down from the fence, but in the darkness she could see nothing. The rain continued to fall and the wind screamed and shouted as it rushed through the bare branches of the trees. Sam went through the gate and around the house to the kitchen door intent upon getting to his mother's bedside.

In the house the neighbour woman sat asleep in a chair before the kitchen stove. The daughter had gone.

Sam went through the house to the parlour and sat down in a chair beside his mother's bed, picking up her hand and holding it in his own. "She must be asleep," he thought.

At the kitchen door Mary Underwood stopped, and, turning, ran away into the darkness along the street. By the kitchen fire the neighbour woman still slept. In the parlour Sam, sitting on the chair beside his mother's bed, looked about him. A lamp burned dimly upon the little stand beside the bed and the light of it fell upon the portrait of a tall, aristocratic-looking woman with rings on her fingers, that hung upon the wall. The picture belonged to Windy and was claimed by him as a portrait of his mother, and it had once brought on a quarrel between Sam and his sister.

Kate had taken the portrait of the lady seriously, and the boy had come upon her sitting in a chair before it, her hair rearranged and her hands lying in her lap in imitation of the pose maintained so haughtily by the great lady who looked down at her.

"It is a fraud," he had declared, irritated by what he believed his sister's devotion to one of the father's pretensions. "It is a fraud he has picked up somewhere and now claims as his mother to make people believe he is something big."

The girl, ashamed at having been caught in the pose, and furious because of the attack upon the authenticity of the portrait, had gone into a spasm of indignation, putting her hands to her ears and stamping on the floor with her foot. Then she had run across the room and dropped upon her knees before a little couch, buried her face in a pillow and shook with anger and grief.

Sam had turned and walked out of the room. The emotions of the sister had seemed to him to have the flavour of one of Windy's outbreaks.

"She likes it," he had thought, dismissing the incident. "She likes believing in lies. She is like Windy and would rather believe in them than not."

MARY UNDERWOOD RAN THROUGH THE rain to John Telfer's house and beat on the door with her fist until Telfer, followed by Eleanor, holding a lamp above her head, appeared at the door. With Telfer she went back through the streets to the front of Sam's house thinking of the terrible choked and disfigured man they should find there. She went along clinging to Telfer's arm as she had clung to Sam's, unconscious of her bare head and scanty attire. In his hand Telfer carried a lantern secured from the stable.

In the road before the house they found nothing. Telfer went up and down swinging the lantern and peering into gutters. The woman walked beside him, her skirts lifted and the mud splashing upon her bare leg.

Suddenly Telfer threw back his head and laughed. Taking her hand he led Mary with a rush up the bank and through the gate.

"What a muddle-headed old fool I am!" he cried. "I am getting old and addle-pated! Windy McPherson is not dead! Nothing could kill that old war horse! He was in at Wildman's grocery after nine o'clock tonight covered with mud and swearing he had been in a fight with Art Sherman. Poor Sam and you—to have come to me and to have found me a stupid ass! Fool! Fool! What a fool I have become!"

In at the kitchen door ran Mary and Telfer, frightening the woman by the stove so that she sprang to her feet and began nervously making the false teeth rattle with her tongue. In the parlour they found Sam, his head upon the edge of the bed, asleep. In his hand he held the cold hand of Jane McPherson. She had been dead for an hour. Mary Underwood stooped over and kissed his wet hair as the neighbour woman came in at the doorway bearing the kitchen lamp, and John Telfer, holding his finger to his lips, commanded silence.

VIII

The funeral of Jane McPherson was a trying affair for her son. He thought that his sister Kate, with the babe in her arms, had become coarsened—she looked frumpish and, while they were in the house, had an air of having quarrelled with her husband when they came out of their bedroom in the morning. During the funeral service Sam sat in the parlour, astonished and irritated by the endless number of women that crowded into the house. They were everywhere, in the kitchen, the sleeping room back of the parlour; and in the parlour, where the dead woman lay in her coffin, they were massed. When the thin-lipped minister, holding a book in his hand, held forth upon the virtues of the dead woman, they wept. Sam looked at the floor and thought that thus they would have wept over the body of the dead Windy, had his fingers but tightened a trifle. He wondered if the minister would have talked in the same way—blatantly and without knowledge—of the virtues of the dead. In a chair at the side of the coffin the bereaved husband, in new black clothes, wept audibly. The baldheaded, officious undertaker kept moving nervously about, intent upon the ritual of his trade.

During the service, a man sitting behind him dropped a note on the floor at Sam's feet. Sam picked it up and read it, glad of something to distract his attention from the voice of the minister, and the faces of the weeping women, none of whom had before been in the house and all of whom he thought strikingly lacking in a sense of the sacredness of privacy. The note was from John Telfer.

"I will not come to your mother's funeral," he wrote. "I respected your mother while she lived and I will leave you alone with her now that she is dead. In her memory I will hold a ceremony in my heart. If I am in Wildman's, I may ask the man to quit selling soap and tobacco for the moment and to close and lock the door. If I am at Valmore's shop, I will go up into his loft and listen to him pounding on the anvil below. If he or Freedom Smith go to your house, I warn them I will cut their friendship. When I see the carriages going through the street and know that the thing is right well done and over, I will buy flowers and take them to Mary Underwood as an appreciation of the living in the name of the dead."

The note cheered and comforted Sam. It gave him back a grip of something that had slipped from him.

"It is good sense, after all," he thought, and realised that even in the days when he was being made to suffer horrors, and in the face of the fact that Jane McPherson's long, hard role was just being played out to the end, the farmer in the field was sowing his corn, Valmore was beating upon his anvil, and John Telfer was writing notes with a flourish. He arose, interrupting the minister's discourse. Mary Underwood had come in just as the minister began talking and had dropped into an obscure corner near the door leading into the street. Sam crowded past the women who stared and the minister who frowned and the baldheaded undertaker who wrung his hands and, dropping the note into her lap, said, oblivious of the people looking and listening with breathless curiosity, "It is from John Telfer. Read it. Even he, hating women as he did, is now bringing flowers to your door."

In the room a wind of whispered comments sprang up. Women, putting their heads together and their hands before their faces, nodded toward the school teacher, and the boy, unconscious of the sensation he had created, went back to his chair and looked again at the floor, waiting until the talk and the singing of songs and the parading through the streets should be ended. Again the minister began reading from the book.

"I have become older than all of these people here," thought the youth. "They play at life and death, and I have felt it between the fingers of my hand."

Mary Underwood, lacking Sam's unconsciousness of the people, looked about with burning cheeks. Seeing the women whispering and putting their heads together, a chill of fear ran through her. Into the room had been thrust the face of an old enemy to her—the scandal of a small town. Picking up the note she slipped out at the door and stole away along the street. The old maternal love for Sam had returned strengthened and ennobled by the terror through which she had passed with him that night in the rain. Going to her house she whistled the collie dog and set out along a country road. At the edge of a grove of trees she stopped, sat down on a log, and read Telfer's note. From the soft ground into which her feet sank there came the warm pungent smell of the new growth. Tears came into her eyes. She thought that in a few days much had come to her. She had got a boy upon whom she could pour out the mother love in her heart, and she had made a friend of Telfer, whom she had long regarded with fear and doubt.

For a month Sam lingered in Caxton. It seemed to him there was something that wanted doing there. He sat with the men at the back of Wildman's, and walked aimlessly through the streets and out of the town along the country roads, where men worked all day in the fields behind sweating horses, ploughing the land. The thrill of spring was in the air, and in the evening a song sparrow sang in the apple tree below his bedroom window. Sam walked and loitered in silence, looking at the ground. In his mind was the dread of people. The talk of the men in the store wearied him and when he went alone into the country he found himself accompanied by the voices of all of those he had come out of town to escape. On the street corner the thin-lipped, brown-bearded minister stopped him and talked of the future life as he had stopped and talked to a bare-legged newsboy.

"Your mother," he said, "has but gone before. It is for you to get into the narrow path and follow her. God has sent this sorrow as a warning to you. He wants you also to get into the way of life and in the end to join her. Begin coming to our church. Join in the work of the Christ. Find truth."

Sam, who had listened without hearing, shook his head and went on. The minister's talk seemed no more than a meaningless jumble of words out of which he got but one thought.

"Find truth," he repeated to himself after the minister, and let his mind play with the idea. "The best men are all trying to do that. They spend their lives at the task. They are all trying to find truth."

He went along the street, pleased with himself because of the interpretation he had put upon the minister's words. The terrible moments in the kitchen followed by his mother's death had put a new look of seriousness into his face and he felt within him a new sense of responsibility to the dead woman and to himself. Men stopped him on the street and wished him well in the city. News of his leaving had become public. Things in which Freedom Smith was concerned were always public affairs.

"He would take a drum with him to make love to a neighbour's wife," said John Telfer.

Sam felt that in a way he was a child of Caxton. Early it had taken him to its bosom; it had made of him a semi-public character; it had encouraged him in his money-making, humiliated him through his father, and patronised him lovingly because of his toiling mother. When he was a boy, scurrying between the legs of the drunkards in Piety Hollow of a Saturday night, there was always some one to speak a word to him of his morals and to shout at him a cheering word of advice. Had he elected to remain there, with the thirty-five hundred dollars already in the Savings Bank—built to that during his years with Freedom Smith—he might soon become one of the town's solid men.

He did not want to stay. He felt that his call was in another place and that he would go there gladly. He wondered why he did not get on the train and be off.

One night when he had been late on the road, loitering by fences, hearing the lonely barking of dogs at distant farmhouses, getting the smell of the new-ploughed ground into his nostrils, he came into town and sat down on a low iron fence that ran along by the platform of the railroad station, to wait for the midnight train north. Trains had taken on a new meaning to him since any day might see him on such a train bound into his new life.

A man, with two bags in his hands, came on the station platform followed by two women.

"Here, watch these," he said to the women, setting the bags upon the platform; "I will go for the tickets," and disappeared into the darkness.

The two women resumed their interrupted talk.

"Ed's wife has been poorly these ten years," said one of them. "It will be better for her and for Ed now that she is dead, but I dread the long ride. I wish she had died when I was in Ohio two years ago. I am sure to be train-sick."

Sam, sitting in the darkness, was thinking of a part of one of John Telfer's old talks with him.

"They are good people but they are not your people. You will go away from here. You will be a big man of dollars, it is plain."

He began listening idly to the two women. The man had a shop for mending shoes on a side street back of Geiger's drug store and the two women, one short and round, one long and thin, kept a small, dingy millinery shop and were Eleanor Telfer's only competitors.

"Well, the town knows her now for what she is," said the tall woman. "Milly Peters says she won't rest until she has put that stuck-up Mary Underwood in her place. Her mother worked in the McPherson house and it was her told Milly. I never heard such a story. To think of Jane McPherson working all these years and then having such goings-on in her house when she lay dying, Milly says that Sam went away early in the evening and came home late with that Underwood thing, half dressed, hanging on his arm. Milly's mother looked out of the window and saw them. Then she ran out by the kitchen stove and pretended to be asleep. She wanted to see what was up. And the bold hussy came right into the house with Sam. Then she went away, and after a while back she came with that John Telfer. Milly is going to see that Eleanor Telfer finds it out. I guess it will bring her down, too. And there is no telling how many other men in this town Mary Underwood is running with. Milly says—"

The two women turned as out of the darkness came a tall figure roaring and swearing. Two hands flashed out and sank into their hair.

"Stop it!" growled Sam, beating the two heads together, "stop your dirty lies!—you ugly she-beasts!"

Hearing the two women screaming the man who had gone for the railroad tickets came running down the station platform followed by Jerry Donlin. Springing forward Sam knocked the shoemaker over the iron fence into a newly spaded flower bed and then turned to the baggage man.

"They were telling lies about Mary Underwood," he shouted. "She tried to save me from killing my father and now they are telling lies about her."

The two women picked up the bags and ran whimpering away along the station platform. Jerry Donlin climbed over the iron fence and confronted the surprised and frightened shoemaker.

"What the Hell are you doing in my flower bed?" he growled.

Hurrying through the streets Sam's mind was in a ferment. Like the Roman emperor he wished that all the world had but one head that he might cut it off with a slash. The town that had seemed so paternal, so cheery, so intent upon wishing him well, now seemed horrible. He thought of it as a great, crawling, slimy thing lying in wait amid the cornfields.

"To be saying that of her, of that white soul!" he exclaimed aloud in the empty street, all of his boyish loyalty and devotion to the woman who had put out a hand to him in his hour of trouble aroused and burning in him.

He wished that he might meet another man and could hit him also a swinging blow on the nose as he had hit the amazed shoemaker. He went to his own house and, leaning on the gate, stood looking at it and swearing meaninglessly. Then, turning, he went again through the deserted streets past the railroad station where, the midnight train having come and gone and Jerry Donlin having gone home for the night, all was dark and quiet. He was filled with horror of what Mary Underwood had seen at Jane McPherson's funeral.

"It is better to be utterly bad than to speak ill of another," he thought.

For the first time he realised another side of village life. In fancy he saw going past him on the dark road a long file of women, women with coarse unlighted faces and dead eyes. Many of the faces he knew. They were the faces of Caxton wives at whose houses he had delivered papers. He remembered how eagerly they had run out of their houses to get the papers and how they hung day after day over the details of sensational murder cases. Once, when a Chicago girl had been murdered in a dive and the details were unusually revolting, two women, unable to restrain their curiosity, had come to the station to wait for the train bringing the newspapers and Sam had heard them rolling the horrid mess over and over on their tongues.

In every city and in every village there is a class of women, the thought of whom paralyses the mind. They live their lives in small, unaired, unsanitary houses, and go on year after year washing dishes and clothes—only their fingers occupied. They read no good books, think no clean thoughts, are made love to as John Telfer had said, with kisses in a darkened room by a shame-faced yokel and, after marrying some such a yokel, live lives of unspeakable blankness. Into the houses of these women come the husbands at evening, tired and uncommunicative, to eat hurriedly and then go again into the streets or, the blessing of utter physical exhaustion having come to them, to sit for an hour in stockinged feet before crawling away to sleep and oblivion.

In these women is no light, no vision. They have instead certain fixed ideas to which they cling with a persistency touching heroism. To the man they have snatched from society they cling also with a tenacity to be measured only by their love of a roof over their heads and the craving for food to put into their stomachs. Being mothers, they are the despair of reformers, the shadow on the vision of dreamers and they put the black dread upon the heart of the poet who cries, "The female of the species is more deadly than the male." At their worst they are to be seen drunk with emotion amid the lurid horrors of a French Revolution or immersed in the secret whispering, creeping terror of a religious persecution. At their best they are mothers of half mankind. Wealth coming to them, they throw themselves into garish display of it and flash upon the sight of Newport or Palm Beach. In their native lair in the close little houses, they sleep in the bed of the man who has put clothes upon their backs and food into their mouths because that is the usage of their kind and give him of their bodies grudgingly or willingly as the laws of their physical needs direct. They do not love, they sell, instead, their bodies in the market place and cry out that man shall witness their virtue because they had had the joy of finding one buyer instead of the many of the red sisterhood. A fierce animalism in them makes them cling to the babe at their breast and in the days of its softness and loveliness they close their eyes and try to catch again an old fleeting dream of their girlhood, a something vague, shadowy, no longer a part of them, brought with the babe out of the infinite. Having passed beyond the land of dreams, they dwell in the land of emotions and weep over the bodies of unknown dead or sit under the eloquence of evangelists, shouting of heaven and of hell—the call to the one being brother to the call of the other—crying upon the troubled air of hot little churches, where hope is fighting in the jaws of vulgarity, "The weight of my sins is heavy on my soul." Along streets they go lifting heavy eyes to peer into the lives of others and to get a morsel to roll upon their heavy tongues. Having fallen upon a side light in the life of a Mary Underwood they return to it again and again as a dog to its offal. Something touching the lives of such as walk in the clean air, dream dreams, and have the audacity to be beautiful beyond the beauty of animal youth, maddens them, and they cry out, running from kitchen door to kitchen door and tearing at the prize like a starved beast who has found a carcass. Let but earnest women found a movement and crowd it forward to the day when it smacks of success and gives promise of the fine emotion of achievement, and they fall upon it with a cry, having hysteria rather than reason as their guiding impulse. In them is all of femininity—and none of it. For the most part they live and die unseen, unknown, eating rank food, sleeping overmuch, and sitting through summer afternoons rocking in chairs and looking at people passing in the street. In the end they die full of faith, hoping for a life to come.

Sam stood upon the road fearing the attacks these women were now making on Mary Underwood. The moon coming up, threw its light on the fields that lay beside the road and brought out their early spring nakedness and he thought them dreary and hideous, like the faces of the women that had been marching through his mind. He drew his overcoat about him and shivered as he went on, the mud splashing him and the raw night air aggravating the dreariness of his thoughts. He tried to revert to the assurance of the days before his mother's illness and to get again the strong belief in his own destiny that had kept him at the money making and saving and had urged him to the efforts to rise above the level of the man who bred him. He didn't succeed. The feeling of age that had settled upon him in the midst of the people mourning over the body of his mother came back, and, turning, he went along the road toward the town, saying to himself: "I will go and talk to Mary Underwood."

While he waited on the veranda for Mary to open the door, he decided that after all a marriage with her might lead to happiness. The half spiritual, half physical love of woman that is the glory and mystery of youth was gone from him. He thought that if he could only drive from her presence the fear of the faces that had been coming and going in his own mind he would, for his own part, be content to live his life as a worker and money maker, one without dreams.

Mary Underwood came to the door wearing the same heavy long coat she had worn on that other night and taking her by the hand Sam led her to the edge of the veranda. He looked with content at the pine trees before the house, thinking that some benign influence must have guided the hand that planted them there to stand clothed and decent amid the barrenness of the land at the end of winter.

"What is it, boy?" asked the woman, and her voice was filled with anxiety. The maternal passion again glowing in her had for days coloured all her thoughts, and with all the ardour of an intense nature she had thrown herself into her love of Sam. Thinking of him, she felt in fancy the pangs of birth, and in her bed at night relived with him his boyhood in the town and built again her plans for his future. In the day time she laughed at herself and said tenderly, "You are an old fool."

Brutally and frankly Sam told her of the thing he had heard on the station platform, looking past her at the pine trees and gripping the veranda rail. From the dead land there came again the smell of the new growth as it had come to him on the road before the revelation at the railroad station.

"Something kept telling me not to go away," he said. "It must have been in the air—this thing. Already these evil crawling things were at work. Oh, if only all the world, like you and Telfer and some of the others here, had an appreciation of the sense of privacy."

Mary Underwood laughed quietly.

"I was more than half right when, in the old days, I dreamed of making you a man at work upon the things of the mind," she said. "The sense of privacy indeed! What a fellow you have become! John Telfer's method was better than my own. He has given you the knack of saying things with a flourish."

Sam shook his head.

"Here is something that cannot be faced down with a laugh," he said stoutly. "Here is something at you—it is tearing at you—it has got to be met. Even now women are waking up in bed and turning the matter over in their minds. Tomorrow they will be at you again. There is but one way and we must take it. You and I will have to marry."

Mary looked at the serious new lines of his face.

"What a proposal!" she cried.

On an impulse she began singing, her voice fine and strong running through the quiet night.

"He rode and he thought of her red, red lips,"

she sang, and laughed again.

"You should come like that," she said, and then, "you poor muddled boy. Don't you know that I am your new mother?" she added, taking hold of his two arms and turning him about facing her. "Don't be absurd. I don't want a husband or a lover. I want a son of my own and I have found him. I adopted you here in this house that night when you came to me sick and covered with mud. As for these women—away with them—I'll face them down—I did it once before and I'll do it again. Go to your city and make your fight. Here in Caxton it is a woman's fight."

"It is horrible. You don't understand," Sam protested.

A grey, tired look came into Mary Underwood's face.

"I understand," she said. "I have been on that battlefield. It is to be won only by silence and tireless waiting. Your very effort to help would make the matter worse."

The woman and the tall boy, suddenly become a man, stood in thought. She was thinking of the end toward which her life was drifting. How differently she had planned it. She thought of the college in Massachusetts and of the men and women walking under the elm trees there.

"But I have got me a son and I am going to keep him," she said aloud, putting her hand on Sam's arm.

Very serious and troubled, Sam went down the gravel path toward the road. He felt there was something cowardly in the part she had given him to play, but he could see no alternative.

"After all," he reflected, "it is sensible—it is a woman's battle."

Half way to the road he stopped and, running back, caught her in his arms and gave her a great hug.

"Good-bye, little Mother," he cried and kissed her upon the lips.

And she, watching him as he went again down the gravel path, was overcome with tenderness. She went to the back of the porch and leaning against the house put her head upon her arm. Then turning and smiling through her tears she called after him.

"Did you crack their heads hard, boy?" she asked.

FROM MARY'S HOUSE SAM WENT to his own. On the gravel path an idea had come to him. He went into the house and, sitting down at the kitchen table with pen and ink, began writing. In the sleeping room back of the parlour he could hear Windy snoring. He wrote carefully, erasing and writing again. Then, drawing up a chair before the kitchen fire, he read over and over what he had written, and putting on his coat went through the dawn to the house of Tom Comstock, editor of the *Caxton Argus*, and roused him out of bed.

"I'll run it on the front page, Sam, and it won't cost you anything," Comstock promised. "But why run it? Let the matter drop."

"I shall just have time to pack and get the morning train for Chicago," Sam thought.

Early the evening before, Telfer, Wildman, and Freedom Smith, at Valmore's suggestion, had made a visit to Hunter's jewelry store. For an hour they bargained, selected, rejected, and swore at the jeweller. When the choice was made and the gift lay shining against white cotton in a box on the counter Telfer made a speech.

"I will talk straight to that boy," he declared, laughing. "I am not going to spend my time training his mind for money making and then have him fail me. I shall tell him that if he doesn't make money in that Chicago I shall come and take the watch from him."

Putting the gift into his pocket Telfer went out of the store and along the street to Eleanor's shop. He strutted through the display room and into the workshop where Eleanor sat with a hat on her knee.

"What am I going to do, Eleanor?" he demanded, standing with legs spread apart and frowning down upon her, "what am I going to do without Sam?"

A freckle-faced boy opened the shop door and threw a newspaper on the floor. The boy had a ringing voice and quick brown eyes. Telfer went again through the display room, touching with his cane the posts upon which hung the finished hats, and whistling. Standing before the shop, with the cane hooked upon his arm, he rolled a cigarette and watched the boy running from door to door along the street.

"I shall have to be adopting a new son," he said musingly.

After Sam left, Tom Comstock stood in his white nightgown and re-read the statement just given him. He read it over and over, and then, laying it on the kitchen table, filled and lighted a corncob pipe. A draft of wind blew into the room under the kitchen door chilling his thin shanks so that he drew his bare feet, one after the other, up behind the protective walls of his nightgown.

"On the night of my mother's death," ran the statement, "I sat in the kitchen of our house eating my supper when my father came in and began shouting and talking loudly, disturbing my mother who was asleep. I put my hand at his throat and squeezed until I thought he was dead, and carried him around the house and threw him into the road. Then I ran to the house of Mary Underwood, who was once my schoolteacher, and told her what I had done. She took me home, awoke John Telfer, and then went to look for the body of my father, who was not dead after all. John McPherson knows this is true, if he can be made to tell the truth."

Tom Comstock shouted to his wife, a small nervous woman with red cheeks, who set up type in the shop, did her own housework, and gathered most of the news and advertising for *The Argus*.

"Ain't that a slasher?" he asked, handing her the statement Sam had written.

"Well, it ought to stop the mean things they are saying about Mary Underwood," she snapped. Then, taking the glasses from her nose, and looking at Tom, who, while he did not find time to give her much help with *The Argus*, was the best checker player in Caxton and had once been to a state tournament of experts in that sport, she added, "Poor Jane McPherson, to have had a son like Sam and no better father for him than that liar Windy. Choked him, eh? Well, if the men of this town had any spunk they would finish the job."

BOOK II

I

For two years Sam lived the life of a travelling buyer, visiting towns in Indiana, Illinois, and Iowa, and making deals with men who, like Freedom Smith, bought the farmers' products. On Sundays he sat in chairs before country hotels and walked in the streets of strange towns, or, getting back to the city at the week end, went through the downtown streets and among the crowds in the parks with young men he had met on the road. From time to time he went to Caxton and sat for an hour with the men in Wildman's, stealing away later for an evening with Mary Underwood.

In the store he heard news of Windy, who was laying close siege to the farmer's widow he later married, and who seldom appeared in Caxton. In the store he saw the boy with freckles on his nose—the same John Telfer had watched running along Main Street on the night when he went to show Eleanor the gold watch bought for Sam and who sat now on the cracker barrel in the store and later went with Telfer to dodge the swinging cane and listen to the eloquence poured out on the night air. Telfer had not got the chance to stand with a crowd about him at the railroad station and make a parting speech to Sam, and in secret he resented the loss of that opportunity. After turning the matter over in his mind and thinking of many fine flourishes and ringing periods to give colour to the speech he had been compelled to send the gift by mail. And Sam, while the gift had touched him deeply and had brought back to his mind the essential solid goodness of the town amid the cornfields, so that he lost much of the bitterness aroused by the attack upon Mary Underwood, had been able to make but a tame and halting reply to the four. In his room in Chicago he had spent an evening writing and rewriting, putting in and taking out flourishes, and had ended by sending a brief line of thanks.

Valmore, whose affection for the boy had been a slow growth and who, now that he was gone, missed him more than the others, once spoke to Freedom Smith of the change that had come over young McPherson. Freedom sat in the wide old phaeton in the road before Valmore's shop as the blacksmith walked around the grey mare, lifting her feet and looking at the shoes.

"What has happened to Sam—he has changed so much?" he asked, dropping a foot of the mare and coming to lean upon the front wheel. "Already the city has changed him," he added regretfully.

Freedom took a match from his pocket and lighted the short black pipe.

"He bites off his words," continued Valmore; "he sits for an hour in the store and then goes away, and doesn't come back to say good-bye when he leaves town. What has got into him?"

Freedom gathered up the reins and spat over the dashboard into the dust of the road. A dog idling in the street jumped as though a stone had been hurled at him.

"If you had something he wanted to buy you would find he talked all right," he exploded. "He skins me out of my eyeteeth every time he comes to town and then gives me a cigar wrapped in tinfoil to make me like it."

For some months after his hurried departure from Caxton the changing, hurrying life of the city profoundly interested the tall strong boy from the Iowa village, who had the cold, quick business stroke of the money-maker combined with an unusually active interest in the problems of life and of living. Instinctively he looked upon business as a great game in which many men sat, and in which the capable, quiet ones waited patiently until a certain moment and then pounced upon what they would possess. With the quickness and accuracy of a beast at the kill they pounced and Sam felt that he had that stroke, and in his deals with country buyers used it ruthlessly. He knew the vague, uncertain look that came into the eyes of unsuccessful business men at critical moments and watched for it and took advantage of it as a successful prize fighter watches for a similar vague, uncertain look in the eyes of an opponent.

He had found his work, and had the assurance and the confidence that comes with that discovery. The stroke that he saw in the hand of the successful business men about him is the stroke also of the master painter, scientist, actor, singer, prize fighter. It was the hand of Whistler, Balzac, Agassiz, and Terry McGovern. The sense of it had been in him when as a boy he watched the totals grow in the yellow bankbook, and now and then he recognised it in Telfer talking on a country road. In the city where men of wealth and power in affairs rubbed elbows with him in the street cars and walked past him in hotel lobbies he watched and waited saying to himself, "I also will be such a one."

Sam had not lost the vision that had come to him when as a boy he walked on the road and listened to the talk of Telfer, but he now thought of himself as one who had not only a hunger for achievement but also a knowledge of where to look for it. At times he had stirring dreams of vast work to be done by his hand that made the blood race in him, but for the most part he went his way quietly, making friends, looking about him, keeping his mind busy with his own thoughts, making deals.

During his first year in the city he lived in the house of an ex-Caxton family named Pergrin that had been in Chicago for several years, but that still continued to send its members, one at a time, to spend summer vacations in the Iowa village. To these people he carried letters handed him during the month after his mother's death, and letters regarding him had come to them from Caxton. In the house, where eight people sat down to dinner, only three besides himself were Caxton-bred, but thoughts and talk of the town pervaded the house and crept into every conversation.

"I was thinking of old John Moore today—does he still drive that team of black ponies?" the housekeeping sister, a mild-looking woman of thirty, would ask of Sam at the dinner table, breaking in on a conversation of baseball, or a tale by one of the boarders of a new office building to be erected in the Loop.

"No, he don't," Jake Pergrin, a fat bachelor of forty who was foreman in a machine shop and the man of the house, would answer. So long had Jake been the final authority in the house on affairs touching Caxton that he looked upon Sam as an intruder. "John told me last summer when I was home that he intended to sell the blacks and buy mules," he would add, looking at the youth challengingly.

The Pergrin family was in fact upon foreign soil. Living amid the roar and bustle of Chicago's vast west side, it still turned with hungry heart toward the place of corn and of steers, and wished that work for Jake, its mainstay, could be found in that paradise.

Jake Pergrin, a bald-headed man with a paunch, stubby iron-grey moustache, and a dark line of machine oil encircling his finger nails so that they stood forth separately like formal flower beds at the edge of a lawn, worked industriously from Monday morning until Saturday night, going to bed at nine o'clock, and until that hour wandering, whistling, from room to room through the house, in a pair of worn carpet slippers, or sitting in his room practising on a violin. On Saturday evening, the habits formed in his Caxton days being strong in him, he came home with his pay in his pocket, settled with the two sisters for the week's living, sat down to dinner neatly shaved and combed, and then disappeared upon the troubled waters of the town. Late on Sunday evening he re-appeared, with empty pockets, unsteady step, blood-shot eyes, and a noisy attempt at self-possessed unconcern, to hurry upstairs and crawl into bed in preparation for another week of toil and respectability. The man had a certain Rabelaisian sense of humour and kept score of the new ladies met on his weekly flights by pencil marks upon his bedroom wall. He once took Sam upstairs to show his record. A row of them ran half around the room.

Besides the bachelor there was a sister, a tall gaunt woman of thirty-five who taught school, and the housekeeper, thirty, mild, and blessed with a remarkably sweet speaking voice. Then there was a medical student in the front room, Sam in an alcove off the hall, a grey-haired woman stenographer, whom Jake called Marie Antoinette, and a buyer from a wholesale dry-goods house, with a vivacious, fun-loving little Southern wife.

The women in the Pergrin house seemed to Sam tremendously concerned about their health and each evening talked of the matter, he thought, more than his mother had talked during her illness. While Sam lived with them they were all under the influence of a strange sort of faith healer and took what they called "Health Suggestion" treatments. Twice each week the faith healer came to the house, laid his hands upon their backs and took their money. The treatment afforded Jake a never-ending source of amusement and in the evening he went through the house putting his hands upon the backs of the women and demanding money from them, but the dry-goods buyer's wife, who for years had coughed at night, slept peacefully after some weeks of the treatment and the cough did not return while Sam remained in the house.

In the house Sam had a standing. Glowing tales of his shrewdness in business, his untiring industry, and the size of his bank account, had preceded him from Caxton, and these tales the Pergrins, in their loyalty to the town and to all the products of the town, did not allow to shrink in the re-telling. The housekeeping sister, a kindly woman, became fond of Sam, and in his absence would boast of him to chance callers or to the boarders gathered in the living room in the evening. She it was who laid the foundation of the medical student's belief that Sam was a kind of genius in money matters, a belief that enabled him later to make a successful assault upon a legacy which came to that young man.

Frank Eckardt, the medical student, Sam took as a friend. On Sunday afternoons they went to walk in the streets, or, taking two girl friends of Frank's, who were also students at the medical school, on their arms, they went to the park and sat upon benches under the trees.

For one of these young women Sam conceived a regard that approached tenderness. Sunday after Sunday he spent with her, and once, walking through the park on an evening in the late fall, the dry brown leaves rustling under their feet and the sun going down in red splendour before their eyes, he took her hand and walked in silence, feeling tremendously alive and vital as he had felt on that other night walking under the trees of Caxton with the dark-skinned daughter of banker Walker.

That nothing came of the affair and that after a time he did not see the girl again was due, he thought, to his own growing interest in money making and to the fact that there was in her, as in Frank Eckardt, a blind devotion to something that he could not himself understand.

Once he had a talk with Eckardt of the matter. "She is fine and purposeful like a woman I knew in my home town," he said, thinking of Eleanor Telfer, "but she will not talk to me of her work as sometimes she talks to you. I want her to talk. There is something about her that I do not understand and that I want to understand. I think that she likes me and once or twice I have thought she would not greatly mind my making love to her, but I do not understand her just the same."

One day in the office of the company for which he worked Sam became acquainted with a young advertising man named Jack Prince, a brisk, very much alive young fellow who made money rapidly, spent it lavishly, and had friends and acquaintances in every office, every hotel lobby, every bar room and restaurant in the down-town section of the city. The chance acquaintance rapidly grew into friendship. The clever, witty Prince made a kind of hero of Sam, admiring his reserve and good sense and boasting of him far and wide through the town. With Prince, Sam occasionally went on mild carouses, and, once, in the midst of thousands of people sitting about tables and drinking beer at the Coliseum on Wabash Avenue, he and Prince got into a fight with two waiters, Prince declaring he had been cheated and Sam, although he thought his friend in the wrong, striking out with his fist and dragging Prince through the door and into a passing street car in time to avoid a rush of other waiters hurrying to the aid of the one who lay dazed and sputtering on the sawdust floor.

After these evenings of carousal, carried on with Jack Prince and with young men met on trains and about country hotels, Sam spent hour after hour walking about town absorbed in his own thoughts and getting his own impressions of what he saw. In the affairs with the young men he played, for the most part, a passive rôle, going with them from place to place and drinking until they became loud and boisterous, or morose and quarrelsome, and then slipping away to his own room, amused or irritated as the circumstances, or the temperament of his companions, had made or marred the joviality of the evening. On his nights alone, he put his hands into his pockets and walked for endless miles through the lighted streets, getting in a dim way a realisation of the hugeness of life. All of the faces going past him, the women in their furs, the young men with cigars in their mouths going to the theatres, the bald old men with watery eyes, the boys with bundles of newspapers under their arms, and the slim prostitutes lurking in the hallways, should have interested him deeply. In his youth, and with the pride of sleeping power in him, he saw them only as so many individuals that might some day test their ability against his own. And if he peered at them closely and marked down face after face in the crowds it was as a sitter in the great game of business that he looked, exercising his mind by imagining this or that one arrayed against him in deals, and planning the method by which he would win in the imaginary struggle.

There was at that time in Chicago a place, to be reached by a bridge above the Illinois Central Railroad track, that Sam sometimes visited on stormy nights to watch the lake lashed by the wind. Great masses of water moving swiftly and silently broke with a roar against wooden piles, backed by hills of stone and earth, and the spray from the broken waves fell upon Sam's face and on winter nights froze on his coat. He had learned to smoke, and leaning upon the railing of the bridge would stand for hours with a pipe in his mouth looking at the moving water, filled with awe and admiration of the silent power of it.

One night in September, when he was walking alone in the streets, an incident happened that showed him also a silent power within himself, a power that startled and for the moment frightened him. Walking into a little street back of Dearborn, he was suddenly aware of the faces of women looking out at him through small square windows cut in the fronts of the houses. Here and there, before and behind him, were the faces; voices called, smiles invited, hands beckoned. Up and down the street went men looking at the sidewalk, their coats turned up about their necks, their hats pulled down over their eyes. They looked at the faces of the women pressed against the little squares of glass and then, turning, suddenly, sprang in at the doors of the houses as if pursued. Among the walkers on the sidewalk were old men, men in shabby coats whose feet scuffled as they hurried along, and young boys with the pink of virtue in their cheeks. In the air was lust, heavy and hideous. It got into Sam's brain and he stood hesitating and uncertain, startled, nerveless, afraid. He remembered a story he had once heard from John Telfer, a story of the disease and death that lurks in the little side streets of cities, and ran into Van Buren Street and from that into lighted State. He climbed up the stairway of the elevated railroad and jumping on the first train went away south to walk for hours on a gravel roadway at the edge of the lake in Jackson Park. The wind from the lake and the laughter and talk of people passing under the lights cooled the fever in him, as once it had been cooled by the eloquence of John Telfer, walking on the road near Caxton, and with his voice marshalling the armies of the standing corn.

Into Sam's mind came a picture of the cold, silent water moving in great masses under the night sky and he thought that in the world of men there was a force as resistless, as little understood, as little talked of, moving always forward, silent, powerful—the force of sex. He wondered how the force would be broken in his own case, against what breakwater it would spend itself. At midnight, he went home across the city and crept into his alcove in the Pergrin house, puzzled and for the time utterly tired. In his bed, he turned his face to the wall and resolutely closing his eyes tried to sleep. "There are things not to be understood," he told himself. "To live decently is a matter of good sense. I will keep thinking of what I want to do and not go into such a place again."

One day, when he had been in Chicago two years, there happened an incident of another sort, an incident so grotesque, so Pan-like, so full of youth, that for days after it happened he thought of it with delight, and walked in the streets or sat in a passenger train laughing joyfully at the remembrance of some new detail of the affair.

Sam, who was the son of Windy McPherson and who had more than once ruthlessly condemned all men who put liquor into their mouths, got drunk, and for eighteen hours went shouting poetry, singing songs, and yelling at the stars like a wood god on the bend.

Late on an afternoon in the early spring he sat with Jack Prince in DeJonge's restaurant in Monroe Street. Prince, his watch lying before him on the table and the thin stem of a wine glass between his fingers, talked to Sam of the man for whom they had been waiting a half hour.

"He will be late, of course," he exclaimed, refilling Sam's glass. "The man was never on time in his life. To keep an appointment promptly would take something from him. It would be like the bloom of youth gone from the cheeks of a maiden."

Sam had already seen the man for whom they waited. He was thirty-five, small and narrow-shouldered, with a little wrinkled face, a huge nose, and a pair of eyeglasses that hooked over his ears. Sam had seen him in a Michigan Avenue club with Prince solemnly pitching silver dollars at a chalk mark on the floor with a group of serious, solid-looking old men.

"They are the crowd that have just put through the big deal in Kansas oil stock and the little one is Morris, who handled the publicity for them," Prince had explained.

Later, when they were walking down Michigan Avenue, Prince talked at length of Morris, whom he admired immensely. "He is the best advertising and publicity man in America," he declared. "He isn't a four-flusher, as I am, and does not make as much money, but he can take another man's ideas and express them so simply and forcibly that they tell the man's story better than he knew it himself. And that's all there is to advertising."

He began laughing.

"It is funny to think of it. Tom Morris will do a job of work and the man for whom he does it will swear that he did it himself, that every pat phrase on the printed page Tom has turned out, is one of his own. He will howl like a beast at paying Tom's bill, and then the next time he will try to do the job himself and make a hopeless muddle of it so that he has to send for Tom only to see the trick done over again like shelling corn off the cob. The best men in Chicago send for him."

Into the restaurant came Tom Morris bearing under his arm a huge pasteboard portfolio. He seemed hurried and nervous. "I am on my way to the office of the International Biscuit Turning Machine Company," he explained to Prince. "I can't stop at all. I have here the layout of a circular designed to push on to the market some more of that common stock of theirs that hasn't paid a dividend for ten years."

Thrusting out his hand, Prince dragged Morris into a chair. "Never mind the Biscuit Machine people and their stock," he commanded; "they will always have common stock to sell. It is inexhaustible. I want you to meet McPherson here who will some day have something big for you to help him with."

Morris reached across the table and took Sam's hand; his own was small and soft like that of a woman. "I am worked to death," he complained; "I have my eye on a chicken farm in Indiana. I am going down there to live."

For an hour the three men sat in the restaurant while Prince talked of a place in Wisconsin where the fish should be biting. "A man has told me of the place twenty times," he declared; "I am sure I could find it on a railroad folder. I have never been fishing nor have you, and Sam here comes from a place to which they carry water in wagons over the plains."

The little man who had been drinking copiously of the wine looked from Prince to Sam. From time to time he took off his glasses and wiped them with a handkerchief. "I don't understand your being in such society," he announced; "you have the solid, substantial look of a bucket-shop man. Prince here will get nowhere. He is honest, sells wind and his charming society, and spends the money that he gets, instead of marrying and putting it in his wife's name."

Prince arose. "It is useless to waste time in persiflage," he began and then turning to Sam, "There is a place in Wisconsin," he said uncertainly.

Morris picked up the portfolio and with a grotesque effort at steadiness started for the door followed by Prince and Sam walking with wavering steps. In the street Prince took the portfolio out of the little man's hand. "Let your mother carry it, Tommy," he said, shaking his finger under Morris's nose. He began singing a lullaby. "When the bough bends the cradle will fall."

The three men walked out of Monroe and into State Street, Sam's head feeling strangely light. The buildings along the street reeled against the sky. A sudden fierce longing for wild adventure seized him. On a corner Morris stopped, took the handkerchief from his pocket and again wiped his glasses. "I want to be sure that I see clearly," he said; "it seems to me that in the bottom of that last glass of wine I saw three of us in a cab with a basket of life oil on the seat between us going to the station to catch the train for that place Jack's friend told fish lies about."

The next eighteen hours opened up a new world to Sam. With the fumes of liquor rising in his brain, he rode for two hours on a train, tramped in the darkness along dusty roads and, building a bonfire in a woods, danced in the light of it upon the grass, holding the hands of Prince and the little man with the wrinkled face. Solemnly he stood upon a stump at the edge of a wheatfield and recited Poe's "Helen," taking on the voice, the gestures and even the habit of spreading his legs apart, of John Telfer. And then overdoing the last, he sat down suddenly on the stump, and Morris, coming forward with a bottle in his hand said, "Fill the lamp, man—the light of reason has gone out."

From the bonfire in the woods and Sam's recital from the stump, the three friends emerged again upon the road, and a belated farmer driving home half asleep on the seat of his wagon caught their attention. With the skill of an Indian boy the diminutive Morris sprang upon the wagon and thrust a ten dollar bill into the farmer's hand. "Lead us, O man of the soil!" he shouted, "Lead us to a gilded palace of sin! Take us to a saloon! The life oil gets low in the can!"

Beyond the long, jolting ride in the wagon Sam never became quite clear. In his mind ran vague notions of a wild carousal in a country tavern, of himself acting as bartender, and a huge red-faced woman rushing here and there under the direction of a tiny man, dragging reluctant rustics to the bar and commanding them to keep on drinking the beer that Sam drew until the last of the ten dollars given to the man of the wagon should have gone into her cash drawer. Also, he thought that Jack Prince had put a chair upon the bar and that he sat on it explaining to the hurrying drawer of beer that although the Egyptian kings had built great pyramids to celebrate themselves they never built anything more gigantic than the jag Tom Morris was building among the farm hands in the room.

Later Sam thought that he and Jack Prince tried to sleep under a pile of grain sacks in a shed and that Morris came to them weeping because every one in the world was asleep and most of them lying under tables.

And then, his head clearing, Sam found himself with the two others walking again upon the dusty road in the dawn and singing songs.

On the train, with the help of a Negro porter, the three men tried to efface the dust and the stains of the wild night. The pasteboard portfolio containing the circular for the Biscuit Machine Company was still under Jack Prince's arm and the little man, wiping and re-wiping his glasses, peered at Sam.

"Did you come with us or are you a child we have adopted here in these parts?" he asked.

II

I t was a wonderful place, that South Water Street in Chicago where Sam came to make his business start in the city, and it was proof of the dry unresponsiveness in him that he did not sense more fully its meaning and its message. All day the food stuff of a vast city flowed through the narrow streets. Blue-shirted, broad-shouldered teamsters from the tops of high piled wagons bawled at scurrying pedestrians. On the sidewalks in boxes, bags, and barrels, lay oranges from Florida and California, figs from Arabia, bananas from Jamaica, nuts from the hills of Spain and the plains of Africa, cabbages from Ohio, beans from Michigan, corn and potatoes from Iowa. In December, fur-coated men hurried through the forests of northern Michigan gathering Christmas trees that found their way to warm firesides through the street. And summer and winter a million hens laid the eggs that were gathered there, and the cattle on a thousand hills sent their yellow butter fat packed in tubs and piled upon trucks to add to the confusion.

Into this street Sam walked, thinking little of the wonder of these things and thinking haltingly, getting his sense of the bigness of it in dollars and cents. Standing in the doorway of the commission house for which he was to work, strong, well clad, able and efficient, he looked through the streets, seeing and hearing the hurry and the roar and the shouting of voices, and then with a smile upon his lips went inside. In his brain was an unexpressed thought. As the old Norse marauders looked at the cities sitting in their splendour on the Mediterranean so looked he. "What loot!" a voice within him said, and his brain began devising methods by which he should get his share of it.

Years later, when Sam was a man of big affairs, he drove one day in a carriage through the streets and turning to his companion, a grey-haired, dignified Boston man who sat beside him, said, "I worked here once and used to sit on a barrel of apples at the edge of the sidewalk thinking how clever I was to make more money in one month than the man who raised the apples made in a year."

The Boston man, stirred by the sight of so much foodstuff and moved to epigram by his mood, looked up and down the street.

"The foodstuff of an empire rattling o'er the stones," he said.

"I should have made more money here," answered Sam dryly.

The commission firm for which Sam worked was a partnership, not a corporation, and was owned by two brothers. Of the two Sam thought that the elder, a tall, bald, narrow-shouldered man, with a long narrow face and a suave manner, was the real master, and represented most of the ability in the partnership. He was oily, silent, tireless. All day he went in and out of the office and warehouses and up and down the crowded street, sucking nervously at an unlighted cigar. He was a great worker in a suburban church, but a shrewd and, Sam suspected, an unscrupulous business man. Occasionally the minister or some of the women of the suburban church came into the office to talk with him, and Sam was amused at the thought that Narrow Face, when he talked of the affairs of the church, bore a striking resemblance to the brown-bearded minister of the church in Caxton.

The other brother was a far different sort, and, in business, Sam thought, a much inferior man. He was a heavy, broad-shouldered, square-faced man of about thirty, who sat in the office dictating letters and who stayed out two or three hours to lunch. He sent out letters signed by him on the firm's stationery with the title of General Manager, and Narrow Face let him do it. Broad Shoulders had been educated in New England and even after several years away from his college seemed more interested in it than in the welfare of the business. For a month or more in the spring he took most of the time of one of the two stenographers employed by the firm writing letters to graduates of Chicago high schools to induce them to go East to finish their education; and when a graduate of the college came to Chicago seeking employment, he closed his desk and spent entire days going from place to place, introducing, urging, recommending. Sam noticed, however, that when the firm employed a new man in their own office or on the road it was Narrow-Face who chose the man.

Broad-shoulders had been a famous football player in his day and wore an iron brace on his leg. The offices, like most of the offices on the street, were dark and narrow, and smelled of decaying vegetables and rancid butter. Noisy Greek and Italian hucksters wrangled on the sidewalk in front, and among these went Narrow-Face hurrying about making deals.

In South Water Street Sam did well, multiplying his thirty-six hundred dollars by ten during the three years that he stayed there, or went out from there to towns and cities directing a part of the great flowing river of foodstuff through his firm's front door.

With almost his first day on the street he began seeing on all sides of him opportunity for gain, and set himself industriously at work to get his hand upon money with which to take advantage of the chances that he thought lay so invitingly about. Within a year he had made much progress. From a woman on Wabash Avenue he got six thousand dollars, and he planned and executed a coup that gave him the use of twenty thousand dollars that had come as a legacy to his friend, the medical student, who lived at the Pergrin house.

Sam had eggs and apples lying in warehouse against a rise; game, smuggled across the state line from Michigan and Wisconsin, lay frozen in cold storage tagged with his name and ready to be sold at a long profit to hotels and fashionable restaurants; and there were even secret bushels of corn and wheat lying in other warehouses along the Chicago River ready to be thrown on the market at a word from him, or, the margins by which he kept his hold on the stuff not being forthcoming, at a word from a LaSalle Street broker.

Getting the twenty thousand dollars out of the hands of the medical student was a turning point in Sam's life. Sunday after Sunday he walked with Eckardt in the streets or loitered with him in the parks thinking of the money lying idle in the bank and of the deals he might be turning with it in the street or on the road. Daily he saw more clearly the power of cash. Other commission merchants along South Water Street came running into the office of his firm with tense, anxious faces asking Narrow-Face to help them over rough spots in the day's trading. Broad-Shoulders, who had no business ability but who had married a rich woman, went on month after month taking half the profits brought in by the ability of his tall, shrewd brother, and Narrow-Face, who had taken a liking for Sam and who occasionally stopped for a word with him, spoke of the matter often and eloquently.

"Spend your time with no one who hasn't money to help you," he said; "on the road look for the men with money and then try to get it. That's all there is to business—money-getting." And then looking across to the desk of his brother he would add, "I would kick half the men in business out of it if I could, but I myself must dance to the tune that money plays."

One day Sam went to the office of an attorney named Webster, whose reputation for the shrewd drawing of contracts had come to him from Narrow-Face.

"I want a contract drawn that will give me absolute control of twenty thousand dollars with no risk on my part if I lose the money and no promise to pay more than seven per cent if I do not lose," he said.

The attorney, a slender, middle-aged man with a swarthy skin and black hair, put his hands on the desk before him and looked at the tall young man.

"What collateral?" he asked.

Sam shook his head. "Can you draw such a contract that will be legal and what will it cost me?" he asked.

The lawyer laughed good naturedly. "I can draw it of course. Why not?"

Sam, taking a roll of bills from his pocket, counted the amount upon the table.

"Who are you anyway?" asked Webster. "If you can get twenty thousand and without collateral you're worth knowing. I might be getting up a gang to rob a mail train."

Sam did not answer. He put the contract in his pocket and went home to his alcove at the Pergrins. He wanted to get by himself and think. He did not believe that he would by any chance lose Frank Eckardt's money, but he knew that Eckardt himself would draw back from the kind of deals that he expected to make with the money, that they would frighten and alarm him, and he wondered if he was being honest.

In his own room after dinner Sam studied carefully the agreement drawn by Webster. It seemed to him to cover what he wanted covered, and having got it well fixed in his mind he tore it up. "There is no use his knowing I have been to a lawyer," he thought guiltily.

Getting into bed, he began building plans for the future. With more than thirty thousand dollars at his command he thought that he should be able to make headway rapidly. "In my hands it will double itself every year," he told himself and getting out of bed he drew a chair to the window and sat down, feeling strangely alive and awake like a young man in love. He saw himself going on and on, directing, managing, ruling men. It seemed to him that there was nothing he could not do. "I will run factories and banks and maybe mines and railroads," he thought and his mind leaped forward so that he saw himself, grey, stern, and capable, sitting at a broad desk high in a great stone building, a materialisation of John Telfer's word picture—"You will be a big man of dollars—it is plain."

And then into Sam's mind came another picture. He remembered a

Saturday afternoon when a young man had come running into the office on South Water Street, a young man who owed Narrow-Face a sum of money and could not pay it. He remembered the unpleasant tightening of the mouth and the sudden shrewd hard look in his employer's long narrow face. He had not heard much of the talk, but he was aware of a strained pleading quality in the voice of the young man who had said over and over slowly and painfully, "But, man, my honour is at stake," and of a coldness in the answering voice replying persistently, "With me it is not a matter of honour but of dollars, and I am going to get them."

From the alcove window Sam looked out upon a vacant lot covered with patches of melting snow. Beyond the lot facing him stood a flat building, and the snow, melting on the roof, made a little stream that ran down some hidden pipe and rattled out upon the ground. The noise of the falling water and the sound of distant footsteps going homeward through the sleeping city brought back thoughts of other nights when as a boy in Caxton he had sat thus, thinking disconnected thoughts.

Without knowing it Sam was fighting one of the real battles of his life, a battle in which the odds were very much against the quality in him that got him out of bed to look at the snow-clad vacant lot.

There was in the youth much of the brute trader, blindly intent upon gain; much of the quality that has given America so many of its so-called great men. It was the quality that had sent him in secret to Lawyer Webster to protect himself without protecting the simple credulous young medical student, and that had made him say as he came home with the contract in his pocket, "I will do what I can," when in truth he meant, "I will get what I can."

There may be business men in America who do not get what they can, who simply love power. One sees men here and there in banks, at the heads of great industrial trusts, in factories and in great mercantile houses of whom one would like to think thus. They are the men who one dreams have had an awakening, who have found themselves; they are the men hopeful thinkers try to recall again and again to the mind.

To these men America is looking. It is asking them to keep the faith, to stand themselves up against the force of the brute trader, the dollar man, the man who with his one cunning wolf quality of acquisitiveness has too long ruled the business of the nation.

I have said that the sense of equity in Sam fought an unequal battle. He was in business, and young in business, in a day when all America was seized with a blind grappling for gain. The nation was drunk with it, trusts were being formed, mines opened; from the ground spurted oil and gas; railroads creeping westward opened yearly vast empires of new land. To be poor was to be a fool; thought waited, art waited; and men at their firesides gathered their children around them and talked glowingly of men of dollars, holding them up as prophets fit to lead the youth of the young nation.

Sam had in him the making of the new, the commanding man of business. It was that quality in him that made him sit by the window thinking before going to the medical student with the unfair contract, and the same quality had sent him forth night after night to walk alone in the streets when other young men went to theatres or to walk with girls in the park. He had, in truth, a taste for the lonely hours when thought grows. He was a step beyond the youth who hurries to the theatre or buries himself in stories of love or adventure. He had in him something that wanted a chance.

In the flat building across the vacant lot a light appeared at a window and through the lighted window he saw a man clad in pajamas who propped a sheet of music against a dressing-table and who had a shining silver horn in his hand. Sam watched, filled with mild curiosity. The man, not reckoning on an onlooker at so late an hour, began an elaborate and amusing schedule of personation. He opened the window, put the horn to his lips and then turning bowed before the lighted room as before an audience. He put his hand to his lips and blew kisses about, then put the horn to his lips and looked again at the sheet of music.

The note that came out of the window on the still air was a failure, it flattened into a squawk. Sam laughed and pulled down the window. The incident had brought back to his mind another man who bowed to a crowd and blew upon a horn. Getting into bed he pulled the covers about him and went to sleep. "I will get Frank's money if I can," he told himself, settling the matter that had been in his mind. "Most men are fools and if I do not get his money some other man will."

On the next afternoon Eckardt had lunch down town with Sam. Together they went to a bank where Sam showed the profits of deals he had made and the growth of his bank account, going afterward into South Water Street where Sam talked glowingly of the money to be made by a shrewd man who knew the ways of the street and had a head upon his shoulders.

"That's just it," said Frank Eckardt, falling quickly into the trap Sam had set, and hungering for profits; "I have money but no head on my shoulders for using it. I wish you would take it and see what you can do."

With a thumping heart Sam went home across the city to the Pergrin house, Eckardt beside him in the elevated train. In Sam's room the agreement was written out by Sam and signed by Eckardt. At dinner time they had the drygoods buyer in to sign as witness.

And the agreement turned out to Eckardt's advantage. In no year did Sam return him less than ten per cent, and in the end gave back the principal more than doubled so that Eckardt was able to retire from the practice of medicine and live upon the interest of his capital in a village near Tiffin, Ohio.

With the thirty thousand dollars in his hands Sam began to reach out and extend the scope of his ventures. He bought and sold constantly, not only eggs, butter, apples, and grain, but also houses and building lots. Through his head marched long rows of figures. Deals worked themselves out in detail in his brain as he went about town drinking with young men, or sat at dinner in the Pergrin house. He even began working over in his head various schemes for getting into the firm by which he was employed, and thought that he might work upon Broad-Shoulders, getting hold of his interest and forcing himself into control. And then, the fear of Narrow-Face holding him back and his growing success in deals keeping his mind occupied, he was suddenly confronted by an opportunity that changed entirely the plans he was making for himself.

Through Jack Prince's suggestion Colonel Tom Rainey of the great Rainey Arms Company sent for him and offered him a position as buyer of all the materials used in their factories.

It was the kind of connection Sam had unconsciously been seeking—a company, strong, old, conservative, known throughout the world. There was, in the talk with Colonel Tom, a hint of future opportunities to get stock in the company and perhaps to become eventually an official— these things were of course remote—to be dreamed of and worked toward—the company made it a part of its policy.

Sam said nothing, but already he had decided to accept the place, and was thinking of a profitable arrangement touching percentages on the amount saved in buying that had worked out so well for him during his years with Freedom Smith.

Sam's work for the firearms company took him off the road and confined him to an office all day long. In a way he regretted this. The complaints he had heard among travelling men in country hotels with regard to the hardship of travel meant nothing to his mind. Any kind of travel was a keen pleasure to him. Against the hardships and discomforts he balanced the tremendous advantages of seeing new places and faces and getting a look into many lives, and he looked back with a kind of retrospective joy on the three years of hurrying from place to place, catching trains, and talking with chance acquaintances met by the way. Also, the years on the road had given him many opportunities for secret and profitable deals of his own.

Over against these advantages the place at Rainey's threw him into close and continuous association with men of big affairs. The offices of the Arms Company occupied an entire floor of one of Chicago's newest and biggest skyscrapers and millionaire stockholders and men high in the service of the state and of the government at Washington came in and went out at the door. Sam looked at them closely. He wanted to have a tilt with them and try if his Caxton and South Water Street shrewdness would keep the head upon his shoulders in LaSalle Street. The opportunity seemed to him a big one and he went about his work quietly and ably, intent upon making the most of it.

The Rainey Arms Company, at the time of Sam's coming with it, was still largely owned by the Rainey family, father and daughter. Colonel Rainey, a grey-whiskered military looking man with a paunch, was the president and largest individual stockholder. He was a pompous, swaggering old fellow with a habit of making the most trivial statement with the air of a judge pronouncing the death sentence, and sat dutifully at his desk day after day looking very important and thoughtful, smoking long black cigars and signing personally piles of letters brought him by the heads of various departments. He looked upon himself as a silent but very important spoke in the government at Washington and every day issued many orders which the men at the heads of departments received with respect and disregarded in secret. Twice he had been prominently mentioned in connection with cabinet positions in the national government, and in talks with his cronies at clubs and restaurants he gave the impression of having actually refused an offer of appointment on both occasions.

Having got himself established as a factor in the management of the business, Sam found many things that surprised him. In every company of which he knew there was some one man to whom all looked for guidance, who at critical moments became dominant, saying "Do this, or that," and making no explanations. In the Rainey Company he found no such man, but, instead, a dozen strong departments, each with its own head and each more or less independent of the others.

Sam lay in his bed at night and went about in the evening thinking of this and of its meaning. Among the department heads there was a great deal of loyalty and devotion to Colonel Tom, and he thought that among them were a few men who were devoted to other interests than their own.

At the same time he told himself there was something wrong. He himself had no such feeling of loyalty and although he was willing to give lip service to the resounding talk of the colonel about the fine old traditions of the company, he could not bring himself to a belief in the idea of conducting a vast business on a system founded upon lip service to traditions, or upon loyalty to an individual.

"There must be loose ends lying about everywhere," he thought and followed the thought with another. "A man will come along, pick up these loose ends, and run the whole shop. Why not I?"

The Rainey Arms Company had made its millions for the Rainey and Whittaker families during the Civil War. Whittaker had been an inventor, making one of the first practical breech-loading guns, and the original Rainey had been a dry-goods merchant in an Illinois town who backed the inventor.

It proved itself a rare combination. Whittaker developed into a wonderful shop manager for his day, and, from the first, stayed at home building rifles and making improvements, enlarging the plant, getting out the goods. The drygoods merchant scurried about the country, going to Washington and to the capitals of the individual states, pulling wires, appealing to patriotism and state pride, taking big orders at fat prices.

In Chicago there is a tradition that more than once he went south of the Dixie line and that following these trips thousands of Rainey-Whittaker rifles found their way into the hands of Confederate soldiers, but this story which increased Sam's respect for the energetic little drygoods merchant, Colonel Tom, his son, indignantly denied. In reality Colonel Tom would have liked to think of the first Rainey as a huge, Jove-like god of arms. Like Windy McPherson of Caxton, given a chance, he would have invented a new ancestor.

After the Civil War, and Colonel Tom's growing to manhood, the Rainey and Whittaker fortunes were merged into one through the marriage of Jane Whittaker, the last of her line, to the only surviving

Rainey, and upon her death her fortune, grown to more than a million, stood in the name of Sue Rainey, twenty-six, the only issue of the marriage.

From the first day, Sam began to forge ahead in the Rainey Company. In the buying end he found a rich field for spectacular money saving and money making and made the most of it. The position as buyer had for ten years been occupied by a distant cousin to Colonel Tom, now dead. Whether the cousin was a fool or a knave Sam could never quite decide and did not greatly care, but after he had got the situation in hand he felt that the man must have cost the company a tremendous sum, which *he* intended to save.

Sam's arrangement with the company gave him, besides a fair salary, half he saved in the fixed prices of standard materials. These prices had stood fixed for years and Sam went into them, cutting right and left, and making for himself during his first year twenty-three thousand dollars. At the end of the year, when the directors asked to have an adjustment made and the percentage contract annulled, he got a generous slice of company stock, the respect of Colonel Tom Rainey and the directors, the fear of some of the department heads, the loyal devotion of others, and the title of Treasurer of the company.

The Rainey Arms Company was in truth living largely upon the reputation built up for it by the first pushing energetic Rainey, and the inventive genius of his partner, Whittaker. Under Colonel Tom it had found new conditions and new competition which he had ignored, or met in a half-hearted way, standing on its reputation, its financial strength, and on the glory of its past achievements. Dry rot ate at its heart. The damage done was not great, but was growing greater. The heads of the departments, in whose hands so much of the running of the business lay, were many of them incompetent men with nothing to commend them but long years of service. And in the treasurer's office sat a quiet young man, barely turned twenty, who had no friends, wanted his own way, and who shook his head over the office traditions and was proud of his unbelief.

Seeing the absolute necessity of working through Colonel Tom, and having a head filled with ideas of things he wanted done, Sam began working to get suggestions into the older man's mind. Within a month after his elevation the two men were lunching together daily and Sam was spending many extra hours behind closed doors in Colonel Tom's office.

Although American business and manufacturing had not yet achieved the modern idea of efficiency in shop and office management, Sam had many of these ideas in his mind and expounded them tirelessly to Colonel Tom. He hated waste; he cared nothing for company tradition; he had no idea, as did the heads of other departments, of getting into a comfortable berth and spending the rest of his days there, and he was bent on managing the great Rainey Company, if not directly, then through Colonel Tom, who, he felt, was putty in his hands.

From his new position as treasurer Sam did not drop his work as buyer, but, after a talk with Colonel Tom, merged the two departments, put in capable assistants of his own, and went on with his work of effacing the tracks of the cousin. For years the company had been overpaying for inferior material. Sam put his own material inspectors into the west side factories and brought several big Pennsylvania steel companies scurrying to Chicago to make restitution. The restitution was stiff, but when Colonel Tom was appealed to, Sam went to lunch with him, bought a bottle of wine, and stiffened his back.

One afternoon in a room in the Palmer House a scene was played out that for days stayed in Sam's mind as a kind of realisation of the part he wanted to play in the business world. The president of a lumber company took Sam into the room, and, laying five one thousand dollar bills upon a table, walked to the window and stood looking out.

For a moment Sam stood looking at the money on the table and at the back of the man by the window, burning with indignation. He felt that he should like to take hold of the man's throat and press as he had once pressed on the throat of Windy McPherson. And then a cold gleam coming into his eyes he cleared his throat and said, "You are short here; you will have to build this pile higher if you expect to interest me."

The man by the window shrugged his shoulders—he was a slender, young-looking man in a fancy waistcoat—and then turning and taking a roll of bills from his pocket he walked to the table, facing Sam.

"I shall expect you to be reasonable," he said, as he laid the bills on the table.

When the pile had reached twenty thousand, Sam reached out his hand and taking it up put it in his pocket. "You will get a receipt for this when I get back to the office," he said; "it is about what you owe our company for overcharges and crooked material. As for our business, I made a contract with another company this morning."

Having got the buying end of the Rainey Arms Company straightened out to his liking, Sam began spending much time in the shops and, through Colonel Tom, forced big changes everywhere. He discharged useless foremen, knocked out partitions between rooms, pushed everywhere for more and better work. Like the modern efficiency man, he went about with a watch in his hand, cutting out lost motion, rearranging, getting his own way.

It was a time of great agitation. The offices and shops buzzed like bees disturbed and black looks followed him about. But Colonel Tom rose to the situation and went about at Sam's heels, swaggering, giving orders, throwing back his shoulders like a man remade. All day long he was at it, discharging, directing, roaring against waste. When a strike broke out in one of the shops because of innovations Sam had forced upon the workmen there, he got upon a bench and delivered a speech—written by Sam—on a man's place in the organisation and conducting of a great modern industry and his duty to perfect himself as a workman.

Silently, the men picked up their tools and started again for their benches and when he saw them thus affected by his words Colonel Tom brought what threatened to be a squally affair to a hurrahing climax by the announcement of a five per cent increase in the wage scale—that was Colonel Tom's own touch and the rousing reception of it brought a glow of pride to his cheeks.

Although the affairs of the company were still being handled by Colonel Tom, and though he daily more and more asserted himself, the officers and shops, and later the big jobbers and buyers as well as the rich LaSalle Street directors, knew that a new force had come into the company. Men began dropping quietly into Sam's office, asking questions, suggesting, seeking favours. He felt that he was getting hold. Of the department heads, about half fought him and were secretly marked for slaughter; the others came to him, expressed approval of what was going on and asked him to look over their departments and to make suggestions for improvements through them. This Sam did eagerly, getting by it their loyalty and support which later stood him in good stead.

In choosing the new men that came into the company Sam also took a hand. The method used was characteristic of his relations with Colonel Tom. If a man applying for a place suited him, he got admission to the colonel's office and listened for half an hour to a talk anent the fine old traditions of the company. If a man did not suit Sam, he did not get to the colonel. "You can't have your time taken up by them," Sam explained.

In the Rainey Company, the various heads of departments were stockholders in the company, and selected from among themselves two men to sit upon the board, and in his second year Sam was chosen as one of these employee directors. During the same year five heads of departments resigning in a moment of indignation over one of Sam's innovations—to be replaced later by two—their stock by a prearranged agreement came back into the company's hands. This stock and another block, secured for him by the colonel, got into Sam's hands through the use of Eckardt's money, that of the Wabash Avenue woman, and his own snug pile.

Sam was a growing force in the company. He sat on the board of directors, the recognised practical head of the business among its stockholders and employees; he had stopped the company's march toward a second place in its industry and had faced it about. All about him, in offices and shops, there was the swing and go of new life and he felt that he was in a position to move on toward real control and had begun laying lines with that end in view. Standing in the offices in LaSalle Street or amid the clang and roar of the shops he tilted up his chin with the same odd little gesture that had attracted the men of Caxton to him when he was a barefoot newsboy and the son of the town drunkard. Through his head went big ambitious projects. "I have in my hand a great tool," he thought; "with it I will pry my way into the place I mean to occupy among the big men of this city and this nation."

S am McPherson, who stood in the shops among the thousands of employees of the Rainey Arms Company, who looked with unseeing eyes at the faces of the men intent upon the operation of machines and saw in them but so many aids to the ambitious projects stirring in his brain, who, while yet a boy, had because of the quality of daring in him, combined with a gift of acquisitiveness, become a master, who was untrained, uneducated, knowing nothing of the history of industry or of social effort, walked out of the offices of his company and along through the crowded streets to the new apartment he had taken on Michigan Avenue. It was Saturday evening at the end of a busy week and as he walked he thought of things he had accomplished during the week and made plans for the one to come. Through Madison Street he went and into State, seeing the crowds of men and women, boys and girls, clambering aboard the cable cars, massed upon the pavements, forming in groups, the groups breaking and reforming, and the whole making a picture intense, confusing, awe-inspiring. As in the shops among the men workers, so here, also, walked the youth with unseeing eyes. He liked it all; the mass of people; the clerks in their cheap clothing; the old men with young girls on their arms going to dine in restaurants; the young man with a wistful look in his eyes waiting for his sweetheart in the shadow of the towering office building. The eager, straining rush of the whole, seemed no more to him than a kind of gigantic setting for action; action controlled by a few quiet, capable men—of whom he intended to be one—intent upon growth.

In State Street he stopped at a shop and buying a bunch of roses came out again upon the crowded street. In the crowd before him walked a woman—tall, freewalking, with a great mass of reddish-brown hair on her head. As she passed through the crowd men stopped and looked back at her, their eyes ablaze with admiration. Seeing her, Sam sprang forward with a cry.

"Edith!" he called, and running forward thrust the roses into her hand. "For Janet," he said, and lifting his hat walked beside her along State to Van Buren Street.

Leaving the woman at a corner Sam came into a region of cheap theatres and dingy hotels. Women spoke to him; young men in flashy overcoats and with a peculiar, assertive, animal swing to their shoulders loitered before the theatres or in the doorways of the hotels; from an upstairs restaurant came the voice of another young man singing a popular song of the street. "There'll be a hot time in the old town tonight," sang the voice.

Over a cross street Sam went into Michigan Avenue, faced by a long narrow park and beyond the railroad tracks by the piles of new earth where the city was trying to regain its lake front. In the cross street, standing in the shadow of the elevated railroad, he had passed a whining, intoxicated old woman who lurched forward and put a hand upon his coat. Sam had flung her a quarter and passed on shrugging his shoulders. Here also he had walked with unseeing eyes; this too was a part of the gigantic machine with which the quiet, competent men of growth worked.

From his new quarters in the top floor of the hotel facing the lake, Sam walked north along Michigan Avenue to a restaurant where Negro men went noiselessly about among white-clad tables, serving men and women who talked and laughed under the shaded lamps had an assured, confident air. Passing in at the door of the restaurant, a wind, blowing over the city toward the lake, brought the sound of a voice floating with it. "There'll be a hot time in the old town tonight," again insisted the voice.

After dining Sam got on a grip car of the Wabash Avenue Cable, sitting on the front seat and letting the panorama of the town roll up to him. From the region of cheap theatres he passed through streets in which saloons stood massed, one beside another, each with its wide garish doorway and its dimly lighted "Ladies' Entrance," and into a region of neat little stores where women with baskets upon their arms stood by the counters and Sam was reminded of Saturday nights in Caxton.

The two women, Edith and Janet Eberly, met through Jack Prince, to one of whom Sam had sent the roses at the hands of the other, and from whom he had borrowed the six thousand dollars when he was new in the city, had been in Chicago for five years when Sam came to know them. For all of the five years they had lived in a two-story frame building that had been a residence in Wabash Avenue near Thirty-ninth Street and that was now both a residence and a grocery store. The apartment upstairs, reached by a stairway at the side of the grocery, had in the five years, and under the hand of Janet Eberly, become a thing of beauty, perfect in the simplicity and completeness of its appointment.

The two women were the daughters of a farmer who had lived in one of the middle western states facing the Mississippi River. Their grandfather had been a noted man in the state, having been one of its first governors and later serving it in the senate in Washington. There was a county and a good-sized town named for him and he had once been talked of as a vice-presidential possibility but had died at Washington before the convention at which his name was to have been put forward. His one son, a youth of great promise, went to West Point and served brilliantly through the Civil War, afterward commanding several western army posts and marrying the daughter of another army man. His wife, an army belle, died after having borne him the two daughters.

After the death of his wife Major Eberly began drinking, and to get away from the habit and from the army atmosphere where he had lived with his wife, whom he loved intensely, took the two little girls and returned to his home state to settle on a farm.

About the county where the two girls grew to womanhood, their father, Major Eberly, got the name of a character, seeing people but seldom and treating rudely the friendly advances of his farmer neighbours. He would sit in the house for days poring over books, of which he had a great many, and hundreds of which were now on open shelves in the apartment of the two girls. These days of study, during which he would brook no intrusion, were followed by days of fierce industry during which he led team after team to the field, ploughing or reaping day and night with no rest except to eat.

At the edge of the Eberly farm there was a little wooden country church surrounded by a hay field, and on Sunday mornings during the summer the ex-army man was always to be found in the field, running some noisy, clattering agricultural implement up and down under the windows of the church and disturbing the worship of the country folk; in the winter he drew a pile of logs there and went on Sunday mornings to split firewood under the church windows. While his daughters were small he was several times haled into court and fined for cruel neglect of his animals. Once he locked a great herd of fine sheep in a shed and went into the house and stayed for days intent upon his books so that many of them suffered cruelly for want of food and water. When he was taken into court and fined, half the county came to the trial and gloated over his humiliation.

To the two girls the father was neither cruel nor kind, leaving them largely to themselves but giving them no money, so that they went about in dresses made over from those of the mother, that lay piled in trunks in the attic. When they were small, an old Negro woman, an ex-servant of the army belle, lived with and mothered them, but when Edith was a girl of ten this woman went off home to Tennessee, so that the girls were thrown on their own resources and ran the house in their own way.

Janet Eberly was, at the beginning of her friendship with Sam, a slight woman of twenty-seven with a small expressive face, quick nervous fingers, black piercing eyes, black hair and a way of becoming so absorbed in the exposition of a book or the rush of a conversation that her little intense face became transfigured and her quick fingers clutched the arm of her listener while her eyes looked into his and she lost all consciousness of his presence or of the opinions he may have expressed. She was a cripple, having fallen from the loft of a barn in her youth injuring her back so that she sat all day in a specially made reclining wheeled chair.

Edith was a stenographer, working in the office of a publisher down town, and Janet trimmed hats for a milliner a few doors down the street from the house in which they lived. In his will the father left the money from the sale of the farm to Janet, and Sam used it, insuring his life for ten thousand dollars in her name while it was in his possession and handling it with a caution entirely absent from his operations with the money of the medical student. "Take it and make money for me," the little woman had said impulsively one evening shortly after the beginning of their acquaintance and after Jack Prince had been talking flamboyantly of Sam's ability in affairs. "What is the good of having a talent if you do not use it to benefit those who haven't it?"

Janet Eberly was an intellect. She disregarded all the usual womanly points of view and had an attitude of her own toward life and people. In a way she had understood her hard-driven, grey-haired father and during the time of her great physical suffering they had built up a kind of understanding and affection for each other. After his death she wore a miniature of him, made in his boyhood, on a chain about her neck. When Sam met her the two immediately became close friends, sitting for hours in talk and coming to look forward with great pleasure to the evenings spent together.

In the Eberly household Sam McPherson was a benefactor, a wonder-worker. In his hands the six thousand dollars was bringing two thousand a year into the house and adding immeasurably to the air of comfort and good living that prevailed there. To Janet, who managed the house, he was guide, counsellor, and something more than friend.

Of the two women it was the strong, vigorous Edith, with the reddish-brown hair and the air of physical completeness that made men stop to look at her on the street, who first became Sam's friend.

Edith Eberly was strong of body, given to quick flashes of anger, stupid intellectually and hungry to the roots of her for wealth and a place in the world. She had heard, through Jack Prince, of Sam's money making and of his ability and prospects and, for a time, had designs upon his affections. Several times when they were alone together she gave his hand a characteristically impulsive squeeze and once upon the stairway beside the grocery store offered him her lips to kiss. Later there sprang up between her and Jack Prince a passionate love affair, dropped finally by Prince through fear of her violent fits of anger. After Sam had met Janet Eberly and had become her loyal friend and henchman all show of affection or even of interest between him and Edith was at an end and the kiss upon the stairs was forgotten.

GOING UP THE STAIRWAY AFTER the ride in the cable car Sam stood beside Janet's wheel chair in the room at the front of the apartment facing Wabash Avenue. The chair was by the window and faced an open coal fire in a grate she had had built into the wall of the house. Outside, through an open arched doorway, Edith moved noiselessly about taking dishes from a little table. He knew that after a time Jack Prince would come and take her to the theatre, leaving Janet and him to finish their talk.

Sam lighted his pipe and between puffs began talking, making a statement that he knew would arouse her, and Janet, putting her hand impulsively on his shoulder, began tearing the statement to bits.

"You talk!" she broke out. "Books are not full of pretence and lies; you business men are—you and Jack Prince. What do you know of books? They are the most wonderful things in the world. Men sit writing them and forget to lie, but you business men never forget. You and books! You haven't read books, not real ones. Didn't my father know; didn't he save himself from insanity through books? Do I not, sitting here, get the real feel of the movement of the world through the books that men write? Suppose I saw those men. They would swagger and strut and take themselves seriously just like you or Jack or the grocer down stairs. You think you know what's going on in the world. You think you are doing things, you Chicago men of money and action and growth. You are blind, all blind."

The little woman, a light, half scorn, half amusement in her eyes, leaned forward and ran her fingers through Sam's hair, laughing down into the astonished face he turned up to her.

"Oh, I'm not afraid, in spite of what Edith and Jack Prince say of you," she went on impulsively. "I like you all right and if I were a well woman I should make love to you and marry you and then see to it there was something in this world for you besides money and tall buildings and men and machines that make guns."

Sam grinned. "You are like your father, driving the mowing machine up and down under the church windows on Sunday mornings," he declared; "you think you could remake the world by shaking your fist at it. I should like to go and see you fined in a court room for starving sheep."

Janet, closing her eyes and lying back in her chair, laughed with delight and declared that they would have a splendid quarrelsome evening.

After Edith had gone out, Sam sat through the evening with Janet, listening to her exposition of life and what she thought it should mean to a strong capable fellow like himself, as he had been listening ever since their acquaintanceship began. In the talk, and in the many talks they had had together, talks that rang in his ears for years, the little black-eyed woman gave him a glimpse into a whole purposeful universe of thought and action of which he had never dreamed, introducing him to a new world of men: methodical, hard-thinking Germans, emotional, dreaming Russians, analytical, courageous Norwegians, Spaniards and Italians with their sense of beauty, and blundering, hopeful Englishmen wanting so much and getting so little; so that at the end of the evening he went out of her presence feeling strangely small and insignificant against the great world background she had drawn for him.

Sam did not understand Janet's point of view. It was all too new and foreign to everything life had taught him, and in his mind he fought her ideas doggedly, clinging to his own concrete, practical thoughts and hopes, but on the train homeward bound, and in his own room later, he turned over and over in his mind the things she had said and tried in a dim way to grasp the bigness of the conception of human life she had got sitting in a wheel chair and looking down into Wabash Avenue.

Sam loved Janet Eberly. No word of that had ever passed between them and he had seen her hand flash out and grasp the shoulder of Jack

Prince when she was laying down to him some law of life as she saw it, as it had so often shot out and grasped his own, but had she been able to spring out of the wheel chair he should have taken her hand and gone with her to the clergyman within the hour and in his heart he knew that she would have gone with him gladly.

Janet died suddenly during the second year of Sam's work for the gun company without a direct declaration of affection from him, but during the years when they were much together he thought of her as in a sense his wife and when she died he was desolate, overdrinking night after night and wandering aimlessly through the deserted streets during hours when he should have been asleep. She was the first woman who ever got hold of and stirred his manhood, and she awoke something in him that made it possible for him later to see life with a broadness and scope of vision that was no part of the pushing, energetic young man of dollars and of industry who sat beside her wheeled chair during the evenings on Wabash Avenue.

After Janet's death, Sam did not continue his friendship with Edith, but turned over to her the ten thousand dollars to which the six thousand of Janet's money had grown in his hands and did not see her again.

IV

One night in April Colonel Tom Rainey of the great Rainey Arms Company and his chief lieutenant, young Sam McPherson, treasurer and chairman of the board of directors of the company, slept together in a room in a St. Paul hotel. It was a double room with two beds, and Sam, lying on his pillow, looked across the bed to where the colonel's paunch protruding itself between him and the light from a long narrow window, made a round hill above which the moon just peeped. During the evening the two men had sat for several hours at a table in the grill down stairs while Sam discussed a proposition he proposed making to a St. Paul jobber the next day. The account of the jobber, a large one, had been threatened by Lewis, the Jew manager of the Edwards Arms Company, the Rainey Company's only important western rival, and Sam was full of ideas to checkmate the shrewd trade move the Jew had made. At the table, the colonel had been silent and taciturn, an unusual attitude of mind for him, and Sam lay in bed and looked at the moon gradually working its way over the undulating abdominal hill, wondering what was in his mind. The hill dropped, showing the full face of the moon, and then rose again obliterating it.

"Sam, were you ever in love?" asked the colonel, with a sigh.

Sam turned and buried his face in the pillow and the white covering of his bed danced up and down. "The old fool, has it come to that with him?" he asked himself. "After all these years of single life is he going to begin running after women now?"

He did not answer the colonel's question. "There are breakers ahead for you, old boy," he thought, the figure of quiet, determined, little Sue Rainey, the colonel's daughter, as he had seen her on the rare occasions when he had dined at the Rainey home or she had come into the LaSalle Street offices, coming into his mind. With a quiver of enjoyment of the mental exercise, he tried to imagine the colonel as a swaggering blade among women.

The colonel, oblivious of Sam's mirth and of his silence regarding his experience in the field of love, began talking, making amends for the silence in the grill. He told Sam that he had decided to take to himself a new wife, and confessed that the view of the matter his daughter might take worried him. "Children are so unfair," he complained; "they forget about a man's feelings and can't realise that his heart is still young."

With a smile on his lips, Sam began trying to picture a woman's lying in his place and looking at the moon over the pulsating hill. The colonel continued talking. He grew franker, telling the name of his beloved and the circumstances of their meeting and courtship. "She is an actress, a working girl," he said feelingly. "I met her at a dinner given by Will Sperry one evening and she was the only woman there who did not drink wine. After the dinner we went for a drive together and she told me of her hard life, of her fight against temptations, and of her brother, an artist, she is trying to get started in the world. We have been together a dozen times and have written letters, and, Sam, we have discovered an affinity for each other."

Sam sat up in bed. "Letters!" he muttered. "The old dog is going to get himself involved." He dropped again upon the pillow. "Well, let him. Why need I bother myself?"

The colonel, having begun talking, could not stop. "Although we have seen each other only a dozen times, a letter has passed between us every day. Oh, if you could see the letters she writes. They are wonderful."

A worried sigh broke from the colonel. "I want Sue to invite her to the house, but I am afraid," he complained; "I am afraid she will be wrong-headed about it. Women are such determined creatures. She and my Luella should meet and know each other, but if I go home and tell her she may make a scene and hurt Luella's feelings."

The moon had risen, shedding its light in Sam's eyes, and he turned his back to the colonel and prepared to sleep. The naive credulity of the older man had touched a spring of mirth in him and from time to time the covering of his bed continued to quiver suggestively.

"I would not hurt her feelings for anything. She is the squarest little woman alive," the voice of the colonel announced. The voice broke and the colonel, who habitually roared forth his sentiments, began to dither. Sam wondered if his feelings had been touched by the thoughts of his daughter or of the lady from the stage. "It is a wonderful thing," half sobbed the colonel, "when a young and beautiful woman gives her whole heart into the keeping of a man like me."

It was a week later before Sam heard more of the affair. Looking up from his desk in the offices in LaSalle Street one morning, he found Sue Rainey standing before him. She was a small athletic looking woman with black hair, square shoulders, cheeks browned by the sun and wind, and quiet grey eyes. She stood facing Sam's desk and pulled off a glove while she looked down at him with amused, quizzical eyes. Sam rose, and leaning over the flat-topped desk, took her hand, wondering what had brought her there.

Sue Rainey did not mince matters, but plunged at once into an explanation of the purpose of her visit. From birth she had lived in an atmosphere of wealth. Although she was not counted a beautiful woman, she had, because of her wealth and the charm of her person, been much courted. Sam, who had talked briefly with her a half dozen times, had long had a haunting curiosity to know more of her personality. As she stood there before him looking so wonderfully well-kept and confident he thought her baffling and puzzling.

"The colonel," she began, and then hesitated and smiled. "You, Mr. McPherson, have become a figure in my father's life. He depends upon you very much. He tells me that he has talked with you concerning a Miss Luella London from the theatre, and that you have agreed with him that the colonel and she should marry."

Sam watched her gravely. A flicker of mirth ran through him, but his face was grave and disinterested.

"Yes?" he said, looking into her eyes. "Have you met Miss London?"

"I have," answered Sue Rainey. "Have you?"

Sam shook his head.

"She is impossible," declared the colonel's daughter, clutching the glove held in her hand and staring at the floor. A flush of anger rose in her cheeks. "She is a crude, hard, scheming woman. She colours her hair, she cries when you look at her, she hasn't even the grace to be ashamed of what she is trying to do, and she has got the colonel into a fix."

Sam looked at the brown of Sue Rainey's cheek and thought the texture of it beautiful. He wondered why he had heard her called a plain woman. The heightened colour brought to her face by her anger had, he thought, transfigured her. He liked her direct, forceful way of putting the matter of the colonel's affair, and felt keenly the compliment implied by her having come to him. "She has self-respect," he told himself, and felt a thrill of pride in her attitude as though it had been inspired by himself.

"I have been hearing of you a great deal," she continued, glancing up at him and smiling. "At our house you are brought to the table with the soup and taken away with the liqueur. My father interlards his table talk, and introduces all of his wise new axioms on economy and efficiency and growth, with a constant procession of 'Sam says' and 'Sam thinks.'

And the men who come to the house talk of you also. Teddy Foreman says that at directors' meetings they all sit about like children waiting for you to tell them what to do."

She threw out her hand with an impatient little gesture. "I am in a hole," she said. "I might handle my father but I cannot handle that woman."

While she had been talking to him Sam looked past her and out at a window. When her eyes wandered from his face he looked again at her brown firm cheeks. From the beginning of the interview he had been intending to help her.

"Give me the lady's address," he said; "I'll go look her over."

Three evenings later Sam took Miss Luella London to a midnight supper at one of the town's best restaurants. She knew the motive of his taking her, as he had been quite frank in the few minutes' talk near the stage door of the theatre when the engagement was made. As they ate, they talked of the plays at the Chicago theatres, and Sam told her a story of an amateur performance that had once taken place in the hall over Geiger's drug store in Caxton when he was boy. In the performance Sam had taken the rôle of a drummer boy killed on the field of battle by a swaggering villain in a grey uniform, and John Telfer, in the rôle of villain, had become so in earnest that, a pistol not exploding at a critical moment, he had chased Sam about the stage trying to hit him with the butt of the weapon while the audience roared with delight at the realism of Telfer's rage and at the frightened boy begging for mercy.

Luella London laughed heartily at Sam's story and then, the coffee being served, she fingered the handle of the cup and a shrewd look came into her eyes.

"And now you are a big business man and have come to see me about Colonel Rainey," she said.

Sam lighted a cigar.

"Just how much are you counting on this marriage between yourself and the colonel?" he asked bluntly.

The actress laughed and poured cream into her coffee. A line came and went on her forehead between her eyes. Sam thought she looked capable.

"I have been thinking of what you told me at the stage door," she said, and a childlike smile played about her lips. "Do you know, Mr. McPherson, I can't just figure you. I can't just see how you get into this. Where are your credentials, anyway?"

Sam, keeping his eyes upon her face, took a jump into the dark.

"It's this way," he said, "I'm something of an adventurer myself. I fly the black flag. I come from where you do. I had to reach out my hand and take what I wanted. I do not blame you in the least, but it just happens that I saw Colonel Tom Rainey first. He is my game and I do not propose to have you fooling around. I am not bluffing. You have got to get off him."

Leaning forward, he stared at her intently, and then lowered his voice. "I've got your record. I know the man you used to live with. He's going to help me get you if you do not drop it."

Sitting back in his chair Sam watched her gravely. He had taken the odd chance to win quickly by a bluff and had won. But Luella London was not to be defeated without a struggle.

"You lie," she cried, half springing from her chair. "Frank has never—"

"Oh yes, Frank has," answered Sam, turning as though to call a waiter; "I will have him here in ten minutes if you wish to be shown."

Picking up a fork the woman began nervously picking holes in the table cloth and a tear appeared upon her cheek. She took a handkerchief from a bag that hung hooked over the back of a chair at the side of the table and wiped her eyes.

"All right! All right!" she said, bracing herself, "I'll drop it. If you've dug up Frank Robson you've got me. He'll do anything you say for a piece of money."

For some minutes the two sat in silence. A tired look had come into the woman's eyes.

"I wish I was a man," she said. "I get whipped at everything I tackle because I'm a woman. I'm getting past my money-making days in the theatre and I thought the colonel was fair game."

"He is," answered Sam dispassionately, "but you see I beat you to it. He's mine."

Glancing cautiously about the room, he took a roll of bills from his pocket and began laying them one at a time upon the table.

"Look here," he said, "you've done a good piece of work. You should have won. For ten years half the society women of Chicago have been trying to marry their daughters or their sons to the Rainey fortune. They had everything to help them, wealth, good looks, and a standing in the world. You have none of these things. How did you do it?

"Anyway," he went on, "I'm not going to see you trimmed. I've got ten thousand dollars here, as good Rainey money as ever was printed. You sign this paper and then put the roll in your purse."

"That's square," said Luella London, signing, and with the light coming back into her eyes.

Sam beckoned to the proprietor of the restaurant whom he knew and had him and a waiter sign as witnesses.

Luella London put the roll of bills into her purse.

"What did you give me that money for when you had me beat anyway?" she asked.

Sam lighted a fresh cigar and folding the paper put it in his pocket.

"Because I like you and I admire your skill," he said, "and anyway I did not have you beaten until right now."

They sat studying the people getting up from the tables and going through the door to waiting carriages and automobiles, the well-dressed women with assured airs serving Sam's mind to make a contrast for the woman who sat with him.

"I presume you are right about women," he said musingly, "it must be a stiff game for you if you like winning on your own hook."

"Winning! We don't win." The lips of the actress drew back showing her white teeth. "No woman ever won who tried to play a straight fighting game for herself."

Her voice grew tense and the lines upon her forehead reappeared.

"Woman can't stand alone," she went on, "she is a sentimental fool. She reaches out her hand to some man and that in the end beats her. Why, even when she plays the game as I played it against the colonel some rat of a man like Frank Robson, for whom she has given up everything worth while to a woman, sells her out."

Sam looked at her hand, covered with rings, lying on the table.

"Let's not misunderstand each other," he said quietly, "do not blame Frank for this. I never knew him. I just imagined him."

A puzzled look came into the woman's eyes and a flush rose in her cheeks.

"You grafter!" she sneered.

Sam called to a passing waiter and ordered a fresh bottle of wine.

"What's the use being sore?" he asked. "It's simple enough. You staked against a better mind. Anyway you have the ten thousand, haven't you?"

Luella reached for her purse.

"I don't know," she said, "I'll look. Haven't you decided to steal it back yet?"

Sam laughed.

"I'm coming to that," he said, "don't hurry me."

For several minutes they sat eyeing each other, and then, with an earnest ring in his voice and a smile on his lips, Sam began talking again.

"Look here!" he said, "I'm no Frank Robson and I do not like giving a woman the worst of it. I have been studying you and I can't see you running around loose with ten thousand dollars of real money on you. You do not fit into the picture and the money will not last a year in your hands.

"Give it to me," he urged; "let me invest it for you. I'm a winner. I'll double it for you in a year."

The actress stared past Sam's shoulder to where a group of young men sat about a table drinking and talking loudly. Sam began telling an anecdote of an Irish baggage man in Caxton. When he had finished he looked at her and laughed.

"As that shoemaker looked to Jerry Donlin so you, as the colonel's wife, looked to me," he said. "I had to make you get out of my flower bed."

A gleam of resolution came into the wandering eyes of Luella London and she took the purse from the back of the chair and brought out the roll of bills.

"I'm a sport," she said, "and I'm going to lay a bet on the best horse I ever saw. You may trim me, but I always would take a chance."

Turning, she called a waiter and, handing him a bill from her purse, threw the roll on the table.

"Take the pay for the spread and the wine we have had out of that," she said, handing him the loose bill and then turning to Sam. "You ought to beat the world. Anyway your genius gets recognition from me. I pay for this party and when you see the colonel say good-bye to him for me."

The next day, at his request, Sue Rainey called at the offices of the Arms Company and Sam handed her the paper signed by Luella London. It was an agreement on her part to divide with Sam, half and half, any money she might be able to blackmail out of Colonel Rainey.

The colonel's daughter glanced from the paper to Sam's face.

"I thought so," she said, and a puzzled look came into her eyes. "But I do not understand this. What does this paper do and what did you pay for it?"

"The paper," Sam answered, "puts her in a hole and I paid ten thousand dollars for it."

Suc Rainey laughed and taking a checkbook from her handbag laid it on the desk and sat down.

"Do you get your half?" she asked.

"I get it all," answered Sam, and then leaning back in his chair launched into an explanation. When he had told her of the talk in the restaurant she sat with the checkbook lying before her and with the puzzled look still in her eyes.

Without giving her time for comment, Sam plunged into the midst of what had been in his mind to say to her.

"The woman will not bother the colonel any more," he declared; "if that paper won't hold her something else will. She respects me and she is afraid of me. We had a talk after she had signed the paper and she gave me the ten thousand dollars to invest for her. I promised to double it for her within a year and I want to make good. I want you to double it now. Make the check for twenty thousand."

Sue Rainey wrote the check, making it payable to bearer, and pushed it across the table.

"I cannot say that I understand yet," she confessed. "Did you also fall in love with her?"

Sam grinned. He was wondering whether he would be able to get into words just what he wanted to tell her of the actress soldier of fortune. He looked across the table at her frank grey eyes and then on an impulse decided that he would tell it straight out as though she had been a man.

"It's like this," he said. "I like ability and good brains and that woman has them. She isn't a good woman, but nothing in her life has made her want to be good. All her life she has been going the wrong way, and now she wants to get on her feet and squared around. That's what she was after the colonel for. She did not want to marry him, she wanted to make him give her the start she was after. I got the best of her because somewhere there is a snivelling little whelp of a man who has taken all the good and the fineness out of her and who now stands ready to sell her out for a few dollars. I imagined there would be such a man when I saw her and I bluffed my way through to him. But I do not want to whip a woman, even in such an affair, through the cheapness of some man. I want to do the square thing by her. That's why I asked you to make that check for twenty thousand."

Sue Rainey rose and stood by the desk looking down at him. He was thinking how wonderfully clear and honest her eyes.

"And what about the colonel?" she asked. "What will he think of all this?"

Sam walked around the desk and took her hand.

"We'll have to agree not to consider him," he said. "We really did that you know when we started this thing. I think we can depend upon Miss London's putting the finishing touches on the job."

And Miss London did. She sent for Sam a week later and put tweny-five hundred dollars into his hand.

"That's not to invest for me," she said, "that's for yourself. By the agreement I signed with you we were to split anything I got out of the colonel. Well, I went light. I only got five thousand dollars."

With the money in his hand Sam stood by the side of a little table in her room looking at her.

"What did you tell the colonel?" he asked.

"I called him up here to my room last night and lying here in bed I told him that I had just discovered I was the victim of an incurable disease. I told him that within a month I would be in bed for keeps and asked him to marry me at once and to take me away with him to some quiet place where I could die in his arms."

Coming over to Sam, Luella London put a hand upon his arm and laughed.

"He began to beg off and make excuses," she went on, "and then I brought out his letters to me and talked straight. He wilted at once and paid the five thousand dollars I asked for the letters without a murmur. I might have made it fifty and with your talent you ought to get all he has in six months."

Sam shook hands with her and told her of his success in doubling the money she had put into his hands. Then putting the twenty-five hundred dollars in his pocket he went back to his desk. He did not see her again and when, through a lucky market turn, he had increased the twenty thousand dollars she had left with him to twenty-five, he placed it in the hands of a trust company for her and forgot the incident. Years later he heard that she was running a fashionable dressmaking establishment in a western city.

And Colonel Tom Rainey, who had for months talked of nothing but factory efficiency and of what he and young Sam McPherson were going to do in the way of enlarging the business, began the next morning a tirade against women that lasted the rest of his life.

V

S ue Rainey had long touched the fancy of the youths of Chicago society who, while looking at her trim little figure and at the respectable size of the fortune behind it, were yet puzzled and disconcerted by her attitude toward themselves. On the wide porches at golf clubs, where young men in white trousers lounged and smoked cigarettes, and in the down-town clubs, where the same young men spent winter afternoons playing Kelly pool, they spoke of her, calling her an enigma. "She'll end by being an old maid," they declared, and shook their heads at the thought of so good a connection dangling loosely in the air just without their reach. From time to time, one of the young men tore himself loose from the group that contemplated her, and, with an opening volley of books, candy, flowers and invitations to theatres, charged down upon her, only to have the youthful ardour of his attack cooled by her prolonged attitude of indifference. When she was twenty-one, a young English cavalry officer, who came to Chicago to ride in the horse show had, for some weeks, been seen much in her company and a report of their engagement had been whispered through the town and talked of about the nineteenth hole at the country clubs. The rumour proved to be without foundation, the attraction to the cavalry officer having been a certain brand of rare old wine the colonel had stored in his cellar and a feeling of brotherhood with the swaggering old gun maker, rather than the colonel's quiet little daughter.

After the beginning of his acquaintanceship with her, and all during the days when he stirred things up in the offices and shops of the gun company, tales of the assiduous and often needy young men who were camped on her trail reached Sam's ears. They would be in at the office to see and talk with the colonel, who had several times confided to Sam that his daughter Sue was already past the age at which right-minded young women should marry, and in the absence of the father two or three of them had formed a habit of stopping for a word with Sam, whom they had met through the colonel or Jack Prince. They declared that they were "squaring themselves with the colonel." Not a difficult thing to do, Sam thought, as he drank the wine, smoked the cigars, and ate the dinners of all without prejudice. Once, at luncheon, Colonel Tom discussed these young men with Sam, pounding on a table so that the glasses jumped about, and calling them damned upstarts.

For his own part, Sam did not feel that he knew Sue Rainey, and although, after their first meeting one evening at the Rainey house, he had been pricked by a mild curiosity concerning her, no opportunity to satisfy it had presented itself. He knew that she was athletic, travelled much, rode, shot, and sailed a boat; and he had heard Jack Prince speak of her as a woman of brains, but, until the incident of the colonel and Luella London threw them for the moment into the same enterprise and started him thinking of her with real interest, he had seen and talked with her for but brief passing moments brought about by their mutual interest in the affairs of her father.

After Janet Eberly's sudden death, and while he was yet in the midst of his grief at her loss, Sam had his first long talk with Sue Rainey. It was in Colonel Tom's office, and Sam, walking hurriedly in, found her sitting at the colonel's desk and staring out of the window at a broad expanse of flat roofs. A man, climbing a flag pole to replace a slipped rope, caught his attention and standing by the window looking at the minute figure clinging to the swaying pole, he began talking of the absurdity of human endeavour.

The colonel's daughter listened respectfully to his rather obvious banalities and getting up from her chair came to stand beside him. Sam turned slyly to look at her firm brown cheeks as he had looked on the morning when she had come to see him about Luella London and was struck by the thought that she in some faint way reminded him of Janet Eberly. In a moment, and rather to his own surprise, he burst into a long speech telling of Janet, of the tragedy of her loss and something of the beauty of her life and character.

The nearness of his loss and the nearness also of what he thought might be a sympathetic listener spurred him and he found himself getting a kind of relief for the aching sense of loss for his dead comrade by heaping praises upon her life.

When he had finished saying what was in his mind, he stood by the window feeling awkward and embarrassed. The man who climbed the flag pole having put the rope through the ring at the top slid suddenly down the pole and thinking for the moment that he had fallen Sam made a quick clutch at the air with his hand. His gripping fingers closed over Sue Rainey's hand.

He turned, amused by the incident, and began making a halting explanation. There were tears in Sue Rainey's eyes.

"I wish I had known her," she said and drew her hand from between his fingers. "I wish you had known me better that I also might have known your Janet. They are rare—such women. They are worth much to know. Most women like most men—"

She made an impatient gesture with her hand and Sam, turning, walked toward the door. He felt that he might not trust himself to answer her. For the first time since coming to manhood he felt that tears might at any moment come into his eyes. Grief for the loss of Janet surged through him disconcerting and engulfing him.

"I have been doing you an injustice," said Sue Rainey, looking at the floor. "I have thought of you as something different from what you are. There is a story I heard of you which gave me a wrong impression."

Sam smiled. Having conquered the commotion within himself, he laughed and explained the incident of the man who had slid down the pole.

"What was the story you heard?" he asked.

"It was a story a young man told at our house," she explained hesitatingly, refusing to be carried away from her mood of seriousness. "It was about a little girl you saved from drowning and a purse made up and given you. Why did you take the money?"

Sam looked at her squarely. The story was one that Jack Prince had delight in telling. It concerned an incident of his early business life in the city.

One afternoon, when he was still in the employ of the commission firm, he had taken a party of men for a trip on an excursion steamer on the lake. He had a project into which he wanted them to go with him and had taken them aboard the steamer to get them together and present the merits of his scheme. During the trip a little girl had fallen overboard and Sam, springing after her, had brought her safely aboard the boat.

On the excursion steamer a cheer had arisen. A young man in a broad-brimmed cowboy hat ran about taking up a collection. People crowded forward to grasp Sam's hand and he had accepted the money collected and had put it in his pocket.

Among the men aboard the boat were several who, while they did not draw back from going into Sam's project, had thought his taking the money not manly. They had told the story, and it had come to the ears of Jack Prince, who never tired of repeating it and always ended the story with the request that the listener ask Sam why he had taken the money.

Now in Colonel Tom's office facing Sue Rainey, Sam made the explanation that had so delighted Jack Prince.

"The crowd wanted to give me the money," he said, slightly perplexed. "Why shouldn't I have taken it? I did not save the little girl for the money, but because she was a little girl; and the money paid for my ruined clothes and the expenses of the trip."

With his hand on the doorknob he looked steadily at the woman before him.

"And I wanted the money," he announced, a ring of defiance in his voice. "I have always wanted money, any money I could get."

Sam went back to his own office and sat down at his desk. He had been surprised by the cordiality and friendliness Sue Rainey had shown toward him. On an impulse, he wrote a letter, defending his position in the matter of the money taken on the excursion steamer and setting forth something of the attitude of his mind toward money and business affairs.

"I cannot see myself believing in the rot most business men talk," he wrote at the end of the letter. "They are full of sentiment and ideals which are not true. Having a thing to sell they always say it is the best, although it may be third rate. I do not object to that. What I do object to is the way they have of nursing a hope within themselves that the third rate thing is first rate until the hope becomes a belief. In the talk I had with that actress Luella London I told her that I myself flew the black flag. Well, I do. I would lie about goods to sell them, but I would not lie to myself. I will not stultify my own mind. If a man crosses swords with me in a business deal and I come out of the affair with the money, it is no sign that I am the greater rascal, rather it is a sign that I am the keener man."

With the note lying before him on the desk Sam wondered why he had written it. It seemed to him an accurate and straightforward statement of the business creed he had adopted for himself, but a rather absurd note to write to a woman. And then, not allowing himself time to reconsider his action, he addressed an envelope and going out into the general offices dropped it into the mail chute.

"It will let her know where I stand anyway," he thought, with a return of the defiant mood in which he had told her the motive of his action on the boat.

Within the next ten days after the talk in Colonel Tom's office Sam saw Sue Rainey several times coming to or going from her father's office. Once, meeting in the little lobby by the office entrance, she stopped and put out her hand which Sam took awkwardly. He had a feeling that she would not have regretted an opportunity to continue the sudden little intimacy that had sprung up between them in the few minutes' talk of Janet Eberly. The feeling did not come from vanity but from a belief in Sam that she was in some way lonely and wanting companionship. Although she had been much courted she lacked, he thought, the talent for comradeship or quick friendliness. "Like Janet she is more than half intellect," he told himself, and felt a pang of regret for the slight disloyalty of the further thought that there was in Sue a something more substantial and solid than there had been in Janet.

Suddenly Sam began wondering whether or not he would like to marry Sue Rainey. His mind played with the idea. He took it with him to bed, and it went with him all day in his hurried trips through offices and shops. The thought having come to him persisted, and he began seeing her in a new light. The odd half awkward little movements of her hands, and their expressiveness, the brown fine texture of her cheeks, the clearness and honesty of her grey eyes, the quick sympathy and understanding of his feeling for Janet, and the subtle flattery of the notion he had got that she was interested in him—all of these things came and went in his mind while he ran through columns of figures and laid plans for the expansion of the business of the Arms Company. Unconsciously he began to make her a part of his plans for the future.

Later, Sam discovered that during the days after the first talk together the thought of a marriage between them was in Sue's mind also. After the talk she went home and stood for an hour before the glass studying herself and she once told Sam that in her bed that night she shed tears because she had never been able to arouse in a man the note of tenderness that had been in his voice when he talked to her of Janet.

And then two months after the first talk they had another. Sam, who had not allowed his grief over the loss of Janet or his nightly efforts to drown the sting of it in hard drinking, to check the big forward movement that he felt he was getting into the work of the offices and shops, sat one afternoon deeply absorbed in a pile of factory cost sheets. His shirt sleeves were rolled to the elbow, showing his white muscular forearms. He was absorbed, intent upon the sheets.

"I stepped in," said a voice above his head.

Glancing up quickly, Sam sprang to his feet. "She must have been there some minutes looking down at me," he thought, and had a thrill of pleasure in the thought.

Into his mind came the contents of the letter he had written her, and he wondered if after all he had been a fool, and whether the thoughts of a marriage with her were but vagaries. "Perhaps it would not be attractive to either her or myself when we came up to it," he decided.

"I stepped in," she began again. "I have been thinking. Some things you said—in the letter and when you talked of your friend Janet who died—some things of men and women and work. You may not remember them. I—I got interested. I—are you a socialist?"

"I believe not," Sam answered, wondering what had given her that thought. "Are you?"

'She laughed and shook her head.

"Just what are you?" she went on. "What do you believe? I am curious to know. I thought your note—you will pardon me—I thought it a kind of pretence."

Sam winced. A shadow of doubt of the sincerity of his business philosophy crossed his mind accompanied by the swaggering figure of Windy McPherson. He came around the desk and leaning against it looked at her. His secretary had gone out of the room and they were alone together. Sam laughed.

"There was a man in the town where I was raised used to say that I was a little mole working underground, intent upon worms," he said, and then, waving his arms toward the papers on the desk, added, "I am a business man. Isn't that enough? If you could go with me through some of these cost sheets you would agree they are needed."

He turned and faced her again.

"What should I be doing with beliefs?" he asked.

"Well, I think you have them—some kind of beliefs," she insisted, "you must have them. You get things done. You should hear the men talk of you. Sometimes at the house they are quite foolish about what a wonderful fellow you are and what you are doing here. They say that you drive on and on. What drives you? I want to know."

For the moment Sam half suspected that she was secretly laughing at him. Finding her quite serious he started to reply and then stopped, regarding her.

The silence between them went on and on. A clock on the wall ticked loudly.

Sam stepped nearer to her and stood looking down into the face she slowly turned up to his.

"I want to have a talk with you," he said, and his voice broke. He had the illusion of a hand gripping at his throat.

In a flash he had definitely decided that he would try to marry her. Her interest in the motives of his life had clinched the sort of half decision he had made. In an illuminating moment during the prolonged silence between them he had seen her in a new light. The feeling of vague intimacy brought to him by his thoughts of her became a fixed belief that she belonged to him—was a part of him—and he was charmed with her manner, and her person, standing there, as with a gift given him.

And then into his mind came a hundred other thoughts, clamouring thoughts, come out of the hidden parts of him. He began to think that she could lead the way on a road he wanted to travel. He thought of her wealth and what it would mean to a man filled with his hunger for power. And through these thoughts shot others. Something in her had taken hold of him—something that had been also in Janet. He was curious concerning her curiosity about his beliefs, and wanted to question her concerning her own beliefs. He could see none of Colonel Tom's blustering incompetence in her and thought her filled with truth as a deep spring is filled with clear water. He believed she would give him something, something that all his life he had been wanting. An old aching hunger that had haunted his nights as a boy came back and he thought that at her hand it might be fed.

"I—I must read a book about socialism," he said lamely.

Again they stood in silence, she looking at the floor, he past her head and out at the window. He could not bring himself to speak again of the proposed talk. He had a boyish dread of having her notice the tremor in his voice.

Colonel Tom came into the room, bursting with an idea Sam had given him at the lunch hour and which in working its way into his mind had become to the colonel's entirely honest belief an idea of his own. The interruption brought to Sam an intense feeling of relief and he began talking of the colonel's idea as though it had taken him unawares.

Sue, walking to a window, began tying and untying the curtain cord. When Sam, raising his eyes, looked at her, he caught her eyes watching him intently and she smiled, continuing to look at him squarely. It was his eyes that first broke away.

From that day Sam's mind was afire with thoughts of Sue Rainey. In his room he sat, or going into Grant Park stood by the lake, looking at the silent, moving water as he had looked in the days when he first came to the city. He did not dream of having her in his arms or of kissing her lips; he thought, instead, with a glowing heart, of a life lived with her. He wanted to walk beside her through the streets, to have her come suddenly in at his office door, to look into her eyes and to have her question him, as she had questioned, concerning his beliefs and his hopes. He thought that in the evening he would like to go to a house of his own and find her sitting there waiting for him. All the charm of his aimless, half-dissolute way of life died in him, and he believed that with her he could begin to live more fully and completely. From the moment when he had definitely decided that he wanted Sue as a wife, Sam stopped overdrinking, going to his room or walking through the streets or in the parks instead of seeking his old companions in the clubs and drinking places. Sometimes pushing his bed to the window overlooking the lake, he would undress immediately after dinner and opening the window would spend half the night watching the lights of boats far away over the water and thinking of her. He would imagine her in the room, moving here and there, and coming occasionally to put her hand in his hair and look down at him as Janet had done, helping by her sane talk and quiet ways to get his life straightened out for good living.

And when he had fallen asleep the face of Sue Rainey came to visit his dreams. One night he thought she had become blind and sat in the room with sightless eyes saying over and over like one demented, "Truth, truth, give me back the truth that I may see," and he awoke sick with horror at the thought of the look of suffering that had been in her face. Never did Sam dream of having her in his arms or of raining kisses on her lips and neck as he had dreamed of other women who in the past had won his favour.

For all that he thought of her so constantly and built so confidently his dream of a life to be spent with her, months passed before he saw her again. Through Colonel Tom he learned that she had gone for a visit to the East and he went earnestly about his work, keeping his mind on his business during the day and only in the evening allowing himself to become absorbed in thoughts of her. He had a feeling that although he had said nothing she knew of his desire for her and that she wanted time to think it over. Several times in the evening in his room he wrote her long letters filled with minute, boyish explanations of his thoughts and motives, letters which after writing he immediately destroyed. A woman of the west side, with whom he had once had an affair, met him one day on the street, and put her hand familiarly on his arm and for the moment reawakened in him an old desire. After leaving her he did not go back to the office, but taking a south-bound car, spent the afternoon walking in Jackson Park, watching the children at play on the grass, sitting on benches under the trees, getting out of his body and his mind the insistent call of the flesh that had come back to him.

Then in the evening, he came suddenly upon Sue riding a spirited black horse in a bridle path at the upper end of the park. It was just at the grey beginning of night. Stopping the horse, she sat looking at him and going to her he put a hand on the bridle.

"We might have that talk," he said.

She smiled down at him and the colour began to rise in her brown cheeks.

"I have been thinking of it," she said, the familiar serious look coming into her eyes. "After all what have we to say to each other?"

Sam watched her steadily.

"I have a lot of things to say to you," he announced. "That is to say— well—I have, if things are as I hope." She got off the horse and they stood together by the side of the path. Sam never forgot the few minutes of silence that followed. The wide prospects of green sward, the golf player trudging wearily toward them through the uncertain light, his bag upon his shoulder, the air of physical fatigue with which he walked, bending slightly forward, the faint, soft sound of waves washing over a low beach, and the intense waiting look on the face she turned up to him, made an impression on his mind that stayed with him through life. It seemed to him that he had arrived at a kind of culmination, a starting point, and that all the vague shadowy uncertainties that had, in reflective moments, flitted through his mind, were to be brushed away by some act, some word, from the lips of this woman. With a rush he realised how consistently he had been thinking of her and how enormously he had been counting on her falling in with his plans, and the realisation was followed by a sickening moment of fear. How little he actually knew of her and of her way of thought. What assurance had he that she would not laugh, jump back upon the horse, and ride away? He was afraid as he had never been afraid before. Dumbly his mind groped about for a way to begin. Expressions he had caught and noted in her strong serious little face when he had achieved but a mild curiosity concerning her came back to visit his mind and he tried desperately to build an instant idea of her from these. And then turning his face from her he plunged directly into his thoughts of the past months as though she had been sharing talking to the colonel.

"I have been thinking we might marry, you and I," he said, and cursed himself for the blundering bluntness of the declaration.

"You do get things done, don't you?" she replied, smiling.

"Why should you have been thinking anything of the sort?"

"Because I want to live with you," he said; "I have been talking to the colonel."

"About marrying me?" She seemed about to begin laughing.

He hurried on. "No, not that. We talked about you. I could not let him alone. He might have known. I kept making him talk. I made him tell me about your ideas. I felt I had to know."

Sam faced her.

"He thinks your ideas absurd. I do not. I like them. I like you. I think you are beautiful. I do not know whether I love you or not, but for weeks I have been thinking of you and clinging to you and saying over and over to myself, 'I want to live my life with Sue Rainey.' I did not expect to go at it this way. You know me. What you do not know I will tell you."

"Sam McPherson, you are a wonder," she said, "and I do not know but that I will marry you in the end, but I can't tell now. I want to know a lot of things. I want to know if you are ready to believe what I believe and to live for what I want to live."

The horse, growing restless, began tugging at the bridle and she spoke to him sharply. She plunged into a description of a man she had seen on the lecture platform during her visit to the East and Sam looked at her with puzzled eyes.

"He was beautiful," she said. "He was past sixty but looked like a boy of twenty-five, not in his body, but in an air of youth that hung over him. He stood there before the people talking, quiet, able, efficient. He was clean. He had lived clean, body and mind. He had been companion and co-worker with William Morris, and once he had been a mine boy in Wales, but he had got hold of a vision and lived for it. I did not hear what he said, but I kept thinking, 'I want a man like that.'

"Can you accept my beliefs and live for what I want to live?" she persisted.

Sam looked at the ground. It seemed to him that he was going to lose her, that she would not marry him.

"I am not accepting beliefs or ends in life blindly," he said stoutly, "but I want them. What are your beliefs? I want to know. I think I haven't any myself. When I reach for them they are gone. My mind shifts and changes. I want something solid. I like solid things. I want you."

"When can we meet and talk everything over thoroughly?"

"Now," answered Sam bluntly, some look in her face changing his whole viewpoint. Suddenly it seemed as though a door had been opened, letting in a strong light upon the darkness of his mind. His confidence had come back to him. He wanted to strike and keep on striking. The blood rushed through his body and his brain began working rapidly. He felt sure of ultimate success.

Taking her hand, and leading the horse, he began walking with her along the path. Her hand trembled in his and as though answering a thought in his mind she looked up at him and said,

"I am not different from other women, although I do not accept your offer. This is a big moment for me, perhaps the biggest moment of my life. I want you to know that I feel that, though I do want certain things more than I want you or any other man."

There was a suggestion of tears in her voice and Sam had a feeling that the woman in her wanted him to take her into his arms, but something within him told him to wait and to help her by waiting. Like her he wanted something more than the feel of a woman in his arms. Ideas rushed through his head; he thought that she was going to give him some bigger idea than he had known. The figure she had drawn for him of the old man who stood on the platform, young and beautiful, the old boyish need of a purpose in life, the dreams of the last few weeks—all of these were a part of the eager curiosity in him. They were like hungry little animals waiting to be fed. "We must have it all out here and now," he told himself. "I must not let myself be swept away by a rush of feeling and I must not let her be.

"Do not think," he said, "that I haven't tenderness for you. I am filled with it. But I want to have our talk. I want to know what you expect me to believe and how you want me to live."

He felt her hand stiffen in his.

"Whether or not we are worth while to each other," she added.

"Yes," he said.

And then she began to talk, telling him in a quiet steady voice that steadied something in him what she wanted to make out of her life. Her idea was one of service to mankind through children. She had seen girl friends of hers, with whom she had gone to school, grow up and marry. They had wealth and education, fine well-trained bodies, and they had been married only to live lives more fully devoted to pleasure. One or two who had married poor men had only done so to satisfy a passion in themselves, and after marriage had joined the others in the hungry pursuit of pleasure.

"They do nothing at all," she said, "to repay the world for the things given them, the wealth and well-trained bodies and the disciplined minds. They go through life day after day and year after year wasting themselves and come in the end to nothing but indolent, slovenly vanity."

She had thought it all out and had tried to plan for herself a life with other ends, and wanted a husband in accord with her ideas.

"That isn't so difficult," she said, "I can find a man whom I can control and who will believe as I believe. My money gives me that power. But I want him to be a real man, a man of ability, a man who does things for himself, one fitted by his life and his achievements to be the father of children who do things. And so I began thinking about you. I got the men who come to the house to talk of you."

She hung her head and laughed like a bashful boy.

"I know much of the story of your early life out in that Iowa town," she said. "I got the story of your life and your achievements out there from some one who knew you well."

The idea seemed wonderfully simple and beautiful to Sam. It seemed to add tremendously to the dignity and nobility of his feeling for her. He stopped in the path and swung her about facing him. They were alone in that end of the park. The soft darkness of the summer night had settled over them. In the grass at their feet a cricket sang loudly. He made a movement to take her into his arms.

"It is wonderful," he said.

"Wait," she demanded, putting her hand against his shoulder. "It isn't so simple. I am wealthy. You are able and you have a kind of undying energy in you. I want to give both my wealth and your ability to children—our children. That will not be easy for you. It means giving up your dreams of power. Perhaps I shall lose courage. Women do after two or three have come. You will have to furnish that. You will have to make a mother of me and keep making a mother of me. You will have to be a new kind of father with something maternal in you. You will have to be patient and studious and kind. You will have to think of these things at night instead of thinking of your own advancement. You will have to live wholly for me because I am to be their mother, giving me your strength and courage and your good sane outlook on things. And then when they come you will have to give all these things to them day after day in a thousand little ways."

Sam took her into his arms and for the first time in his memory the hot tears stood in his eyes.

The horse, unattended, wheeled, threw up his head and trotted off down the path. They let him go, walking along after him hand in hand like two happy children. At the entrance to the park they came up to him, held by a park policeman. She got on the horse and Sam stood beside her looking up.

"I'll tell the colonel in the morning," he said.

"What will he say?" she murmured, musingly.

"Damned ingrate," Sam mimicked the colonel's blustering throat tones.

She laughed and picked up the reins. Sam laid his hand on hers.

"How soon?" he asked.

She put her head down near his.

"We'll waste no time," she said, blushing.

And then in the presence of a park policeman, in the street by the entrance to the park with the people passing up and down, Sam had his first kiss from Sue Rainey's lips.

After she rode away Sam walked. He had no sense of the passing of time, wandering through street after street, rearranging and readjusting his outlook on life. What she had said had stirred every vestige of sleeping nobility in him. He thought that he had got hold of the thing he had unconsciously been seeking all his life. His dreams of control of the Rainey Arms Company and the other big things he had planned in business seemed, in the light of their talk, so much nonsense and vanity. "I will live for this! I will live for this!" he kept saying over and over to himself. He imagined he could see the little white things lying in Sue's arms, and his new love for her and for what they were to accomplish together ran through him and hurt him so that he felt like shouting in the darkened streets. He looked up at the sky and saw the stars and thought they looked down on two new and glorious beings living on the earth.

At a corner he turned and came into a quiet residence street where frame houses stood in the midst of little green lawns and thoughts of his boyhood in the Iowa town came back to him. And then his mind moving forward, he remembered nights in the city when he had stolen away to the arms of women. Hot shame burned in his cheeks and his eyes felt hot.

"I must go to her—I must go to her at her house—now—tonight—and tell her all of these things, and beg her to forgive me," he thought.

And then the absurdity of such a course striking him he laughed aloud.

"It cleanses me! this cleanses me!" he said to himself.

He remembered the men who had sat about the stove in Wildman's grocery when he was a boy and the stories they sometimes told. He remembered how he, as a boy in the city, had run through the crowded streets fleeing from the terror of lust. He began to understand how distorted, how strangely perverted, his whole attitude toward women and sex had been. "Sex is a solution, not a menace—it is wonderful," he told himself without knowing fully the meaning of the word that had sprung to his lips.

When, at last, he turned into Michigan Avenue and went toward his apartment, the late moon was just mounting the sky and a clock in one of the sleeping houses was striking three.

VI

One evening, six weeks after the talk in the gathering darkness in Jackson Park, Sue Rainey and Sam McPherson sat on the deck of a Lake Michigan steamer watching the lights of Chicago blink out in the distance. They had been married that afternoon in Colonel Tom's big house on the south side; and now they sat on the deck of the boat, being carried out into darkness, vowed to motherhood and to fatherhood, each more or less afraid of the other. They sat in silence, looking at the blinking lights and listening to the low voices of their fellow passengers, also sitting in the chairs along the deck or strolling leisurely about, and to the wash of the water along the sides of the boat, eager to break down a little reserve that the solemnity of the marriage service had built up between them.

A picture floated in Sam's mind. He saw Sue, all in white, radiant and wonderful, coming toward him down a broad stairway, toward him, the newsboy of Caxton, the smuggler of game, the roisterer, the greedy moneygetter. All during those six weeks he had been waiting for this hour when he should sit beside the little grey-clad figure, getting from her the help he wanted in the reconstruction of his life. Without being able to talk as he had thought of talking, he yet felt assured and easy in his mind. In the moment when she had come down the stairway he had been half overcome by a feeling of intense shame, a return of the shame that had swept over him that night when she had given her word and he had walked hour after hour through the streets. It had seemed to him that from among the guests standing about should arise a voice crying, "Stop! Do not go on! Let me tell you of this fellow—this McPherson!" And then he had seen her holding to the arm of swaggering, pretentious Colonel Tom and he had taken her hand to become one with her, two curious, feverish, strangely different human beings, taking a vow in the name of their God, with the flowers banked about them and the eyes of people upon them.

When Sam had gone to Colonel Tom the morning after that evening in Jackson Park, there had been a scene. The old gun maker had blustered and roared and forbidden, pounding on his desk with his fist. When Sam remained cool and unimpressed, he had stormed out of the room slamming the door and shouting, "Upstart! Damned upstart!" and Sam had gone smiling back to his desk, mildly disappointed. "I told Sue he would say 'Ingrate,'" he thought, "I am losing my skill at guessing just what he will do and say."

The colonel's rage had been short-lived. Within a week he was boasting of Sam to chance callers as "the best business man in America," and in the face of a solemn promise given Sue was telling news of the approaching marriage to every newspaper man he knew. Sam suspected him of secretly calling on the telephone those newspapers whose representatives had not crossed his trail.

During the six waiting weeks there had been little of love making between Sue and Sam. They had talked instead, or, going into the country or to the parks, had walked under the trees consumed with a curious eager passion of suspense. The idea she had given him in the park grew in Sam's brain. To live for the young things that would presently come to them, to be simple, direct, and natural, like the trees or the beasts of the field, and then to have the native honesty of such a life illuminated and ennobled by a mutual intelligent purpose to make their young something finer and better than the things in Nature by the intelligent use of their own good minds and bodies. In the shops and on the streets the hurrying men and women took on a new significance to him. He wondered what secret mighty purpose might be in their lives, and read a newspaper report of an engagement or a marriage with a little jump of the heart. He looked at the girls and the women at work over the typewriting machines in the office, with questioning eyes, asking himself why they did not seek marriage openly and determinedly, and saw a healthy single woman as so much wasted material, as a machine for producing healthy new life standing idle and unused in the great workshop of the universe. "Marriage is a port, a beginning, a point of departure, from which men and women go forth upon the real voyage of life," he told Sue one evening as they walked in the park. "All that goes before is but a preparation, a building. The pains and the triumphs of all unmarried people are but the good oak planks being driven into place to make the vessel fit for the real voyage." Or, again, one night when they were in a rowboat on the lagoon in the park and all about them in the darkness was the plash of oars in the water, the screams of excited girls, and the sound of voices calling, he let the boat float in against the shores of a little island and crept along the boat to kneel, with his head in her lap and whisper, "It is not the love of a woman that grips me, Sue, but the love of life. I have had a peep into the great mystery. This—this is why we are here—this justifies us."

Now that she sat beside him, her shoulder against his own, being carried away with him into darkness and privacy, the personal side of his love for her ran through Sam like a flame and, turning, he drew her head down upon his shoulder.

"Not yet, Sam," she whispered, "not with these hundreds of people sleeping and drinking and thinking and going about their affairs almost within touch of our hands."

They got up and walked along the swaying deck. Out of the north the clean wind called to them, the stars looked down upon them, and in the darkness in the bow of the boat they parted for the night silently, speechless with happiness and with a dear, unmentioned secret between them.

At dawn they landed at a little lumbering town, where boat, blankets, and camping kit had gone before. A river flowed down out of the woods passing the town, going under a bridge and turning the wheel of a sawmill that stood by the shore of the river facing the lake. The clean sweet smell of the new-cut logs, the song of the saws, the roar of the water tumbling over a dam, the cries of the blue-shirted lumbermen working among the floating logs above the dam, filled the morning air, and above the song of the saws sang another song, a breathless, waiting song, the song of love and of life singing in the hearts of husband and wife.

In a little roughly-built lumberman's hotel they ate breakfast in a room overlooking the river. The proprietor of the hotel, a large red-faced woman in a clean calico dress, was expecting them and, having served the breakfast, went out of the room grinning good naturedly and closing the door behind her. Through the open window they looked at the cold swiftly-flowing river and at a freckled-faced boy who carried packages wrapped in blankets and put them in a long canoe tied to a little wharf beside the hotel. They ate and sat staring at each other like two strange boys, saying nothing. Sam ate little. His heart pounded in his breast.

On the river he sank his paddle deep into the water, pulling against the current. During the six weeks' waiting in Chicago she had taught him the essentials of the canoeist's art and, now, as he shot the canoe under the bridge and around a bend of the river out of sight of the town, a superhuman strength seemed in his arms and back. Before him in the prow of the boat sat Sue, her straight muscular little back bending and straightening again. By his side rose towering hills clothed with pine trees, and piles of cut logs lay at the foot of the hills along the shore.

At sunset they landed in a little cleared space at the foot of a hill and on the top of the hill, with the wind blowing across it, they made their first camp. Sam brought boughs and spread them, lapped like feathers in the wings of a bird, and carried blankets up the hill, while Sue, at the foot, near the overturned boat, built a fire and prepared their first cooked meal out of doors. In the failing light, Sue got out her rifle and gave Sam his first lesson in marksmanship, his awkwardness making the lesson half a jest. And then, in the soft stillness of the young night, with the first stars coming into the sky and the clean cold wind blowing into their faces, they went arm in arm up the hill under the trees to where the tops of the trees rolled and pitched like the stormy waters of a great sea before their eyes, and lay down together for their first long tender embrace.

There is a special kind of fine pleasure in getting one's first knowledge of the great outdoors in the company of a woman a man loves and to have that woman an expert, with a keen appetite for the life, adds point and flavour to the experience. In his busy striving, nickel-seeking boyhood in the town surrounded by hot cornfields, and in his young manhood of scheming and money hunger in the city, Sam had not thought of vacations and resting places. He had walked on country roads with John Telfer and Mary Underwood, listening to their talk, absorbing their ideas, blind and deaf to the little life in the grass, in the leafy branches of the trees and in the air about him. In clubs, and about hotels and barrooms in the city, he had heard men talk of life in the open, and had said to himself, "When my time comes I will taste these things."

And now he did taste them, lying on his back on the grass along the river, floating down quiet little side streams in the moonlight, listening to the night call of birds, or watching the flight of frightened wild things as he pushed the canoe into the quiet depths of the great forest about them.

At night, under the little tent they had brought, or beneath the blankets under the stars, he slept lightly, awakening often to look at Sue lying beside him. Perhaps the wind had blown a wisp of hair across her face and her breath played with it, tossing it about; perhaps just the quiet of her expressive little face charmed and held him, so that he turned reluctantly to sleep again thinking that he might, with pleasure, go on looking at her all night.

For Sue the days also passed lightly. She also awoke in the night and lay looking at the man sleeping beside her, and once she told Sam that when he awoke she feigned sleep dreading to rob him of the pleasure that she knew these secret love passages gave to both.

They were not alone in those northern woods. Everywhere along the rivers and on the shores of little lakes they found people, to Sam a new kind of people, who dropped all the ordinary things of life, and ran away to the woods and the streams to spend long happy months in the open. He discovered with surprise that these adventurers were men of modest fortunes, small manufacturers, skilled workingmen, retail merchants. One with whom he talked was a grocer from a town in Ohio, and when Sam asked him if the coming to the woods with his family for an eight-weeks stay did not endanger the success of his business he agreed with Sam that it did, nodding his head and laughing.

"But there would be a lot more danger in not leaving it," he said, "the danger of having my boys grow up to be men without my having any real fun with them."

Among all of the people they met Sue passed with a sort of happy freedom that confounded Sam, as he had formed a habit of thinking of her always as one shut within herself. Many of the people they saw she knew, and he came to believe that she had chosen the place for their love making because she admired and held in high favour the lives of these people of the out-of-doors and wanted her lover to be in some way like them. Out of the solitude of the woods, along the shores of little lakes, they called to her as she passed, demanding that she come ashore and show her husband, and among them she sat talking of other seasons and of the inroads of the lumber men upon their paradise. "The Burnhams were this year on the shores of Grant Lake, the two school teachers from Pittsburgh would come early in August, the Detroit man with the crippled son was building a cabin on the shores of Bone River."

Sam sat among them in silence, renewing constantly his admiration for the wonder of Sue's past life. She, the daughter of Colonel Tom, the woman rich in her own right, to have made her friends among these people; she, who had been pronounced an enigma by the young men of Chicago, to have been secretly all of these years the companion and fellow spirit of these campers by the lakes.

For six weeks they led a wandering, nomadic life in that half wild land, for Sue six weeks of tender love making, and of the expression of every thought and impulse of her fine nature, for Sam six weeks of readjustment and freedom, during which he learned to sail a boat, to shoot, and to get the fine taste of that life into his being.

And then one morning they came again to the little lumber town at the mouth of the river and sat upon the pier waiting for the Chicago boat. They were bound once more into the world, and to that life together that was the foundation of their marriage and that was to be the end and aim of their two lives.

If Sam's life from boyhood had been, on the whole, barren and empty of many of the sweeter things, his life during the next year was strikingly full and complete. In the office he had ceased being the pushing upstart tramping on the toes of tradition and had become the son of Colonel Tom, the voter of Sue's big stock holdings, the practical, directing head and genius of the destinies of the company. Jack Prince's loyalty had been rewarded, and a huge advertising campaign made the name and merits of the Rainey Arms Company's wares known to all reading Americans. The muzzles of Rainey-Whittaker rifles, revolvers, and shotguns looked threateningly out at one from the pages of the great popular magazines, brown fur-clad hunters did brave deeds before one's eyes, kneeling upon snow-topped crags preparing to speed winged death to waiting mountain sheep; huge open-mouthed bears rushed down from among the type at the top of the pages and seemed about to devour cool deliberate sportsmen who stood undaunted, swinging their trusty Rainey-Whittakers into place, and presidents, explorers, and Texas gun fighters loudly proclaimed the merits of Rainey-Whittakers to a gun-buying world. It was for Sam and for Colonel Tom a time of big dividends, mechanical progress, and contentment.

Sam stayed diligently at work in the offices and in the shops, but kept within himself a reserve of strength and resolution that might have gone into the work. With Sue he took up golf and morning rides on horseback, and with Sue he sat during the long evenings, reading aloud, absorbing her ideas and her beliefs. Sometimes for days they were like two children, going off together to walk on country roads and to sleep in country hotels. On these walks they went hand in hand or, bantering each other, raced down long hills to lie panting in the grass by the roadside when they were out of breath.

Near the end of the first year she told him one night of the realisation of their hopes and they sat through the evening alone by the fire in her room, filled with the white wonder of it, renewing to each other all the fine vows of their early love-making days.

Sam never succeeded in recapturing the flavour of those days. Happiness is a thing so vague, so indefinite, so dependent on a thousand little turns of the events of the day, that it only visits the most fortunate and at rare intervals, but Sam thought that he and Sue touched almost ideal happiness constantly during that time. There were weeks and even months of their first year together that later passed out of Sam's memory entirely, leaving only a sense of completeness and well being. He could remember, perhaps, a winter walk in the moonlight by the frozen lake, or a visitor who sat and talked an evening away by their fire. But at the end he had to come back to this: that something sang in his heart all day long and that the air tasted better, the stars shone more brightly, and the wind and the rain and the hail upon the window panes sang more sweetly in his ears. He and the woman who lived with him had wealth, position, and infinite delight in the presence and the persons of each other, and a great idea burned like a lamp in a window at the end of the road they travelled.

Meanwhile, in the world about him events came and went. A president was elected, the grey wolves were being hunted out of the Chicago city council, and a strong rival to his company flourished in his own city. In other days he would have been down upon this rival fighting, planning, working for its destruction. Now he sat at Sue's feet, dreaming and talking to her of the brood that under their care should grow into wonderful reliant men and women. When Lewis, the talented sales manager of the Edwards Arms Company, got the business of a Kansas City jobber, he smiled, wrote a sharp letter to his man in that territory, and went for an afternoon of golf with Sue. He had completely and wholly accepted Sue's conception of life. "We have wealth for any emergency," he said to himself, "and we will live our lives for service to mankind through the children that will presently come into our house."

After their marriage Sam found that Sue, for all her apparent coldness and indifference, had in Chicago, as in the northern woods, her own little circle of men and women. Some of these people Sam had met during the engagement, and now they began gradually coming to the house for an evening with the McPhersons. Sometimes there would be several of them for a quiet dinner at which there was much good talk, and after which Sue and Sam sat for half the night, continuing some vein of thought brought to them. Among the people who came to them, Sam shone resplendent. In some indefinable way he thought they paid court to him and the thought flattered him immensely. The college professor who had talked brilliantly through an evening turned to Sam for approval of his conclusions, a writer of tales of cowboy life asked him to help him over a difficulty in the stock market, and a tall black-haired painter paid him the rare compliment of repeating one of Sam's remarks as his own. It was as though, in spite of their talk, they thought him the most gifted of them all, and for a time he was puzzled by their attitude. Jack Prince came, sat at one of the dinner parties, and explained.

"You have got what they want and cannot get—the money," he said.

After the evening when Sue told him the great news they gave a dinner. It was a sort of welcoming party for the coming guest, and, while the people at the table ate and talked, Sue and Sam, from opposite ends of the table, lifted high their glasses and, looking into each other's eyes, drank off the health of him who was to come, the first of the great family, the family that was to have two lives lived for its success.

At the table sat Colonel Tom with his broad white shirt front, his white, pointed beard, and his grandiloquent flow of talk; at Sue's side sat Jack Prince, pausing in his open admiration of Sue to cast an eye on the handsome New York girl at Sam's end of the table or to puncture, with a flash of his terse common sense, some balloon of theory launched by Williams of the University, who sat on the other side of Sue; the artist, who hoped for a commission to paint Colonel Tom, sat opposite him bewailing the dying out of fine old American families; and a serious-faced little German scientist sat beside Colonel Tom smiling as the artist talked. The man, Sam fancied, was laughing at them both, perhaps at all of them. He did not mind. He looked at the scientist and at the other faces up and down the table and then at Sue. He saw her directing and leading the talk; he saw the play of muscles about her strong neck and the fine firmness of her straight little body, and his eyes grew moist and a lump came into his throat at the thought of the secret that lay between them.

And then his mind ran back to another night in Caxton when first he sat eating among strange people at Freedom Smith's table. He saw again the tomboy girl and the sturdy boy and the lantern swinging in Freedom's hand in the close little stable; he saw the absurd housepainter trying to blow the bugle in the street; and the mother talking to her boy of death through the summer evening; the fat foreman making the record of his loves on the walls of his room, the narrow-faced commission man rubbing his hands before a group of Greek hucksters, and then this—this home with its safety and its secret high aim and him sitting there at the head of it all. Like the novelist, it seemed to him that he should admire and bow his head before the romance of destiny. He thought his station, his wife, his country, his end in life, when rightly seen, the very apex of life on the earth, and to him in his pride it seemed that he was in some way the master and maker of it all.

VII

L ate one evening, some weeks after the McPhersons had given the dinner party in secret celebration of the future arrival of what was to be the first of the great family, they came together down the steps of a north side house to their waiting carriage. They had spent, Sam thought, a delightful evening. The Grovers were people of whose friendship he was particularly proud and since his marriage with Sue he had taken her often for an evening to the house of the venerable surgeon. Doctor Grover was a scholar, a man of note in the medical world, and a rapid and absorbing talker and thinker on any subject that aroused his interest. A certain youthful enthusiasm in his outlook on life had attracted to him the devotion of Sue, who, since meeting him through Sam, had counted him a marked addition to their little group of friends. His wife, a white-haired, plump little woman, was, though apparently somewhat diffident, in reality his intellectual equal and companion, and Sue in a quiet way had taken her as a model in her own effort toward complete wifehood.

During the evening, spent in a rapid exchange of opinions and ideas between the two men, Sue had sat in silence. Once when he looked at her Sam thought that he had surprised an annoyed look in her eyes and was puzzled by it. During the remainder of the evening her eyes refused to meet his and she looked instead at the floor, a flush mounting her cheeks.

At the door of the carriage Frank, Sue's coachman, stepped on the hem of her gown and tore it. The tear was slight, the incident Sam thought entirely unavoidable, and as much due to a momentary clumsiness on the part of Sue as to the awkwardness of Frank. The man had for years been a loyal servant and a devoted admirer of Sue's.

Sam laughed and taking Sue by the arm started to help her in at the carriage door.

"Too much gown for an athlete," he said, pointlessly.

In a flash Sue turned and faced the coachman.

"Awkward brute," she said, through her teeth.

Sam stood on the sidewalk dumb with astonishment as Frank turned and climbed to his seat without waiting to close the carriage door. He felt as he might have felt had he, as a boy, heard profanity from the lips of his mother. The look in Sue's eyes as she turned them on Frank struck him like a blow and in a moment his whole carefully built-up conception of her and of her character had been shaken. He had an impulse to slam the carriage door after her and walk home.

They drove home in silence, Sam feeling as though he rode beside a new and strange being. In the light of passing street lamps he could see her face held straight ahead and her eyes staring stonily at the curtain in front. He didn't want to reproach her; he wanted to take hold of her arm and shake her. "I should like to take the whip from in front of Frank's seat and give her a sound beating," he told himself.

At the house Sue jumped out of the carriage and, running past him in at the door, closed it after her. Frank drove off toward the stables and when Sam went into the house he found Sue standing half way up the stairs leading to her room and waiting for him.

"I presume you do not know that you have been openly insulting me all evening," she cried. "Your beastly talk there at the Grovers—it was unbearable—who are these women? Why parade your past life before me?"

Sam said nothing. He stood at the foot of the stairs and looked up at her and then, turning, just as she, running up the stairs, slammed the door of her own room, he went into the library. A wood fire burned in the grate and he sat down and lighted his pipe. He did not try to think the thing out. He felt that he was in the presence of a lie and that the Sue who had lived in his mind and in his affections no longer existed, that in her place there was this other woman, this woman who had insulted her own servant and had perverted and distorted the meaning of his talk during the evening.

Sitting by the fire filling and refilling his pipe, Sam went carefully over every word, gesture, and incident of the evening at the Grovers and could get hold of no part of it that he thought might in fairness serve as an excuse for the outburst. In the upper part of the house he could hear Sue moving restlessly about and he had satisfaction in the thought that her mind was punishing her for so strange a seizure. He and Grover had perhaps been somewhat carried away, he told himself; they had talked of marriage and its meaning and had both declared somewhat hotly against the idea that the loss of virginity in women was in any sense a bar to honourable marriage, but he had said nothing that he thought could have been twisted into an insult to Sue or to Mrs. Grover. He had thought the talk rather good and clearly thought out and had come out of the house exhilarated and secretly preening himself with the thought that he had talked unusually forcefully and well. In any event what had been said had been said before in Sue's presence and he thought that he could remember her having, in the past, expressed similar ideas with enthusiasm.

Hour after hour he sat in the chair before the dying fire. He dozed and his pipe dropped from his hand and fell upon the stone hearth. A kind of dumb misery and anger was in him as over and over endlessly his mind kept reviewing the events of the evening.

"What has made her think she can do that to me?" he kept asking himself.

He remembered certain strange silences and hard looks from her eyes during the past weeks, silences and looks that in the light of the events of the evening became pregnant with meaning.

"She has a temper, a beast of a temper. Why shouldn't she have been square and told me?" he asked himself.

The clock had struck three when the library door opened quietly and Sue, clad in a dressing gown through which the new roundness of her lithe little figure was plainly apparent, came into the room. She ran across to him and putting her head down on his knee wept bitterly.

"Oh, Sam!" she said, "I think I am going insane. I have been hating you as I have not hated since I was an evil-tempered child. A thing I worked years to suppress in me has come back. I have been hating myself and the baby. For days I have been fighting the feeling in me, and now it has come out and perhaps you have begun hating me. Can you love me again? Will you ever forget the meanness and the cheapness of it? You and poor innocent Frank—Oh, Sam, the devil was in me!"

Reaching down, Sam took her into his arms and cuddled her like a child. A story he had heard of the vagaries of women at such times came back to him and was as a light illuminating the darkness of his mind.

"I understand now," he said. "It is a part of the burden you carry for us both."

For some weeks after the outbreak at the carriage door events ran smoothly in the McPherson house. One day as he stood in the stable door Frank came round the corner of the house and, looking up sheepishly from under his cap, said to Sam: "I understand about the missus. It is the baby coming. We have had four of them at our house," and Sam, nodding his head, turned and began talking rapidly of his plans to replace the carriages with automobiles.

But in the house, in spite of the clearing up of the matter of Sue's ugliness at the Grovers, a subtle change had taken place in the relationship of the two. Although they were together facing the first of the events that were to be like ports-of-call in the great voyage of their lives, they were not facing it with the same mutual understanding and kindly tolerance with which they had faced smaller things in the past—a disagreement over the method of shooting a rapid in a river or the entertainment of an undesirable guest. The inclination to fits of temper loosens and disarranges all the little wires of life. The tune will not get itself played. One stands waiting for the discord, strained, missing the harmony. It was so with Sam. He began feeling that he must keep a check upon his tongue and that things of which they had talked with great freedom six months earlier now annoyed and irritated his wife when brought into an after-dinner discussion. To Sam, who, during his life with Sue, had learned the joy of free, open talk upon any subject that came into his mind and whose native interest in life and in the motives of men and women had blossomed in the large leisure and independence of the last year, this was trying. It was, he thought, like trying to hold free and open communion with the people of an orthodox family, and he fell into a habit of prolonged silences, a habit that later, he found, once formed, unbelievably hard to break.

One day in the office a situation arose that seemed to demand Sam's presence in Boston on a certain date. For months he had been carrying on a trade war with some of the eastern manufacturers in his line and an opportunity for the settlement of the trouble in a way advantageous to himself had, he thought, arisen. He wanted to handle the matter himself and went home to explain to Sue. It was at the end of a day when nothing had occurred to irritate her and she agreed with him that he should not be compelled to trust so important a matter to another.

"I am no child, Sam. I will take care of myself," she said, laughing.

Sam wired his New York man asking him to make the arrangements for the meeting in Boston and picked up a book to spend the evening reading aloud to her.

And then, coming home the next evening he found her in tears and when he tried to laugh away her fears she flew into a black fit of anger and ran out of the room.

Sam went to the 'phone and called his New York man, thinking to instruct him in regard to the conference in Boston and to give up his own plans for the trip. When he had got his man on the wire, Sue, who had been standing outside the door, rushed in and put her hand over the mouthpiece of the 'phone.

"Sam! Sam!" she cried. "Do not give up the trip! Scold me! Beat me! Do anything, but do not let me go on making a fool of myself and destroying your peace of mind! I shall be miserable if you stay at home because of what I have said!"

Over the 'phone came the insistent voice of Central and putting her hand aside Sam talked to his man, letting the engagement stand and making some detail of the conference answer as his need of calling.

Again Sue was repentant and again after her tears they sat before the fire until his train time, talking like lovers.

To Buffalo in the morning came a wire from her.

"Come back. Let business go. Cannot stand it," she had wired.

While he sat reading the wire the porter brought another.

"Please, Sam, pay no attention to any wire from me. I am all right and only half a fool."

Sam was irritated. "It is deliberate pettiness and weakness," he thought, when an hour later the porter brought another wire demanding his immediate return. "The situation calls for drastic action and perhaps one good stinging reproof will stop it for all time."

Going into the buffet car he wrote a long letter calling her attention to the fact that a certain amount of freedom of action was due him, and saying that he intended to act upon his own judgment in the future and not upon her impulses.

Having begun to write Sam went on and on. He was not interrupted, no shadow crossed the face of his beloved to tell him he was hurting and he said all that was in his mind to say. Little sharp reproofs that had come into his mind but that had been left unsaid now got themselves said and when he had dumped his overloaded mind into the letter he sealed and mailed it at a passing station.

Within an hour after the letter had left his hands Sam regretted it. He thought of the little woman bearing the burden for them both, and things Grover had told him of the unhappiness of women in her condition came back to haunt his mind so that he wrote and sent off to her a wire asking her not to read the letter he had mailed and assuring her that he would hurry through the Boston conference and get back to her at once.

When Sam returned he knew that in an evil moment Sue had opened and read the letter sent from the train and was surprised and hurt by the knowledge. The act seemed like a betrayal. He said nothing, going about his work with a troubled mind and watching with growing anxiety her alternate fits of white anger and fearful remorse. He thought her growing worse daily and became alarmed for her health.

And, then, after a talk with Grover he began to spend more and more time with her, forcing her to take with him daily, long walks in the open air. He tried valiantly to keep her mind fixed on cheerful things and went to bed happy and relieved when a day ended that did not bring a stormy passage between them.

There were days during that period when Sam thought himself near insanity. With a light in her grey eyes that was maddening Sue would take up some minor thing, a remark he had made or a passage he had quoted from some book, and in a dead, level, complaining tone would talk of it until his head reeled and his fingers ached from the gripping of his hands to keep control of himself. After such a day he would steal off by himself and, walking rapidly, would try through pure physical fatigue to force his mind to give up the remembrance of the persistent, complaining voice. At times he would give way to fits of anger and strew impotent oaths along the silent street, or, in another mood, would mumble and talk to himself, praying for strength and courage to keep his own head during the ordeal through which he thought they were passing together. And when he returned from such a walk and from such a struggle with himself it often occurred that he would find her waiting in the arm chair before the fire in her room, her mind clear and her little face wet with the tears of her repentance.

And then the struggle ended. With Doctor Grover it had been arranged that Sue should be taken to the hospital for the great event, and they drove there hurriedly one night through the quiet streets, the recurring pains gripping Sue and her hands clutching his. An exalted cheerfulness had hold of them. Face to face with the actual struggle for the new life Sue was transfigured. Her voice rang with triumph and her eyes glistened.

"I am going to do it," she cried; "my black fear is gone. I shall give you a child—a man child. I shall succeed, my man Sam. You shall see. It will be beautiful."

When the pain gripped she gripped at his hand, and a spasm of physical sympathy ran through him. He felt helpless and ashamed of his helplessness.

SHERWOOD ANDERSON

At the entrance to the hospital grounds she put her face down upon his knees so that the hot tears ran through his hands.

"Poor, poor old Sam, it has been horrible for you."

At the hospital Sam walked up and down in the corridor through the swinging doors at the end of which she had been taken. Every vestige of regret for the trying months now lying behind had passed, and he paced up and down the corridor feeling that he had come to one of those huge moments when a man's brain, his grasp of affairs, his hopes and plans for the future, all of the little details and trivialities of his life, halt, and he waits anxious, breathless, expectant. He looked at a little clock on a table at the end of the corridor, half expecting it to stop also and wait with him. His marriage hour that had seemed so big and vital seemed now, in the quiet corridor, with the stone floor and the silent white-clad, rubber-shod nurses passing up and down and in the presence of this greater event, to have shrunk enormously. He walked up and down peering at the clock, looking at the swinging door and biting at the stem of his empty pipe.

And then through the swinging door came Grover.

"We can get the child, Sam, but to get it we shall have to take a chance with her. Do you want to do that? Do not wait. Decide."

Sam sprang past him toward the door.

"You bungler," he cried, and his voice rang through the long quiet corridor. "You do not know what this means. Let me go."

Doctor Grover, catching him by the arm, swung him about. The two men stood facing each other.

"You stay here," said the doctor, his voice remaining quiet and firm; "I will attend to things. Your going in there would be pure folly now. Now answer me—do you want to take the chance?"

"No! No!" Sam shouted. "No! I want her—Sue—alive and well, back through that door."

A cold gleam came into his eyes and he shook his fist before the doctor's face.

"Do not try deceiving me about this. By God, I will—"

Turning, Doctor Grover ran back through the swinging door leaving Sam staring blankly at his back. A nurse, one whom he had seen in Doctor Grover's office, came out of the door and taking his arm, walked beside him up and down the corridor. Sam put his arm around her shoulder and talked. An illusion that it was necessary to comfort her came to him.

"Do not worry," he said. "She will be all right. Grover will take care of her. Nothing can happen to little Sue."

The nurse, a small, sweet-faced, Scotch woman, who knew and admired Sue, wept. Some quality in his voice had touched the woman in her and the tears ran in a little stream down her cheeks. Sam continued talking, the woman's tears helping him to regain his grip upon himself.

"My mother is dead," he said, an old sorrow revisiting him. "I wish that you, like Mary Underwood, would be a new mother to me."

When the time came that he could be taken to the room where Sue lay, his self-possession had returned to him and his mind had begun blaming the little dead stranger for the unhappiness of the past months and for the long separation from what he thought was the real Sue. Outside the door of the room into which she had been taken he stopped, hearing her voice, thin and weak, talking to Grover.

"Unfit—Sue McPherson unfit," said the voice, and Sam thought it was filled with an infinite weariness.

He ran through the door and dropped on his knees by her bed. She turned her eyes to him smiling bravely.

"The next time we'll make it," she said.

The second child born to the young McPhersons arrived out of time. Again Sam walked, this time through the corridor of his own house and without the consoling presence of the sweet-faced Scotch woman, and again he shook his head at Doctor Grover who came to him consoling and reassuring.

After the death of the second child Sue lay for months in bed. In his arms, in her own room, she wept openly in the presence of Grover and the nurses, crying out against her unfitness. For several days she refused to see Colonel Tom, harbouring in her mind the notion that he was in some way responsible for her physical inability to bear living children, and when she got up from her bed, she remained for months white and listless but grimly determined upon another attempt for the little life she so wanted to feel in her arms.

During the days of her carrying the second baby she had again the fierce ugly attacks of temper that had shattered Sam's nerves, but having learned to understand, he went quietly about his work, trying as far as in him lay to close his ears to the stinging, hurtful things she sometimes said; and the third time, it was agreed between them that if they were again unsuccessful they would turn their minds to other things.

"If we do not succeed this time we might as well count ourselves

SHERWOOD ANDERSON

through with each other for good," she said one day in one of the fits of cold anger that were a part of child bearing with her.

That second night when Sam walked in the hospital corridor he was beside himself. He felt like a young recruit called to face an unseen enemy and to stand motionless and inactive in the presence of the singing death that ran through the air. He remembered a story, told when he was a child by a fellow soldier who had come to visit his father, of the prisoners at Andersonville creeping in the darkness past armed sentries to a little pool of stagnant water beyond the dead line, and felt that he too was creeping unarmed and helpless in the neighbourhood of death. In a conference at his house between the three some weeks before, it had been decided, after tearful insistence on the part of Sue and a stand on the part of Grover, who declared that he would not remain on the case unless permitted to use his own judgment, that an operation should be performed.

"Take the chances that need be taken," Sam had said to Grover after the conference; "she will never stand another defeat. Give her the child."

In the corridor it seemed to Sam that hours had passed and still he stood motionless waiting. His feet felt cold and he had the impression that they were wet although the night was dry and a moon shone outside. When, from a distant part of the hospital, a groan reached his ears he shook with fright and had an inclination to cry out. Two young interns clad in white passed.

"Old Grover is doing a Caesarian section," said one of them; "he is getting out of date. Hope he doesn't bungle it."

In Sam's ears rang the remembrance of Sue's voice, the Sue who that first time had gone into the room behind the swinging doors with the determined smile on her face. He thought he could see again the white face looking up from the wheeled cot on which they had taken her through the door.

"I am afraid, Dr. Grover—I am afraid I am unfit," he had heard her say as the door closed.

And then Sam did a thing for which he cursed himself the rest of his life. On an impulse, and maddened by the intolerable waiting, he walked to the swinging doors and, pushing them open, stepped into the operating room where Grover was at work upon Sue.

The room was long and narrow, with floors, walls and ceiling of white cement. A great glaring light, suspended from the ceiling, threw its rays directly down on a white-clad figure lying on a white metal operating table. On the walls of the room were other glaring lights set in shining glass reflectors. And, here and there through an intense, expectant atmosphere, moved and stood silently a group of men and women, faceless, hairless, with only their strangely vivid eyes showing through the white masks that covered their faces.

Sam, standing motionless by the door, looked about with wild, half-seeing eyes. Grover worked rapidly and silently, taking from time to time little shining instruments from a swinging table close at his hand. The nurse standing beside him looked up toward the light and began calmly threading a needle. And in a white basin on a little stand at the side of the room lay the last of Sue's tremendous efforts toward new life, the last of their dreams of the great family.

Sam closed his eyes and fell. His head, striking against the wall, aroused him and he struggled to his feet.

Without stopping his work, Grover began swearing.

"Damn it, man, get out of here."

Sam groped with his hand for the door. One of the white-clad, ghoulish figures started toward him. And then with his head reeling and his eyes closed he backed through the door and, running along the corridor and down a flight of broad stairs, reached the open air and darkness. He had no doubt of Sue's death.

"She is gone," he muttered, hurrying bareheaded along the deserted streets.

Through street after street he ran. Twice he came out upon the shores of the lake, and, then turning, went back into the heart of the city through streets bathed in the warm moonlight. Once he turned quickly at a corner and stepping into a vacant lot stood behind a high board fence as a policeman strolled along the street. Into his head came the idea that he had killed Sue and that the blue-clad figure walking with heavy tread on the stone pavement was seeking him to take him back to where she lay white and lifeless. Again he stopped, before a little frame drugstore on a corner, and sitting down on the steps before it cursed God openly and defiantly like an angry boy defying his father. Some instinct led him to look at the sky through the tangle of telegraph wires overhead.

"Go on and do what you dare!" he cried. "I will not follow you now. I shall never try to find you after this."

Presently he began laughing at himself for the instinct that had led him to look at the sky and to shout out his defiance and, getting up, wandered on. In his wanderings he came to a railroad track where a freight train groaned and rattled over a crossing. When he came up to it he jumped upon an empty coal car, falling as he climbed, and cutting his face upon the sharp pieces of coal that lay scattered about the bottom of the car.

The train ground along slowly, stopping occasionally, the engine shrieking hysterically.

After a time he got out of the car and dropped to the ground. On all sides of him were marshes, the long rank marsh grasses rolling and tossing in the moonlight. When the train had passed he followed it, walking stumblingly along. As he walked, following the blinking lights at the end of the train, he thought of the scene in the hospital and of Sue lying dead for that—that ping livid and shapeless on the table under the lights.

Where the solid ground ran up to the tracks Sam sat down under a tree. Peace came over him. "This is the end of things," he thought, and was like a tired child comforted by its mother. He thought of the sweet-faced nurse who had walked with him that other time in the corridor of the hospital and who had wept because of his fears, and then of the night when he had felt the throat of his father between his fingers in the squalid little kitchen. He ran his hands along the ground. "Good old ground," he said. A sentence came into his mind followed by the figure of John Telfer striding, stick in hand, along a dusty road. "Here is spring come and time to plant out flowers in the grass," he said aloud. His face felt swollen and sore from the fall in the freight car and he lay down on the ground under a tree and slept.

When he woke it was morning and grey clouds were drifting across the sky. Within sight, down a road, a trolley car went past into the city. Before him, in the midst of the marsh, lay a low lake, and a raised walk, with boats tied to the posts on which it stood, ran down to the water. He went down the walk, bathed his bruised face in the water, and boarding a car went back into the city.

In the morning air a new thought took possession of him. The wind ran along a dusty road beside the car track, picking up little handfuls of dust and playfully throwing them about. He had a strained, eager feeling like some one listening for a faint call out of the distance.

"To be sure," he thought, "I know what it is, it is my wedding day. I am to marry Sue Rainey today."

At the house he found Grover and Colonel Tom standing in the breakfast room. Grover looked at his swollen, distorted face. His voice trembled.

"Poor devil!" he said. "You have had a night!"

Sam laughed and slapped Colonel Tom on the shoulder.

"We will have to begin getting ready," he said. "The wedding is at ten. Sue will be getting anxious."

Grover and Colonel Tom took him by the arm and began leading him up the stairs, Colonel Tom weeping like a woman.

"Silly old fool," thought Sam.

When, two weeks later, he again opened his eyes to consciousness Sue sat beside his bed in a reclining chair, her little thin white hand in his.

"Get the baby!" he cried, believing anything possible. "I want to see the baby!"

She laid her head down on the pillow.

"It was gone when you saw it," she said, and put an arm about his neck.

When the nurse came back she found them, their heads together upon the pillow, crying weakly like two tired children.

VIII

The blow given the plan of life so carefully thought out and so eagerly accepted by the young McPhersons threw them back upon themselves. For several years they had been living upon a hill top, taking themselves very seriously and more than a little preening themselves with the thought that they were two very unusual and thoughtful people engaged upon a worthy and ennobling enterprise. Sitting in their corner immersed in admiration of their own purposes and in the thoughts of the vigorous, disciplined, new life they were to give the world by the combined efficiency of their two bodies and minds they were, at a word and a shake of the head from Doctor Grover, compelled to remake the outline of their future together.

All about them the rush of life went on, vast changes were impending in the industrial life of the people, cities were doubling and tripling their population, a war was being fought, and the flag of their country flew in the ports of strange seas, while American boys pushed their way through the tangled jungles of strange lands carrying in their hands Rainey-Whittaker rifles. And in a huge stone house, set in a broad expanse of green lawns near the shores of Lake Michigan, Sam McPherson sat looking at his wife, who in turn looked at him. He was trying, as she also was trying, to adjust himself to the cheerful acceptance of their new prospect of a childless life.

Looking at Sue across the dinner table or seeing her straight, wiry body astride a horse riding beside him through the parks, it seemed to Sam unbelievable that a childless womanhood was ever to be her portion, and more than once he had an inclination to venture again upon an effort for the success of their hopes. But when he remembered her still white face that night in the hospital, her bitter, haunting cry of defeat, he turned with a shudder from the thought, feeling that he could not go with her again through that ordeal; that he could not again allow her to look forward through weeks and months toward the little life that never came to lie upon her breast or to laugh up into her face.

And yet Sam, son of that Jane McPherson who had won the admiration of the men of Caxton by her ceaseless efforts to keep her family afloat and clean handed, could not sit idly by, living upon the income of his own and Sue's money. The stirring, forward-moving world called to him; he looked about him at the broad, significant movements in business and finance, at the new men coming into prominence and apparently finding a way for the expression of new big ideas, and felt his youth stirring in him and his mind reaching out to new projects and new ambitions.

Given the necessity for economy and a hard long-drawn-out struggle for a livelihood and competence, Sam could conceive of living his life with Sue and deriving something like gratification from just her companionship, and her partnership in his efforts—here and there during the waiting years he had met men who had found such gratification—a foreman in the shops or a tobacconist from whom he bought his cigars—but for himself he felt that he had gone with Sue too far upon another road to turn that way now with anything like mutual zeal or interest. At bottom, his mind did not run strongly toward the idea of the love of women as an end in life; he had loved, and did love, Sue with something approaching religious fervour, but the fervour was more than half due to the ideas she had given him and to the fact that with him she was to have been the instrument for the realisation of those ideas. He was a man with children in his loins and he had given up his struggles for business eminence for the sake of preparing himself for a kind of noble fatherhood of children, many children, strong children, fit gifts to the world for two exceptionally favoured lives. In all of his talks with Sue this idea had been present and dominant. He had looked about him and in the arrogance of his youth and in the pride of his good body and mind had condemned all childless marriages as a selfish waste of good lives. With her he had agreed that such lives were without point and purpose. Now he remembered that in the days of her audacity and daring she had more than once expressed the hope that in case of a childless issue to their marriage one or the other of them would have the courage to cut the knot that tied them and venture into another effort at right living at any cost.

In the months after Sue's last recovery, and during the long evenings, as they sat together or walked under the stars in the park, the thought of these talks was often in Sam's mind and he found himself beginning to speculate on her present attitude and to wonder how bravely she would meet the idea of a separation. In the end he decided that no such thought was in her mind, that face to face with the tremendous actuality she clung to him with a new dependence, and a new need of his companionship. The conviction of the absolute necessity of children as a justification for a man and woman living together had, he thought, burned itself more deeply into his brain than into hers; to him it clung, coming back again and again to his mind, causing him to turn here and there restlessly, making readjustments, seeking new light. The old gods being dead he sought new gods.

In the meantime he sat in his house facing his wife, losing himself in the books recommended to him years before by Janet, thinking his own thoughts. Often in the evening he would look up from his book or from his preoccupied staring at the fire to find her eyes looking at him.

"Talk, Sam; talk," she would say; "do not sit there thinking."

Or at another time she would come to his room at night and putting her head down on the pillow beside his would spend hours planning, weeping, begging him to give her again his love, his old fervent, devoted love.

This Sam tried earnestly and honestly to do, going with her for long walks when the new call, the business had begun to make to him, would have kept him at his desk, reading aloud to her in the evening, urging her to shake off her old dreams and to busy herself with new work and new interests.

Through the days in the office he went in a kind of half stupor. An old feeling of his boyhood coming back to him, it seemed to him, as it had seemed when he walked aimlessly through the streets of Caxton after the death of his mother, that there remained something to be done, an accounting to be made. Even at his desk with the clatter of typewriters in his ears and the piles of letters demanding his attention, his mind slipped back to the days of his courtship with Sue and to those days in the north woods when life had beat strong within him, and every young, wild thing, every new growth renewed the dream that filled his being. Sometimes on the street, or walking in the park with Sue, the cries of children at play cut across the sombre dulness of his mind and he shrank from the sound and a kind of bitter resentment took possession of him. When he looked covertly at Sue she talked of other things, apparently unconscious of his thoughts.

Then a new phase of life presented itself. To his surprise he found himself looking with more than passing interest at women in the streets, and an old hunger for the companionship of strange women came back to him, in some way coarsened and materialised. One evening at the theatre a woman, a friend of Sue's and the childless wife of a business friend of his own, sat beside him. In the darkness of the playhouse her shoulder nestled down against his. In the excitement of a crisis on the stage her hand slipped into his and her fingers clutched and held his fingers.

Animal desire seized and shook him, a feeling without sweetness, brutal, making his eyes burn. When between the acts the theatre was again flooded with light he looked up guiltily to meet another pair of eyes equally filled with guilty hunger. A challenge had been given and received.

In their car, homeward bound, Sam put the thoughts of the woman away from him and taking Sue in his arms prayed silently for some help against he knew not what.

"I think I will go to Caxton in the morning and have a talk with Mary Underwood," he said.

After his return from Caxton Sam set about finding some new interest to occupy Sue's mind. He had spent an afternoon talking to Valmore, Freedom Smith, and Telfer and thought there was a kind of flatness in their jokes and in their ageing comments on each other. Then he had gone from them for his talk with Mary. Half through the night they had talked, Sam getting forgiveness for not writing and getting also a long friendly lecture on his duty toward Sue. He thought she had in some way missed the point. She had seemed to suppose that the loss of the children had fallen singly upon Sue. She had not counted upon him, and he had depended upon her doing just that. He had come as a boy to his mother wanting to talk of himself and she had wept at the thought of the childless wife and had told him how to set about making her happy.

"Well, I will set about it," he thought on the train coming home; "I will find for her this new interest and make her less dependent upon me. Then I also will take hold anew and work out for myself a programme for a way of life."

One afternoon when he came home from the office he found Sue filled indeed with a new idea. With glowing cheeks she sat beside him through the evening and talked of the beauties of a life devoted to social service.

"I have been thinking things out," she said, her eyes shining. "We must not allow ourselves to become sordid. We must keep to the vision. We must together give the best in our lives and our fortunes to mankind. We must make ourselves units in the great modern movements for social uplift."

Sam looked at the fire and a chill feeling of doubt ran through him.

He could not see himself as a unit in anything. His mind did not run out toward the thought of being one of the army of philanthropists or rich social uplifters he had met talking and explaining in the reading rooms of clubs. No answering flame burned in his heart as it had burned that evening by the bridle path in Jackson Park when she had expounded another idea. But the thought of a need of new interest for her coming to him, he turned to her smiling.

"It sounds all right but I know nothing of such things," he said.

After that evening Sue began to get a hold upon herself. The old fire came back into her eyes and she went about the house with a smile upon her face and talked through the evenings to her silent, attentive husband of the life of usefulness, the full life. One day she told him of her election to the presidency of a society for the rescue of fallen women, and he began seeing her name in the newspapers in connection with various charity and civic movements. At the house a new sort of men and women began appearing at the dinner table; a strangely earnest, feverish, half fanatical people, Sam thought, with an inclination toward corsetless dresses and uncut hair, who talked far into the night and worked themselves into a sort of religious zeal over what they called their movement. Sam found them likely to run to startling statements, noticed that they sat on the edges of their chairs when they talked, and was puzzled by their tendency toward making the most revolutionary statements without pausing to back them up. When he questioned a statement made by one of these people, he came down upon him with a rush that quite carried him away and then, turning to the others, looked at them wisely like a cat that has swallowed a mouse. "Ask us another question if you dare," their faces seemed to be saying, while their tongues declared that they were but students of the great problem of right living.

With these new people Sam never made any progress toward real understanding and friendship. For a time he tried honestly to get some of their own fervent devotions to their ideas and to be impressed by what they said of their love of man, even going with them to some of their meetings, at one of which he sat among the fallen women gathered in, and listened to a speech by Sue.

The speech did not make much of a hit, the fallen women moving restlessly about. A large woman, with an immense nose, did better. She talked with a swift, contagious zeal that was very stirring, and, listening to her, Sam was reminded of the evening when he sat before another zealous talker in the church at Caxton and Jim Williams, the barber, tried to stampede him into the fold with the lambs. While the woman talked a plump little member of the *demi monde* who sat beside Sam wept copiously, but at the end of the speech he could remember nothing of what had been said and he wondered if the weeping woman would remember.

To express his determination to continue being Sue's companion and partner, Sam during one winter taught a class of young men at a settlement house in the factory district of the west side. The class in his hands was unsuccessful. He found the young men heavy and stupid with fatigue after the day of labour in the shops and more inclined to fall asleep in their chairs, or wander away, one at a time, to loaf and smoke on a nearby corner, than to stay in the room listening to the man reading or talking before them.

When one of the young women workers came into the room, they sat up and seemed for the moment interested. Once Sam heard a group of them talking of these women workers on a landing in a darkened stairway. The experience startled Sam and he dropped the class, admitting to Sue his failure and his lack of interest and bowing his head before her accusation of a lack of the love of men.

Later by the fire in his own room he tried to draw for himself a moral from the experience.

"Why should I love these men?" he asked himself. "They are what I might have been. Few of the men I have known have loved me and some of the best and cleanest of them have worked vigorously for my defeat. Life is a battle in which few men win and many are defeated and in which hate and fear play their part with love and generosity. These heavy-featured young men are a part of the world as men have made it. Why this protest against their fate when we are all of us making more and more of them with every turn of the clock?"

During the next year, after the fiasco of the settlement house class, Sam found himself drifting more and more rapidly away from Sue and her new viewpoint of life. The growing gulf between them showed itself in a thousand little household acts and impulses, and every time he looked at her he thought her more apart from him and less a part of the real life that went on within him. In the old days there had been something intimate and familiar in her person and in her presence. She had seemed like a part of him, like the room in which he slept or the coat he wore on his back, and he had looked into her eyes as thoughtlessly and with as little fear of what he might find there as he looked at his own hands. Now when his eyes met hers they dropped, and one or the other of them began talking hurriedly like a person who has a consciousness of something he must conceal.

Down town Sam took up anew his old friendship and intimacy with Jack Prince, going with him to clubs and drinking places and often spending evenings among the clever, money-wasting young men who laughed and made deals and talked their way through life at Jack's side. Among these young men a business associate of Jack's caught his attention and in a few weeks an intimacy had sprung up between Sam and this man.

Maurice Morrison, Sam's new friend, had been discovered by Jack Prince working as a sub-editor on a country daily down the state. There was, Sam thought, something of the Caxton dandy, Mike McCarthy, in the man, combined with prolonged and fervent, although somewhat periodic attacks of industry. In his youth he had written poetry and at one time had studied for the ministry, and in Chicago, under Jack Prince, he had developed into a money maker and led the life of a talented, rather unscrupulous man of the world. He kept a mistress, often overdrank, and Sam thought him the most brilliant and convincing talker he had ever heard. As Jack Prince's assistant he had charge of the Rainey Company's large advertising expenditure, and the two men being thrown often together a mutual regard grew up between them. Sam believed him to be without moral sense; he knew him to be able and honest and he found in the association with him a fund of odd little sweetnesses of character and action that lent an inexpressible charm to the person of his friend.

It was through Morrison that Sam had his first serious misunderstanding with Sue. One evening the brilliant young advertising man dined at the McPhersons'. The table, as usual, was filled with Sue's new friends, among them a tall, gaunt man who, with the arrival of the coffee, began in a high-pitched, earnest voice to talk of the coming social revolution. Sam looked across the table and saw a light dancing in Morrison's eyes. Like a hound unleashed he sprang among Sue's friends, tearing the rich to pieces, calling for the onward advance of the masses, quoting odds and ends of Shelley and Carlyle, peering earnestly up and down the table, and at the end quite winning the hearts of the women by a defence of fallen women that stirred the blood of even his friend and host.

Sam was amused and a trifle annoyed. The whole thing was, he knew, no more than a piece of downright acting with just the touch of sincerity in it that was characteristic of the man but that had no depth or real meaning. During the rest of the evening he watched Sue, wondering if she too had fathomed Morrison and what she thought of his having taken the role of star from the long gaunt man, who had evidently been booked for that part and who sat at the table and wandered afterward among the guests, annoyed and disconcerted.

Late that night Sue came into his room and found him reading and smoking by the fire.

"Cheeky of Morrison, dimming your star," he said, looking at her and laughing apologetically.

Sue looked at him doubtfully.

"I came in to thank you for bringing him," she said; "I thought him splendid."

Sam looked at her and for a moment was tempted to let the matter pass. And then his old inclination to be always open and frank with her asserted itself and he closed the book and rising stood looking down at her.

"The little beast was guying your crowd," he said, "but I do not want him to guy you. Not that he wouldn't try. He has the audacity for anything."

A flush arose to her cheeks and her eyes gleamed.

"That is not true, Sam," she said coldly. "You say that because you are becoming hard and cold and cynical. Your friend Morrison talked from his heart. It was beautiful. Men like you, who have a strong influence over him, may lead him away, but in the end a man like that will come to give his life to the service of society. You should help him; not assume an attitude of unbelief and laugh at him."

Sam stood upon the hearth smoking his pipe and looking at her. He was thinking how easy it would have been in the first year after their marriage to have explained Morrison. Now he felt that he was but making a bad matter worse, but went on determined to stick to his policy of being entirely honest with her.

"Look here, Sue," he began quietly, "be a good sport. Morrison was joking. I know the man. He is the friend of men like me because he wants to be and because it pays him to be. He is a talker, a writer, a talented, unscrupulous word-monger. He is making a big salary by taking the ideas of men like me and expressing them better than we can ourselves. He is a good workman and a generous, open-hearted fellow with a lot of nameless charm in him, but a man of convictions he is not. He could talk tears into the eyes of your fallen women, but he would be a lot more likely to talk good women into their state."

Sam put a hand upon her shoulder.

"Be sensible and do not be offended," he went on: "take the fellow for what he is and be glad for him. He hurts little and cheers a lot. He could make a convincing argument in favour of civilisation's return to cannibalism, but really, you know, he spends most of his time thinking and writing of washing machines and ladies' hats and liver pills, and most of his eloquence after all only comes down to 'Send for catalogue, Department K' in the end."

Sue's voice was colourless with passion when she replied.

"This is unbearable. Why did you bring the fellow here?"

Sam sat down and picked up his book. In his impatience he lied to her for the first time since their marriage.

"First, because I like him and second, because I wanted to see if I couldn't produce a man who could outsentimentalise your socialist friends," he said quietly.

Sue turned and walked out of the room. In a way the action was final and marked the end of understanding between them. Putting down his book Sam watched her go and some feeling he had kept for her and that had differentiated her from all other women died in him as the door closed between them. Throwing the book aside he sprang to his feet and stood looking at the door.

"The old goodfellowship appeal is dead," he thought. "From now on we will have to explain and apologise like two strangers. No more taking each other for granted."

Turning out the light he sat again before the fire to think his way through the situation that faced him. He had no thought that she would return. That last shot of his own had crushed the possibility of that.

The fire was getting low in the grate and he did not renew it. He looked past it toward the darkened windows and heard the hum of motor cars along the boulevard below. Again he was the boy of Caxton hungrily seeking an end in life. The flushed face of the woman in the theatre danced before his eyes. He remembered with shame how he had, a few days before, stood in a doorway and followed with his eyes the figure of a woman who had lifted her eyes to him as they passed in the street. He wished that he might go out of the house for a walk with

John Telfer and have his mind filled with eloquence of the standing corn, or sit at the feet of Janet Eberly as she talked of books and of life. He got up and turning on the lights began preparing for bed.

"I know what I will do," he said, "I will go to work. I will do some real work and make some more money. That's the place for me."

And to work he went, real work, the most sustained and clearly thought-out work he had done. For two years he was out of the house at dawn for a long bracing walk in the fresh morning air, to be followed by eight, ten and even fifteen hours in the office and shops; hours in which he drove the Rainey Arms Company's organisation mercilessly and, taking openly every vestige of the management out of the hands of Colonel Tom, began the plans for the consolidation of the American firearms companies that later put his name on the front pages of the newspapers and got him the title of a Captain of Finance.

There is a widespread misunderstanding abroad regarding the motives of many of the American millionaires who sprang into prominence and affluence in the days of change and sudden bewildering growth that followed the close of the Spanish War. They were, many of them, not of the brute trader type, but were, instead, men who thought and acted quickly and with a daring and audacity impossible to the average mind. They wanted power and were, many of them, entirely unscrupulous, but for the most part they were men with a fire burning within them, men who became what they were because the world offered them no better outlet for their vast energies.

Sam McPherson had been untiring and without scruples in the first hard, quick struggle to get his head above the great unknown body of men there in the city. He had turned aside from money getting when he heard what he took to be a call to a better way of life. Now with the fires of youth still in him and with the training and discipline that had come from two years of reading, of comparative leisure and of thought, he was prepared to give the Chicago business world a display of that tremendous energy that was to write his name in the industrial history of the city as one of the first of the western giants of finance.

Going to Sue, Sam told her frankly of his plans.

"I want a free hand in the handling of your stock in the company," he said. "I cannot lead this new life of yours. It may help and sustain you but it gets no hold on me. I want to be myself now and lead my own life in my own way. I want to run the company, really run it. I cannot stand idly by and let life go past. I am hurting myself and you standing here looking on. Also I am in a kind of danger of another kind that I want to avoid by throwing myself into hard, constructive work."

Without question Sue signed the papers he brought her. A flash of her old frankness toward him came back.

"I do not blame you, Sam," she said, smiling bravely. "Things have not gone right, as we both know, but if we cannot work together at least let us not hurt each other."

When Sam returned to give himself again to affairs, the country was just at the beginning of the great wave of consolidation which was finally to sweep all of the financial power of the country into a dozen pairs of competent and entirely efficient hands. With the sure instinct of the born trader Sam had seen this movement coming and had studied it. Now he began to act. Going to that same swarthy-faced lawyer who had drawn the contract for him to secure control of the medical student's twenty thousand dollars and who had jokingly invited him to become one of a band of train robbers, he told him of his plans to begin working toward a consolidation of all the firearms companies of the country.

Webster wasted no time in joking now. He laid out the plans, adjusted and readjusted them to suit Sam's shrewd suggestions, and when a fee was mentioned shook his head.

"I want in on this," he said. "You will need me. I am made for this game and have been waiting for a chance to get at it. Just count me in as one of the promoters if you will."

Sam nodded his head. Within a week he had formed a pool of his own company's stock controlling, as he thought, a safe majority and had begun working to form a similar pool in the stock of his only big western rival.

This last job was not an easy one. Lewis, the Jew, had been making constant headway in that company just as Sam had made headway in the Rainey Company. He was a money maker, a sales manager of rare ability, and, as Sam knew, a planner and executor of business coups of the first class.

Sam did not want to deal with Lewis. He had respect for the man's ability in driving sharp bargains and felt that he would like to have the whip in his own hands when it came to the point of dealing with him. To this end he began visiting bankers and the men who were head of big western trust companies in Chicago and St. Louis. He went about his work slowly, feeling his way and trying to get at each man by some effective appeal, buying the use of vast sums of money by a promise of common stock, the bait of a big active bank account, and, here and there, by the hint of a directorship in the big new consolidated company.

For a time the project moved slowly; indeed there were weeks and months when it did not appear to move at all. Working in secret and with extreme caution Sam encountered many discouragements and went home in the evening day after day to sit among Sue's guests with a mind filled with his own plans and with an indifferent ear turned to the talk of revolution, social unrest, and the new class consciousness of the masses, that rattled and crackled up and down his dinner table. He thought that it must be trying to Sue. He was so evidently not interested in her interests. At the same time he thought that he was working toward what he wanted out of life and went to bed at night believing that he was finding, and would find, a kind of peace in just thinking clearly along one line day after day.

One day Webster, who had wanted to be in on the deal, came to Sam's office and gave his project its first great boost toward success. He, like Sam, thought he saw clearly the tendencies of the times, and was greedy for the block of common stock that Sam had promised should come to him with the completion of the enterprise.

"You are not using me," he said, sitting down before Sam's desk. "What is blocking the deal?"

Sam began to explain and when he had finished Webster laughed.

"Let's get at Tom Edwards of the Edward Arms Company direct," he said, and then, leaning over the desk, "Edwards is a vain little peacock and a second rate business man," he declared emphatically. "Get him afraid and then flatter his vanity. He has a new wife with blonde hair and big soft blue eyes. He wants prominence. He is afraid to venture upon big things himself but is hungry for the reputation and gain that comes through big deals. Use the method the Jew has used; show him what it means to the yellow-haired woman to be the wife of the president of the big consolidated Arms Company. THE EDWARDS CONSOLIDATED, eh? Get at Edwards. Bluff him and flatter him and he is your man."

Sam wondered. Edwards was a small grey-haired man of sixty with something dry and unresponsive about him. Being a silent man, he had created an impression of remarkable shrewdness and ability. After a lifetime spent in hard labour and in the practice of the most rigid economy he had come up to wealth, and had got into the firearms business through Lewis, and it was counted one of the brightest stars in that brilliant Hebrew's crown that he had been able to lead Edwards with him in his daring and audacious handling of the company's affairs.

Sam looked at Webster across the desk and thought of Tom Edwards as the figurehead of the firearms trust.

"I was saving the frosting on the cake for my own Tom," he said; "it was a thing I wanted to hand the colonel."

"Let us see Edwards this evening," said Webster dryly.

Sam nodded, and late that night made the deal that gave him control of the two important western companies and put him in position to move on the eastern companies with every prospect of complete success. To Edwards he went with an exaggerated report of the support he had already got for his project, and having frightened him offered him the presidency of the new company and promised that it should be incorporated under the name of The Edwards Consolidated Firearms Company of America.

The eastern companies fell quickly. With Webster Sam tried on them the old dodge of telling each that the other two had agreed to come in, and it worked.

With the coming in of Edwards and the options given by the eastern companies Sam began to get also the support of the LaSalle Street bankers. The firearms trust was one of the few big consolidations managed wholly in the west, and after two or three of the bankers had agreed to help finance Sam's plan the others began asking to be taken into the underwriting syndicate he and Webster had formed. Within thirty days after the closing of the deal with Tom Edwards Sam felt that he was ready to act.

For several months Colonel Tom had known something of the plans Sam had on foot, and had made no protest. He had in fact given Sam to understand that his stock would be voted with Sue's, controlled by Sam, and with the stock of the other directors who knew of and hoped to share in the profits of Sam's deal. The old gunmaker had all of his life believed that the other American firearms companies were but shadows destined to disappear before the rising sun of the Rainey Company, and thought of Sam's project as an act of providence to further this desirable end.

At the moment of his acquiescence in Webster's plan, for landing Tom Edwards, Sam had a moment of doubt, and now, with the success of his project in sight, he began to wonder how the blustering old man would look upon Edwards as the titular head of the big company and upon the name of Edwards in the title of the company.

For two years Sam had seen little of the colonel, who had given up all pretence to an active part in the management of the business and who, finding Sue's new friends disconcerting, seldom appeared at the house, living at the clubs, playing billiards all day long, or sitting in the club windows boasting to chance listeners of his part in the building of the Rainey Arms Company.

With a mind filled with doubt Sam went home and put the matter before Sue. She was dressed and ready for an evening at the theatre with a party of friends and the talk was brief.

"He will not mind," she said indifferently. "Go ahead and do what you want to do."

Sam rode back to the office and called his lieutenants about him. He felt that the thing might as well be done and over, and with the options in his hands, and the ability he thought he had to control his own company, he was ready to come out into the open and get the deal cleaned up.

The morning papers that carried the story of the proposed big new consolidation of firearms companies carried also an almost life-size halftone of Colonel Tom Rainey, a slightly smaller one of Tom Edwards, and grouped about these, small pictures of Sam, Lewis, Prince, Webster, and several of the eastern men. By the size of the half-tone, Sam, Prince, and Morrison had tried to reconcile Colonel Tom to Edwards' name in the title of the new company and to Edwards' coming election as president. The story also played up the past glories of the Rainey Company and its directing genius, Colonel Tom. One phrase, written by Morrison, brought a smile to Sam's lips.

"This grand old patriarch of American business, retired now from active service, is like a tired giant, who, having raised a brood of young giants, goes into his castle to rest and reflect and to count the scars won in many a hard-fought battle."

Morrison laughed as he read it aloud.

"It ought to get the colonel," he said, "but the newspaper man who prints it should be hung."

"They will print it all right," said Jack Prince.

And they did print it; going from newspaper office to newspaper office Prince and Morrison saw to that, using their influence as big buyers of advertising space and even insisting upon reading proof on their own masterpiece.

But it did not work. Early the next morning Colonel Tom appeared at the offices of the arms company with blood in his eye, and swore that the consolidation should not be put through. For an hour he stormed up and down in Sam's office, his outbursts of wrath varied by periods of childlike pleading for the retention of the name and glory of the Raineys. When Sam shook his head and went with the old man to the meeting that was to pass upon his action and sell the Rainey Company, he knew that he had a fight on his hands.

The meeting was a stormy one. Sam made a talk telling what had been done and Webster, voting some of Sam's proxies, made a motion that Sam's offer for the old company be accepted.

And then Colonel Tom fired his guns. Walking up and down in the room before the men, sitting at a long table or in chairs tilted against the walls, he began talking with all of his old flamboyant pomposity of the past glories of the Rainey Company. Sam watched him quietly thinking of the exhibition as something detached and apart from the business of the meeting. He remembered a question that had come into his head when he was a schoolboy and had got his first peep into a school history. There had been a picture of Indians at the war dance and he had wondered why they danced before rather than after battle. Now his mind answered the question.

"If they had not danced before they might never have got the chance," he thought, and smiled to himself.

"I call upon you men here to stick to the old colours," roared the colonel, turning and making a direct attack upon Sam. "Do not let this ungrateful upstart, this son of a drunken village housepainter, that I picked up from among the cabbages of South Water Street, win you away from your loyalty to the old leader. Do not let him steal by trickery what we have won only by years of effort."

The colonel, leaning on the table, glared about the room. Sam felt relieved and glad of the direct attack.

"It justifies what I am going to do," he thought.

When Colonel Tom had finished Sam gave a careless glance at the old man's red face and trembling fingers. He had no doubt that the outburst of eloquence had fallen upon deaf ears and without comment put Webster's motion to the vote.

To his surprise two of the new employé directors voted their stock with Colonel Tom's, and a third man, voting his own stock as well as that of a wealthy southside real estate man, did not vote. On a count the stock represented stood deadlocked and Sam, looking down the table, raised his eyebrows to Webster.

"Move we adjourn for twenty-four hours," snapped Webster, and the motion carried.

Sam looked at a paper lying before him on the table. During the count of the vote he had been writing over and over on the sheet of paper this sentence.

"The best men spend their lives seeking truth."

Colonel Tom walked out of the room like a conqueror, declining to speak to Sam as he passed, and Sam looked down the table at Webster and made a motion with his head toward the man who had not voted.

Within an hour Sam's fight was won. Pouncing upon the man representing the stock of the south-side investor, he and Webster did not go out of the room until they had secured absolute control of the Rainey Company and the man who had refused to vote had put twenty-five thousand dollars into his pocket. The two employeé directors Sam marked for slaughter. Then after spending the afternoon and early evening with the representatives of the eastern companies and their attorneys he drove home to Sue.

It was past nine o'clock when his car stopped before the house and, going at once to his room, he found Sue sitting before his fire, her arms thrown above her head and her eyes staring at the burning coals.

As Sam stood in the doorway looking at her a wave of resentment swept over him.

"The old coward," he thought, "he has brought our fight here to her."

Hanging up his coat he filled his pipe and drawing up a chair sat beside her. For five minutes Sue sat staring into the fire. When she spoke there was a touch of hardness in her voice.

"When everything is said, Sam, you do owe a lot to father," she observed, refusing to look at him.

Sam said nothing and she went on.

"Not that I think we made you, father and I. You are not the kind of man that people make or unmake. But, Sam, Sam, think what you are doing. He has always been a fool in your hands. He used to come home here when you were new with the company and talk of what he was doing. He had a whole new set of ideas and phrases; all that about waste and efficiency and orderly working toward a definite end. It did not fool me. I knew the ideas, and even the phrases he used to express them, were not his and I was not long finding out they were yours, that it was simply you expressing yourself through him. He is a big helpless child, Sam, and he is old. He hasn't much longer to live. Do not be hard, Sam. Be merciful."

Her voice did not tremble but tears ran down her rigid face and her expressive hands clutched at her dress.

"Can nothing change you? Must you always have your own way?" she added, still refusing to look at him.

"It is not true, Sue, that I always want my own way, and people do change me; you have changed me," he said.

She shook her head.

"No, I have not changed you. I found you hungry for something and you thought I could feed it. I gave you an idea that you took hold of and made your own. I do not know where I got it, from some book or hearing some one talk, I suppose. But it belonged to you. You built it and fostered it in me and coloured it with your own personality. It is your idea today. It means more to you than all this firearms trust that the papers are full of."

She turned to look at him, and put out her hand and laid it in his.

"I have not been brave," she said. "I am standing in your way. I have had a hope that we would get back to each other. I should have freed you but I hadn't the courage, I hadn't the courage. I could not give up the dream that some day you would really take me back to you."

Getting out of her chair she dropped to her knees and putting her head in his lap, shook with sobs. Sam sat stroking her hair. Her agitation was so great that her muscular little back shook with it.

Sam looked past her at the fire and tried to think clearly. He was not greatly moved by her agitation, but with all his heart he wanted to think things out and get at the right and the honest thing to do.

"It is a time of big things," he said slowly and with an air of one explaining to a child. "As your socialists say, vast changes are going on. I do not believe that your socialists really sense what these changes mean, and I am not sure that I do or that any man does, but I know they mean something big and I want to be in them and a part of them; all big men do; they are struggling like chicks in the shell. Why, look here! What I am doing has to be done and if I do not do it another man will. The colonel has to go. He will be swept aside. He belongs to something old and outworn. Your socialists, I believe, call it the age of competition."

"But not by us, not by you, Sam," she plead. "After all, he is my father."

A stern look came into Sam's eyes.

"It does not ring right, Sue," he said coldly; "fathers do not mean much to me. I choked my own father and threw him into the street when I was only a boy. You knew about that. You heard of it when you went to find out about me that time in Caxton. Mary Underwood told you. I did it because he lied and believed in lies. Do not your friends say that the individual who stands in the way should be crushed?"

She sprang to her feet and stood before him.

"Do not quote that crowd," she burst out. "They are not the real thing. Do you suppose I do not know that? Do I not know that they come here because they hope to get hold of you? Haven't I watched them and seen the look on their faces when you have not come or have not listened to their talk? They are afraid of you, all of them. That's why they talk so bitterly. They are afraid and ashamed that they are afraid."

"Like the workers in the shop?" he asked, musingly.

"Yes, like that, and like me since I failed in my part of our lives and had not the courage to get out of the way. You are worth all of us and for all our talk we shall never succeed or begin to succeed until we make men like you want what we want. They know that and I know it."

"And what do you want?"

"I want you to be big and generous. You can be. Failure cannot hurt you. You and men like you can do anything. You can even fail. I cannot. None of us can. I cannot put my father to that shame. I want you to accept failure."

Sam got up and taking her by the arm led her to the door. At the door he turned her about and kissed her on the lips like a lover.

"All right, Sue girl, I will do it," he said, and pushed her through the door. "Now let me sit down by myself and think things out."

It was a night in September and a whisper of the coming frost was in the air. He threw up the window and took long breaths of the sharp air and listened to the rumble of the elevated road in the distance. Looking up the boulevard he saw the lights of the cyclists making a glistening stream that flowed past the house. A thought of his new motor car and of all of the wonder of the mechanical progress of the world ran through his mind.

"The men who make machines do not hesitate," he said to himself; "even though a thousand fat-hearted men stood in their way they would go on."

A line of Tennyson's came into his mind.

SHERWOOD ANDERSON

"And the nation's airy navies grappling in the central blue," he quoted, thinking of an article he had read predicting the coming of airships.

He thought of the lives of the workers in steel and iron and of the things they had done and would do.

"They have," he thought, "freedom. Steel and iron do not run home to carry the struggle to women sitting by the fire."

He walked up and down the room.

"Fat old coward. Damned fat old coward," he muttered over and over to himself.

It was past midnight when he got into bed and began trying to quiet himself for sleep. In his dreams he saw a fat man with a chorus girl hanging to his arm kicking his head about a bridge above a swiftly flowing stream.

When he got down to the breakfast room the next morning Sue had gone. By his plate he found a note saying that she had gone for Colonel Tom and would take him to the country for the day. He walked to the office thinking of the incapable old man who, in the name of sentiment, had beaten him in what he thought the big enterprise of his life.

At his desk he found a message from Webster. "The old turkey cock has fled," it said; "we should have saved the twenty-five thousand."

On the phone Webster told Sam of an early visit to the club to see Colonel Tom and that the old man had left the city, going to the country for the day. It was on Sam's lips to tell of his changed plans but he hesitated.

"I will see you at your office in an hour," he said.

Outside again in the open air Sam walked and thought of his promise. Down by the lake he went to where the railroad with the lake beyond stopped him. Upon the old wooden bridge looking over the track and down to the water he stood as he had stood at other crises in his life and thought over the struggle of the night before. In the clear morning air, with the roar of the city behind him and the still waters of the lake in front, the tears, and the talk with Sue seemed but a part of the ridiculous and sentimental attitude of her father, and the promise given her insignificant and unfairly won. He reviewed the scene carefully, the talk and the tears and the promise given as he led her to the door. It all seemed far away and unreal like some promise made to a girl in his boyhood.

"It was never a part of all this," he said, turning and looking at the towering city before him.

For an hour he stood on the wooden bridge. He thought of Windy McPherson putting the bugle to his lips in the streets of Caxton and again there sounded in his ears the roaring laugh of the crowd; again he lay in the bed beside Colonel Tom in that northern city and saw the moon rising over the round paunch and heard the empty chattering talk of love.

"Love," he said, still looking toward the city, "is a matter of truth, not lies and pretence."

Suddenly it seemed to him that if he went forward truthfully he should get even Sue back again some time. His mind lingered over the thoughts of the loves that come to a man in the world, of Sue in the wind-swept northern woods and of Janet in her wheel-chair in the little room where the cable cars ran rumbling under the window. And he thought of other things, of Sue reading papers culled out of books before the fallen women in the little State Street hall, of Tom Edwards with his new wife and his little watery eyes, of Morrison and the long-fingered socialist fighting over words at his table. And then pulling on his gloves he lighted a cigar and went back through the crowded streets to his office to do the thing he had determined on.

At the meeting that afternoon the project went through without a dissenting voice. Colonel Tom being absent, the two employé directors voted with Sam with almost panicky haste as Sam looking across at the well-dressed, cool-headed Webster, laughed and lighted a fresh cigar. And then he voted the stock Sue had intrusted to him for the project, feeling that in doing so he was cutting, perhaps for all time, the knot that bound them.

With the completion of the deal Sam stood to win five million dollars, more money than Colonel Tom or any of the Raineys had ever controlled, and had placed himself in the eyes of the business men of Chicago and New York where before he had placed himself in the eyes of Caxton and South Water Street. Instead of another Windy McPherson failing to blow his bugle before the waiting crowd, he was still the man who made good, the man who achieved, the kind of man of whom America boasts before the world.

He did not see Sue again. When the news of his betrayal reached her she went off east taking Colonel Tom with her, and Sam closed the house, even sending a man there for his clothes. To her eastern address, got from her attorney, he wrote a brief note offering to make over to her or to Colonel Tom his entire winnings from the deal and closed it with the brutal declaration, "At the end I could not be an ass, even for you."

To this note Sam got a cold, brief reply telling him to dispose of her stock in the company and of that belonging to Colonel Tom, and naming an eastern trust company to receive the money. With Colonel Tom's help she had made a careful estimate of the values of their holdings at the time of consolidation and refused flatly to accept a penny beyond that amount.

Sam felt that another chapter of his life was closed. Webster, Edwards, Prince, and the eastern men met and elected him chairman of the board of directors of the new company and the public bought eagerly the river of common stock he turned upon the market, Prince and Morrison doing masterful work in the moulding of public opinion through the press. The first board meeting ended with a dinner at which wine flowed in rivulets and Edwards, getting drunk, stood up at his place and boasted of the beauty of his young wife. And Sam, at his desk in his new offices in the Rookery, settled down grimly to the playing of his role as one of the new kings of American business.

IX

The story of Sam's life there in Chicago for the next several years ceases to be the story of a man and becomes the story of a type, a crowd, a gang. What he and the group of men surrounding him and making money with him did in Chicago, other men and other groups of men have done in New York, in Paris, in London. Coming into power with the great expansive wave of prosperity that attended the first McKinley administration, these men went mad of money making. They played with great industrial institutions and railroad systems like excited children, and a man of Chicago won the notice and something of the admiration of the world by his willingness to bet a million dollars on the turn of the weather. In the years of criticism and readjustment that followed this period of sporadic growth, writers have told with great clearness how the thing was done, and some of the participants, captains of industry turned penmen, Caesars become ink-slingers, have bruited the story to an admiring world.

Given the time, the inclination, the power of the press, and the unscrupulousness, the thing that Sam McPherson and his followers did in Chicago in not difficult. Advised by Webster and the talented Prince and Morrison to handle his publicity work, he rapidly unloaded his huge holdings of common stock upon an eager public, keeping for himself the bonds which he hypothecated at the banks to increase his working capital while continuing to control the company. When the common stock was unloaded, he, with a group of fellow spirits, began an attack upon it through the stock market and in the press, and bought it again at a low figure, holding it ready to unload when the public should have forgotten.

The annual advertising expenditure of the firearms trust ran into millions and Sam's hold upon the press of the country was almost unbelievably strong. Morrison rapidly developed unusual daring and audacity in using this instrument and making it serve Sam's ends. He suppressed facts, created illusions, and used the newspapers as a whip to crack at the heels of congressmen, senators, and legislators, of the various states, when such matters as appropriation for firearms came before them.

And Sam, who had undertaken the consolidation of the firearms companies, having a dream of himself as a great master in that field, a sort of American Krupp, rapidly awoke from the dream to take the bigger chances for gain in the world of speculation. Within a year he dropped Edwards as head of the firearms trust and in his place put Lewis, with Morrison as secretary and manager of sales. Guided by Sam these two, like the little drygoods merchant of the old Rainey Company, went from capital to capital and from city to city making contracts, influencing news, placing advertising contracts where they would do the most good, fixing men.

And in the meantime Sam, with Webster, a banker named Crofts who had profited largely in the firearms merger, and sometimes Morrison or Prince, began a series of stock raids, speculations, and manipulations that attracted country-wide attention, and became known to the newspaper reading world as the McPherson Chicago crowd. They were in oil, railroads, coal, western land, mining, timber, and street railways. One summer Sam, with Prince, built, ran to a profit, and sold to advantage a huge amusement park. Through his head day after day marched columns of figures, ideas, schemes, more and more spectacular opportunities for gain. Some of the enterprises in which he engaged, while because of their size they seemed more dignified, were of reality of a type with the game smuggling of his South Water Street days, and in all of his operations it was his old instinct for bargains and for the finding of buyers together with Webster's ability for carrying through questionable deals that made him and his followers almost constantly successful in the face of opposition from the more conservative business and financial men of the city.

Again Sam led a new life, owning running horses at the tracks, memberships in many clubs, a country house in Wisconsin, and shooting preserves in Texas. He drank steadily, played poker for big stakes, kept in the public prints, and day after day led his crew upon the high seas of finance. He did not dare think and in his heart he was sick of it. Sick to the soul, so that when thought came to him he got out of his bed to seek roistering companions or, getting pen and paper, sat for hours figuring out new and more daring schemes for money making. The great forward movement in modern industry of which he had dreamed of being a part had for him turned out to be a huge meaningless gamble with loaded dice against a credulous public. With his followers he went on day after day doing deeds without thought. Industries were organised and launched, men employed and thrown out of employment, towns wrecked by the destruction of an industry and other towns made by the building of other industries. At a whim of his a thousand men began building a city on an Indiana sand hill, and at a wave of his hand another thousand men of an Indiana town sold their homes, with the chicken houses in the back-yards and vines trained by the kitchen doors, and rushed to buy sections of the hill plotted off for them. He did not stop to discuss with his followers the meaning of the things he did. He told them of the profits to be made and then, having done the thing, he went with them to drink in bar rooms and to spend the evening or afternoon singing songs, visiting his stable of runners or, more often, sitting silently about the card table playing for high stakes. Making millions through the manipulation of the public during the day, he sometimes sat half the night struggling with his companions for the possession of thousands.

Lewis, the Jew, the only one of Sam's companions who had not followed him in his spectacular money making, stayed in the office of the firearms company and ran it like the scientific able man of business he was. While Sam remained chairman of the board of the company and had an office, a desk, and the name of leadership there, he let Lewis run the place, and spent his own time upon the stock exchange or in some corner with Webster and Crofts planning some new money making raid.

"You have the better of it, Lewis," he said one day in a reflective mood; "you thought I had cut the ground from under you when I got Tom Edwards, but I only set you more firmly in a larger place."

He made a movement with his hand toward the large general offices with the rows of busy clerks and the substantial look of work being done.

"I might have had the work you are doing. I planned and schemed with that end in view," he added, lighting a cigar and going out at the door.

"And the money hunger got you," laughed Lewis, looking after him, "the hunger that gets Jews and Gentiles and all who feed it."

One might have come upon the McPherson Chicago crowd about the old Chicago stock exchange on any day during those years, Crofts, tall, abrupt, and dogmatic; Morrison, slender, dandified, and gracious; Webster, well-dressed, suave, gentlemanly, and Sam, silent, restless, and often morose and ugly. Sometimes it seemed to Sam that they were all unreal, himself and the men with him. He watched his companions cunningly. They were constantly posing before the passing crowd of brokers and small speculators. Webster, coming up to him on the floor of the exchange, would tell him of a snowstorm raging outside with the air of a man parting with a long-cherished secret. His companions went from one to the other vowing eternal friendships, and then, keeping spies upon each other, they hurried to Sam with tales of secret betrayals. Into any deal proposed by him they went eagerly, although sometimes fearfully, and almost always they won. And with Sam they made millions through the manipulation of the firearms company, and the Chicago and Northern Lake Railroad which he controlled.

In later years Sam looked back upon it all as a kind of nightmare. It seemed to him that never during that period had he lived or thought sanely. The great financial leaders that he saw were not, he thought, great men. Some of them, like Webster, were masters of craft, or, like Morrison, of words, but for the most part they were but shrewd, greedy vultures feeding upon the public or upon each other.

In the meantime Sam was rapidly degenerating. His paunch became distended, and his hands trembled in the morning. Being a man of strong appetites, and having a determination to avoid women, he almost constantly overdrank and overate, and in the leisure hours that came to him he hurried eagerly from place to place, avoiding thought, avoiding sane quiet talk, avoiding himself.

All of his companions did not suffer equally. Webster seemed made for the life, thriving and expanding under it, putting his winnings steadily aside, going on Sunday to a suburban church, avoiding the publicity connecting his name with race horses and big sporting events that Crofts sought and to which Sam submitted. One day Sam and Crofts caught him in an effort to sell them out to a group of New York bankers in a mining deal and turned the trick on him instead, whereupon he went off to New York to become a respectable big business man and the friend of senators and philanthropists.

Crofts was a man with chronic domestic troubles, one of those men who begin each day by cursing their wives before their associates and yet continue living with them year after year. There was a kind of rough squareness in the man, and after the completion of a successful deal he would be as happy as a boy, pounding men on the back, shaking with laughter, throwing money about, making crude jokes. After Sam left Chicago he finally divorced his wife and married an actress from the vaudeville stage and after losing two-thirds of his fortune in an effort to capture control of a southern railroad, went to England and, coached by the actress wife, developed into an English country gentleman.

And Sam was a man sick. Day after day he went on drinking more and more heavily, playing for bigger and bigger stakes, allowing himself less and less thought of himself. One day he received a long letter from John Telfer telling of the sudden death of Mary Underwood and berating him for his neglect of her.

"She was ill for a year and without an income," wrote Telfer. Sam noticed that the man's hand had begun to tremble. "She lied to me and told me you had sent her money, but now that she is dead I find that though she wrote you she got no answer. Her old aunt told me."

Sam put the letter into his pocket and going into one of his clubs began drinking with a crowd of men he found idling there. He had paid little attention to his correspondence for months. No doubt the letter from Mary had been received by his secretary and thrown aside with the letters of thousands of other women, begging letters, amorous letters, letters directed at him because of his wealth and the prominence given his exploits by the newspapers.

After wiring an explanation and mailing a check the size of which filled John Telfer with admiration, Sam with a half dozen fellow roisterers spent the late afternoon and evening going from saloon to saloon through the south side. When he got to his apartments late that night, his head was reeling and his mind filled with distorted memories of drinking men and women and of himself standing on a table in some obscure drinking place and calling upon the shouting, laughing hangers-on of his crowd of rich money spenders to think and to work and to seek Truth.

He went to sleep in his chair, his mind filled with the dancing faces of dead women, Mary Underwood and Janet and Sue, tear-stained faces calling to him. When he awoke and shaved he went out into the street and to another down-town club.

"I wonder if Sue is dead, too," he muttered, remembering his dream.

At the club he was called to the telephone by Lewis, who asked him to come at once to his office at the Edwards Consolidated. When he got there he found a wire from Sue. In a moment of loneliness and despondency over the loss of his old business standing and reputation, Colonel Tom had shot himself in a New York hotel.

Sam sat at his desk, fingering the yellow paper lying before him and fighting to get his head clear.

"The old coward. The damned old coward," he muttered; "any one could have done that."

When Lewis came into Sam's office he found his chief sitting at his desk fingering the telegram and muttering to himself. When Sam handed him the wire he came around and stood beside Sam, his hand upon his shoulder.

"Well, do not blame yourself for that," he said, with quick understanding.

"I don't," Sam muttered; "I do not blame myself for anything. I am a result, not a cause. I am trying to think. I am not through yet. I am going to begin again when I get things thought out."

Lewis went out of the room leaving him to his thoughts. For an hour he sat there reviewing his life. When he came to the day that he had humiliated Colonel Tom, there came back to his mind the sentence he had written on the sheet of paper while the vote was being counted. "The best men spend their lives seeking truth."

Suddenly he came to a decision and, calling Lewis, began laying out a plan of action. His head cleared and the ring came back into his voice. To Lewis he gave an option on his entire holdings of Edwards Consolidated stocks and bonds and to him also he entrusted the clearing up of deal after deal in which he was interested. Then, calling a broker, he began throwing a mass of stock on the market. When Lewis told him that Crofts was 'phoning wildly about town to find him, and was with the help of another banker supporting the market and taking Sam's stocks as fast as offered, he laughed and giving Lewis instructions regarding the disposal of his monies walked out of the office, again a free man and again seeking the answer to his problem.

He made no attempt to answer Sue's wire. He was restless to get at something he had in his mind. He went to his apartments and packed a bag and from there disappeared saying goodbye to no one. In his mind was no definite idea of where he was going or what he was going to do. He knew only that he would follow the message his hand had written. He would try to spend his life seeking truth.

BOOK III

I

O ne day when the youth Sam McPherson was new in the city he went on a Sunday afternoon to a down-town theatre to hear a sermon. The sermon was delivered by a small dark-skinned Boston man, and seemed to the young McPherson scholarly and well thought out.

"The greatest man is he whose deeds affect the greatest number of lives," the speaker had said, and the thought had stuck in Sam's mind. Now walking along the street carrying his travelling bag, he remembered the sermon and the thought and shook his head in doubt.

"What I have done here in this city must have affected thousands of lives," he mused, and felt a quickening of his blood at just letting go of his thoughts as he had not dared do since that day when, by breaking his word to Sue, he had started on his career as a business giant.

He began to think of the quest on which he had started and had keen satisfaction in the thought of what he should do.

"I will begin all over and come up to Truth through work," he told himself. "I will leave the money hunger behind me, and if it returns I will come back here to Chicago and see my fortune piled up and the men rushing about the banks and the stock exchange and the court they pay to such fools and brutes as I have been, and that will cure me."

Into the Illinois Central Station he went, a strange spectacle. A smile came to his lips as he sat on a bench along the wall between an immigrant from Russia and a small plump farmer's wife who held a banana in her hand and gave bites of it to a rosy-cheeked babe lying in her arms. He, an American multimillionaire, a man in the midst of his money-making, one who had realised the American dream, to have sickened at the feast and to have wandered out of a fashionable club with a bag in his hand and a roll of bills in his pocket and to have come on this strange quest—to seek Truth, to seek God. A few years of the fast greedy living in the city, that had seemed so splendid to the Iowa boy and to the men and women who had lived in his town, and then a woman had died lonely and in want in that Iowa town, and half across the continent a fat blustering old man had shot himself in a New York hotel, and here he sat.

Leaving his bag in the care of the farmer's wife, he walked across the room to the ticket window and standing there watched the people with definite destinations in mind come up, lay down money, and taking their tickets go briskly away. He had no fear of being known. Although his name and his picture had been upon the front pages of Chicago newspapers for years, he felt so great a change within himself from just the resolution he had taken that he had no doubt of passing unnoticed.

A thought struck him. Looking up and down the long room filled with its strangely assorted clusters of men and women a sense of the great toiling masses of people, the labourers, the small merchants, the skilled mechanics, came over him.

"These are the Americans," he began telling himself, "these people with children beside them and with hard daily work to be done, and many of them with stunted or imperfectly developed bodies, not Crofts, not Morrison and I, but these others who toil without hope of luxury and wealth, who make up the armies in times of war and raise up boys and girls to do the work of the world in their turn."

He fell into the line moving toward the ticket window behind a sturdy-looking old man who carried a box of carpenter tools in one hand and a bag in the other, and bought a ticket to the same Illinois town to which the old man was bound.

In the train he sat beside the old man and the two fell into quiet talk—the old man talking of his family. He had a son, married and living in the Illinois town to which he was going, of whom he began boasting. The son, he said, had gone to that town and had prospered there, owning a hotel which his wife managed while he worked as a builder.

"Ed," he said, "keeps fifty or sixty men going all summer. He has sent for me to come and take charge of a gang. He knows well enough I will get the work out of them."

From Ed the old man drifted into talk of himself and his life, telling bare facts with directness and simplicity and making no effort to disguise a slight turn of vanity in his success.

"I have raised seven sons and made them all good workmen and they are all doing well," he said.

He told of each in detail. One, who had taken to books, was a mechanical engineer in a manufacturing town in New England. The mother of his children had died the year before and of his three daughters two had married mechanics. The third, Sam gathered, had not done well and from something the old man said he thought she had perhaps gone the wrong way there in Chicago.

To the old man Sam talked of God and of a man's effort to get truth out of life.

"I have thought of it a lot," he said.

The old man was interested. He looked at Sam and then out at the car window and began talking of his own beliefs, the substance of which Sam could not get.

"God is a spirit and lives in the growing corn," said the old man, pointing out the window at the passing fields.

He began talking of churches and of ministers, against whom he was filled with bitterness.

"They are dodgers. They do not get at things. They are damned dodgers, pretending to be good," he declared.

Sam talked of himself, saying that he was alone in the world and had money. He said that he wanted work in the open air, not for the money it would bring him, but because his paunch was large and his hand trembled in the morning.

"I've been drinking," he said, "and I want to work hard day after day so that my muscles may become firm and sleep come to me at night."

The old man thought that his son could find Sam a place.

"He's a driver—Ed is," he said, laughing, "and he won't pay you much. Ed don't let go of money. He's a tight one."

Night had come when they reached the town where Ed lived, and the three men walked over a bridge, beneath which roared a waterfall, toward the long poorly-lighted main street of the town and Ed's hotel. Ed, a young, broad-shouldered man, with a dry cigar stuck in the corner of his mouth, led the way. He had engaged Sam standing in the darkness on the station platform, accepting his story without comment.

"I'll let you carry timbers and drive nails," he said, "that will harden you up."

On the way over the bridge he talked of the town.

"It's a live place," he said, "we are getting people in here."

"Look at that!" he exclaimed, chewing at the cigar and pointing to the waterfall that foamed and roared almost under the bridge. "There's a lot of power there and where there's power there will be a city."

At Ed's hotel some twenty men sat about a long low office. They were, for the most part, middle-aged working men and sat in silence reading and smoking pipes. At a table pushed against the wall a bald-headed young man with a scar on his cheek played solitaire with a greasy pack of cards, and in front of him and sitting in a chair tilted against the wall a sullen-faced boy idly watched the game. When the three men came into the office the boy dropped his chair to the floor and stared at Ed who stared back at him. It was as though a contest of some sort went on between them. A tall neatly-dressed woman, with a brisk manner and pale, inexpressive, hard blue eyes, stood back of a little combined desk and cigar case at the end of the room, and as the three walked toward her she looked from Ed to the sullen-faced boy and then again at Ed. Sam concluded she was a woman bent on having her own way. She had that air.

"This is my wife," said Ed, introducing Sam with a wave of his hand and passing around the end of the desk to stand by her side.

Ed's wife twirled the hotel register about facing Sam, nodded her head, and then, leaning over the desk, bestowed a quick kiss upon the leathery cheek of the old carpenter.

Sam and the old man found a place in chairs along the wall and sat down among the silent men. The old man pointed to the boy in the chair beside the card players.

"Their son," he whispered cautiously.

The boy looked at his mother, who in turn looked steadily at him, and got up from his chair. Back of the desk Ed talked in low tones to his wife. The boy, stopping before Sam and the old man and still looking toward the woman, put out his hand which the old man took. Then, without speaking, he went past the desk and through a doorway, and began noisily climbing a flight of stairs, followed by his mother. As they climbed they berated each other, their voices rising to a high pitch and echoing through the upper part of the house.

Ed, coming across to them, talked to Sam about the assignment of a room, and the men began looking at the stranger; noting his fine clothes, their eyes filled with curiosity.

"Selling something?" asked a large red-haired young man, rolling a quid of tobacco in his mouth.

"No," replied Sam shortly, "going to work for Ed."

The silent men in chairs along the wall dropped their newspapers and stared, and the bald-headed young man at the table sat with open mouth, a card held suspended in the air. Sam had become, for the moment, a centre of interest and the men stirred in their chairs and began to whisper and point to him.

A large, watery-eyed man, with florid cheeks, clad in a long overcoat with spots down the front, came in at the door and passed through the room bowing and smiling to the men. Taking Ed by the arm he disappeared into a little barroom, where Sam could hear him talking in low tones.

After a little while the florid-faced man came and put his head through the barroom door into the office.

"Come on, boys," he said, smiling and nodding right and left, "the drinks are on me."

The men got up and filed into the bar, the old man and Sam remaining seated in their chairs. They began talking in undertones.

"I'll start 'em thinking—these men," said the old man.

From his pocket he took a pamphlet and gave it to Sam. It was a crudely written attack upon rich men and corporations.

"Some brains in the fellow who wrote that," said the old carpenter, rubbing his hands together and smiling.

Sam did not think so. He sat reading it and listening to the loud, boisterous voices of the men in the barroom. The florid-faced man was explaining the details of a proposed town bond issue. Sam gathered that the water power in the river was to be developed.

"We want to make this a live town," said the voice of Ed, earnestly.

The old man, leaning over and putting his hand beside his mouth, began whispering to Sam.

"I'll bet there is a capitalist deal back of that power scheme," he said.

He nodded his head up and down and smiled knowingly.

"If there is Ed will be in on it," he added. "You can't lose Ed. He's a slick one."

He took the pamphlet from Sam's hand and put it in his pocket.

"I'm a socialist," he explained, "but don't say anything. Ed's against 'em."

The men filed back into the room, each with a freshly-lighted cigar in his mouth, and the florid-faced man followed them and went out at the office door.

"Well, so long, boys," he shouted heartily.

Ed went silently up the stairs to join the mother and boy, whose voices could still be heard raised in outbursts of wrath from above as the men took their former chairs along the wall.

"Well, Bill's sure all right," said the red-haired young man, evidently expressing the opinion of the men in regard to the florid-faced man.

A small bent old man with sunken cheeks got up and walking across the room leaned against the cigar case.

"Did you ever hear this one?" he asked, looking about.

Obviously no answer could be given and the bent old man launched into a vile pointless anecdote of a woman, a miner, and a mule, the crowd giving close attention and laughing uproariously when he had finished. The socialist rubbed his hands together and joined in the applause.

"That was a good one, eh?" he commented, turning to Sam.

Sam, picking up his bag, climbed the stairway as the red-haired young man launched into another tale, slightly less vile. In his room to which Ed, meeting him at the top of the stairs, led him, still chewing at the unlighted cigar, he turned out the light and sat on the edge of the bed. He was as homesick as a boy.

"Truth," he muttered, looking through the window to the dimly-lighted street. "Do these men seek truth?"

The next day he went to work, wearing a suit of clothes bought from Ed. He worked with Ed's father, carrying timbers and driving nails as directed by him. In the gang with him were four men, boarders at Ed's hotel, and four other men who lived in the town with their families. At the noon hour he asked the old carpenter how the men from the hotel, who did not live in the town, could vote on the question of the power bonds. The old man grinned and rubbed his hands together.

"I don't know," he said. "I suppose Ed tends to that. He's a slick one, Ed is."

At work, the men who had been so silent in the office of the hotel were alert and wonderfully busy, hurrying here and there at a word from the old man and sawing and nailing furiously. They seemed bent upon outdoing each other and when one fell behind they laughed and shouted at him, asking him if he had decided to quit for the day. But though they seemed determined to outdo him the old man kept ahead of them all, his hammer beating a rattling tattoo upon the boards all day. At the noon hour he had given each of the men one of the pamphlets from his pocket and on the way back to his hotel in the evening he told Sam that the others had tried to show him up.

"They wanted to see if I had juice in me," he explained, strutting beside Sam with an amusing little swagger of his shoulders.

Sam was sick with fatigue. His hands were blistered, his legs felt weak, and a terrible thirst burned in his throat. All day he had gone grimly ahead, thankful for every physical discomfort, every throb of his strained, tired muscles. In his weariness and in his efforts to keep pace with the others he had forgotten Colonel Tom and Mary Underwood.

　　　　　　　　　　　　　　　　SHERWOOD ANDERSON

All during that month and into the next Sam stayed with the old man's gang. He ceased thinking, and only worked desperately. An odd feeling of loyalty and devotion to the old man came over him and he felt that he too must prove that he had the juice in him. At the hotel he went to bed immediately after the silent dinner, slept, awoke aching, and went to work again.

One Sunday one of the men of his gang came to Sam's room and invited him to go with a party of the workers into the country. They went in boats, carrying with them kegs of beer, to a deep ravine clothed on both sides by heavy woods. In the boat with Sam sat the red-haired young man, who was called Jake and who talked loudly of the time they would have in the woods, and boasted that he was the instigator of the trip.

"I thought of it," he said over and over again.

Sam wondered why he had been invited. It was a soft October day and in the ravine he sat looking at the trees splashed with colour and breathing deeply of the air, his whole body relaxed, grateful for the day of rest. Jake came and sat beside him.

"What are you?" he asked bluntly. "We know you are no working man."

Sam told him a half-truth.

"You are right enough about that; I have money enough not to have to work. I used to be a business man. I sold guns. But I have a disease and the doctors have told me that if I do not work out of doors part of me will die."

The man from his own gang who had invited him on the trip came up to them, bringing Sam a foaming glass of beer. He shook his head.

"The doctor says it will not do," he explained to the two men.

The red-haired man called Jake began talking.

"We are going to have a fight with Ed," he said. "That's what we came up here to talk about. We want to know where you stand. We are going to see if we can't make him pay as well for the work here as men are paid for the same work in Chicago."

Sam lay back upon the grass.

"All right," he said. "Go ahead. If I can help I will. I'm not so fond of Ed."

The men began talking among themselves. Jake, standing among them, read aloud a list of names among which was the name Sam had written on the register at Ed's hotel.

"It's a list of the names of men we think will stick together and vote together on the bond issue," he explained, turning to Sam. "Ed's in that and we want to use our votes to scare him into giving us what we want. Will you stay with us? You look like a fighter."

Sam nodded and getting up joined the men about the beer kegs. They began talking of Ed and of the money he had made in the town.

"He's done a lot of town work here and there's been graft in all of it," explained Jake emphatically. "It's time he was being made to do the right thing."

While they talked Sam sat watching the men's faces. They did not seem vile to him now as they had seemed that first evening in the hotel office. He began thinking of them silently and alertly at work all day long, surrounded by such influences as Ed and Bill, and the thought sweetened his opinion of them.

"Look here," he said, "tell me of this matter. I was a business man before I came here and I may be able to help you fellows get what you want."

Getting up, Jake took Sam's arm and they walked down the ravine, Jake explaining the situation in the town.

"The game," he said, "is to make the taxpayers pay for a millrace to be built for the development of the water power in the river and then, by a trick, to turn it over to a private company. Bill and Ed are both in the deal and they are working for a Chicago man named Crofts. He's been up here at the hotel with Bill talking to Ed. I've figured out what they are up to." Sam sat down upon a log and laughed heartily.

"Crofts, eh?" he exclaimed. "Say, we will fight this thing. If Crofts has been up here you can depend upon it there is some size to the deal. We will just smash the whole crooked gang for the good of the town."

"How would you do that?" asked Jake.

Sam sat down on a log and looked at the river flowing past the mouth of the ravine.

"Just fight," he said. "Let me show you something."

He took a pencil and slip of paper from his pocket, and, with the voices of the men about the beer kegs in his ears and the red-haired man peering over his shoulder, began writing his first political pamphlet. He wrote and erased and changed words and phrases. The pamphlet was a statement of facts as to the value of water power, and was addressed to the taxpayers of the community. He warmed to the subject, saying that a fortune lay sleeping in the river, and that the town, by the exercise of a little discretion now, could build with that fortune a beautiful city belonging to the people.

"This fortune in the river rightly managed will pay the expenses of government and give you control of a great source of revenue forever," he wrote. "Build your millrace, but look out for a trick of the politicians. They are trying to steal it. Reject the offer of the Chicago banker named Crofts. Demand an investigation. A capitalist has been found who will take the water power bonds at four per cent and back the people in this fight for a free American city." Across the head of the pamphlet Sam wrote the caption, "A River Paved With Gold," and handed it to Jake, who read it and whistled softly.

"Good!" he said. "I will take this and have it printed. It will make Bill and Ed sit up."

Sam took a twenty-dollar bill from his pocket and gave it to the man.

"To pay for the printing," he said. "And when we have them licked I am the man who will take the four per cent bonds."

Jake scratched his head. "How much do you suppose the deal is worth to Crofts?"

"A million, or he would not bother," Sam answered.

Jake folded the paper and put it in his pocket.

"This would make Bill and Ed squirm, eh?" he laughed.

Going home down the river the men, filled with beer, sang and shouted as the boats, guided by Sam and Jake, floated along. The night fell warm and still and Sam thought he had never seen the sky so filled with stars. His brain was busy with the idea of doing something for the people.

"Perhaps here in this town I shall make a start toward what I am after," he thought, his heart filled with happiness and the songs of the tipsy workmen ringing in his ears.

All through the next few weeks there was an air of something astir among the men of Sam's gang and about Ed's hotel. During the evening Jake went among the men talking in low tones, and once he took a three days' vacation, telling Ed that he did not feel well and spending the time among the men employed in the plough works up the river. From time to time he came to Sam for money.

"For the campaign," he said, winking and hurrying away.

Suddenly a speaker appeared and began talking nightly from a box before a drug store on Main Street, and after dinner the office of Ed's hotel was deserted. The man on the box had a blackboard hung on a pole, on which he drew figures estimating the value of the power in the river, and as he talked he grew more and more excited, waving his arms and inveighing against certain leasing clauses in the bond proposal. He declared himself a follower of Karl Marx and delighted the old carpenter who danced up and down in the road and rubbed his hands.

"It will come to something—this will—you'll see," he declared to Sam.

One day Ed appeared, riding in a buggy, at the job where Sam worked, and called the old man into the road. He sat pounding one hand upon the other and talking in a low voice. Sam thought the old man had perhaps been indiscreet in the distribution of the socialistic pamphlets. He seemed nervous, dancing up and down beside the buggy and shaking his head. Then hurrying back to where the men worked he pointed over his shoulder with his thumb.

"Ed wants you," he said, and Sam noticed that his voice trembled and his hand shook.

In the buggy Ed and Sam rode in silence. Again Ed chewed at an unlighted cigar.

"I want to talk with you," he had said as Sam climbed into the buggy.

At the hotel the two men got out of the buggy and went into the office. Inside the door Ed, who came behind, sprang forward and pinioned Sam's arms with his own. He was as powerful as a bear. His wife, the tall woman with the inexpressive eyes, came running into the room, her face drawn with hatred. In her hand she carried a broom and with the handle of this she struck Sam several swinging blows across the face, accompanying each blow with a half scream of rage and a volley of vile names. The sullen-faced boy, alive now and with eyes burning with zeal, came running down the stairs and pushed the woman aside. He struck Sam time after time in the face with his fist, laughing each time as Sam winced under the blows.

Sam struggled furiously to escape Ed's powerful grasp. It was the first time he had ever been beaten and the first time he had faced hopeless defeat. The wrath within him was so intense that the jolting impact of the blows seemed a secondary matter to the need of escaping Ed's vice-like grasp.

Suddenly Ed turned and, pushing Sam before him, threw him through the office door and into the street. In falling his head struck against a hitching post and he lay stunned. When he partially recovered from the fall Sam got up and walked along the street. His face was swollen and bruised and his nose bled. The street was deserted and the assault upon him had been unnoticed.

He went to a hotel on Main Street—a more pretentious place than Ed's, near the bridge leading to the station—and as he passed in he saw, through an open door, Jake, the red-haired man, leaning against the bar and talking to Bill, the man with the florid face. Sam, paying for a room, went upstairs and to bed.

In the bed, with cold bandages on his bruised face, he tried to get the situation in hand. Hatred for Ed ran through his veins. His hands clenched, his brain whirled, and the brutal, passionate faces of the woman and the boy danced before his eyes.

"I'll fix them, the brutal bullies," he muttered aloud.

And then the thought of his quest came back to his mind and quieted him. Through the window came the roar of the waterfall, broken by noises of the street. As he fell asleep they mingled with his dreams, sounding soft and quiet like the low talk of a family about the fire of an evening.

He was awakened by a noise of pounding on his door. At his call the door opened and the face of the old carpenter appeared. Sam laughed and sat up in bed. Already the cold bandages had soothed the throbbing of his bruised face.

"Go away," begged the old man, rubbing his hands together nervously. "Get out of town."

He put his hand to his mouth and talked in a hoarse whisper, looking back over his shoulder through the open door. Sam, getting out of bed, began filling his pipe.

"You can't beat Ed, you fellows," added the old man, backing out at the door. "He's a slick one, Ed is. You better get out of town."

Sam called a boy and gave him a note to Ed asking for his clothes and for the bag in his room, and to the boy he gave a large bill, asking him to pay anything due. When the boy came back bringing the clothes and the bag he returned the bill unbroken.

"They're scared about something up there," he said, looking at Sam's bruised face.

Sam dressed carefully and went down into the street. He remembered that he had never seen a printed copy of the political pamphlet written in the ravine and realised that Jake had used it to make money for himself.

"Now I shall try something else," he thought.

It was early evening and crowds of men coming down the railroad track from the plough works turned to right and left as they reached Main Street. Sam walked among them, climbing a little hilly side street to a number he had got from a clerk at the drug store before which the socialist had talked. He stopped at a little frame house and a moment after knocking was in the presence of the man who had talked night after night from the box in the street. Sam had decided to see what could be done through him. The socialist was a short, fat man, with curly grey hair, shiny round cheeks, and black broken teeth. He sat on the edge of his bed and looked as if he had slept in his clothes. A corncob pipe lay smoking among the covers of the bed, and during most of the talk he sat with one shoe held in his hand as though about to put it on. About the room in orderly piles lay stack after stack of paper-covered books. Sam sat down in a chair by the window and told his mission.

"It is a big thing, this power steal that is going on here," he explained. "I know the man back of it and he would not bother with a small affair. I know they are going to make the city build the millrace and then steal it. It will be a big thing for your party about here if you take hold and stop them. Let me tell you how it can be done."

He explained his plan, and told of Crofts and of his wealth and dogged, bullying determination. The socialist seemed beside himself. He pulled on the shoe and began running hurriedly about the room.

"The time for the election," Sam went on, "is almost here. I have looked into this thing. We must beat this bond issue and then put through a square one. There is a train out of Chicago at seven o'clock, a fast train. You get fifty speakers out here. I will pay for a special train if necessary and I will hire a band and help stir things up. I can give you facts enough to shake this town to the bottom. You come with me and 'phone to Chicago. I will pay everything. I am McPherson, Sam McPherson of Chicago."

The socialist ran to a closet and began pulling on his coat. The name affected him so that his hand trembled and he could scarcely get his arm into the coat sleeve. He began to apologise for the appearance of the room and kept looking at Sam with the air of one not able to believe what he had heard. As the two men walked out of the house he ran ahead holding doors open for Sam's passage.

"And you will help us, Mr. McPherson?" he exclaimed. "You, a man of millions, will help us in this fight?"

Sam had a feeling that the man was going to kiss his hand or do something equally ridiculous. He had the air of a club door man gone off his head.

At the hotel Sam stood in the lobby while the fat man waited in a telephone booth.

"I will have to 'phone Chicago, I will simply have to 'phone Chicago. We socialists don't do anything like this offhand, Mr. McPherson," he had explained as they walked along the street.

When the socialist came out of the booth he stood before Sam shaking his head. His whole attitude had changed, and he looked like a man caught doing a foolish or absurd thing.

"Nothing doing, nothing doing, Mr. McPherson," he said, starting for the hotel door.

At the door he stopped and shook his finger at Sam.

"It won't work," he said, emphatically. "Chicago is too wise."

Sam turned and went back to his room. His name had killed his only chance to beat Crofts, Jake, Bill and Ed. In his room he sat looking out of the window into the street.

"Where shall I take hold now?" he asked himself.

Turning out the lights he sat listening to the roar of the waterfall and thinking of the events of the last week.

"I have had a time," he thought. "I have tried something and even though it did not work it has been the best fun I have had for years."

The hours slipped away and night came on. He could hear men shouting and laughing in the street, and going downstairs he stood in a hallway at the edge of the crowd that gathered about the socialist. The orator shouted and waved his hand. He seemed as proud as a young recruit who has just passed through his first baptism of fire.

"He tried to make a fool of me—McPherson of Chicago—the millionaire—one of the capitalist kings—he tried to bribe me and my party."

In the crowd the old carpenter was dancing in the road and rubbing his hands together. With the feeling of a man who had finished a piece of work or turned the last leaf of a book, Sam went back to his hotel.

"In the morning I shall be on my way," he thought.

A knock came at the door and the red-haired man came in. He closed the door softly and winked at Sam.

"Ed made a mistake," he said, and laughed. "The old man told him you were a socialist and he thought you were trying to spoil the graft.

He is scared about that beating you got and mighty sorry. He's all right—
Ed is—and he and Bill and I have got the votes. What made you stay
under cover so long? Why didn't you tell us you were McPherson?"

Sam saw the hopelessness of any attempt to explain. Jake had
evidently sold out the men. Sam wondered how.

"How do you know you can deliver the votes?'" he asked, trying to
lead Jake on.

Jake rolled the quid in his mouth and winked again.

"It was easy enough to fix the men when Ed, Bill and I got together,"
he said. "You know about the other. There's a clause in the act authorising
the bond issue, a sleeper, Bill calls it. You know more about that than I
do. Anyway the power will be turned over to the man we say."

"But how do I know you can deliver the votes?"

Jake threw out his hand impatiently.

"What do they know?" he asked sharply. "What they want is more
wages. There's a million in the power deal and they can't any more
realise a million than they can tell what they want to do in Heaven.
I promised Ed's fellows the city scale. Ed can't kick. He'll make a
hundred thousand as it stands. Then I promised the plough works gang
a ten per cent raise. We'll get it for them if we can, but if we can't, they
won't know it till the deal is put through."

Sam walked over and held open the door.

"Good night," he said.

Jake looked annoyed.

"Ain't you even going to make a bid against Crofts?" he asked. "We
ain't tied to him if you do better by us. I'm in this thing because you put
me in. That piece you wrote up the river scared 'em stiff. I want to do
the right thing by you. Don't be sore about Ed. He wouldn't a done it
if he'd known."

Sam shook his head and stood with his hand still on the door.

"Good night," he said again. "I am not in it. I have dropped it. No
use trying to explain."

For weeks and months Sam led a wandering vagabond life, and surely a stranger or more restless vagabond never went upon the road. In his pocket he had at almost any time from one to five thousand dollars, his bag went on from place to place ahead of him, and now and then he caught up with it, unpacked it, and wore a suit of his former Chicago clothes upon the streets of some town. For the most part, however, he wore the rough clothes bought from Ed, and, when these were gone, others like them, with a warm canvas outer jacket, and for rough weather a pair of heavy boots lacing half way up the legs. Among the people, he passed for a rather well-set-up workman with money in his pocket going his own way.

During all those months of wandering, and even when he had returned to something nearer his former way of life, his mind was unsettled and his outlook on life disturbed. Sometimes it seemed to him that he, among all men, was a unique, an innovation. Day after day his mind ground away upon his problem and he was determined to seek and to keep on seeking until he found for himself a way of peace. In the towns and in the country through which he passed he saw the clerks in the stores, the merchants with worried faces hurrying into banks, the farmers, brutalised by toil, dragging their weary bodies homeward at the coming of night, and told himself that all life was abortive, that on all sides of him it wore itself out in little futile efforts or ran away in side currents, that nowhere did it move steadily, continuously forward giving point to the tremendous sacrifice involved in just living and working in the world. He thought of Christ going about seeing the world and talking to men, and thought that he too would go and talk to them, not as a teacher, but as one seeking eagerly to be taught. At times he was filled with longing and inexpressible hopes and, like the boy of Caxton, would get out of bed, not now to stand in Miller's pasture watching the rain on the surface of the water, but to walk endless miles through the darkness getting the blessed relief of fatigue into his body and often paying for and occupying two beds in one night.

Sam wanted to go back to Sue; he wanted peace and something like happiness, but most of all he wanted work, real work, work that would demand of him day after day the best and finest in him so that he would be held to the need of renewing constantly the better impulses of his mind. He was at the top of his life, and the few weeks of hard physical exertion as a driver of nails and a bearer of timbers had begun to restore his body to shapeliness and strength, so that he was filled anew with all of his native restlessness and energy; but he was determined that he would not again pour himself out in work that would react upon him as had his money making, his dream of beautiful children, and this last half-formed dream of a kind of financial fatherhood to the Illinois town.

The incident with Ed and the red-haired man had been his first serious effort at anything like social service achieved through controlling or attempting to influence the public mind, for his was the type of mind that runs to the concrete, the actual. As he sat in the ravine talking to Jake, and, later, coming home in the boat under the multitude of stars, he had looked up from among the drunken workmen and his mind had seen a city built for a people, a city independent, beautiful, strong, and free, but a glimpse of a red head through a barroom door and a socialist trembling before a name had dispelled the vision. After his return from hearing the socialist, who in his turn was hedged about by complicated influences, and in those November days when he walked south through Illinois, seeing the late glory of the trees and breathing the fine air, he laughed at himself for having had the vision. It was not that the red-haired man had sold him out, it was not the beating given him by Ed's sullen-faced son or the blows across the face at the hands of his vigorous wife—it was just that at bottom he did not believe the people wanted reform; they wanted a ten per cent raise in wages. The public mind was a thing too big, too complicated and inert for a vision or an ideal to get at and move deeply.

And then, walking on the road and struggling to find truth even within himself, Sam had to come to something else. At bottom he was no leader, no reformer. He had not wanted the free city for a free people, but as a work to be done by his own hand. He was McPherson, the money maker, the man who loved himself. The fact, not the sight of Jake hobnobbing with Bill or the timidity of the socialist, had blocked his way to work as a political reformer and builder.

Tramping south between the rows of shocked corn he laughed at himself. "The experience with Ed and Jake has done something for me," he thought. "They bullied me. I have been a kind of bully myself and what has happened has been good medicine for me."

Sam walked the roads of Illinois, Ohio, New York, and other states, through hill country and flat country, in the snow drifts of winter and through the storms of spring, talking to people, asking their way of life and the end toward which they worked. At night he dreamed of Sue, of his boyhood struggles in Caxton, of Janet Eberly sitting in her chair and talking of writers of books, or, visualising the stock exchange or some garish drinking place, he saw again the faces of Crofts, Webster, Morrison, and Prince intent and eager as he laid before them some scheme of money making. Sometimes at night he awoke, seized with horror, seeing Colonel Tom with the revolver pressed against his head; and sitting in his bed, and all through the next day he talked aloud to himself.

"The damned old coward," he shouted into the darkness of his room or into the wide peaceful prospect of the countryside.

The idea of Colonel Tom as a suicide seemed unreal, grotesque, horrible. It was as though some round-cheeked, curly-headed boy had done the thing to himself. The man had been so boyishly, so blusteringly incompetent, so completely and absolutely without bigness and purpose.

"And yet," thought Sam, "he has found strength to whip me, the man of ability. He has taken revenge, absolute and unanswerable, for the slight I put upon the little play world in which he had been king."

In fancy Sam could see the great paunch and the little white pointed beard sticking up from the floor in the room where the colonel lay dead, and into his mind came a saying, a sentence, the distorted remembrance of a thought he had got from a book of Janet's or from some talk he had heard, perhaps at his own dinner table.

"It is horrible to see a fat man with purple veins in his face lying dead."

At such times he hurried along the road like one pursued. People driving past in buggies and seeing him and hearing the stream of talk that issued from his lips, turned and watched him out of sight. And Sam, hurrying and seeking relief from the thoughts in his mind, called to the old commonsense instincts within himself as a captain marshals his forces to withstand an attack.

"I will find work. I will find work. I will seek Truth," he said.

Sam avoided the larger towns or went hurriedly through them, sleeping night after night at village hotels or at some hospitable farmhouse, and daily he increased the length of his walks, getting real satisfaction from the aching of his legs and from the bruising of his unaccustomed feet on the hard road. Like St. Jerome, he had a wish to beat upon his body and subdue the flesh. In turn he was blown upon by the wind, chilled by the winter frost, wet by the rains, and warmed by the sun. In the spring he swam in rivers, lay on sheltered hillsides watching the cattle grazing in the fields and the white clouds floating across the sky, and constantly his legs became harder and his body more flat and sinewy. Once he slept for a night in a straw stack at the edge of a woods and in the morning was awakened by a farmer's dog licking his face.

Several times he came up to vagabonds, umbrella menders and other roadsters, and walked with them, but he found in their society no incentive to join in their flights across country on freight trains or on the fronts of passenger trains. Those whom he met and with whom he talked and walked did not interest him greatly. They had no end in life, sought no ideal of usefulness. Walking and talking with them, the romance went out of their wandering life. They were utterly dull and stupid, they were, almost without exception, strikingly unclean, they wanted passionately to get drunk, and they seemed to be forever avoiding life with its problems and responsibilities. They always talked of the big cities, of "Chi" and "Cinci" and "Frisco," and were bent upon getting to one of these places. They condemned the rich and begged and stole from the poor, talked swaggeringly of their personal courage and ran whimpering and begging before country constables. One of them, a tall, leering youth in a grey cap, who came up to Sam one evening at the edge of a village in Indiana, tried to rob him. Full of his new strength and with the thought of Ed's wife and the sullen-faced son in his mind, Sam sprang upon him and had revenge for the beating received in the office of Ed's hotel by beating this fellow in his turn. When the tall youth had partially recovered from the beating and had staggered to his feet, he ran off into the darkness, stopping when well out of reach to hurl a stone that splashed in the mud of the road at Sam's feet.

Everywhere Sam sought people who would talk to him of themselves. He had a kind of faith that a message would come to him out of the mouth of some simple, homely dweller of the villages or the farms. A woman, with whom he talked in the railroad station at Fort Wayne, Indiana, interested him so that he went into a train with her and travelled all night in the day coach, listening to her talk of her three sons, one of whom had weak lungs and had, with two younger brothers, taken up government land in the west. The woman had been with them for some months, helping them to get a start.

"I was raised on a farm and knew things they could not know," she told Sam, raising her voice above the rumble of the train and the snoring of fellow passengers.

She had worked with her sons in the field, ploughing and planting, had driven a team across country, carrying boards for the building of a house, and had grown brown and strong at the work.

"And Walter is getting well. His arms are as brown as my own and he has gained eleven pounds," she said, rolling up her sleeves and showing her heavy, muscular forearms.

She planned to take her husband, a machinist working in a bicycle factory in Buffalo, and her two grown daughters, clerks in a drygoods store, with her and return to the new country, and having a sense of her hearer's interest in her story, she talked of the bigness of the west and the loneliness of the vast, silent plains, saying that they sometimes made her heart ache. Sam thought she had in some way achieved success, although he did not see how her experience could serve as a guide to him.

"You have got somewhere. You have got hold of a truth," he said, taking her hand when he got off the train at Cleveland, at dawn.

At another time, in the late spring, when he was tramping through southern Ohio, a man drove up beside him, and pulling in his horse, asked, "Where are you going?" adding genially, "I may be able to give you a lift."

Sam looked at him and smiled. Something in the man's manner or in his dress suggesting the man of God, he assumed a bantering air.

"I am on my way to the New Jerusalem," he said seriously. "I am one who seeks God."

The young minister picked up his reins with a look of alarm, but when he saw a smile playing about the corners of Sam's mouth, he turned the wheels of his buggy.

"Get in and come along with me and we will talk of the New Jerusalem," he said.

On the impulse Sam got into the buggy, and driving along the dusty road, told the essential parts of his story and of his quest for an end toward which he might work.

"It would be simple enough if I were without money and driven by hard necessity, but I am not. I want work, not because it is work and will bring me bread and butter, but because I need to be doing something that will satisfy me when I am done. I do not want so much to serve men as to serve myself. I want to get at happiness and usefulness as for years I got at money making. There is a right way of life for such a man as me, and I want to find that way."

The young minister, who was a graduate of a Lutheran seminary at Springfield, Ohio, and had come out of college with a very serious outlook on life, took Sam to his house and together they sat talking half the night. He had a wife, a country girl with a babe lying at her breast, who got supper for them, and who, after supper, sat in the shadows in a corner of the living-room listening to their talk.

The two men sat together. Sam smoked his pipe and the minister poked at a coal fire that burned in a stove. They talked of God and of what the thought of God meant to men; but the young minister did not try to give Sam an answer to his problem; on the contrary, Sam found him strikingly dissatisfied and unhappy in his way of life.

"There is no spirit of God here," he said, poking viciously at the coals in the stove. "The people here do not want me to talk to them of God. They have no curiosity about what He wants of them nor of why He has put them here. They want me to tell them of a city in the sky, a kind of glorified Dayton, Ohio, to which they can go when they have finished this life of work and of putting money in the savings bank."

For several days Sam stayed with the clergyman, driving about the country with him and talking of God. In the evening they sat in the house, continuing their talks, and on Sunday Sam went to hear the man preach in his church.

The sermon was a disappointment to Sam. Although his host had talked vigorously and well in private, his public address was stilted and unnatural.

"The man," thought Sam, "has no feeling for public address and is not treating his people well in not giving them, without reservation, the ideas he has expounded to me in his house." He decided there was something to be said for the people who sat patiently listening week after week and who gave the man the means of a living for so lame an effort.

One evening when Sam had been with them for a week the young wife came to him as he stood on the little porch before the house.

"I wish you would go away," she said, standing with her babe in her arms and looking at the porch floor. "You stir him up and make him dissatisfied."

Sam stepped off the porch and hurried off up the road into the darkness. There had been tears in the wife's eyes.

　　　　　　　　　　　　　　　　　　SHERWOOD ANDERSON

In June he went with a threshing crew, working among labourers and eating with them in the fields or about the crowded tables of farmhouses where they stopped to thresh. Each day Sam and the men with him worked in a new place and had as helpers the farmer for whom they threshed and several of his neighbours. The farmers worked at a killing pace and the men of the threshing crew were expected to keep abreast of each new lot of them day after day. At night the threshermen, too weary for talk, crept into the loft of a barn, slept until daylight and then began another day of heartbreaking toil. On Sunday morning they went for a swim in some creek and in the afternoon sat in a barn or under the trees of an orchard sleeping or indulging in detached, fragmentary bits of talk, talk that never rose above a low, wearisome level. For hours they would try to settle a dispute as to whether a horse they had seen at some farm during the week had three, or four, white feet, and one man in the crew never talked at all, sitting on his heels through the long Sunday afternoons and whittling at a stick with his pocket knife.

The threshing outfit with which Sam worked was owned by a man named Joe, who was in debt for it to the maker and who, after working with the men all day, drove about the country half the night making deals with farmers for other days of threshing. Sam thought that he looked constantly on the point of collapse through overwork and worry, and one of the men, who had been with Joe through several seasons, told Sam that at the end of the season their employer did not have enough money left from his season of work to pay the interest on the debt for his machines and that he continually took jobs for less than the cost of doing them.

"One has to keep going," said Joe, when one day Sam began talking to him on the matter.

When told to keep Sam's wage until the end of the season he looked relieved and at the end of the season came to Sam, looking more worried and said that he had no money.

"I will give you a note bearing good interest if you can let me have a little time," he said.

Sam took the note and looked at the pale, drawn face peering out of him from the shadows at the back of the barn.

"Why do you not drop the whole thing and begin working for some one else?" he asked.

Joe looked indignant.

"A man wants independence," he said.

When Sam got again upon the road he stopped at a little bridge over a stream, and tearing up Joe's note watched the torn pieces of it float away upon the brown water.

III

Through the summer and early fall Sam continued his wanderings. The days on which something happened or on which something outside himself interested or attracted him were special days, giving him food for hours of thought, but for the most part he walked on and on for weeks, sunk in a kind of healing lethargy of physical fatigue. Always he tried to get at people who came into his way and to discover something of their way of life and the end toward which they worked, and many an open-mouthed, staring man and woman he left behind him on the road and on the sidewalks of the villages. He had one principle of action; whenever an idea came into his mind he did not hesitate, but began trying at once the practicability of living by following the idea, and although the practice brought him to no end and only seemed to multiply the difficulties of the problem he was striving to work out, it brought him many strange experiences.

At one time he was for several days a bartender in a saloon in a town in eastern Ohio. The saloon was in a small wooden building facing a railroad track and Sam had gone in there with a labourer met on the sidewalk. It was a stormy night in September at the end of his first year of wandering and while he stood by a roaring coal stove, after buying drinks for the labourer and cigars for himself, several men came in and stood by the bar drinking together. As they drank they became more and more friendly, slapping each other on the back, singing songs and boasting. One of them got out upon the floor and danced a jig. The proprietor, a round-faced man with one dead eye, who had himself been drinking freely, put a bottle upon the bar and coming up to Sam, began complaining that he had no bartender and had to work long hours.

"Drink what you want, boys, and then I'll tell you what you owe," he said to the men standing along the bar.

Watching the men who drank and played like school boys about the room, and looking at the bottle sitting on the bar, the contents of which had for the moment taken the sombre dulness out of the lives of the workmen, Sam said to himself, "I will take up this trade. It may appeal to me. At least I shall be selling forgetfulness and not be wasting my life with this tramping on the road and thinking."

The saloon in which he worked was a profitable one and although in an obscure place had made its proprietor what is called "well fixed." It had a side door opening into an alley and one went up this alley to the main street of the town. The front door looking upon the railroad tracks was but little used, perhaps at the noon hour two or three young men from the freight depot down the tracks would come in by it and stand about drinking beer, but the trade that came down the alley and in at the side door was prodigious. All day long men hurried in at this door, took drinks and hurried out again, looking up the alley and running quickly when they found the way clear. These men all drank whiskey, and when Sam had worked for a few days in the place he once made the mistake of reaching for the bottle when he heard the door open.

"Let them ask for it," said the proprietor gruffly. "Do you want to insult a man?"

On Saturday the place was filled all day with beer-drinking farmers, and at odd hours on other days men came in, whimpering and begging drinks. When alone in the place, Sam looked at the trembling fingers of these men and put the bottle before them, saying, "Drink all you want of the stuff."

When the proprietor was in, the men who begged drinks stood a moment by the stove and then went out thrusting their hands into their coat pockets and looking at the floor.

"Bar flies," the proprietor explained laconically.

The whiskey was horrible. The proprietor mixed it himself and put it into stone jars that stood under the bar, pouring it out of these into bottles as they became empty. He kept on display in glass cases bottles of well known brands of whiskey, but when a man came in and asked for one of these brands Sam handed him a bottle bearing that label from beneath the bar, a bottle previously filled by Al from the jugs of his own mixture. As Al sold no mixed drinks Sam was compelled to know nothing the bartender's art and stood all day handing out Al's poisonous stuff and the foaming glasses of beer the workingmen drank in the evening.

Of the men coming in at the side door, a shoe merchant, a grocer, the proprietor of a restaurant, and a telegraph operator interested Sam most. Several times each day these men would appear, glance back over their shoulders at the door, and then turning to the bar would look at Sam apologetically.

"Give me a little out of the bottle, I have a bad cold," they would say, as though repeating a formula.

At the end of the week Sam was on the road again. The rather bizarre notion that by staying there he would be selling forgetfulness of life's unhappiness had been dispelled during his first day's duty, and his curiosity concerning the customers was his undoing. As the men came in at the side door and stood before him Sam leaned over the bar and asked them why they drank. Some of the men laughed, some swore at him, and the telegraph operator reported the matter to Al, calling Sam's question an impertinence.

"You fool, don't you know better than to be throwing stones at the bar?" Al roared, and with an oath discharged him.

IV

One fine warm morning in the fall Sam was sitting in a little park in the centre of a Pennsylvania manufacturing town watching men and women going through the quiet streets to the factories and striving to overcome a feeling of depression aroused by an experience of the evening before. He had come into town over a poorly made clay road running through barren hills, and, depressed and weary, had stood on the shores of a river, swollen by the early fall rains, that flowed along the edges of the town.

Before him in the distance he had looked into the windows of a huge factory, the black smoke from which added to the gloom of the scene that lay before him. Through the windows of the factory, dimly seen, workers ran here and there, appearing and disappearing, the glare of the furnace fire lighting now one, now another of them, sharply. At his feet the tumbling waters that rolled and pitched over a little dam fascinated him. Looking closely at the racing waters his head, light from physical weariness, reeled, and in fear of falling he had been compelled to grip firmly the small tree against which he leaned. In the back yard of a house across the stream from Sam and facing the factory four guinea hens sat on a board fence, their weird, plaintive cries making a peculiarly fitting accompaniment to the scene that lay before him, and in the yard itself two bedraggled fowls fought each other. Again and again they sprang into the fray, striking out with bills and spurs. Becoming exhausted, they fell to picking and scratching among the rubbish in the yard, and when they had a little recovered renewed the struggle. For an hour Sam had looked at the scene, letting his eyes wander from the river to the grey sky and to the factory belching forth its black smoke. He had thought that the two feebly struggling fowls, immersed in their pointless struggle in the midst of such mighty force, epitomised much of man's struggle in the world, and, turning, had gone along the sidewalks and to the village hotel, feeling old and tired. Now on the bench in the little park, with the early morning sun shining down through the glistening rain drops clinging to the red leaves of the trees, he began to lose the sense of depression that had clung to him through the night.

A young man who walked in the park saw him idly watching the hurrying workers, and stopped to sit beside him.

SHERWOOD ANDERSON

"On the road, brother?" he asked.

Sam shook his head, and the other began talking.

"Fools and slaves," he said earnestly, pointing to the men and women passing on the sidewalk. "See them going like beasts to their bondage? What do they get for it? What kind of lives do they lead? The lives of dogs."

He looked at Sam for approval of the sentiment he had voiced.

"We are all fools and slaves," said Sam, stoutly.

Jumping to his feet the young man began waving his arms about.

"There, you talk sense," he cried. "Welcome to our town, stranger. We have no thinkers here. The workers are like dogs. There is no solidarity among them. Come and have breakfast with me."

In the restaurant the young man began talking of himself. He was a graduate of the University of Pennsylvania. His father had died while he was yet in school and had left him a modest fortune, upon the income of which he lived with his mother. He did no work and was enormously proud of the fact.

"I refuse to work! I scorn it!" he declared, shaking a breakfast roll in the air.

Since leaving school he had devoted himself to the cause of the socialist party in his native town, and boasted of the leadership he had already achieved. His mother, he declared, was disturbed and worried because of his connection with the movement.

"She wants me to be respectable," he said sadly, and added, "What's the use trying to explain to a woman? I can't get her to see the difference between a socialist and a direct-action anarchist and I've given up trying. She expects me to end by blowing somebody up with dynamite or by getting into jail for throwing bricks at the borough police."

He talked of a strike going on among some girl employés of a Jewish shirtwaist factory in the town, and Sam, immediately interested, began asking questions, and after breakfast went with his new acquaintance to the scene of the strike.

The shirtwaist factory was located in a loft above a grocery store, and on the sidewalk in front of the store three girl pickets were walking up and down. A flashily dressed Hebrew, with a cigar in his mouth and his hands in his trousers pockets, stood in the stairway leading to the loft and looked closely at the young socialist and Sam. From his lips came a stream of vile words which he pretended to be addressing to the empty air. When Sam walked towards him he turned and ran up the stairs, shouting oaths over his shoulder.

Sam joined the three girls, and began talking to them, walking up and down with them before the grocery store.

"What are you doing to win?" he asked when they had told him of their grievances.

"We do what we can!" said a Jewish girl with broad hips, great motherly breasts, and fine, soft, brown eyes, who appeared to be a leader and spokesman among the strikers. "We walk up and down here and try to get a word with the strikebreakers the boss has brought in from other towns, when they go in and come out."

Frank, the University man, spoke up. "We are putting up stickers everywhere," he said. "I myself have put up hundreds of them."

He took from his coat pocket a printed slip, gummed on one side, and told Sam that he had been putting them on walls and telegraph poles about town. The thing was vilely written. "Down with the dirty scabs" was the heading in bold, black letters across the top.

Sam was shocked at the vileness of the caption and at the crude brutality of the text printed on the slip.

"Do you call women workers names like that?" he asked.

"They have taken our work from us," the Jewish girl answered simply and began again, telling the story of her sister strikers and of what the low wage had meant to them and to their families. "To me it does not so much matter; I have a brother who works in a clothing store and he can support me, but many of the women in our union have only their wage here with which to feed their families."

Sam's mind began working on the problem.

"Here," he declared, "is something definite to do, a battle in which I will pit myself against this employer for the sake of these women."

He put away from him his experience in the Illinois town, telling himself that the young woman walking beside him would have a sense of honour unknown to the red-haired young workman who had sold him out to Bill and Ed.

"I failed with my money," he thought, "now I will try to help these girls with my energy."

Turning to the Jewish girl he made a quick decision.

"I will help you get your places back," he said.

Leaving the girls he went across the street to a barber shop where he could watch the entrance to the factory. He wanted to think out a method of procedure and wanted also to look at the girl strikebreakers as they came to work. After a time several girls came along the street and turned in at the stairway. The flashily dressed Hebrew with the cigar still in his mouth was again by the stairway entrance. The three pickets running forward accosted the file of girls going up the stairs, one of whom, a young American girl with yellow hair, turned and shouted something over her shoulder. The man called Frank shouted back and the Hebrew took the cigar out of his mouth and laughed heartily. Sam filled and lighted his pipe, a dozen plans for helping the striking girls running through his mind.

During the morning he went into the grocery store on the corner, a saloon in the neighbourhood, and returned to the barber shop talking to men of the strike. He ate his lunch alone, still thinking of the three girls patiently walking up and down before the stairway. Their ceaseless walking seemed to him a useless waste of energy.

"They should be doing something more definite," he thought.

After lunch he joined the soft-eyed Jewish girl and together they walked along the street talking of the strike.

"You cannot win this strike by just calling nasty names," he said. "I do not like that 'dirty scab' sticker Frank had in his pocket. It cannot help you and only antagonises the girls who have taken your places. Here in this part of town the people want to see you win. I have talked to the men who come into the saloon and the barber shop across the street and you already have their sympathy. You want to get the sympathy of the girls who have taken your places. Calling them dirty scabs only makes martyrs of them. Did the yellow-haired girl call you a name this morning?"

The Jewish girl looked at Sam and laughed bitterly.

"Rather; she called me a loud-mouthed street walker."

They continued their walk along the street, across the railroad track and a bridge, and into a quiet residence street. Carriages stood at the curb before the houses, and pointing to these and to the well-kept houses Sam said, "Men have bought these things for their women."

A shadow fell across the girl's face.

"I suppose all of us want what these women have," she answered. "We do not really want to fight and to stand on our own feet, not when we know the world. What a woman really wants is a man," she added shortly.

Sam began talking and told her of a plan that had come into his mind. He had remembered how Jack Prince and Morrison used to talk about the appeal of the direct personal letter and how effectively it was used by mail order houses.

"We will have a mail order strike here," he said and went on to lay before her the details of his plan. He proposed that she, Frank, and some others of the striking girls, should go about town getting the names and the mail addresses of the girl strikebreakers.

"Get also the names of the keepers of the boarding houses at which these girls live and the names of the men and women who live in the same houses," he suggested. "Then you get the striking girls and women together and have them tell me their stories. We will write letters day after day to the girl strikebreakers, to the women who keep the boarding houses, and to the people who live in the houses and sit at table with them. We won't call names. We will tell the story of what being beaten in this fight means to the women in your union, tell it simply and truthfully as you told it to me this morning."

"It will cost such a lot," said the Jewish girl, shaking her head.

Sam took a roll of bills from his pocket and showed it to her.

"I will pay," he said.

"Why?" she asked, looking at him sharply.

"Because I am a man wanting work just as you want work," he replied, and then went on hurriedly, "It is a long story. I am a rich man wandering about the world seeking Truth. I will not want that known. Take me for granted. You won't be sorry."

Within an hour he had engaged a large room, paying a month's rent in advance, and into the room chairs and table and typewriters had been brought. He put an advertisement in the evening paper for girl stenographers, and a printer, hurried by a promise of extra pay, ran out for him several thousand letter heads across the top of which in bold, black type ran the words, "The Girl Strikers."

That night Sam held, in the room he had engaged, a meeting of the girl strikers, explaining to them his plan and offering to pay all expenses of the fight he proposed to make for them. They clapped their hands and shouted approvingly, and Sam began laying out his campaign.

One of the girls he told off to stand in front of the factory morning and evening.

"I will have other help for you there," he said. "Before you go home tonight there will be a printer here with a bundle of pamphlets I am having printed for you."

Advised by the soft-eyed Jewish girl, he told off others to get additional names for the mailing list he wanted, getting many important ones from girls in the room. Six of the girls he asked to come in the morning to help him with addressing and mailing letters. The Jewish girl he told to take charge of the girls at work in the room—on the morrow to become also an office—and to superintend getting the names.

Frank rose at the back of the room.

"Who are you anyway?" he asked.

"A man with money and the ability to win this strike," Sam told him.

"What are you doing it for?" demanded Frank.

The Jewish girl sprang to her feet.

"Because he believes in these women and wants to help," she explained.

"Rot," said Frank, going out at the door.

It was snowing when the meeting ended, and Sam and the Jewish girl finished their talk in the hallway leading to her room.

"I don't know what Harrigan, the union leader from Pittsburgh, will say to this," she told him. "He appointed Frank to lead and direct the strike here. He doesn't like interference and he may not like your plan. But we working women need men, men like you who can plan and do things. There are too many men living on us. We need men who will work for all of us as the men work for the women in the carriages and automobiles." She laughed and put out a hand to him. "See what you have got yourself into? I want you to be a husband to our entire union."

The next morning four girl stenographers went to work in Sam's strike headquarters, and he wrote his first strike letter, a letter telling the story of a striking girl named Hadaway, whose young brother was sick with tuberculosis. Sam did not put any flourishes in the letter; he felt that he did not need to. He thought that with twenty or thirty such letters, each telling briefly and truthfully the story of one of the striking girls, he should be able to show one American town how its other half lived. He gave the letter to the four girl stenographers with the mailing list he already had and started them writing it to each of the names.

At eight o'clock a man came in to install a telephone and girl strikers began bringing in new names for the mailing list. At nine o'clock three more stenographers appeared and were put to work, and girls who had been in began sending more names over the 'phone. The Jewish girl walked up and down, giving orders, making suggestions. From time to time she ran to Sam's desk and suggested other sources of names for the mailing list. Sam thought that if the other working girls were timid and embarrassed before him this one was not. She was like a general on the field of battle. Her soft brown eyes glowed, her mind worked rapidly, and her voice had a ring in it. At her suggestion Sam gave the girls at the typewriters lists bearing the names of town officials, bankers and prominent business men, and the wives of all these, also presidents of various women's clubs, society women, and charitable organizations. She called reporters from the town's two daily papers and had them interview Sam, and at her suggestion he gave them copies of the Hadaway girl letter to print.

"Print it," he said, "and if you cannot use it as news, make it an advertisement and bring the bill to me."

At eleven o'clock Frank came into the room bringing a tall Irishman, with sunken cheeks, black, unclean teeth, and an overcoat too small for him. Leaving him standing by the door, Frank walked across the room to Sam.

"Come to lunch with us," he said. He jerked his thumb over his shoulder toward the tall Irishman. "I picked him up," he said. "Best brain that's been in town for years. He's a wonder. Used to be a Catholic priest. He doesn't believe in God or love or anything. Come on out and hear him talk. He's great."

Sam shook his head.

"I am too busy. There is work to be done here. We are going to win this strike."

Frank looked at him doubtfully and then about the room at the busy girls.

"I don't know what Harrigan will think of all this," he said. "He doesn't like interferences. I never do anything without writing him. I wrote and told him what you were doing here. I had to, you know. I'm responsible to headquarters."

In the afternoon the Hebrew owner of the shirtwaist factory came in to strike headquarters and, walking through the room took off his hat and sat down by Sam's desk.

"What do you want here?" he asked. "The newspaper boys told me of what you had planned to do. What's your game?"

"I want to whip you," Sam answered quietly, "to whip you good. You might as well get into line. You are going to lose this strike."

"I'm only one," said the Hebrew. "There is an association of us manufacturers of shirtwaists. We are all in this. We all have a strike on our hands. What will you gain if you do beat me here? I'm only a little fellow after all."

Sam laughed and picking up his pen began writing.

"You are unlucky," he said. "I just happened to take hold here. When I have you beaten I will go on and beat the others. There is more money back of me than back of you all, and I am going to beat every one of you."

The next morning a crowd stood before the stairway leading to the factory when the strikebreaking girls came to work. The letters and the newspaper interview had been effective and more than half the strikebreakers did not appear. The others hurried along the street and turned in at the stairway without looking at the crowd. The girl, told off by Sam, stood on the sidewalk passing out pamphlets to the strikebreakers. The pamphlets were headed, "The Story of Ten Girls," and told briefly and pointedly the stories of ten striking girls and what the loss of the strike meant to them and to their families.

After a while there drove up two carriages and a large automobile, and out of the automobile climbed a well-dressed woman who took a bundle of the pamphlets from the girl picket and began passing them about among the people. Two policemen who stood in front of the crowd took off their helmets and accompanied her. The crowd cheered. Frank came hurrying across the street to where Sam stood in front of the barber shop and slapped him on the back.

"You're a wonder," he said.

Sam hurried back to the room and prepared the second letter for the mailing list. Two more stenographers had come to work. He had to send out for more machines. A reporter for the town's evening paper ran up the stairway.

"Who are you?" he asked. "The town wants to know."

From his pocket he took a telegram from a Pittsburgh daily.

"What about mail-order strike plan? Give name and story new strike leader there."

At ten o'clock Frank returned.

"There's a wire from Harrigan," he said. "He's coming here. He wants a mass meeting of the girls for tonight. I've got to get them together. We'll meet here in this room."

In the room the work went on. The list of names for the mailing had doubled. The picket at the shirtwaist factory reported that three more of the strikebreakers had left the plant. The Jewish girl was excited. She went hurrying about the room, her eyes glowing.

"It's great," she said. "The plan is working. The whole town is aroused and for us. We'll win in another twenty-four hours."

And then at seven o'clock that night Harrigan came into the room where Sam sat with the assembled girls, bolting the door behind him. He was a short, strongly built man with blue eyes and red hair. He walked about the room in silence, followed by Frank. Suddenly he stopped and, picking up one of the typewriting machines rented by Sam for the letter writing, raised it above his head and sent it smashing to the floor.

"A hell of a strike leader," he roared. "Look at this. Scab machines!

"Scab stenographers!" he said through his teeth. "Scab printing! Scab everything!"

Picking up a bundle of the letterheads, he tore them across, and walking to the front of the room, shook his fist before Sam's face.

"Scab leader!" he shouted, turning and facing the girls.

The soft-eyed Jewish girl sprang to her feet.

"He's winning for us," she said.

Harrigan walked toward her threateningly.

"Better lose than win a scab victory," he bellowed.

"Who are you anyway? What grafter sent you here?" he demanded, turning to Sam.

He launched into a speech. "I have been watching this fellow, I know him. He has a scheme to break down the union and is being paid by the capitalists."

Sam waited to hear no more. Getting up he pulled on his canvas jacket and started for the door. He saw that already he had involved himself in a dozen violations of the unionist code and the idea of trying to convince Harrigan of his disinterestedness did not occur to him.

"Do not mind me," he said, "I am going."

He walked between the rows of frightened, white-faced girls and unbolted the door, the Jewish girl following. At the head of the stairway leading to the street he stopped and pointed back into the room.

"Go back," he said, handing her a roll of bills. "Carry on the work if you can. Get other machines and new printing. I will help you in secret."

Turning he ran down the stairs, hurried through the curious crowd standing at the foot, and walked rapidly along in front of the lighted stores. A cold rain, half snow, was falling. Beside him walked a young man with a brown pointed beard, one of the newspaper reporters who had interviewed him the day before.

"Did Harrigan trim you?" asked the young man, and then added, laughing, "He told us he intended to throw you down stairs."

Sam walked on in silence, filled with wrath. He turned into a side street and stopped when his companion put a hand upon his arm.

"This is our dump," said the young man, pointing to a long low frame building facing the side street. "Come in and let us have your story. It should be a good one."

Inside the newspaper office another young man sat with his head lying on a flat-top desk. He was clad in a strikingly flashy plaid coat, had a little wizened, good-natured face and seemed to have been drinking. The young man with the beard explained Sam's identity, taking the sleeping man by the shoulder and shaking him vigorously.

"Wake up, Skipper! There's a good story here!" he shouted. "The union has thrown out the mail-order strike leader!"

The Skipper got to his feet and began shaking his head.

"Of course, of course, Old Top, they would throw you out. You've got some brains. No man with brains can lead a strike. It's against the laws of Nature. Something was bound to hit you. Did Roughneck come out from Pittsburgh?" he asked, turning to the young man of the brown beard.

Then reaching above his head and taking a cap that matched his plaid coat from a nail on the wall, he winked at Sam. "Come on, Old Top. I've got to get a drink."

The two men went through a side door and down a dark alley, going in at the back door of a saloon. Mud lay deep in the alley and The Skipper sloshed through it, splattering Sam's clothes and face. In the saloon at a table facing Sam, with a bottle of French wine between them, he began explaining.

"I've a note coming due at the bank in the morning and no money to pay it," he said. "When I have a note coming due I always have no money and I always get drunk. Then next morning I pay the note. I don't know how I do it, but I always come out all right. It's a system— Now about this strike." He plunged into a discussion of the strike while men came in and out, laughing and drinking. At ten o'clock the proprietor locked the front door, drew the curtain, and coming to the back of the room sat down at the table with Sam and The Skipper, bringing another bottle of the French wine from which the two men continued drinking.

"That man from Pittsburgh busted up your place, eh?" he said, turning to Sam. "A man came in here tonight and told me. He sent for the typewriter people and made them take away the machines."

When they were ready to leave, Sam took money from his pocket and offered to pay for the bottle of French wine ordered by The Skipper, who arose and stood unsteadily on his feet.

"Do you mean to insult me?" he demanded indignantly, throwing a twenty-dollar bill on the table. The proprietor gave him back only fourteen dollars.

"I might as well wipe off the slate while you're flush," he observed, winking at Sam.

The Skipper sat down again, taking a pencil and pad of paper from his pocket, and throwing them on the table.

"I want an editorial on the strike for the Old Rag," he said to Sam. "Do one for me. Do something strong. Get a punch into it. I want to talk to my friend here."

Putting the pad of paper on the table Sam began writing his newspaper editorial. His head seemed wonderfully clear, his command of words unusually good. He called the attention of the public to the situation, the struggles of the striking girls and the intelligent fight they had been making to win a just cause, following this with paragraphs pointing out how the effectiveness of the work done had been annulled by the position taken by the labour and socialist leaders.

"These fellows at bottom care nothing for results," he wrote. "They are not thinking of the unemployed women with families to support, they are thinking only of themselves and their puny leadership which they fear is threatened. Now we shall have the usual exhibition of all the old things, struggle, and hatred and defeat."

When he had finished The Skipper and Sam went back through the alley to the newspaper office. The Skipper sloshed again through the mud and carried in his hand a bottle of red gin. At his desk he took the editorial from Sam's hands and read it.

"Perfect! Perfect to the thousandth part of an inch, Old Top," he said, pounding Sam on the shoulder. "Just what the Old Rag wanted to say about the strike." Then climbing upon the desk and putting the plaid coat under his head he went peacefully to sleep, and Sam, sitting beside the desk in a shaky office chair, slept also. At daybreak a black man with a broom in his hand woke them, and going into a long low room filled with presses The Skipper put his head under a water tap and came back waving a soiled towel and with water dripping from his hair.

"Now for the day and the labours thereof," he said, grinning at Sam and taking a long drink out of the gin bottle.

After breakfast he and Sam took up their stand in front of the barber shop opposite the stairway leading to the shirtwaist factory. Sam's girl with the pamphlets was gone as was also the soft-eyed Jewish girl, and in their places Frank and the Pittsburgh leader named Harrigan walked up and down. Again carriages and automobiles stood by the curb, and again a well-dressed woman got out of a machine and went toward three striking girls approaching along the sidewalk. The woman was met by Harrigan, shaking his fist and shouting, and getting back into the machine she drove off. From the stairway the flashily-dressed Hebrew looked at the crowd and laughed.

"Where is the new strike leader—the mail-order strike leader?" he called to Frank.

With the words, a working man with a dinner pail on his arm ran out of the crowd and knocked the Jew back into the stairway.

"Punch him! Punch the dirty scab leader!" yelled Frank, dancing up and down on the sidewalk.

Two policemen running forward began leading the workingman up the street, his dinner pail still clutched in one hand.

"I know something," The Skipper shouted, pounding Sam on the shoulder. "I know who will sign that note with me. The woman Harrigan drove back into her machine is the richest woman in town. I will show her your editorial. She will think I wrote it and it will get her. You'll see." He ran off up the street, shouting back over his shoulder, "Come over to the dump, I want to see you again."

Sam returned to the newspaper office and sat down waiting for The Skipper who, after a time, came in, took off his coat and began writing furiously. From time to time he took long drinks out of the bottle of red gin, and after silently offering it to Sam, continued reeling off sheet after sheet of loosely-written matter.

"I got her to sign the note," he called over his shoulder to Sam. "She was furious at Harrigan and when I told her we were going to attack him and defend you she fell for it quick. I won out by following my system. I always get drunk and it always wins."

At ten o'clock the newspaper office was in a ferment. The little man with the brown pointed beard, and another, kept running to The Skipper asking advice, laying typewritten sheets before him, talking as he wrote.

"Give me a lead. I want one more front page lead," The Skipper kept bawling at them, working like mad.

At ten thirty the door opened and Harrigan, accompanied by Frank, came in. Seeing Sam they stopped, looking at him uncertainly, and at the man at work at the desk.

"Well, speak up. This is no ladies' reception room. What do you fellows want?" snapped The Skipper, glaring at them.

Frank, coming forward, laid a typewritten sheet on the desk, which the newspaper man read hurriedly.

"Will you use it?" asked Frank.

The Skipper laughed.

"Wouldn't change a word of it," he shouted. "Sure I'll use it. It's what I wanted to make my point. You fellows watch me."

Frank and Harrigan went out and The Skipper, rushing to the door, began yelling into the room beyond.

"Hey, you Shorty and Tom, I've got that last lead."

Coming back to his desk he began writing again, grinning as he worked. To Sam he handed the typewritten sheet prepared by Frank.

"Dastardly attempt to win the cause of the working girls by dirty scab leaders and butter-fingered capitalist class," it began, and after this followed a wild jumble of words, words without meaning, sentences without point in which Sam was called a mealy-mouthed mail-order musser and The Skipper was mentioned incidentally as a pusillanimous ink slinger.

"I'll run the stuff and comment on it," declared The Skipper, handing Sam what he had written. It was an editorial inviting the public to read the article prepared for publication by the strike leaders and sympathising with the striking girls that their cause had to be lost because of the incompetence and lack of intelligence of their leaders.

"Hurrah for Roughhouse, the brave man who leads working girls to defeat in order that he may retain leadership and drive intelligent effort out of the cause of labour," wrote The Skipper.

Sam looked at the sheets and out of the window where a snow storm raged. It seemed to him that a crime was being done and he was sick and disgusted at his own inability to stop it. The Skipper lighted a short black pipe and took his cap from a nail on the wall.

"I'm the smoothest little newspaper thing in town and some financier as well," he declared. "Let's go have a drink."

After the drink Sam walked through the town toward the country. At the edge of town where the houses became scattered and the road started to drop away into a deep valley some one helloed behind him.

Turning, he saw the soft-eyed Jewish girl running along a path beside the road.

"Where are you going?" he asked, stopping to lean against a board fence, the snow falling upon his face.

"I'm going with you," said the girl. "You're the best and the strongest man I've ever seen and I'm not going to let you get away. If you've got a wife it don't matter. She isn't what she should be or you wouldn't be walking about the country alone. Harrigan and Frank say you're crazy, but I know better. I am going with you and I'm going to help you find what you want."

Sam wondered. She took a roll of bills from a pocket in her dress and gave it to him.

"I spent three hundred and fourteen dollars," she said.

They stood looking at each other. She put out a hand and laid it on his arm. Her eyes, soft and now glowing with eager light looked into his. Her round breasts rose and fell.

"Anywhere you say. I'll be your servant if you ask it of me."

A wave of hot desire ran through Sam followed by a quick reaction. He thought of his months of weary seeking and his universal failure.

"You are going back to town if I have to drive you there with stones," he told her, and turning ran down the valley leaving her standing by the board fence, her head buried in her arms.

V

One crisp winter evening Sam found himself on a busy street corner in Rochester, N.Y., watching from a doorway the crowds of people hurrying or loitering past him. He stood in a doorway near a corner that seemed to be a public meeting place and from all sides came men and women who met at the corner, stood for a moment in talk, and then went away together. Sam found himself beginning to wonder about the meetings. In the year since he had walked out of the Chicago office his mind had grown more and more reflective. Little things—a smile on the lips of an ill-clad old man mumbling and hurrying past him on the street, or the flutter of a child's hand from the doorway of a farmhouse—had furnished him food for hours of thought. Now he watched with interest the little incidents; the nods, the hand clasps, the hurried stealthy glances around of the men and women who met for a moment at the corner. On the sidewalk near his doorway several middle-aged men, evidently from a large hotel around the corner, were eyeing, with unpleasant, hungry, furtive eyes the women in the crowd.

A large blond woman stepped into the doorway beside Sam. "Waiting for some one?" she asked, smiling and looking steadily at him, with the harried, uncertain, hungry light he had seen in the eyes of the middle-aged men upon the sidewalk.

"What are you doing here with your husband at work?" he ventured.

She looked startled and then laughed.

"Why don't you hit me with your fist if you want to jolt me like that?" she demanded, adding, "I don't know who you are, but whoever you are I want to tell you that I've quit my husband."

"Why?" asked Sam.

She laughed again and stepping over looked at him closely.

"I guess you're bluffing," she said. "I don't believe you know Alf at all. And I'm glad you don't. I've quit Alf, but he would raise Cain just the same, if he saw me out here hustling."

Sam stepped out of the doorway and walked down a side street past a lighted theatre. Along the street women raised their eyes to him and beyond the theatre, a young girl, brushing against him, muttered, "Hello, Sport!"

Sam wanted to get away from the unhealthy, hungry look he had seen in the eyes of the men and women. His mind began working on this side of the lives of great numbers of people in the cities—of the men and women on the street corner, of the woman who from the security of a safe marriage had once thrown a challenge into his eyes as they sat together in the theatre, and of the thousand little incidents in the lives of all modern city men and women. He wondered how much that eager, aching hunger stood in the way of men's getting hold of life and living it earnestly and purposefully, as he wanted to live it, and as he felt all men and women wanted at bottom to live it. When he was a boy in Caxton he was more than once startled by the flashes of brutality and coarseness in the speech and actions of kindly, well-meaning men; now as he walked in the streets of the city he thought that he had got past being startled. "It is a quality of our lives," he decided. "American men and women have not learned to be clean and noble and natural, like their forests and their wide, clean plains."

He thought of what he had heard of London, and of Paris, and of other cities of the old world; and following an impulse acquired through his lonely wanderings, began talking to himself.

"We are no finer nor cleaner than these," he said, "and we sprang from the big clean new land through which I have been walking all these months. Will mankind always go on with that old aching, queerly expressed hunger in its blood, and with that look in its eyes? Will it never shrive itself and understand itself, and turn fiercely and energetically toward the building of a bigger and cleaner race of men?"

"It won't unless you help," came the answer from some hidden part of him.

Sam fell to thinking of the men who write, and of those who teach, and he wondered why they did not, all of them, talk more thoughtfully of vice, and why they so often spent their talents and their energies in futile attacks upon some phase of life, and ended their efforts toward human betterment by joining or promoting a temperance league, or stopping the playing of baseball on Sunday.

As a matter of fact were not many writers and reformers unconsciously in league with the procurer, in that they treated vice and profligacy as something, at bottom, charming? He himself had seen none of this vague charm.

"For me," he reflected, "there have been no François Villons or Sapphos in the tenderloins of American cities. There have been instead only heart-breaking disease and ill health and poverty, and hard brutal faces and torn, greasy finery."

He thought of men like Zola who saw this side of life clearly and how he, as a young fellow in the city, had read the man at Janet Eberly's suggestion and had been helped by him—helped and frightened and made to see. And then there rose before him the leering face of a keeper of a second-hand book store in Cleveland who some weeks before had pushed across the counter to him a paper-covered copy of "Nana's Brother," saying with a smirk, "That's some sporty stuff." And he wondered what he should have thought had he bought the book to feed the imagination the bookseller's comment was intended to arouse.

In the small towns through which Sam walked and in the small town in which he grew to manhood vice was openly crude and masculine. It went to sleep sprawling across a dirty beer-soaked table in Art Sherman's saloon in Piety Hollow, and the newsboy passed it without comment, regretting that it slept and that it had no money with which to buy papers.

"Dissipation and vice get into the life of youth," he thought, coming to a street corner where young men played pool and smoked cigarettes in a dingy poolroom, and turned back toward the heart of the city. "It gets into all modern life. The farmer boy coming up to the city to work hears lewd stories in the smoking car of the train, and the travelling men from the cities tell tales of the city streets to the group about the stove in village stores."

Sam did not quarrel with the fact that youth touched vice. Such things were a part of the world that men and women had made for their sons and daughters to live in, and that night as he wandered in the streets of Rochester he thought that he would like all youth to know, if they could but know, truth. His heart was bitter at the thought of men throwing the glamour of romance over the sordid, ugly things he had been seeing in that city and in every city he had known.

Past him in a street lined with small frame houses stumbled a man far gone in drink, by whose side walked a boy, and Sam's mind leaped back to those first years he had spent in the city and of the staggering old man he had left behind him in Caxton.

"You would think no man better armed against vice and dissipation than that painter's son of Caxton," he reminded himself, "and yet he embraced vice. He found, as all young men find, that there is much misleading talk and writing on the subject. The business men he knew did not part with able assistance because it did not sign the pledge. Ability was too rare a thing and too independent to sign pledges, and the lips-that-touch-liquor-shall-never-touch-mine sentiment among women was reserved for the lips that did not invite."

He began reviewing incidents of carouses he had been on with business men of his acquaintance, of a policeman knocked into a street and of himself, quiet and ably climbing upon tables to make speeches and to shout the innermost secrets of his heart to drunken hangers-on in Chicago barrooms. Normally he had not been a good mixer. He had been one to keep himself to himself. But on these carouses he let himself go, and got a reputation for daring audacity by slapping men on the back and singing songs with them. A glowing cordiality had pervaded him and for a time he had really believed there was such a thing as high flying vice that glistens in the sun.

Now stumbling past lighted saloons, wandering unknown in a city's streets, he knew better. All vice was unclean, unhealthy.

He remembered a hotel in which he had once slept, a hotel that admitted questionable couples. Its halls had become dingy; its windows remained unopened; dirt gathered in the corners; the attendants shuffled as they walked, and leered into the faces of creeping couples; the curtains at the windows were torn and discoloured; strange snarling oaths, screams, and cries jarred the tense nerves; peace and cleanliness had fled the place; men hurried through the halls with hats drawn down over their faces; sunlight and fresh air and cheerful, whistling bellboys were locked out.

He thought of the weary, restless walks taken by the young men from farms and country towns in the streets of the cities; young men believers in the golden vice. Hands beckoned to them from doorways, and women of the town laughed at their awkwardness. In Chicago he had walked in that way. He also had been seeking, seeking the romantic, impossible mistress that lurked at the bottom of men's tales of the submerged world. He wanted his golden girl. He was like the naïve German lad in the South Water Street warehouses who had once said to him—he was a frugal soul—"I would like to find a nice-looking girl who is quiet and modest and who will be my mistress and not charge anything."

Sam had not found his golden girl, and now he knew she did not exist. He had not seen the places called by the preachers the palaces of sin, and now he knew there were no such places. He wondered why youth could not be made to understand that sin is foul and that immorality reeks of vulgarity. Why could not they be told plainly that there are no housecleaning days in the tenderloin?

During his married life men had come to the house who discussed this matter. One of them, he remembered, had maintained stoutly that the scarlet sisterhood was a necessity of modern life and that ordinary decent social life could not go on without it. Often during the past year Sam had thought of the man's talk and his brain had reeled before the thought. In towns and on country roads he had seen troops of little girls come laughing and shouting out of school houses, and had wondered which of them would be chosen for that service to mankind; and now, in his hour of depression, he wished that the man who had talked at his dinner table might be made to walk with him and to share with him his thoughts.

Turning again into a lighted busy thoroughfare of the city, Sam continued his study of the faces in the crowds. To do this quieted and soothed his mind. He began to feel a weariness in his legs and thought with gratitude that he should have a night of good sleep. The sea of faces rolling up to him under the lights filled him with peace. "There is so much of life," he thought, "it must come to some end."

Looking intently at the faces, the dull faces and the bright faces, the faces drawn out of shape and with eyes nearly meeting above the nose, the faces with long, heavy sensual jaws, and the empty, soft faces on which the scalding finger of thought had left no mark, his fingers ached to get a pencil in his hand, or to spread the faces upon canvas in enduring pigments, to hold them up before the world and to be able to say, "Here are the faces you, by your lives, have made for yourselves and for your children."

In the lobby of a tall office building, where he stopped at a little cigar counter to get fresh tobacco for his pipe, he looked so fixedly at a woman clad in long soft furs, that in alarm she hurried out to her machine to wait for her escort, who had evidently gone up the elevator.

Once more in the street, Sam shuddered at the thought of the hands that had laboured that the soft cheeks and the untroubled eyes of this one woman might be. Into his mind came the face and figure of a little Canadian nurse who had once cared for him through an illness—her quick, deft fingers and her muscular little arms. "Another such as she," he muttered, "has been at work upon the face and body of this gentlewoman; a hunter has gone into the white silence of the north to bring out the warm furs that adorn her; for her there has been a tragedy—a shot, and red blood upon the snow, and a struggling beast waving its little claws in the air; for her a woman has worked through the morning, bathing her white limbs, her cheeks, her hair."

For this gentlewoman also there had been a man apportioned, a man like himself, who had cheated and lied and gone through the years in pursuit of the dollars to pay all of the others, a man of power, a man who could achieve, could accomplish. Again he felt within him a yearning for the power of the artist, the power not only to see the meaning of the faces in the street, but to reproduce what he saw, to get with subtle fingers the story of the achievement of mankind into a face hanging upon a wall.

In other days, in Caxton, listening to Telfer's talk, and in Chicago and New York with Sue, Sam had tried to get an inkling of the passion of the artist; now walking and looking at the faces rolling past him on the long street he thought that he did understand.

Once when he was new in the city he had, for some months, carried on an affair with a woman, the daughter of a cattle farmer from Iowa. Now her face filled his vision. How rugged it was, how filled with the message of the ground underfoot; the thick lips, the dull eyes, the strong, bullet-like head, how like the cattle her father had bought and sold. He remembered the little room in Chicago where he had his first love passage with this woman. How frank and wholesome it had seemed. How eagerly both man and woman had rushed at evening to the meeting place. How her strong hands had clasped him. The face of the woman in the motor by the office building danced before his eyes, the face so peaceful, so free from the marks of human passion, and he wondered what daughter of a cattle raiser had taken the passion out of the man who paid for the beauty of that face.

On a side street, near the lighted front of a cheap theatre, a woman, standing alone and half concealed in the doorway of a church, called softly, and turning he went to her.

"I am not a customer," he said, looking at her thin face and bony hands, "but if you care to come with me I will stand a good dinner. I am getting hungry and do not like eating alone. I want some one to talk to me so that I won't get to thinking."

"You're a queer bird," said the woman, taking his arm. "What have you done that you don't want to think?"

Sam said nothing.

"There's a place over there," she said, pointing to the lighted front of a cheap restaurant with soiled curtains at the windows.

Sam kept on walking.

"If you do not mind," he said, "I will pick the place. I want to buy a good dinner. I want a place with clean linen on the table and a good cook in the kitchen."

They stopped at a corner to talk of the dinner, and at her suggestion he waited at a near-by drug store while she went to her room. As he waited he went to the telephone and ordered the dinner and a taxicab. When she returned she had on a clean shirtwaist and had combed her hair. Sam thought he caught the odour of benzine, and guessed she had been at work on the spots on her worn jacket. She seemed surprised to find him still waiting.

"I thought maybe it was a stall," she said.

They drove in silence to a place Sam had in mind, a road-house with clean washed floors, painted walls, and open fires in the private dining-rooms. Sam had been there several times during the month, and the food had been well cooked.

They ate in silence. Sam had no curiosity to hear her talk of herself, and she seemed to have no knack of casual conversation. He was not studying her, but had brought her as he had said, because of his loneliness, and because her thin, tired face and frail body, looking out from the darkness by the church door, had made an appeal.

She had, he thought, a look of hard chastity, like one whipped but not defeated. Her cheeks were thin and covered with freckles, like a boy's. Her teeth were broken and in bad repair, though clean, and her hands had the worn, hardly-used look of his own mother's hands. Now that she sat before him in the restaurant, in some vague way she resembled his mother.

After dinner he sat smoking his cigar and looking at the fire. The woman of the streets leaned across the table and touched him on the arm.

"Are you going to take me anywhere after this—after we leave here?" she said.

"I am going to take you to the door of your room, that's all."

"I'm glad," she said; "it's a long time since I've had an evening like this. It makes me feel clean."

For a time they sat in silence and then Sam began talking of his home town in Iowa, letting himself go and expressing the thoughts that came into his mind. He told her of his mother and of Mary Underwood and she in turn told of her town and of her life. She had some difficulty about hearing which made conversation trying. Words and sentences had to be repeated to her and after a time Sam smoked and looked at the fire, letting her talk. Her father had been a captain of a small steamboat plying up and down Long Island Sound and her mother a careful, shrewd woman and a good housekeeper. They had lived in a Rhode Island village and had a garden back of their house. The captain had not married until he was forty-five and had died when the girl was eighteen, the mother dying a year later.

The girl had not been much known in the Rhode Island village, being shy and reticent. She had kept the house clean and helped the captain in the garden. When her parents were dead she had found herself alone with thirty-seven hundred dollars in the bank and the little home, and had married a young man who was a clerk in a railroad office, and sold the house to move to Kansas City. The big flat country frightened her. Her life there had been unsuccessful. She had been lonely for the hills and the water of her New England village, and she was, by nature, undemonstrative and unemotional, so that she did not get much hold of her husband. He had undoubtedly married her for the little hoard and, by various devices, began getting it from her. A son had been born, for a time her health broke badly, and she discovered through an accident that her husband was spending her money in dissipation among the women of the town.

"There wasn't any use wasting words when I found he didn't care for me or for the baby and wouldn't support us, so I left him," she said in a level, businesslike way.

When she came to count up, after she had got clear of her husband and had taken a course in stenography, there was one thousand dollars of her savings left and she felt pretty safe. She took a position and went to work, feeling well satisfied and happy. And then came the trouble with her hearing. She began to lose places and finally had to be content with a small salary, earned by copying form letters for a mail order medicine man. The boy she put out with a capable German woman, the wife of a gardener. She paid four dollars a week for him and there was clothing to be bought for herself and the boy. Her wage from the medicine man was seven dollars a week.

"And so," she said, "I began going on the street. I knew no one and there was nothing else to do. I couldn't do that in the town where the boy lived, so I came away. I've gone from city to city, working mostly for patent medicine men and filling out my income by what I earned in the streets. I'm not naturally a woman who cares about men and not many of them care about me. I don't like to have them touch me with their hands. I can't drink as most of the girls do; it sickens me. I want to be left alone. Perhaps I shouldn't have married. Not that I minded my husband. We got along very well until I had to stop giving him money. When I found where it was going it opened my eyes. I felt that I had to have at least a thousand dollars for the boy in case anything happened to me. When I found there wasn't anything to do but just go on the streets, I went. I tried doing other work, but hadn't the strength, and when it came to the test I cared more about the boy than I did about myself—any woman would. I thought he was of more importance than what I wanted.

"It hasn't been easy for me. Sometimes when I have got a man to go with me I walk along the street praying that I won't shudder and draw away when he touches me with his hands. I know that if I do he will go away and I won't get any money.

"And then they talk and lie about themselves. I've had them try to work off bad money and worthless jewelry on me. Sometimes they try to make love to me and then steal back the money they have given me. That's the hard part, the lying and the pretence. All day I write the same lies over and over for the patent-medicine men and then at night I listen to these others lying to me."

She stopped talking and leaning over put her cheek down on her hand and sat looking into the fire.

"My mother," she began again, "didn't always wear a clean dress. She couldn't. She was always down on her knees scrubbing around the floor or out in the garden pulling weeds. But she hated dirt. If her dress was dirty her underwear was clean and so was her body. She taught me to be that way and I wanted to be. It came naturally. But I'm losing it all. All evening I have been sitting here with you thinking that my underwear isn't clean. Most of the time I don't care. Being clean doesn't go with what I am doing. I have to keep trying to be flashy outside so that men will stop when they see me on the street. Sometimes when I have done well I don't go on the streets for three or four weeks. Then I clean up my room and bathe myself. My landlady lets me do my washing in the basement at night. I don't seem to care about cleanliness the weeks I am on the streets."

The little German orchestra began playing a lullaby, and a fat German waiter came in at the open door and put more wood on the fire.

SHERWOOD ANDERSON

He stopped by the table and talked about the mud in the road outside. From another room came the silvery clink of glasses and the sound of laughing voices. The girl and Sam drifted back into talk of their home towns. Sam felt that he liked her very much and thought that if she had belonged to him he should have found a basis on which to live with her contentedly. She had a quality of honesty that he was always seeking in people.

As they drove back to the city she put a hand on his arm.

"I wouldn't mind about you," she said, looking at him frankly.

Sam laughed and patted her thin hand. "It's been a good evening," he said, "we'll go through with it as it stands."

"Thanks for that," she said, "and there is something else I want to tell you. Perhaps you will think it bad of me. Sometimes when I don't want to go on the streets I get down on my knees and pray for strength to go on gamely. Does it seem bad? We are a praying people, we New Englanders."

As he stood in the street Sam could hear her laboured asthmatic breathing as she climbed the stairs to her room. Half way up she stopped and waved her hand at him. The thing was awkwardly done and boyish. Sam had a feeling that he should like to get a gun and begin shooting citizens in the streets. He stood in the lighted city looking down the long deserted street and thought of Mike McCarthy in the jail at Caxton. Like Mike, he lifted up his voice in the night.

"Are you there, O God? Have you left your children here on the earth hurting each other? Do you put the seed of a million children in a man, and the planting of a forest in one tree, and permit men to wreck and hurt and destroy?"

VI

O ne morning, at the end of his second year of wandering, Sam got out of his bed in a cold little hotel in a mining village in West Virginia, looked at the miners, their lamps in their caps, going through the dimly lighted streets, ate a portion of leathery breakfast cakes, paid his bill at the hotel, and took a train for New York. He had definitely abandoned the idea of getting at what he wanted through wandering about the country and talking to chance acquaintances by the wayside and in villages, and had decided to return to a way of life more befitting his income.

He felt that he was not by nature a vagabond, and that the call of the wind and the sun and the brown road was not insistent in his blood. The spirit of Pan did not command him, and although there were certain spring mornings of his wandering days that were like mountain tops in his experience of life, mornings when some strong, sweet feeling ran through the trees, and the grass, and the body of the wanderer, and when the call of life seemed to come shouting and inviting down the wind, filling him with delight of the blood in his body and the thoughts in his brain, yet at bottom and in spite of these days of pure joy he was, after all, a man of the towns and the crowds. Caxton and South Water Street and LaSalle Street had all left their marks on him, and so, throwing his canvas jacket into a corner of the room in the West Virginia hotel, he returned to the haunts of his kind.

In New York he went to an uptown club where he owned a membership and into the grill where he found at breakfast an actor acquaintance named Jackson.

Sam dropped into a chair and looked about him. He remembered a visit he had made there some years before with Webster and Crofts and felt again the quiet elegance of the surroundings.

"Hello, Moneymaker," said Jackson, heartily. "Heard you had gone to a nunnery."

Sam laughed and began ordering a breakfast that made Jackson's eyes open with astonishment.

"You, Mr. Elegance, would not understand a man's spending month after month in the open air seeking a good body and an end in life and then suddenly changing his mind and coming back to a place like this," he observed.

SHERWOOD ANDERSON

Jackson laughed and lighted a cigarette.

"How little you know me," he said. "I would live my life in the open but that I am a mighty good actor and have just finished another long New York run. What are you going to do now that you are thin and brown? Will you go back to Morrison and Prince and money making?"

Sam shook his head and looked at the quiet elegance of the man before him. How satisfied and happy he looked.

"I am going to try living among the rich and the leisurely," he said.

"They are a rotten crew," Jackson assured him, "and I am taking a night train for Detroit. Come with me. We will talk things over."

On the train that night they got into talk with a broad-shouldered old man who told them of a hunting trip on which he was bound.

"I am going to sail from Seattle," he said, "and go everywhere and hunt everything. I am going to shoot the head off of every big animal kind of thing left in the world and then come back to New York and stay there until I die."

"I will go with you," said Sam, and in the morning left Jackson at Detroit and continued westward with his new acquaintance.

For months Sam travelled and shot with the old man, a vigorous, big-hearted old fellow who, having become wealthy through an early investment in stock of the Standard Oil Company, devoted his life to his lusty, primitive passion for shooting and killing. They went on lion hunts, elephant hunts and tiger hunts, and when on the west coast of Africa Sam took a boat for London, his companion walked up and down the beach smoking black cheroots and declaring the fun was only half over and that Sam was a fool to go.

After the year of the hunt royal Sam spent another year living the life of a gentleman of wealth and leisure in London, New York, and Paris. He went on automobile trips, fished and loafed along the shores of northern lakes, canoed through Canada with a writer of nature books, and sat about clubs and fashionable hotels listening to the talk of the men and women of that world.

Late one afternoon in the spring of the year he went to the village on the Hudson River where Sue had taken a house, and almost immediately saw her. For an hour he followed, watching her quick, active little figure as she walked through the village streets, and wondering what life had come to mean to her, but when, turning suddenly, she would have come face to face with him, he hurried down a side street and took a train to the city feeling that he could not face her empty-handed and ashamed after the years.

In the end he started drinking again, not moderately now, but steadily and almost continuously. One night in Detroit, with three young men from his hotel, he got drunk and was, for the first time since his parting with Sue, in the company of women. Four of them, met in some restaurant, got into an automobile with Sam and the three young men and rode about town laughing, waving bottles of wine in the air, and calling to passers-by in the street. They wound up in a diningroom in a place at the edge of town, where the party spent hours around a long table, drinking, and singing songs.

One of the girls sat on Sam's lap and put an arm about his neck.

"Give me some money, rich man," she said.

Sam looked at her closely.

"Who are you?" he asked.

She began explaining that she was a clerk in a downtown store and that she had a lover who drove a laundry wagon.

"I go on these bats to get money to buy good clothes," she said frankly, "but if Tim saw me here he would kill me."

Putting a bill into her hand Sam went downstairs and getting into a taxicab drove back to his hotel.

After that night he went frequently on carouses of this kind. He was in a kind of prolonged stupor of inaction, talked of trips abroad which he did not take, bought a huge farm in Virginia which he never visited, planned a return to business which he did not execute, and month after month continued to waste his days. He would get out of bed at noon and begin drinking steadily. As the afternoon passed he grew merry and talkative, calling men by their first names, slapping chance acquaintances on the back, playing pool or billiards with skilful young men intent upon gain. In the early summer he got in with a party of young men from New York and with them spent months in sheer idle waste of time. Together they drove high-powered automobiles on long trips, drank, quarrelled, and went on board a yacht to carouse, alone or with women. At times Sam would leave his companions and spend days riding through the country on fast trains, sitting for hours in silence looking out of the window at the passing country and wondering at his endurance of the life he led. For some months he carried with him a young man whom he called a secretary and paid a large salary for his ability to tell stories and sing clever songs, only to discharge him suddenly for telling a foul tale that reminded Sam of another tale told by the stoop-shouldered old man in the office of Ed's hotel in the Illinois town.

From being silent and taciturn, as during the months of his wanderings, Sam became morose and combative. Staying on and on in the empty, aimless way of life he had adopted he yet felt that there was for him a right way of living and wondered at his continued inability to find it. He lost his native energy, grew fat and coarse of body, was pleased for hours by little things, read no books, lay for hours in bed drunk and talking nonsense to himself, ran about the streets swearing vilely, grew habitually coarse in thought and speech, sought constantly a lower and more vulgar set of companions, was brutal and ugly with attendants about hotels and clubs where he lived, hated life, but ran like a coward to sanitariums and health resorts at the wagging of a doctor's head.

BOOK IV

I

One afternoon in early September Sam got on a westward-bound train intending to visit his sister on the farm near Caxton. For years he had heard nothing from Kate, but she had, he knew, two daughters, and he thought he would do something for them.

"I will put them on the Virginia farm and make a will leaving them my money," he thought. "Perhaps I shall be able to make them happy by setting them up in life and giving them beautiful clothes to wear."

At St. Louis he got off the train, thinking vaguely that he would see an attorney and make arrangements about the will, and for several days stayed about the Planters Hotel with a set of drinking companions he had picked up. One afternoon he began going from place to place drinking and gathering companions. An ugly light was in his eyes and he looked at men and women passing in the streets, feeling that he was in the midst of enemies, and that for him the peace, contentment, and good cheer that shone out of the eyes of others was beyond getting.

In the late afternoon, followed by a troop of roistering companions, he came out upon a street flanked with small, brick warehouses facing the river, where steamboats lay tied to floating docks.

"I want a boat to take me and my crowd for a cruise up and down the river," he announced, approaching the captain of one of the boats. "Take us up and down the river until we are tired of it. I will pay what it costs."

It was one of the days when drink would not take hold of him, and he went among his companions, buying drinks and thinking himself a fool to continue furnishing entertainment for the vile crew that sat about him on the deck of the boat. He began shouting and ordering them about.

"Sing louder," he commanded, tramping up and down and scowling at his companions.

A young man of the party who had a reputation as a dancer refused to perform when commanded. Springing forward Sam dragged him out on the deck before the shouting crowd.

"Now dance!" he growled, "or I will throw you into the river."

The young man danced furiously, and Sam marched up and down and looked at him and at the leering faces of the men and women lounging along the deck or shouting at the dancer. The liquor in him beginning to take effect, a queerly distorted version of his old passion for reproduction came to him and he raised his hand for silence.

"I want to see a woman who is a mother," he shouted. "I want to see a woman who has borne children."

A small woman with black hair and burning black eyes sprang from the group gathered about the dancer.

"I have borne children—three of them," she said, laughing up into his face. "I can bear more of them."

Sam looked at her stupidly and taking her by the arm led her to a chair on the deck. The crowd laughed.

"Belle is after his roll," whispered a short, fat man to his companion, a tall woman with blue eyes.

As the steamer, with its load of men and women drinking and singing songs, went up the river past bluffs covered with trees, the woman beside Sam pointed to a row of tiny houses at the top of the bluffs.

"My children are there. They are getting supper now," she said.

She began singing, laughing and waving a bottle to the others sitting along the deck. A youth with heavy features stood upon a chair and sang a song of the street, and, jumping to her feet, Sam's companion kept time with the bottle in her hand. Sam walked over to where the captain stood looking up the river.

"Turn back," he said, "I am tired of this crew."

On the way back down the river the black-eyed woman again sat beside Sam.

"We will go to my house," she said quietly, "just you and me. I will show you the kids."

Darkness was gathering over the river as the boat turned, and in the distance the lights of the city began blinking into view. The crowd had grown quiet, sleeping in chairs along the deck or gathering in small groups and talking in low tones. The black-haired woman began to tell Sam her story.

She was, she said, the wife of a plumber who had left her.

"I drove him crazy," she said, laughing quietly. "He wanted me to stay at home with him and the kids night after night. He used to follow me down town at night begging me to come home. When I wouldn't come he would go away with tears in his eyes. It made me furious. He wasn't a man. He would do anything I asked him to do. And then he ran away and left the kids on my hands."

In the city Sam, with the black-haired woman beside him, rode about in an open carriage, forgetting the children and going from place to place, eating and drinking. For an hour they sat in a box at the theatre, but grew tired of the performance and climbed again into the carriage.

"We will go to my house. I want to have you alone," said the woman.

They drove through street after street of workingmen's houses, where children ran laughing and playing under the lights, and two boys, their bare legs flashing in the lights from the lamps overhead, ran after them, holding to the back of the carriage.

The driver whipped the horses and looked back laughing. The woman got up and kneeling on the seat of the carriage laughed down into the faces of the running boys.

"Run, you little devils," she cried.

They held on, running furiously. Their legs twinkled and flashed under the lights.

"Give me a silver dollar," she said, turning to Sam, and when he had given it to her, threw it ringing upon the pavement under a street lamp. The two boys darted for it, shouting and waving their hands to her.

Swarms of huge flies and beetles circled under the street lamps, striking Sam and the woman in the face. One of them, a great black crawling thing, alighted on her breast, and taking it in her hand she crept forward and dropped it down the neck of the driver.

In spite of his hard drinking during the afternoon and evening, Sam's head was clear and a calm hatred of life burned in him. His mind ran back over the years he had passed since breaking his word to Sue, and a scorn of all effort burned in him.

"It is what a man gets who goes seeking Truth," he thought. "He comes to a fine end in life."

On all sides of him life ran playing on the pavement and leaping in the air. It circled and buzzed and sang above his head in the summer night there in the heart of the city. Even in the sullen man sitting in the carriage beside the black-haired woman it began to sing. The blood climbed through his body; an old half-dead longing, half hunger, half hope awoke in him, pulsating and insistent. He looked at the laughing, intoxicated woman beside him and a feeling of masculine approval shot through him. He began thinking of what she had said before the laughing crowd on the steamer.

"I have borne three children and can bear more."

His blood, stirred by the sight of the woman, awoke his sleeping brain, and he began again to quarrel with life and what life had offered him. He thought that always he would stubbornly refuse to accept the call of life unless he could have it on his own terms, unless he could command and direct it as he had commanded and directed the gun company.

"Else why am I here?" he muttered, looking away from the vacant, laughing face of the woman and at the broad, muscular back of the driver on the seat in front. "Why had I a brain and a dream and a hope? Why went I about seeking Truth?"

His mind ran on in the vein started by the sight of the circling beetles and the running boys. The woman put her head upon his shoulder and her black hair blew against his face. She struck wildly at the circling beetles, laughing like a child when she had caught one of them in her hand.

"Men like me are for some end. They are not to be played with as I have been," he muttered, clinging to the hand of the woman, who, also, he thought, was being tossed about by life.

Before a saloon, on a street where cars ran, the carriage stopped. Through the open front door Sam could see working-men standing before a bar drinking foaming glasses of beer, the hanging lamps above their heads throwing their black shadows upon the floor. A strong, stale smell came out at the door. The woman leaned over the side of the carriage and shouted. "O Will, come out here."

A man clad in a long white apron and with his shirt sleeves rolled to his elbows came from behind the bar and talked to her, and when they had started on she told Sam of her plan to sell her home and buy the place.

"Will you run it?" he asked.

"Sure," she said. "The kids can take care of themselves."

At the end of a little street of a half dozen neat cottages, they got out of the carriage and walked with uncertain steps along a sidewalk skirting a high bluff and overlooking the river. Below the houses a tangled mass of bushes and small trees lay black in the moonlight, and in the distance the grey body of the river showed faint and far away. The undergrowth was so thick that, looking down, one saw only the tops of the growth, with here and there a grey outcrop of rocks that glistened in the moonlight.

Up a flight of stone steps they climbed to the porch of one of the houses facing the river. The woman had stopped laughing and hung heavily on Sam's arm, her feet groping for the steps. They passed through a door and into a long, low-ceilinged room. An open stairway at the

SHERWOOD ANDERSON

side of the room went up to the floor above, and through a curtained doorway at the end one looked into a small dining-room. A rag carpet lay on the floor and about a table, under a hanging lamp at the centre, sat three children. Sam looked at them closely. His head reeled and he clutched at the knob of the door. A boy of perhaps fourteen, with freckles on his face and on the backs of his hands and with reddish-brown hair and brown eyes, was reading aloud. Beside him a younger boy with black hair and black eyes, and with his knees doubled up on the chair in front of him so that his chin rested on them, sat listening. A tiny girl, pale and with yellow hair and dark circles under her eyes, slept in another chair, her head hanging uncomfortably to one side. She was, one would have said, seven, the black-haired boy ten.

The freckle-faced boy stopped reading and looked at the man and woman; the sleeping child stirred uneasily in her chair, and the black-haired boy straightened out his legs and looked over his shoulder.

"Hello, Mother," he said heartily.

The woman walked unsteadily to the curtained doorway leading into the dining-room and pulled aside the curtains.

"Come here, Joe," she said.

The freckle-faced boy arose and went toward her. She stood aside, supporting herself with one hand grasping the curtain. As he passed she struck him with her open hand on the back of the head, sending him reeling into the dining-room.

"Now you, Tom," she called to the black-haired boy. "I told you kids to wash the dishes after supper and to put Mary to bed. Here it is past ten and nothing done and you two reading books again."

The black-haired boy got up and started obediently toward her, but Sam walked rapidly past him and clutched the woman by the arm so that she winced and twisted in his grasp.

"You come with me," he said.

He walked the woman across the room and up the stairs. She leaned heavily on his arm, laughing, and looking up into his face.

At the top of the stairway he stopped.

"We go in here," she said, pointing to a door.

He took her into the room. "You get to sleep," he said, and going out closed the door, leaving her sitting heavily on the edge of the bed.

Downstairs he found the two boys among the dishes in a tiny kitchen off the dining-room. The little girl still slept uneasily in the chair by the table, the hot lamp-light streaming down on her thin cheeks.

Sam stood in the kitchen door looking at the two boys, who looked back at him self-consciously.

"Which of you two puts Mary to bed?" he asked, and then, without waiting for an answer, turned to the taller of the two boys. "Let Tom do it," he said. "I will help you here."

Joe and Sam stood in the kitchen at work with the dishes; the boy, going busily about, showed the man where to put the clean dishes, and got him dry wiping towels. Sam's coat was off and his sleeves rolled up.

The work went on in half awkward silence and a storm went on within Sam's breast. When the boy Joe looked shyly up at him it was as though the lash of a whip had cut down across flesh, suddenly grown tender. Old memories began to stir within him and he remembered his own childhood, his mother at work among other people's soiled clothes, his father Windy coming home drunk, and the chill in his mother's heart and in his own. There was something men and women owed to childhood, not because it was childhood but because it was new life springing up. Aside from any question of fatherhood or motherhood there was a debt to be paid.

In the little house on the bluff there was silence. Outside the house there was darkness and darkness lay over Sam's spirit. The boy Joe went quickly about, putting the dishes Sam had wiped on the shelves. Somewhere on the river, far below the house, a steamboat whistled. The backs of the hands of the boy were covered with freckles. How quick and competent the hands were. Here was new life, as yet clean, unsoiled, unshaken by life. Sam was shamed by the trembling of his own hands. He had always wanted quickness and firmness within his own body, the health of the body that is a temple for the health of the spirit. He was an American and down deep within himself was the moral fervor that is American and that had become so strangely perverted in himself and others. As so often happened with him, when he was deeply stirred, an army of vagrant thoughts ran through his head. The thoughts had taken the place of the perpetual scheming and planning of his days as a man of affairs, but as yet all his thinking had brought him to nothing and had only left him more shaken and uncertain then ever.

The dishes were now all wiped and he went out of the kitchen glad to escape the shy silent presence of the boy. "Has life quite gone from me? Am I but a dead thing walking about?" he asked himself. The presence of the children had made him feel that he was himself but a child, a grown tired and shaken child. There was maturity and manhood somewhere abroad. Why could he not come to it? Why could it not come into him?

The boy Tom returned from having put his sister into bed and the two boys said good night to the strange man in their mother's house. Joe, the bolder of the two, stepped forward and offered his hand. Sam shook it solemnly and then the younger boy came forward.

"I'll be around here tomorrow I think," Sam said huskily.

The boys were gone, into the silence of the house, and Sam walked up and down in the little room. He was restless as though about to start on a new journey and half unconsciously began running his hands over his body wishing it strong and hard as when he tramped the road. As on the day when he had walked out of the Chicago Club bound on his hunt for Truth, he let his mind go so that it played freely over his past life, reviewing and analysing.

For hours he sat on the porch or walked up and down in the room where the lamp still burned brightly. Again the smoke from his pipe tasted good on his tongue and all the night air had a sweetness that brought back to him the walk beside the bridle path in Jackson Park when Sue had given him herself, and with herself a new impulse in life.

It was two o'clock when he lay down upon a couch in the living-room and blew out the light. He did not undress, but threw his shoes on the floor and lay looking at a wide path of moonlight that came through the open door. In the darkness it seemed that his mind worked more rapidly and that the events and motives of his restless years went streaming past like living things upon the floor.

Suddenly he sat up and listened. The voice of one of the boys, heavy with sleep, ran through the upper part of the house.

"Mother! O Mother!" called the sleepy voice, and Sam thought he could hear the little body moving restlessly in bed.

Silence followed. He sat upon the edge of the couch, waiting. It seemed to him that he was coming to something; that his brain that had for hours been working more and more rapidly was about to produce the thing for which he waited. He felt as he had felt that night as he waited in the corridor of the hospital.

In the morning the three children came down the stairs and finished dressing in the long room, the little girl coming last, carrying her shoes and stockings and rubbing her eyes with the back of her hand. A cool morning wind blew up from the river and through the open screened doors as he and Joe cooked breakfast, and later as the four of them sat at the table Sam tried to talk but did not make much progress. His tongue was heavy and the children seemed looking at him with strange questioning eyes. "Why are you here?" their eyes asked.

For a week Sam stayed in the city, coming daily to the house. With the children he talked a little, and in the evening, when the mother had gone away, the little girl came to him. He carried her to a chair on the porch outside and while the boys sat reading under the lamp inside she went to sleep in his arms. Her body was warm and the breath came softly and sweetly from between her lips. Sam looked down the bluffside and saw the country and the river far below, sweet in the moonlight. Tears came into his eyes. Was a new sweet purpose growing within him or were the tears but evidence of self pity? He wondered.

One night the black-haired woman again came home far gone in drink, and again Sam led her up the stairs to see her fall muttering and babbling upon the bed. Her companion, a little flashily dressed man with a beard, had run off at the sight of Sam standing in the living-room under the lamp. The two boys, to whom he had been reading, said nothing, looking self-consciously at the book upon the table and occasionally out of the corner of their eyes at their new friend. In a few minutes they too went up the stairs, and as on that first night, they put out their hands awkwardly.

Through the night Sam again sat in the darkness outside or lay awake on the couch. "I will make a new try, adopt a new purpose in life now," he said to himself.

When the children had gone to school the next morning, Sam took a car and went into the city, going first to a bank to have a large draft cashed. Then he spent many busy hours going from store to store and buying clothes, caps, soft underwear, suit cases, dresses, night clothes, and books. Last of all he bought a large dressed doll. All these things he had sent to his room at the hotel, leaving a man there to pack the trunks and suit cases, and get them to the station. A large, motherly-looking woman, an employé of the hotel, who passed through the hall, offered to help with the packing.

After another visit or two Sam got back upon the car and went again to the house. In his pockets he had several thousands of dollars in large bills. He had remembered the power of cash in deals he had made in the past.

"I will see what it will do here," he thought.

In the house Sam found the black-haired woman lying on a couch in the living-room. As he came in at the door she arose unsteadily and looked at him.

"There's a bottle in the cupboard in the kitchen," she said. "Get me a drink. Why do you hang about here?"

Sam brought the bottle and poured her a drink, pretending to drink with her by putting the bottle to his lips and throwing back his head.

"What was your husband like?" he asked.

"Who? Jack?" she said. "Oh, he was all right. He was stuck on me. He stood for anything until I brought men home here. Then he got crazy and went away." She looked at Sam and laughed.

"I didn't care much for him," she added. "He couldn't make money enough for a live woman."

Sam began talking of the saloon she intended buying.

"The children will be a bother, eh?" he said.

"I have an offer for the house," she said. "I wish I didn't have the kids. They are a nuisance."

"I have been figuring that out," Sam told her. "I know a woman in the East who would take them and raise them. She is wild about kids. I should like to do something to help you. I might take them to her."

"In the name of Heaven, man, lead them away," she laughed, and took another drink from the bottle.

Sam drew from his pocket a paper he had secured from a downtown attorney.

"Get a neighbour in here to witness this," he said. "The woman will want things regular. It releases you from all responsibility for the kids and puts it on her."

She looked at him suspiciously. "What's the graft? Who gets stuck for the fares down east?"

Sam laughed and going to the back door shouted to a man who sat under a tree back of the next house smoking a pipe.

"Sign here," he said, putting the paper before her. "Here is your neighbour to sign as witness. You do not get stuck for a cent."

The woman, half drunk, signed the paper, after a long doubtful look at Sam, and when she had signed and had taken another drink from the bottle lay down again on the couch.

"If any one wakes me up for the next six hours they will get killed," she declared. It was evident she knew little of what she had done, but at the moment Sam did not care. He was again a bargainer, ready to take an advantage. Vaguely he felt that he might be bargaining for an end in life, for purpose to come into his own life.

Sam went quietly down the stone steps and along the little street at the brow of the hill to the car tracks, and at noon was waiting in an automobile outside the door of the schoolhouse when the children came out.

He drove across the city to the Union Station, the three children accepting him and all he did without question. At the station they found the man from the hotel with the trunks and with three bright new suit cases. Sam went to the express office and putting several bills into an envelope sealed and sent it to the woman while the three children walked up and down in the train shed carrying the cases, aglow with the pride of them.

At two o'clock Sam, with the little girl in his arms and with one of the boys seated on either side of him, sat in a stateroom of a New York flyer—bound for Sue.

II

S am McPherson is a living American. He is a rich man, but his money, that he spent so many years and so much of his energy acquiring, does not mean much to him. What is true of him is true of more wealthy Americans than is commonly believed. Something has happened to him that has happened to the others also, to how many of the others? Men of courage, with strong bodies and quick brains, men who have come of a strong race, have taken up what they had thought to be the banner of life and carried it forward. Growing weary they have stopped in a road that climbs a long hill and have leaned the banner against a tree. Tight brains have loosened a little. Strong convictions have become weak. Old gods are dying.

"It is only when you are torn from your mooring and drift like a rudderless ship I am able to come near to you."

The banner has been carried forward by a strong daring man filled with determination.

What is inscribed on it?

It would perhaps be dangerous to inquire too closely. We Americans have believed that life must have point and purpose. We have called ourselves Christians, but the sweet Christian philosophy of failure has been unknown among us. To say of one of us that he has failed is to take life and courage away. For so long we have had to push blindly forward. Roads had to be cut through our forests, great towns must be built. What in Europe has been slowly building itself out of the fibre of the generations we must build now, in a lifetime.

In our father's day, at night in the forests of Michigan, Ohio, Kentucky, and on the wide prairies, wolves howled. There was fear in our fathers and mothers, pushing their way forward, making the new land. When the land was conquered fear remained, the fear of failure. Deep in our American souls the wolves still howl.

THERE WERE MOMENTS AFTER SAM came back to Sue, bringing the three children, when he thought he had snatched success out of the very jaws of failure.

But the thing from which he had all his life been fleeing was still there. It hid itself in the branches of the trees that lined the New England roads where he went to walk with the two boys. At night it looked down at him from the stars.

Perhaps life wanted acceptance from him, but he could not accept. Perhaps his story and his life ended with the home-coming, perhaps it began then.

The home-coming was not in itself a completely happy event. There was a house with a fire at night and the voices of the children. In Sam's breast there was a feeling of something alive, growing.

Sue was generous, but she was not now the Sue of the bridle path in Jackson Park in Chicago or the Sue who had tried to remake the world by raising fallen women. On his arrival at her house, on a summer night, coming in suddenly and strangely with the three strange children—a little inclined toward tears and homesickness—she was flustered and nervous.

Darkness was coming on when he walked up the gravel path from the gate to the house door with the child Mary in his arms and the two boys, Joe and Tom, walking soberly and solemnly beside him. Sue had just come out at the front door and stood regarding them, startled and a little frightened. Her hair was becoming grey, but as she stood there Sam thought her figure almost boyish in its slenderness.

With quick generosity she threw aside the inclination in herself to ask many questions but there was the suggestion of a taunt in the question she did ask.

"Have you decided to come back to me and is this your home-coming?" she asked, stepping down into the path and looking not at Sam but at the children.

Sam did not answer at once, and little Mary began to cry. That was a help.

"They will all be wanting something to eat and a place to sleep," he said, as though coming back to a wife, long neglected, and bringing with him three strange children were an everyday affair.

Although she was puzzled and afraid, Sue smiled and led the way into the house. Lamps were lighted and the five human beings, so abruptly brought together, stood looking at each other. The two boys clung to each other and little Mary put her arms about Sam's neck and hid her face on his shoulder. He unloosed her clutching hands and put her boldly into Sue's arms. "She will be your mother now," he said defiantly, not looking at Sue.

THE EVENING WAS GOT THROUGH, blunderingly by himself, Sam thought, and very nobly by Sue.

There was the mother hunger still alive in her. He had shrewdly counted on that. It blinded her eyes to other things and then a notion had come into her head and there seemed the possibility of doing a peculiarly romantic act. Before that notion was destroyed, later in the evening, both Sam and the children had been installed in the house.

A tall strong Negress came into the room, and Sue gave her instructions regarding food for the children. "They will want bread and milk, and beds must be found for them," she said, and then, although her mind was still filled with the romantic notion that they were Sam's children by some other woman, she took her plunge. "This is Mr. McPherson, my husband, and these are our three children," she announced to the puzzled and smiling servant.

They went into a low-ceilinged room whose windows looked into a garden. In the garden an old Negro with a sprinkling can was watering flowers. A little light yet remained. Both Sam and Sue were glad there was no more. "Don't bring lamps, a candle will do," Sue said, and she went to stand near the door beside her husband. The three children were on the point of breaking forth into sobs, but the Negro woman with a quick intuitive sense of the situation began to chatter, striving to make the children feel at home. She awoke wonder and hope in the breasts of the boys. "There is a barn with horses and cows. Tomorrow old Ben will show you everything," she said, smiling at them.

A THICK GROVE OF ELM and maple trees stood between Sue's house and a road that went down a hill into a New England village, and while Sue and the Negro woman put the children to bed, Sam went there to wait. In the feeble light the trunks of trees could be dimly seen, but the thick branches overhead made a wall between him and the sky. He went back into the darkness of the grove and then returned toward the open space before the house.

He was nervous and distraught and two Sam McPhersons seemed struggling for possession of his person.

There was the man he had been taught by the life about him to bring always to the surface, the shrewd, capable man who got his own way, trampled people underfoot, went plunging forward, always he hoped forward, the man of achievement.

And then there was another personality, a quite different being altogether, buried away within him, long neglected, often forgotten, a timid, shy, destructive Sam who had never really breathed or lived or walked before men.

What of him? The life Sam had led had not taken the shy destructive thing within into account. Still it was powerful. Had it not torn him out of his place in life, made of him a homeless wanderer? How many times it had tried to speak its own word, take entire possession of him.

It was trying again now, and again and from old habit Sam fought against it, thrusting it back into the dark inner caves of himself, back into darkness.

He kept whispering to himself. Perhaps now the test of his life had come. There was a way to approach life and love. There was Sue. A basis for love and understanding might be found with her. Later the impulse could be carried on and into the lives of the children he had found and brought to her.

A vision of himself as a truly humble man, kneeling before life, kneeling before the intricate wonder of life, came to him, but he was again afraid. When he saw Sue's figure, dressed in white, a dim, pale, flashing thing, coming down steps toward him, he wanted to run away, to hide himself in the darkness.

And he wanted also to run toward her, to kneel at her feet, not because she was Sue but because she was human and like himself filled with human perplexities.

He did neither of the two things. The boy of Caxton was still alive within him. With a boyish lift of the head he went boldly to her. "Nothing but boldness will answer now," he kept saying to himself.

THEY WALKED IN THE GRAVEL path before the house and he tried lamely to tell his story, the story of his wanderings, of his seeking. When he came to the tale of the finding of the children she stopped in the path and stood listening, pale and tense in the half light.

Then she threw back her head and laughed, nervously, half hysterically. "I have taken them and you, of course," she said, after he had stepped to her and had put his arm about her waist. "My life alone hasn't turned out to be a very inspiring affair. I had made up my mind to take them and you, in the house there. The two years you have been gone have seemed like an age. What a foolish mistake my mind has made. I thought they must be your own children by some other woman, some woman you had found to take my place. It was an odd notion. Why, the older of the two must be nearly fourteen."

They went toward the house, the Negro woman having, at Sue's command, found food for Sam and respread the table, but at the door he stopped and excusing himself stepped again into the darkness under the trees.

In the house lamps had been lighted and he could see Sue's figure going through a room at the front of the house toward the dining-room. Presently she returned and pulled the shades at the front windows. A place was being prepared for him inside there, a shut-in place in which he was to live what was left of his life.

With the pulling of the shades darkness dropped down over the figure of the man standing just within the grove of trees and darkness dropped down over the inner man also. The struggle within him became more intense.

Could he surrender to others, live for others? There was the house darkly seen before him. It was a symbol. Within the house was the woman, Sue, ready and willing to begin the task of rebuilding their lives together. Upstairs in the house now were the three children, three children who must begin life as he had once done, who must listen to his voice, the voice of Sue and all the other voices they would hear speaking words in the world. They would grow up and thrust out into a world of people as he had done.

To what end?

There was an end. Sam believed that stoutly. "To shift the load to the shoulders of children is cowardice," he whispered to himself.

An almost overpowering desire to turn and run away from the house, from Sue who had so generously received him and from the three new lives into which he had thrust himself and in which in the future he would have to be concerned, took hold of him. His body shook with the strength of it, but he stood still under the trees. "I cannot run away from life. I must face it. I must begin to try to understand these other lives, to love," he told himself. The buried inner thing in him thrust itself up.

How still the night had become. In the tree beneath which he stood a bird moved on some slender branch and there was a faint rustling of leaves. The darkness before and behind was a wall through which he must in some way manage to thrust himself into the light. With his hand before him, as though trying to push aside some dark blinding mass, he moved out of the grove and thus moving stumbled up the steps and into the house.

THE END

Discover more of your favorite classics with Bookfinity™.

- Track your reading with custom book lists.
- Get great book recommendations for your personalized Reader Type.
- Add reviews for your favorite books.
- AND MUCH MORE!

Visit **bookfinity.com** and take the fun Reader Type quiz to get started.

Enjoy our classic and modern companion pairings!